Praise for the Shadowfae Ch

“In this seductive tale of alternate real[illegible] [illegible]ayes uses real settings as a backdrop where gangsters and killers mix with well-defined supernatural characters in an intriguing and tense first-person plot. Add in sizzling sex scenes and dark humor, and this one will take you on a wild ride.”—*RT Book Reviews* (four stars)

“Readers will thoroughly enjoy this entertaining tale of forbidden love. Erica Hayes has a great future ahead of her as a bestselling author.”—*Genre Go Round Reviews*

“Intriguingly dark . . . compellingly emotional and intense. Urban fantasy readers will love the atmosphere.”—*Publishers Weekly*

“Hot, spicy, and well rounded, and the characters were awesome. . . . Great work Erica, I’m waiting for the next round!”—*Tynga’s Urban Fantasy Reviews*

“A thrilling and darkly erotic tale of betrayal, passion, and redemption, *Shadowfae* is a rich novel that will ensnare the senses with lush prose and a deadly vision of the Fae that conjures up fairy tales of old.”—Caitlin Kittredge, bestselling author of *Second Skin*

“*Shadowfae* is a mind-bending blast into a darkness that enfolds and ensnares you from the first page. . . . Pure magic from the word go.”—*Bitten by Books*

SHADOWGLASS

ALSO BY ERICA HAYES

Shadowfae

SHADOWGLASS

ERICA HAYES

St. Martin's Griffin
New York

This is a work of fiction. All of the characters, organizations, and events portrayed in this novel are either products of the author's imagination or are used fictitiously.

Printed in the United States of America. For information, address St. Martin's Press, 175 Fifth Avenue, New York, N.Y. 10010.

Library of Congress Cataloging-in-Publication Data

Hayes, Erica.
Shadowglass / Erica Hayes.—1st ed.
p. cm.
ISBN 978-0-312-57801-5
1. Fairies—Fiction. 2. Magic mirrors—Fiction. I. Title.
PR9619.4.H394S54 2010
823'.92—dc22 2009033888

First Edition: March 2010

10 9 8 7 6 5 4 3 2 1

SHADOWGLASS

1

Stolen diamond bracelets glittered on my wrists in colored nightclub lights, and I laughed, my wings swelling damp in the warm crush of bodies. Midnight at Unseelie Court, dark and fragrant with smoke and sweat. Music ripped my ears like sweet razors, so loud, the air thudded in my lungs and my hair shook to the beat. Strobe lights sliced me, snapshots in time as I danced—here, there, gone.

Blaze wrapped his long white arm around my waist, spilling flames on my shoulder from soft crimson hair. I grinned and wriggled closer, his hot firefae flesh a delicious glory on my skin. Dancing, drinking, diamonds I don't own. Doesn't get sweeter than this.

The floor's packed tonight, a mash of bright fairy wings and rainbow limbs and slick vampire smiles, the air steamy with breath and lust and chemical euphoria. Humans here, too, a few sly ones who can see, but mostly shimmer-eyed and drunk on poison glamour, here for the oblivion. A heady bubble of unreality, this club—no thought, no consequences. Kiss, embrace, dance, love, drown your cares in glorious sensory nectar. A fairy kind of place, no rules, no guilt, the air so glassy with glamour, it might shatter.

Even the name is a fairy joke: Unseelie Court. We fae have no court, no queen or princes or justice. We leave that to demons, gangsters, people who matter.

The smell alone warmed my insides. I'm waterfae, which makes me attuned to moisture, and the wet scent of all that pleasure pressed a sweet ache deep inside me. I shimmied on the crowded dance floor, my silky skirt sticking to my thighs, and lifted my arms in the candy white smoke. My new diamonds sparkled over my wrists, painted blue and green and scarlet by flashing lights. We'd filched them tonight from a glossy apartment in South Yarra, along with a pile of cash and other trinkets.

My skin glowed blue with desire. Shiny things get me all warm and wriggly. I won't get to keep them. We owe the Valenti gang too much protection money. But just for tonight, they're mine. And what harm ever came from something shiny?

Behind me, Blaze rubbed his cheek against my wing, sparks drifting from his pretty red hair. Ooh, tingles, all down my side like sugar. I flexed my shoulders, fluttering golden dust that danced in manic spotlights and rippled in the brittle static of glamour. Blaze is my best friend, a dazzling firefae boy with cute muscles and a cheeky sharp-toothed smile, and his glamour is good. I mean, it's really good. Humans won't see the fine crimson wings like a dragonfly's, the flame dripping from his fingers, his narrow fae-muscled body. They just see a cute redhead with wicked black eyes.

Me? Well, I do my best, but glamour isn't my forte. My nose looks a bit less pointy, my hair more blond than orange, my garish yellow skin fades to human tones. That's about it. Glamour or not, I'm still the same geeky old me.

Blaze slid his arm over my shoulder to offer his fingertip, slick and adorned with a shimmering purple pill.

Naughty boy. I giggled, licked the pill off, and swallowed. It stung bitter, but his finger tasted of sherbet, sparkly and nice.

He rubbed his sharp nose in my hair, and I laughed, my blood hot and urgent, my head awhirl with fizzy-sweet vodka and the thrill of our night's work. Forget the Valentis. Forget the world. Just me and my diamonds, jumping, twirling, dancing until I dropped. Yes.

Next to me a blue-haired vampire kid in leather and his girl kissed, bloody spit trickling on her chin as she swayed to the music, his fingers sliding beneath her skirt. A pair of shirtless trolls scoped for girls, sweat glistening on bulging green muscles and bell-pierced nipples. One winked at me, flicking ragged black hair from his eyes, and I pretended not to see him.

"Spice for Ice!" Blaze yelled, sparks showering. He's allowed to make fun of my unfortunate name. He sizzled my pointed ear with his tongue. Shivers. Mmm. More tongue, slower and wetter than strictly necessary. Bet he's got a hard-on.

I arched my butt backwards and giggled again. Oh, yeah. He's wearing suction-tight leather pants—how he gets those on, I'll never know—and they don't leave much to the imagination.

I grinned, magical warmth already glowing in my guts. Blaze feels as good as he looks, and when he's sparkled to the eyeballs and high from housebreaking and too much broken glass, he always tries something. But we're just friends. We've got rules, and they don't include dragging each other out the back for a hot dirty shag.

Blaze is my lucky charm. Other guys will laugh at me or hit me or play tricks on me just to watch me cry. Fairy girls get that. It's a harsh fae-taunting world out there. Every week you hear about a new fairy-slasher, a sadist, a murderer on the loose. Fairies aren't people, see. We're whispers, shadows, irrelevancies sheathed in desperate glamour so we won't stand out or offend anyone or make anyone feel uncomfortable. We're just flotsam, bobbing on the surface of real people's lives. We just hang out and party. It's what we're here for. No one cares if we die or hurt or bleed.

But I know I'm safe with Blaze, even if he is a horny little rat.

That hunky troll bumped my hip, his beady black gaze slithering down over my ass, and Blaze snarled wet sparks at him and spun me away.

I snickered, and wriggled to face him, static shifting. He tossed bloodred hair and threw me that dazzling Blaze grin. He cuts his hair short in the back and scrunches it wildly too long at the front so he can shake it back like that and skewer you with his dirty black come-taste-me stare.

But I know he doesn't mean it, not with me. He's just having fun. I tickled his pointy teeth with my claw. "Go rub that thing on someone else, ya dirty whore."

He slid bony fingers over my hip, keeping me just an inch or two away. His scent zinged my nose, fresh like a newly struck match. Rakish golden rings glinted in his pointy ears, and his studded black velvet jacket was cropped at his smooth hip with nothing underneath. Sweat caressed his narrow muscles in all the right places. He flicked his smoldering gaze to the bar for a second, ruby sparks jumping from his lips. "I can taste green. Azure's watching us. Wanna tease her a bit?"

Azure's our other best friend, as pretty and awesome as Blaze. I looked. She was watching us, with that glinting glaze over her eyes that meant trouble. "You're cruel."

"You're scared." He edged closer, sweat-slick skin sliding on my bare midriff. My breasts pressed against his chest, burning.

Already the purple pill flowered deep and hot inside me. It couldn't be desire. I was far too sensible to want Blaze. Indignation lifted my eyebrows. "Am not. I'm sensible."

"To hell with sensible. Let's be reckless. I'm good at reckless." He wetted his plum-red lips, and the smell of that moisture tripped warm dizzy waves in my skull. Hot fae boy. Lips. Diamonds.

I couldn't keep the giggles in any longer, and I shoved him in the chest, tipping him backwards. "What you are is a naughty boy with a hard-on. Get a girlfriend." And I turned and pushed my way through the fragrant crowd, laughter floating from me like starlight on the swelling currents of my high.

Colors tumbled and prismed. My diamonds dazzled me, and I stumbled over my own ankles a few times as I approached the blue neon bar. Azure pointed at me and laughed, pearlescent wings jittering as she swayed on her stool. She wore a jagged-hemmed white dress that left her back bare, and she'd piled her green hair above her head in a wild nest of knots and stolen pearls, a pair of broken chopsticks and a cocktail fork sticking out.

My purple-drugged heart swelled with love and awe. Azure's the pretty one. Her glamour shows some weirdly beautiful supermodel, tall and willowy with wide-spaced almond eyes. Her real appearance is the same, only with shimmering oval wings, and her skin is a dozen perfect shades of pale air-sprite blue.

Whereas my hair looks kinda like mango peel, half green and half moldy orange, and my wings are burnt yellow, ragged and droopy like a sick butterfly's.

Some girls have all the luck.

Azure poked my chin with a sharp claw, her soft breeze playing with my hair. Az is airfae, attuned to air and the atmosphere. "You're drunk, diamond girl."

"Not true. I'm high. You're the one who's drunk." I jumped up and down, unsteady on my heels, until the bar boy noticed me, and he served me two pink vodka lemonades without me asking. Maybe

I was drunker than I thought. Still plenty of stolen cash left, though. I tossed him a crumpled twenty, waving my diamonded wrist grandly. "Keep it, peaches. Stop looking at him like that."

Azure said nothing, and I lurched onto a stool and tickled her slender ribs. "I said, stop staring at him."

"Who?" She tossed her pretty blue head, her wings aflutter, and concentrated too hard on stirring her drink.

"Oh, I dunno, the woolly mammoth in the corner? Who d'ya think?"

She thumped her chin into her hand and her elbow onto the bar, sea-green moisture staining her eyes. "But he's so pretty."

Guilt twinged my happy guts, and I patted her shoulder clumsily. "Yeah, I know. But it's an orchid farm in here, okay? Look around. There's other pretty ones."

"Not like him." She hiccuped and burst into proper tears, her wings flooding verdant.

I sighed. Last month she'd had the hots for some cute blond vampire babe. This week it was Blaze. She'd get over it. But my heart still ached for her. Just because she falls quick doesn't mean she doesn't fall hard. And Blaze is the Court's biggest boy whore. He'll only break her heart.

I slipped my arm around her bony shoulder and pointed to the dance floor, where Blaze was trickling orange flame down some laughing banshee's spine, singeing the ends of her long silver hair. "Look at him. See that girl he's dancing with? In the silver dress? Oh, now he's tongue-kissing her, he's putting his hand up her . . . Yeah. You really want that to be you?"

Az just looked at me, indignant breeze dragging her hair back.

I flushed, vodka-tainted water heating my muscles. Maybe I wasn't quite making my point. "Okay, let's not look at that anymore." Firmly I spun her back around to the bar.

She glared, wet-eyed. "You're a real big help, Ice."

I gulped my vodka, pink fizz shooting fireworks up my nose. "So he's boy candy. Everyone knows that. You also know what a bitch he can be. Whaddaya want me to say?"

"Promise you'll never go with him."

I flushed again, and this time the water burned my cheeks. "What?"

"Butterflies in the sun. I've seen him flirt with you. Promise me you'll never."

"Never flirt with him?" Discomfort twisted, ruining my high. Why dissemble? We were best friends. That's all. Even if I'd wanted to, I didn't have the courage to pursue it further. Believe it or not, I'm not too smooth with the boys, and courage is *not* my middle name.

Azure swatted my shoulder. "You know what I mean."

"Hide and seek, catch-me-if-you-can. It's just games—"

"Promise, Ice. I couldn't bear it."

She stared, so earnest and brimful with tears that I couldn't take it. "Okay, I promise. Call me a pincushion and shove safety pins up my nose if I'm wrong. It's the rules anyway, right?"

"Yeah, I guess." Azure gave a sad half smile.

I hugged her, my hand slipping beneath her delicate wings. "You'll get over him, Az."

She hugged me back, and I felt better. I had nothing to hide. She sniffed, wiping snot on my shoulder. "I wish I was like you, Ice. You're the sensible one."

I thought of Blaze's tongue in my ear and giggled. "Yeah, that's me: sense, dense, intense. Dripping out my ears, it is. Of course you wanna be me. Why wouldn't you? You're only the prettiest, cleverest girl in the whole world."

She kissed me, a sugary taste of sky-blue lips, and gamely wiped her tears away in green streaks. "You're nice. Let's get drunk and find some boys."

Meaning she'd get prettily tipsy, I'd get smashed, she'd find more boys than she had hands for, and I'd get the leftovers who were too plain to interest her and too shitfaced to care she was a hundred times more beautiful than me. But what are best friends for?

"Yes yes yes." I paid for two more drinks, and we clinked glasses and chugged. Sugar and alcohol burst into my brain like flares, and my nose fizzed.

Azure gasped. "Raspberries and ice cream. More."

"Careful, there's a fairyslasher on the loose."

She snorted. "S'always a fairyslasher. More."

I ordered more, and we chugged again. This time the froth did come out my nose, laced with plummy drug-charmed mirth. I laughed, splurting pink bubbles onto the guy next to me. "Whoa. Sorry, dude." I yanked up my skirt hem to wipe his arm clean, but the frills were too short. My heels skidded from under me, and I landed in his lap in a giggling, spluttering heap.

Oops. I craned my neck up to apologize, and my laughter strangled.

Not again.

Dark blue skin dusted with copper, so smooth and perfect, it's unreal. Black hair so crisp, it curled jagged. Eyes the velvety gray of softened steel. Long narrow wings like silver-shot glass.

My senses tumbled, intoxicated in hot metal scent. Warm midnight blue hands steadied me, and my belly melted inside like chocolate fudge sauce on ice cream, running everywhere. I inhaled, molten iron and hot fairy skin. . . .

Fluid scorched into my wing veins, swelling them tight. I held my breath. *Calm, Ice. He's touching you. You've practically got your face in his lap. Say something really cool and seductive.*

"Oh. Um. Hi, Indigo. It's me."

Yeah. That *so* wasn't it.

Effortlessly, Indigo lifted me to my feet. Rusty wing-glitter shimmered warm on my shoulders. His coppery claws grazed my wrist, and tiny electric shocks crackled up my arms, sparking my diamonds blue.

I stared, my fingerpads itching. He wore black, as usual, jeans and a sleeveless shirt that showed off lean blue arms.

I wanted to rub my cheek against them, tickle my tongue along his biceps. Metalfae are usually twisted, hunchbacked little monsters with razor metal teeth and an attitude. Indigo—well, he's tall and sculpted and moves light, like a cat burglar, but he's still got razor metal teeth and an attitude. Licking is strictly off-limits, especially for a no-account geek girl like me.

He surveyed me back, steely eyes cool. "Nice diamonds."

His dark quicksilver voice broke my skin out in bumps. I tugged my skirt shyly down over my butt, my skin zinging all over under his scrutiny. My tank top was splashed with pink drink, and my nipples poked the wet fabric, painfully visible. I caught myself fiddling with my hair and yanked my hand away, embarrassment squirming inside. I so wanted to be like Azure, elegant and gorgeous, instead of gangly and yellow and pointy-nosed like me.

At least I had a shiny score to impress him with. Not that it'd impress him much. He was the real deal, Indigo. Not just a petty con artist. I wanted to be him when I grew up. "What? Oh, yeah, thanks. They're not mine. You like 'em?"

He gave me a dark silver-fanged smile, and my tongue tingled. Like candies, Indigo's smiles. Make your mouth water, but you only get one when you've been a very good girl. Probably rot your teeth, too.

He tinkled a copper claw along my glittering bracelets. "Pretty. They suit you."

My cheeks sizzled at his compliment. "Yeah? Wow. I mean . . .

Thanks, you look great, too. I mean, not that you don't always look gr . . . *Well*, that is. You look well." Shit.

Indigo brushed pink froth from lean denim-clad thighs, electricity arcing between his fingers.

Great. Not only had I snorted my drink on him, but I'd spilled his as well. Metalfae rust, doncha know. Good job, Ice. Well done. "Sorry 'bout the drink. I'll get you another one—"

"It's okay. I was finished anyway." He adjusted brittle silver wings, and hard fae muscles did sexy things inside his shirt. I stared, my fingerpads burning to touch that narrow body packed tight with faelight flesh. He's bigger than Blaze, stronger, harder. His muscles, I mean. I can only dream about the rest.

My mouth crinkled inside. This so wasn't going the way I'd imagined it.

Every time I saw him, it was like this: I made a gibbering fool of myself and then spent the time until I saw him again thinking of all the cool things I should've said.

I licked my sharp teeth. He didn't make it easy, so dark and silent and all. Guess he was shy. "So . . . Umm . . . You got anything happening? Me and my friends, we're always—"

"Not right now." His coppery lashes glinted.

"I mean, not that you need our help or anything, but we're real good, like tonight, there was this alarm system wired into the window when we smashed it, and me and Blaze—"

"Ice." Clipped, like he didn't want to listen to me or something.

"Yeah?"

"I'm kind of in the middle of something."

I peered around him. A blond banker type, sleek black suit and golden rings, sipping a bottled green drink through a straw. He glinted black eyes at me, and ash drifted from golden lashes.

I shivered. Spooky. Maybe a client, he looked rich enough. I fluffed my wings out as prettily as I could, grubbing up the dregs of my courage. "Oh, sure. Hi. I'll wait. Maybe after, we could go for pizza or something—"

"Ice?"

"Yeah?" My pulse fluttered. I held my breath. *Please say yes, and I'll never tease Azure about Blaze again.*

He stared at the bar, his elegant jaw tight. "Leave us alone? Please?"

Nausea warmed my stomach. I swallowed, beestung. "Fine. Sure, Indigo. Later." And I walked away, flicking a little updraft to keep my step light.

Embarrassment and alcohol burned my skin. For the fairy of my dreams, he sure was a condescending asshole. That was like ten times he'd brushed me off like that. Why did I set myself up for this? I was so over him.

Fluid boiled in my wings, and my head swirled. Azure smirked at me from the bar, but I ignored her. Just because he'd never turn her down. I made it halfway to the dance floor before my feet tangled and I fell, my kneecaps banging into grippy metal. Nice move. That'd impress him.

I chanced a look up, and he wasn't even watching me. Prick. I scrabbled to get up, my plastic heels slipping on the metal. My ankle twisted, and I yelped, my palm slapping into the floor. "Ow! Shit."

A blue-eyed vampire boy slipped his cold hand in mine and lifted me gracefully to my feet. His black hair scrunched wild in his eyes, blond roots showing. "You okay, fairy lady?"

Nice teeth, white and twinkling sharp. Narrow pretty face, lashes long and green, sexy sapphire stud in his violet-dyed eyebrow. Kinda cute. All the same, too thin, too much eyeliner, smelled of meat and cigarettes. Not my type. No one else was my type with Indigo in the room. And guys who paid attention to me were usually trouble, the kind of guys who liked me because I looked desperate enough to be a sure thing. And it wasn't always a good time they were after.

But at least this one had manners. I slid my arms around his neck, glancing over his shoulder in case Indigo was looking this time. He wasn't. Damn it. "Sure, sweetie. Wanna dance?"

Her sugarbright scent recedes, and Indigo exhales bitter iron temptation. His thighs are still sticky with rum and pink vodka, and imprints of her tiny hands still scorch his skin, too pleasant. She hasn't given up on him. Like she wants to be his girlfriend or something, and the world knows Indigo doesn't do girlfriends, not anymore.

He does thieving, chasing, fleeing from pissed-off hellspawn. Girlfriends just get in the way.

Indigo scrapes wetness from his thighs, wanting to lick his fingers. Silly mango girl has no idea. Pretty amateurs like her should stick to taunting electric alarms and swiping diamonds from faeblind humans. Not playing in the dark where the monsters are.

Indigo flexes tense wings again, raining glitter. Still, something bright and clean about her refreshes his metal-laced blood. Sweet. Charmingly inept. Innocent. Precious things he lost a long time ago.

But not harmless. Ice is never harmless, with that cheeky smile and cute pointy nose and beguiling amber eyes and tempting skin the lost color of sunflowers. In his darker moments, he can admit her awe strokes his ego. Not for a moment harmless, that wide worshipful glow in her eyes, the way her fingers twitch when he touches her, the way she wets her lips without thinking when he gets too close. . . .

His copper claws tingle. Rust crunches along the silvery edges of his wings, and he cracks it off with an electric jitter. Iron-scented particles puff, littering the ash-strewn floor. Better she never knows what hell is like. Better he forgets her. She's probably false anyway. The rest are.

Beside him, the demon lord sips his lime vodka drink, blond ringlets tickling his cheek. Immaculate black suit, lime tie, golden cuff links, the distant smell of thunder. Soft boyish face, fresh with rosy lips, and his voice splits the numbing music effortlessly. "Do you have it?"

Indigo tightens his fingers around the ridged metal sphere, and something evil inside slithers against his palm. He's thieved a demoness's lair for this, and it's not the first time he's stolen it. He should be wise to its tricks by now. Still, giving it up again crawls a hot snake of false regret into his guts. Maybe he should take it home, keep it for his very own, where no one else can see. . . .

The damn thing's gnawing at his mind again. He clunks the heavy sphere on the bar. Good riddance. The demon better keep his end of the bargain. "We done?"

Kane taps blue nails on his bottle, and the sphere rolls across the glass to his waiting hand. It flowers in his palm, iron triangles flashing open like razor-curved petals to reveal the gleaming mirror inside. Kane smiles, childlike, his black eyes swirling green. "You looked, didn't you? I warned you."

Indigo clenches steely teeth in denial. Maybe he's peeked into the glass, drawn by the shimmering silver surface. Wouldn't be the first time. He's a fairy. He likes shiny things. So what? That was days ago. Nothing's happened. Has it?

A sly new whisper rustles warning in his ears. He ignores it. The mirror winks, triumphant, and he drags his gaze away, his stomach twisting. "Are we done?"

"Oh, yes, we're done. For now." Kane admires the glass in colored strobe lights, green sparks playing in his hair. "Who's that pretty yellow child? She smells like strawberries."

"Mind your fucking business." Jealousy shoots hot quicksilver into Indigo's blood. He itches to look over his shoulder, warn her, make sure she's all right, and the irony heats his claws molten. His fingertips scorch. The whispers in his head grow louder, more insistent, mocking him, eating at his reason like acid. His vision flickers like an electricity surge, mirrorshiny images of tangled limbs and fresh auburn hair and blood, and he lights blindly up from his stool with a twist of quivering wings, Kane's empty laughter stinging.

Nausea claws his guts as he staggers away like he's drunk, though he's had only one. Music rocks his ears like motion sickness. A table bangs into his hip, metal crunching, and someone curses, but he doesn't stop or apologize. He tries to focus, but limbs and eyes and fairy wings swim before him, running together like watercolors, wrapping him in a stinging cocoon of gabbling colors. His limbs hurt and yearn. His mouth stings with chrome. His teeth ache like he's grinding them on glass. Something's not right. It's that cursed mirror again.

A slick giggle slides around in his head, and dread wipes his skin with hot grease, but it's too late. Something dark and warm like a snake darts with jagged teeth for his senses, and before he can do anything, the world snaps black.

2

Outside the club, the stormy midnight sky burns orange with reflected city lights, and ozone drenches the pregnant air. No breeze relieves the heat under the cantilever where blue neon gloats on stressed metal walls and queued wannabe starlets, colored glitter makeup and sparkling fairy wings. From inside, the bass throbs, a tantalizing promise of oblivion.

Across the street, pale twins watch in shadow, hands linked. Bleached faces, sapphire eyes, features sharp and identical. Soft white hair curls on their collars in the humidity, and street dust smears their matching white suits. Their arrival in this forsaken city was swift and untidy, crash-landing them to their knees on dirty concrete. It doesn't matter. They don't intend to stay long.

"Here." The first twin speaks, voice neither male nor female, blue gaze unflinching.

The second twin's voice is indistinguishable. "He is inside."

"The demon lord."

"Kane."

"We must face him. We will not fail."

The second twin's smooth brow creases. "We must not fail. I want to go home. I do not like this heat, Akash. The city is . . . not as I expected. People are free."

"People are not free, Indra. It is as Shadow told us. The city is stolen by this demon. We will take it back. We will not fail."

The sharp rip of an engine turns two heads simultaneously, and the twins stare at a leather-vested biker and his girl climbing off a gleaming black bike and staggering up the street with his tattooed arm around her shoulder. The boy is tall, handsome, muscular, his greased dark hair pulled back in a ponytail. The girl walks unsteadily in delicate heels, makeup smeared, her clammy skin shining under loops and studs and rings of metal.

"A big one," Akash remarks.

"And a little one," Indra adds.

Akash sniffs the air. "She is his possession."

Indra sniffs the air. "He is her . . . protector."

"They are in love. Like us."

"Like us. Perfect."

"Perfect," agrees Akash.

The twins look at each other and smile, and walk hand in hand toward the couple.

The biker girl points, ragged black hair falling over multipierced ears, and hitches her leather skirt up with a drunken laugh. "Look, it's Mary-Kate and Ashley."

Her boyfriend laughs, dragging his studded lips over hers as they stop before the twins. "Yeah. Hey, bitches. Your movies suck."

"Yeah. And you killed Heath, you slut." The girl flicks her cigarette, deliberate, and dark ash smears on Akash's white suit.

Akash frowns. It's possible. "I do not remember Heath."

The boy flips a pearly switchblade from his pocket and flicks the spring, his dark eyes glassy. "Sure you do, Mary-Kate. Hand over your fucking cash, bitch."

A chain of silver skulls glints around the boy's neck, rubies glowing bright in the eye sockets. Interesting choice. The twins look at each other and smile. Two identical white hands flash out, each grabbing a sweaty throat.

"Whatthef—!" The boy clutches at Akash's arm, the knife slipping from his fingers. Akash squeezes harder. Blood runs scarlet under white nails, and the boy's eyes bulge, his face purpling.

Akash drags him forward and forces a kiss on his mouth.

The boy convulses, but Akash doesn't let go. Bloody froth drips from their kiss. The boy's limbs jerk, muscles locked hard like stone. His body judders one last time, and Akash's white form crumples to the pavement, lifeless.

The boy lifts his head, and his once-brown eyes glow sapphire blue.

Akash rolls muscular shoulders, stretching in his new body. He lifts his arm, admiring the light glinting on his chains, and bloody claw marks on his throat seethe and vanish in a wisp of steam.

A good disguise. He tosses his ponytail over his shoulder, heaves in a breath, and lets it out. "Perfect." His voice settles, no longer flat and echoless but the boy's bourbon-cracked baritone.

Indra shakes new black hair from her face and smiles, flexing long white legs in strappy heels. "Perfect."

Akash plucks the switchblade from the smeared pavement and flips it over his fingers, a perfect copy of the boy's flourish. The once-twins link hands, tarnished skull rings clinking together, and step out into the street toward the club. Behind them, discarded white bodies crumple in the dust.

Inside, Angelo Valenti swallows the dregs of blood-tainted wine and thumps the glass on the bar, excitement still burning in his blood. The death of his gang rival, Dante, still arcs his nerves, and his vampire senses flower wild with a thousand scents of blood and flesh and salty skin. He slams his fist on the bar, enjoying the twinge of pain. "Fuckin' DiLuca scum. They got it coming. Now it's time to crush 'em."

Beside him, Tony LaFaro chugs back a beer, scaly hands slipping on the bottle. Ange's faeborn second is calm, unruffled as always. Doesn't mean he's not enjoying it. Tony thrives on bloody war. It's what he's good at. "So you wanna do all three in one night?"

"Yeah. Sal's two nephews and that bitch of a mother. Give 'em no time to fuckin' text each other." Ange orders another wine, his gaze lingering on the blond bargirl's succulent vein-blue breast as she pours. Famine wets his mouth, stinging his fangs hot. She's fresh. Virgin. No smell of other scum on her. Jade, Kane's gift girl, always stinks of other men. This one's clean.

Fury and hungry desire flush his balls tight. Jade's a filthy whore. Even fed Dante before he died. Next time Ange sees her, she'll be sorry.

Tony scratches his flat yellow nose with a crusty claw. "Kane know about this?"

"No one knows. Not Kane, not Sonny. I don't want word getting out. We case it first. Then we bring Kane in." Ange drinks deep, the wine a dark premonition of the girl's virgin blood. His cock jerks hard, delicious and uncomfortable.

Tony sucks the lemon from his beer with a forked tongue and lifts his pointed chin toward the mirrored wall. "What about him?"

Ange glances, and spits on the floor. "Joey? That snake-ass freak? Forget about it."

"He's clever." Clear inner eyelids flicker like a lizard's. Tony disapproves.

Ange snarls, his mouth watering. "He's a cringing dog. Just the kind of DiLuca boss I want. Joey stays."

Tony shrugs. "Whatever you say, mate."

"Yeah." Ange gulps his glass empty and flicks the girl a hundred, flashing sharp teeth. "Another one, love. Keep the change."

She takes it, greedy eyes glazing. Done deal. She fills his glass, and too swift for her to see, he grabs her slender white wrist. She gasps, and wine drops splash his sleeve.

He leans closer, inhaling her unsullied perfume. Her pulse thumps sweetly in his palm. "What time you finish?"

She licks purple-painted lips, tempted. "Two thirty."

"Make it now."

Joey DiLuca lounges against the mirrored wall wreathed in green neon smoke, his black fedora tilted over unblinking eyes. He knows LaFaro's watching him. He doesn't care. He watches the mirror pass from the blue fairy to Kane, and his skin ripples, warmth flooding his cold blood.

Leathery black webs crackle from the skin between his long pale fingers, slicing at his cigarette. He sucks in a nicotine lungful and grits his teeth hard to suppress the shift. Last night, Kane murdered Joey's cousin, Dante, boss of the DiLuca family. So now Kane's business is Joey's business, and Kane just showed a weakness that makes Joey want to crawl to the floor and slither.

Joey holds the smoke, adrenaline scintillating. Dante would have liked this—the stalking, the shadows, the plots. His twisted sense of justice thrived on it; his jealous vampire nature devoured it. He'd have laughed that chaos-bright laugh, snorted a river of stinging fairy sparkle, and ghosted off to eat. Joey liked watching Dante eat.

Liked the blood, the sighs, the way their skin paled as they emptied. Liked watching them gasp and fight and die, helpless. Liked to bug out, slide closer, rub his scales on their cooling bodies.

He exhales, smoke rolling. Dante's dead, murdered, brilliant lifeblood sucked out by Kane's cowardly bitch of a succubus. And the DiLuca matriarch despises Joey. He's alone, and the DiLuca clan won't bend to his will if he can't show them what he's made of.

He tosses his glowing cigarette away and taps his lacquered black cane on the metal floor to get Mina's attention. "See that?"

His mad banshee bodyguard yowls and stalks a few paces in her shiny black catsuit, her long spike-heeled boots kicking up sparks. "I see a fairy with a steel spike rammed so far up his ass, his teeth rust, and the luckiest hellspawn in town. I say we waste them."

Joey smiles. She's young, wired. A fresh counterpoint for his cold blood. "That metal ball is Delilah's. She'll want it back."

Mina cartwheels, sleek ultramarine hair flying, her reflection a black blur in the mirror-tiled wall. She lands in a graceful crouch and cracks a grating banshee laugh, full green-painted lips curling. "Delilah? That demon whore? We don't need her, master. We DiLucas owned this city once. We'll own it again without no purple hellbitch to hide behind."

Joey's sinuses vibrate sweetly with her movement. She's no relation, but he doesn't hold that against her. Mina is his protégée. She owes him her life. She's the only person he dares trust.

The snake inside gnaws again, and he wets his lips with a forking tongue. Little stray girls grow up so fast. "Valenti have Kane, and they're stronger by the day. We need Delilah. If we can return that ball, she'll owe us a favor. We'll watch Kane, see what he does."

Mina spears Kane on a ruby-eyed glare, her black-sheened thighs quivering to spring. "Fuck that. Let's kick his ass and take it."

"Ever try kicking a demon's ass, Mina?"

"Always a first time— Ow, for fuck's sake!"

Joey snakes out a black-scaled hand and locks her wrist tight. Minions need discipline. Especially the pretty ones.

She struggles, green nails clawing, but Joey's stronger than he looks. Anger and desire swirl green in her crimson eyes. "Dante's dead! Our cousin's dead and them Valenti assholes did it. D'ya forget that? D'ya even care?"

Angry black spines spring from Joey's shoulder blades inside his jacket, and he flings her hard into the mirror and rams his cane crosswise into her slender throat.

Her skull cracks into the glass. Shards tinkle on steel, and splinters pierce her blue hair. He stares, unblinking, inches from her eyes. No one questions his loyalty to the family. Not even Mina, who knows him better than most. "Say that to me again, and I'll chew your nipples off."

Mina pales. Scarlet trickles from her scalp, staining her forehead and running into her bell-pierced brow. Very fetching, glass in that fresh young skin. Joey likes the smooth slide of glass on his reptile tongue. Her leather-taut breasts press into him, her hip bones sharp and arousing. All that glass and blood make him hard. She'll like that. He smiles, faint.

She flinches, and scrabbles for her knives. Joey jams the cane in harder, forcing her head back, and his poisoned black claws slice her straining forearm.

Her tight body quivers. She chokes, and her wrist tendons pop. Her knife clatters to the floor, her fingers numb, and a conciliatory hum gurgles in her throat. "I'm sorry—"

"I know you want to hunt down the brass-bangled slut who killed Dante." Joey's hot breath wets her mouth. "I know you want to slit Ange Valenti's throat and watch him bleed. When we've won, you can do that. I promise. But to win, we need Delilah. Tell me why."

She tastes trembling lips, tempting him. "But—"

"Why, Mina?" Joey jams his thigh into her hot lap. She smells tasty, bleeding in broken glass over the delicate scent of female skin, and his sinuses quiver, pleasured. He wonders if she knows how long it can take for a snake to come.

She croons, seductive, nails scraping the glass at her sides. "Because you say so."

"Yeah. Because I say so. Don't cross me, little girl."

"Yes, master." She parts raw green lips and leans in.

For a moment he believes it, and their mouths mash together, shocking and bright with lust. She tastes of sugar, aching on his palate. Seductive song blossoms deep in her throat, the vibration stroking pleasure into his burning sinuses. The delicate forks of his tongue flicker in the tiny gaps between her teeth, and sensation sparks in his balls.

But it's not right. She's young, supple, attractive, and he's an inhuman creature, black and twisted inside even when he hasn't shifted. She's lying. She has to be.

Joey shoves his cane in tight one last time, just to taste her salty phlegm, and jerks away from her. Fuck.

She chokes and clutches the scarlet welt across her throat, glass fragments crunching beneath her heels. Her pretty voice cracks. "Jesus, Joey, you're a real prick, you know that?"

Joey flips his cane vertical and squelches his fingerwebs away, discomfort boiling his blood that he let her fool him even for an instant. He won't allow it again, no matter how he craves her. "I pay you to fight for me, Mina. Not to fuck me. If you think you can screw your way out of taking a bullet, think again."

A whiff of damp snakeskin slides in Kane's nose, and disgusted ash bursts from his golden hair to coat the bar.

He scratches at a stain on the bar with a sulky claw, gouging the glass deep. Stinky snakeshifter and his girl, plotting to tempt a demoness. Let him plot. Delilah, ex-mirror-owner, a saucy young newcomer with ambitions beyond her power. A bug on Kane's windshield, so petty, the demon court doesn't even bother to tell him she's here, and crafty blue Indigo had no trouble stealing this snarky mirror from under her jealous purple nose.

Delilah is trespassing. This is Kane's city. Here, baubles belong to Kane. Everything belongs to Kane. Delilah should know that.

Sweet and venomous in his palm, the mirror whispers, sly tentacles of hate crawling into his blood.

He slurps the last of his sticky green drink and peers into the glass. "Hello, shyness."

The mirror giggles, and tugs, grasping for Kane's heart.

"No. Bad." He blinks, and warning scorches the air like a shock wave. The glass bar splits from one side to the other, the crunch lost in the screaming din.

The mirror sees what he is, and quails.

"Naughty thing. Don't sulk." He snaps the metal rosette shut and drops it into his pocket, disappointed. Such a coveted bauble, this mirror that shows people's secrets, back at last where it belongs. The power-crazed demon courtiers have bickered over it for decades, stolen and bribed and cajoled it back and forth like delicious soulcandy. But in the end, it's just wrapped iron and rivets, coated in rusty grunge and tart with hatred. Twisted by too many centuries in hell. Crush it, drop it in the vault, never listen to its nasty giggle again. So sad.

A sigh sears his throat like fever. Nothing is any fun tonight, not even naughty baubles and their splintered blue thieves. Not with this horrid ache in his heart. Kane knows what it is. He's figured out that much, though emotions often confuse him. He misses his pretty Jade, his succubus, his slate-eyed girl.

Reflections glare at him from the fractured neon bar, colored lights, eyes, shadows of rainbow limbs. Sweat sticks his shirt to his back, and he tugs his silken tie loose. The stale air slicks his insides with sickness, and he longs for the cool of home, where everything smells right and he doesn't have to pretend. But home is quiet, blank, bereft, and at least the club has sounds and people and the warm feeling of *not alone* on his skin.

He could call her. Her magical bangles bind her to him. He could drag her here in minutes with the itching compulsion of thrall. But a ghost of delicious sensation tingles his skin when he thinks of her, and dirty envy leaches through his bones like poison. He doesn't need the mirror to see Jade. He can feel exactly what she's doing right now. Every sigh and gasp and perfect caress. She and her lover, thrall-slaves both.

Kane's nails blacken, and he shakes angry sparks from his hair, his flowering teeth jabbing inside his mouth. He owns her. He could make her come here with a thought. But he doesn't want to see her flushed and alive from another man's loving, her lips wet and her pretty hair all mussed and her flesh swollen and her skin coated in the beautiful earthy scent of her sex.

Not when they're together by choice. Not when she means it. She's pleasured a thousand men at Kane's order. This is different.

He crunches sharp teeth, and pain flashes on his tongue, the taste of blood sour and hot like betrayal. If she can fuck around, so can he. The memory of strawberries whispers temptation into his blood, and he closes his eyes and inhales, searching for one he likes.

Scents mix like spilled chemicals, blood and fairy dust and perfumed sweat, the dry insect smell of wing fibers, the brittle ash of a banshee's song, the hot glassy shine of vampire eyes and skimming over it all like oily grime on a puddle, a sick celestial sweetness.

Honey and flowers. Trouble.

Kane's eyes snap open, tense fingers smearing charcoal on the bar.

They're here. Cool white twins, their vapid stink oozing. He spied them arriving tonight, falling from the sky, splat on the ground in a shaft of fetid light like the vermin they are. This is Kane's city now. They don't belong here. The battle for Melbourne's souls was over a long time ago.

Fury flushes his brassy hair blue, and he jerks up from his stool and stalks onto the crowded floor. The saccharine reek draws him on, through the writhing crowd who shuffle aside for him without volition. Past mortals glued in hot blind embraces, past whirling fae dancers and sleepy-eyed vampires feeding slowly, draped on bloody couches. Past the corner bar where Angelo Valenti, Kane's first vampire minion, shares dark wine with his scaly faeborn second and plots a spree of bloody DiLuca deaths now that Dante's gone. Past the bright mirrored wall where Joey DiLuca sucks on another glowing cigarette and leather-wrapped banshee Mina radiates frustrated lust in a sleek fall of ultrablue hair.

DiLuca maggots. He should crush them to pulp. But right now he doesn't care.

Beneath the mezzanine, dim and humid, shadowed bodies stretching and curling as they take their pleasure, be it chemicals, caresses, malicious fairy memory. On the floor, a dragon-tattooed banshee snorts a glittering golden line from a little mirror and passes it on, wetness glazing her eyes. A half-naked human girl moans under twin vampire boys, their fangs ripping delicately at her throat, their snowy hair shimmering in green neon as they share a bloody kiss. A shining glass fairy with silver-spun hair shoots up with glowing violet junk, color veining slowly up his translucent arm. Fairies bite, scuttle, twist each other's bodies in drug-numbed coupling. A long wet sniff, a flutter of moist scarlet wings, sighs and groans and the dark salty taste of sex.

In the corner, the sickly smell pools like hot sulfur, and there they stand, showered in ultraviolet from distant fluorescents, dumb like brainless insects in their stolen bodies. A dark-haired boy wearing a leather vest and buckles, strong thighs, smooth sun-browned skin, tattoos curving on his shoulders, a line of tarnished studs in one ear. Beautiful young face, soft plum lips, a hint of stubble.

That one stinks the worst.

The other is just a faintly foul underling, a black-maned waif in a short skirt and halter, smeared dark lipstick, brows ringed with piercings and a red-berry jewel flashing in her navel. High heels she can't stand up in, straps too tight around tattooed ankles.

Not blending in, not drinking or kissing or sniffing sparkle. Too fucking superior for that. Just standing there, waiting to get their own way as they always do. Both smiling stupidly. Both with unearthly angel-blue eyes. Both greasy with the stink of get-the-fuck-out-of-my-city.

The pair stares, sapphire irises aglitter. Kane doesn't pause. He stalks up, claws springing, and grabs the boy-thing's throat. "Name yourself."

Around them, people blink and back away, or pretend not to see.

The boy chokes, clutching at Kane's gold-linked wrist. The girl-thing whirls, striking at Kane with inhuman strength.

He glances at her, and blinks.

A shimmering black wave of compulsion crashes, and she cries out and staggers, red-skinned, hair crinkling in fresh heat.

Too easy.

Kane crushes his thumb in harder, forcing the boy to his knees. Scarlet blood sizzles on his knuckles like acid. Pain stabs, but he doesn't let go. He coats his voice with grasping duress, dragging invisible black hooks through the boy's blood. "I said, name yourself, aberration."

The boy splutters, tears spilling on his cheeks, and Kane relaxes, just enough to let him talk. Spit dribbles onto Kane's bloodstained hand as the boy forces the sounds out. "Akash. Indra. Curse your blood, demon."

Kane's hair tumbles longer, a deep angry blue. He hisses charcoal smoke, and somewhere behind him, glass shatters. He yanks the boy's greasy ponytail back and crunches razor teeth an inch from the boy's ring-pierced nose. "This is my city, Akash. You won't like it here. You'll not steal back a single soul from me. Go back to where you came from, and tell Shadow I said fuck you. Got it?"

He doesn't wait for an answer, but rips his claws away and strides off, the air around him shimmering with hate.

Akash spits warm sour liquid onto the metal floor, his new body flowering with sensation. Unpleasant. Fresh. Addictive. He wipes blood from the demon-poisoned wounds in his throat, and this time they don't heal.

Indra hugs her knees, still shivering on the floor. Pain clouds her pretty voice. "I do not like this, Akash. I want to go home."

Akash swallows, and warm pain spreads like sunshine. Dazzled, he wobbles to his feet, offering Indra his hand. "He is stronger than we."

She rises, clutching his hand in both of hers, and her gaze slips. "He cannot be. They told us he was weak."

Akash breathes once, again. Pressure in the lungs, bones moving, skin stretching. Delightful. Water stings his eyes, making it hard to see. He blinks, and it's gone. Wonderful.

Even the horrible electric din of the club pleases his ears, and the ache in his injured throat slides delicious fingers of pain down his chest. And the sounds that wrap around him in the dark, sighs and whimpers and muffled moans, they're sounds of agony, yet they're sultry and wet with deep pleasure. He slips a bloodstained finger into his mouth, and it stings. His tongue flares alive with heady sensation, disgusting yet beautiful.

What a strange, bright, painful world.

He gazes around with fresh, suspicious eyes. The sky never lies. There must be a reason for this discrepancy. "Things are not as they told us, Indra. This will not be easy after all. People are free. Kane is strong. Pain is . . . happy."

"No." Indra clutches him closer, her new dark-painted mouth pursed. "The sky is never wrong. It is not true."

"It must be. Kane has corrupted this place. If we are to take the city back, we must watch him, and find his power's source." Akash stretches, blood coursing warm through new muscles, and strokes her pretty new hair with a smile. "Do not be afraid, my love. I have a plan."

3

Some indeterminate time later, I wobbled back to the bar for another drink, my beer-stained diamonds flashing like drunken stars. Blaze was long gone, no doubt up to his boy-whore eyeballs in sparkle and moonshine, shagging some hot babe into next week. Azure jived it up on the dance floor, sharing kisses and breaking hearts. I couldn't see Indigo. Probably home in front of the mirror, polishing those sexy blue muscles and feeling superior. Bastard. I'm so over him.

Me? I was dead thirsty, me. Sweat and spilled drink blotted my clothes, and the world shone starbright with poison-pill euphoria. My thighs ached sweetly from limboing about on the dance floor, my nipples stung permanently erect and I was skidding rapidly from *horny as hell* toward *I'll screw anything* from thinking too much about Indigo's thighs and rubbing up against that pretty emo vampire boy.

Pity about him. Terrific kisser, even if he tasted of meat, and he did this amazing thing with his tongue on my collarbone that melted my knees to custard. But our romance came to an abrupt end when we established that anything deeper than a love bite was out of the question. Sorry, cutie. I'm horny, but I'm not suicidal.

I scrabbled in my bag for more stolen cash—no point just leaving it there—and paid for two more vodkas. Down with one, sugar hurting my throat. Alcohol hit my stomach and burst like a firework, stoking the unrequited heat inside me. I'd also pushed away a hard-eyed human boy with a scary smile who stroked my wings far too accurately for someone who wasn't supposed to see them, and a grinning green spriggan who tried to chew the point off my ear.

Sulkily I crunched the ice, muttering to myself as my vision swayed. Always it's the blood, the memory trade, the nasty games. God, doesn't anyone just have sex anymore?

The second drink went down smoother and hotter than the first. My skin sizzled for contact, my fingerpads itching. A few more of these and I'd be fair game.

Well, good. I wanted to be fair game. I wasn't asking for much. I just wanted to go home with someone who thought I was cute, who didn't want to swallow my blood or finger through my memories or chew my ears off. Who didn't care that I'm not gorgeous like Azure, that I can't dance and always say the wrong thing or that I'm only a petty thief.

Who didn't think he was better than me. Not pointing any fingers or anything.

I wiped a sticky pink smear from my lips and stretched lust-swollen wings, indignation cooking a fine fat pudding in my guts. Fine. He can be like that. Screw being the sensible one, always trying to impress with how smart and cool and with it I am. Screw not wanting to be laughed at. I believe I'll go back out on that dance floor and make a screaming idiot of myself. That might get me laid.

White dust like snowflakes lighted on my arm. I shook it off, but more fell, and when I brushed at it, it smeared black.

Ash.

The rich scent of wind and thunder dizzied me, and I turned, reeling.

Black eyes, shiny like gems. Golden hair tumbling on a perfect brow. Soft cheekbones, gentle red lips.

Indigo's sinister client, he of the ashen lashes and kill-you-cold glance.

Cute, except for that smell. That smell was beyond cute. It did things between my legs I thought you needed a showerhead for. I wanted to squeeze my thighs together, rub my wings in his gilded hair and purr.

And he hadn't even spoken. Usually it's the sweet talk that gets me all gooey. Shoulda known Indigo wouldn't work for just some boring banker.

I swallowed, dry. Too much to hope I'd come up with something supercool to say. "Umm . . . Hi. Indigo's friend, right?"

"Indigo needs more friends than he knows." He shifted on his stool and gave a tiny smile. Perfect teeth, no fangs, no venom. Even better.

"Huh? I mean, yeah. You're right. Can I get you another . . . What flavor's that, lime? Sure. And one of mine, thanks." I paid for the drinks, and Thunderboy didn't stop me. Good sign or bad? I cataloged his perfect suit, his spotless nails, the golden rings glittering on his slender fingers as he rolled them over something rusty and round.

Indigo's loot? Curiosity heated my interest to sizzling. "What's that you got there?"

"A mirror." He slipped his old straw into the new drink.

"Doesn't look l— Whoa. What happened to your hand, dude?"

"What?"

"Your hand. It's like, burnt or something."

"Oh." He surveyed the mangled skin like he'd forgotten it, even though the weeping welt must've hurt like a bastard. He flexed his reddened fingers, and the burn paled and dried, shrinking to nothing. Gone. Just smooth white skin, flushed with blood. "Nothing, I think."

Fluid stretched my wing membranes tight. Freaky. But sexy. My gaze dragged to the lickable glimpse of throat at his loosened collar. Another whiff of that amazing stormy scent dazzled me. I crossed one ankle over the other, squeezing my burning thighs together. *Okay, that's it, I'm yours. I don't know what you are, and I really don't care. I think I'll climb on your lap and beg now, if you don't mind.*

He finished his drink with a slurp and spun on his stool to face me, black eyes drunk on something that may or may not have been me. "You smell nice. Come here."

"Me?" The word slipped out before I could stop it, because my pulse squeezed my throat and popped it out. I darted a glance behind me, to make sure he wasn't talking to Azure over my shoulder or something. Was this my lucky night or what? Maybe he was sparkly, or drunk. Or maybe he just hadn't noticed how clumsy and stupid and tongue-tied I was. There had to be a catch.

"You." He blinked, and the air between us shuddered, black with crawling hellcraft.

My will burned away like a mirage, and reckless desire flooded me. I clunked my empty glass back on the bar. He grasped my wrist with cold fingers and yanked me onto his lap.

I fluttered upward, settling myself, and his sudden explosive heat burst up through me like sunburn. Okay. Impressive. He was hard for something, all right. Might as well pretend it's me.

I pressed down, enjoying the feel of him. My tiny skirt bunched tight at the tops of my thighs, and I tried to remember what kind of underwear I had on. Hopefully something sexy that wouldn't get in the way. I bent closer to sniff him, flickering my wings lightly, and snowy ash swirled in my downdraft. God, his hair smelled fantastic, like burnt foliage after rain.

He slid shameless hands up my back to grasp the sensitive joints where my wings met my shoulders. Dirty boy. I gasped, giggling, and he pulled me down to him, his lips a burning inch from mine. His easy strength spiked shivering pleasure up my spine.

His delicious charcoal breath slid into my mouth. "You like this?"

"Uh-huh." I liked it, all right. Desire spread desperate fingers inside me, and I flooded. Swelling throbbed in my wings, hot moisture flushed under my skin, hot water dripped from my hair to slide over my shoulders. My sex oozed heat, and now I was really making a mess on his lap.

Sudden fear clutched my guts with razor claws. I wanted us alone, sweaty, naked, and I knew nothing about him, not even his name. Fairy girls get hurt like this. They get raped and slashed and end up in the gutter bleeding. Good one, Ice. This is what happens when you forget your fear. "Umm . . . Is this where we exchange names?"

"If you think it's important." He flicked his tongue over my bottom lip, searing.

Thirst ravaged my throat. I shivered, and slid my arms around his neck, and his hair grew a couple of inches, flooding sky blue at the ends. Kinky. "I'm Ice."

"Kane." He kissed me, hard and black and sinful, and my mind glugged, as if water filled my braincase. The inside of his mouth was hot, his lips slick, his teeth sharp and salty. His tongue chased mine, wrapped, tugged. I drank him, tension dragging a sharp ache from my sex. Oh, yes. Don't wake me up just yet. . . .

Hang on. What did he say?

Belated shock spiked me, and I broke off, my nipples tweaking hard. "You don't mean . . . *the* Kane? As in, demon-lord-more-money-than-god-send-my-skanky-ass-to-hell-if-I-piss-you-off Kane?"

He sniffed my breasts, his tongue hungry on my wet top. "Changed your mind, strawberry girl?"

My nerves twitched to wriggle off him and run. I knew he'd compelled me. I knew I didn't normally act like this. My common sense smothered me, cloggy like glue, and for a moment I inhaled it and choked for air. But my instinct for fun squirmed like a wet worm to be free, and longing bubbled inside me, melting my ice-walled fear.

A sexy, powerful demon didn't pick me up every day. No one picked me up most of the time, and part of me wanted everyone to see this. I wanted to show Azure she wasn't the only one who attracted classy guys. I wanted Blaze to see I didn't live for his sparkle-drenched come-ons, and I wanted Indigo to know that just because I wasn't good enough for him didn't mean everyone else thought I was a waste of space.

And Kane was a gang lord from hell, not a fairyslasher or a murderer. So long as I kept my mouth shut and didn't do anything stupid, everything would be okay. Right?

Besides, if I didn't get laid soon, I'd probably melt.

"Change my mind? No way, beautiful." I fluttered and slid my hands underneath me to get at him. No one would mind if we screwed right here. Enough people were doing it on the couches and the dance floor. Besides, this guy owned the world. He could do whatever he wanted, and he wanted to do me.

My pulse surged, flattered, and my bruised heart swelled. *So there, Indigo. Tell me I'm not good enough now.*

I parted damp black cloth, and his smooth hard flesh sizzled on my palm. I shivered, dripping all over with sweat and watery desire. *Oh, yeah. Gimme that, hot and hard and deep.*

But Kane dragged my hand away. "No. My turn. Tell me if you like it." He wrapped one arm around my hips so I couldn't move, and slid sharp fingers beneath my underwear.

His fingertip slid along my wet flesh, searching. Hot relief washed me, and sensation took root, spreading, intensifying into pleasure that worked through my muscles deep into my bones. I sighed, shifting to let him in. He stroked me, circling my entrance with a teasing fingernail, and then unerringly found my most sensitive spot and tortured it.

I gasped at exquisite pressure, my flesh swelling hard under his touch. He caressed the perfect spot, so accurate, it was spooky. Sensation scalded like boiling water, so good, I groaned. He pressed harder, faster. Tension coiled hard inside me, a sharp delicious ache that only hurt worse and felt better. I couldn't breathe. I was trapped. My water gushed, soaking his clever hand to the wrist, and a too-abrupt orgasm crashed into my belly like a waterfall. I gasped and clutched at his hair, my wings jerking.

When the pressure subsided, I caught my breath with a sigh. Wow. That was . . . mechanical. Unpleasant. Humiliating. I wanted to do it again right away.

"Tell me if you liked it." Kane tickled me with a sharp claw.

My muscles spasmed again, and I pushed his fingers away with a breathless giggle. I was so taking him home. "Gimme a moment. Why d'ya keep asking that? Bruised ego?"

He just stared, and crushed my hand in his, licking his lips. "Maybe she lied. Tell me."

My happy heart deflated, just by a whisper. Did his girlfriend dump him? Did she fake it? Tell him he's a shitty lover? Maybe he doesn't really think I'm sexy. Maybe I'm just a revenge shag.

The idea gave me shivers all over again. Well, so's he, kinda. And why the hell not? He's attractive, willing, and talented. I'm horny. Who cares? Screw sensible, remember?

Let's be reckless, whispered Blaze in my memory, and relief spiked hard that he hadn't waited a few more hours to hit on me.

I swallowed, uncomfortable sympathy buzzing my blood. "If

you're asking if that felt good, honey, the answer's fuck yes. Feel my pulse, I'm still shakin' here. That ain't vodka all over your hand. Whatever she told you, you're a real hot shag, okay?"

"She said she liked it." A crease tainted his handsome brow, and his hot black eyes clouded sky blue.

My pulse rippled. *No, you don't, cutie. Too late to back off now. No way are we losing this mood over some absent demon-tricking orgasm-faking screw-with-your-mind bitch. She isn't here. I am.*

I trailed suggestive fingers into his lap, where he'd by no means lost that impressive hard-on. I stroked, and he closed his eyes, ash dusting his pretty golden lashes. I leaned forward to whisper in his ear and flexed my legs around him, flicking out my wings in a puff of yellow dust so I wouldn't fall. "Everything feels just fine to me. But maybe I'd better check you out properly just to make sure. Y'know, see where it fits and all. Make sure it tastes right." I nuzzled his throat, his stormy scent breaking bumps out on my scalp. "Wanna go somewhere and give it a try? I promise not to fake it . . . if you'll promise I won't need to."

Shiver. Did I just deal with a demon?

Too late. He fingered my nipple, teasing, stabbing anticipation deep into my body, and when he opened his eyes, they glinted black and hard once more. "You'll tell me if you like it."

He pinched, and pleasure spiked harder. I arched to press my breast into his hand, searching for more, delight and pride warming my skin along with desire. *Ice, you've done okay.* "Honey, if you do it right, you'll hear all about it."

The mezzanine, green neon smoke glowing. Needle freaks and sparkle sniffers sprawl on the rippled steel floor, lost in chemical contentment or rage. In the corner, a skinny girl sprawls on her back, crooning in pleasure as a pair of vampire boys feed, one at her naked breast, the other between her legs, her skirt scrunched high. Next to her, a drooling black spriggan crouches and slams his misshapen head into the wall, over and over, violet blood smearing. People dance, drink, screw, pass out, and at the pitted steel railing, a razor-nerved fairy named Ebony stretches tense dark arms in the urgent thud of bass.

The sultry air swims on his skin, delicious. The familiar smells wash over him, sweat and fresh lust and the rich iron honey of blood, creamy longing, dusty loneliness, the sharp salt of fury and bitter oblivion. His pale wings spread, twitched by his speeding pulse. What a beautiful night to be alive.

He stretches again, blood rippling warm and alive in his limbs, and leans over the rail to hunt.

Below, where dancers throng and strobe lights crack the air like glass, the yellow fairy girl flirts on a jealous demon lord's lap, her gasps as he pleasures her inaudible from here but beautiful.

"Ice." The sibilant tingles Ebony's tongue, pleasant. Her skin would do the same. The clumsy one, always falling over her own feet and biting her tongue on careless words. Indigo's girl, if you ask anyone but Indigo. Poor frightened thing, always so serious. More charming when she's drunk and carefree.

He's watched her dance with her toxic friends, blush and fidget under Indigo's glance, pour pink poison down her throat to steel her nerves. He feels for her, this frightened girl. He knows what it's like to dread the gaze of others, their accusations, their contempt. And now she's squirming breathless on a demon's lap with no thought or care. Beautiful, unfettered thing.

The demon lord tucks her hand in his elbow and walks her away, and Ebony giggles, imagining Indigo's envy. He knows Indigo well, after so many years, and Indigo's too fucking stubborn and cowardly to admit he wants her. Ebony wouldn't be so circumspect.

Courage, yellow girl. Stretch for the stars. That rusty blue thief isn't worth your sweet pity, not yet. Once Eb's finished with him, he'll be a new man and we'll see who's clumsy then.

But for now, Ebony's itchy inside, that nasty squirming hunger that must be fed. Emptiness must be filled. Itches must be scratched. Another thing Indigo doesn't understand, and Indy's so fucking itchy, his skin bleeds.

Ebony flutters down the metal steps, lighting on the floor eight feet below with a magnetic snap. A human girl stares, starved bruises ringing her glassy eyes. She stuffs a split hank of black hair in her mouth and chews. "How'd you do that?"

He catalogs her, eager but cautious. Thin, dusty black dress hanging from bony shoulders, cheeks hollow, lips cracked, wristbones prominent under stretched skin where fresh scars crisscross old. His pulse twinkles. Delicately, he inhales. Sickness, twisting like starved tissue. Hatred. Despair. No fear. His blood swells with that familiar desire, and he smiles at her and lets his glamour flicker to dazzle her with what he really looks like. "Easy. I can do magic."

Pupils dilate in tired blue irises, and she licks dry lips, fixated. "Wish I could do magic. I'd magic myself right the fuck out of here."

He drifts closer, the updraft heated by longing, and slides a hot knuckle under her chin. So tight and shiny, her skin, so vulnerable. "I'll magic you away, if you like."

Her eyes brighten, hope shining dully like reflected starlight. She doesn't move, doesn't shrink away. She knows. She wants this. "Yeah? Where to?"

"Wherever you imagine." He sniffs her lips, the chlorine taste of starvation and vomit. Perfect.

She swallows. "Will it hurt?"

"Only if you want it to." A lie. He's in control. This will happen the way *he* wants it to. No, the way he needs it to. Wanting is insignificant. This is a compulsion. A gravity-scale inevitability.

He captures her hand and pulls her with him, and they weave between fights and sweating couples and giggling drug-sharing fae toward the alloy-barred fire exit.

The grimy back alley stinks of garbage and sour meat, the air shimmering with imminent rain. Under a glowing midnight sky, he pulls her into his arms against the garbage skip and traps her there, her damp hair plastering to the metal. Her body feels broken and sore against him, like a worn-out doll. He sniffs her sunken face, brushes his mouth across her pin-pierced earlobe, and his skin sparks with electric anticipation. Soon, they'll be together. He'll make sure she never leaves. "Say yes."

"Yes." Unerring. Unafraid. Perfect.

"Good girl." He nibbles at her lips, and when she doesn't struggle, he cups her head in one hand and opens her for a kiss. Her delicious groan slides over his tongue, and he wriggles his thigh in between her legs, ready.

She misunderstands, fumbling cold fingers into his lap. He's hard, but it's not for the reason she thinks. He drifts his hand down the back of her neck, pressing to find the bones, sliding his palm over the ridges. They feel good, knobbly and fragile like china. The base of her skull is cool against his thumb, smooth and round, her ripped hair rough.

He tightens his grip, sharp claws slicing her skin. He jerks his wrist, hard, and simultaneously clips her under the chin with the sharp heel of his other hand.

Snap.

He pulls back to watch, holding her with his thigh. She's not dead. Panic flowers her rolling pupils and slackens her cheeks, and shock fills her mouth with drool. Her fingers jerk uselessly. Paralyzed.

The knowledge hits her, and she screams, high and breathy like dust, the only cry she can manage. No one will hear.

His pulse stings with pleasure at the hoarse sound, and his erection swells tight and sore. Not long now. "Nearly there, sweet. Don't cry." Tenderly, he fingers tears from her lashes and licks them to taste her salty sorrow. He searches with his thumb for the pulse in her throat.

Her eyes widen, bloodshot. She tries to croak out words. "No . . . changed . . . my mind . . . stop it. . . ."

But she can't move. Can't escape. Can't break his heart with lies and cruel laughter. He pierces her with his steely claw, and twists. Blood runs, warm and alive on his hand, down his arm, sparkling thickly all over his skin. It feels good.

She screams again in rage and denial, thrashing her head back and forth, but the blood only squirts harder from the gash in her throat. Such a little thing, moving her hand to close the wound.

Ebony grabs her hair to hold her head still and sniffs, reveling in the rank stink of fright. "Hush. It'll take a minute or two. Enjoy it. It's what you wanted."

Blood spills faster, darker, plopping on the ground like thin ketchup. Her terror-wide pupils glaze over as she realizes she's dying, and urgency hitches Ebony's breath. "Come on, sweet. Give in for me."

Her jaw jerks, quivering her blanched lips. He waits with shaking limbs for the surrender that means she's his forever. Then her face slackens, and release rips through him. Molten heat, sharp in his guts like an iron spike, dragging stinging liquid from him along with his groan. His heart overflows with fondness and desperate relief. He clutches his lover close, slicking his cheek in her precious blood, but it's fleeting, this connection they have, after only a brief second it's gone, and he whines in desolation and scrabbles his claws through her hair, but by the time he's finished, she's dead.

4

I laid my cheek against the damp creamy sheet and let my arm dangle over the edge. My fingerpads trailed over pale carpet, my stolen diamonds glittering in golden downlights. Across the bedroom the window lay open, warm fruity breeze from some dark garden caressing my back. I tried to breathe slowly, but it hurt deep inside. My wings ached from too much water, and I let them drape over my back like limp cloth. My lips stung, abused. I licked them, bitter ash still fresh. A horrid taste, but I liked it.

I giggled, still drunk, weary pleasure echoing deep inside me. *Screwed senseless by a demon lord. Wait till I tell Azure and Blaze. They'll never believe it. I still don't believe it.*

Kane trailed a gentle finger down my spine, and my sated hormones rippled, still warm. Purr. If I rolled over, he'd kiss me, coax me, make me gasp again. Fatigue didn't seem to be an issue, at least not for him. "Mmm. Honey, it's gotta be five in the morning. Don't you ever need sleep?"

"No." He followed his finger with his lips, and I shivered as he kissed the small of my back and moved lower.

Okay, stupid question. Just another weird thing about him. The longer I stayed here, the more my skin wriggled underneath like a cold eel.

He'd kept his promise, at least. We'd done it in his car, up against the front door, and over the sofa in the lounge before we'd even made it to his bedroom. I'd lost count of how many times I'd come, and every time it happened, I disliked him a little more.

It wasn't that he humiliated me, as some guys had. He wasn't one of those people who beat up on fairies to make himself feel good. I'd asked him to use protection—you just never knew—and he hadn't minded. But even when he came inside me, he was distant and calculating, like he wasn't really there. Like he'd studied a book to learn what to do, how to feel.

He nuzzled my thighs apart, and licked. Mmm. Fresh fluid oozed from me, making my glands ache. His burning tongue slipped deeper. Squirmy pleasure glazed my senses, and my claws dug into the carpet. *Sorry, honey, but your mystery girl's right. Something's wrong with you.*

But what you're doing sure feels good. I tucked my limp wings back and rolled over, flexing my tired thigh around his neck. He slid my folds apart with his fingers and delved his tongue inside me, and once again unease pounded my flesh even as my pleasure swelled under his skillful stroking.

Don't be stupid, Ice. Just enjoy it, so you can feel good about yourself next time Indigo brushes you off.

I closed my eyes to concentrate on the sensation. My flesh stung raw under his tongue, scraped clean with friction, my nerves sparking to life. He sucked me, just hard enough, and I whimpered at the rising cramp of delight in my belly. He did it exactly the same way as last time, like he'd memorized my every sigh, each twitch of my limbs.

Creepy. I grabbed his crisp golden hair, pulling him onto me, trying to make him shift, twist, change his angle, take his time, do it my way instead of the fastest way.

He just sucked my clit into his mouth and bit. Pleasure scraped me raw, each spasm wringing hard, but he didn't let go. I gasped, my vision blurring. Damn it.

Dimly, I heard his phone ring, a gloomy church organ tone. He barely let me finish before he wriggled off me to pluck the handset from the floor. He glared at the screen, black eyes shining, and sighed as he picked up. "Angelo."

Downlights gloated over his perfect skin as he leaned on one elbow, golden light teasing his elegant flank. I panted, damp and sore. I wanted to touch him, run my fingers along that smooth thigh, taste the curve of his back. He'd only repeat himself again. It didn't stop me wanting it.

He rolled onto his back, golden hair tumbling on the sheets. His body shone, sweat glistening on perfectly proportioned muscles. No scars. No blemishes. Eerily beautiful, this demon lord. You could fall for him too easily. Whoever this girl of his was, I hoped for her sake she'd gotten out in time. "Not until I get there, Angelo. Can you contain yourself until then?"

Wow. My very own brush with celebrity. Ange Valenti on the phone, Sonny's boss, the scariest vampire in Melbourne after Dante DiLuca. I flopped onto the pillow, my limbs weak and watery. Kane didn't sound pissed off. Not even mildly miffed that we'd been interrupted. Just exasperated that the caller wasn't someone more interesting.

He truly had no clue. No wonder his girlfriend gave up on him.

Sympathy twinged, and the urge to sit him down and explain tickled my spine. But how do you explain emotion or sentiment to someone who has none?

An evil little grin curled his rosy lips. "Good. I like it when

DiLucas bleed. Oh, and call Rajahni Seth, get him to clean up the mess. Tell him I said I'm not sorry." And he hung up, and dropped the phone to the floor.

I stretched, still uncomfortably pleasured. "Kids not playing nice?"

He rose, tossing his hair into place, and flicked me an empty black glance. "Don't steal anything." And he padded across creamy carpet to the bathroom.

Water rushed, flooding the room with steam's sweet scent. Disappointment washed my skin with cool bumps. I'd hoped he'd at least fuck me again before he left. Briefly I considered creeping into the shower with him, and my nerves tingled. All that hot water gushing over me, running his scent over my skin, splashing my wings and flooding in my hair as I knelt and nibbled his thigh and slid him into my mouth, all charcoal and ashen sweat and smooth hard flesh . . .

My taste buds twinged, and reluctantly I swallowed greedy spit. Best not to push my luck with a guy who can send me to hell with one soft golden blink.

I clambered off the bed, my joints creaking, and flicked my wings open to dry them as I wiped myself clean on the sheet. The soft linen scoured the tender flesh between my legs, and I winced and gave up.

I couldn't see my skirt and tank top, and I wandered naked into the dawn-lit lounge before I found them, little blue pools on the floor beside his crumpled white shirt. Pink stains still showed, crusty now. I shook the creases out and dragged the clothes back on over damp skin, tugging the straps around my wings and fastening them tight. My underwear wasn't in evidence. Waste of space anyway.

I glanced around, thieves' habit. Didn't take much notice the first time, what with his tongue wrapped on mine and his hand up my skirt and all. Don't steal anything, he said. Hah. Like I'd want any of this stuff. Big modern town house, expensive white furniture, dull oil paintings, a vase or two. Vast creamy walls that made me long for spray paint. Gleaming wooden floor great for skidding on. Nice big TV for Blaze to smash.

Kane might have a sinister reputation, but his house was dead boring. Wherever he kept his golden demon treasure and screaming minions and rusty hellcursed loot, it wasn't here.

My bag puddled on the floor, and I slung the strap over my head, checking to make sure my phone hadn't fallen out. A drunken text from Blaze. YUFR MIZLE DRIPT! IIEEE!! I kept it, to taunt him with later. Another from Azure, neat and sober, an address in the city. She always does that, in case she doesn't come back. And I'm supposed to be the sensible one. I don't even know what suburb I'm in. The old fear twinged my nerves, and I stamped on it. He hadn't hurt me yet. I'd find my way home, right? I'd be okay.

Swiftly I retrieved Kane's silken jacket from the couch, his stormy scent an unpleasantly pleasant memory. I felt the pockets for cash, and my claws scraped rusty metal.

Indigo's score.

Curiosity spidered over my skin, and with a swift glance over my shoulder, I tugged the sphere out.

Warm velvet steel tingled my palm. It curved seductively, the ridges sharp and tantalizing. I tilted it to the light, and something tumbled inside, like a squidgy and fascinating creature lived in there.

Ooh. A toy. My skin tingled, covetous.

"Hello, squidgy thing." I rolled it in my palm, delight twitching my wings. The thing inside wriggled again, tickling me, and I swear it giggled as the sphere lurched and spilled from my hand.

My heart tilted. I scrabbled wildly for it, and sharp iron petals scythed open in my palm.

Inside, gripped tight by tiny metal claws, a mirror gleamed. Silvery and perfect. Shiny.

I stared. The metal hummed seductively in my hand. My pulse bubbled, and something hot and slick, reminiscent of Kane's tongue, stroked between my legs, pleasuring me. Mmm. Did I mention shiny was my weakness?

I wanted to look. I had to look. My nerves squirmed, and I sniffed over my shoulder once more. Ashen steam, the thick smell of sex and wet demon flesh. Kane was still in the shower. No one would ever know.

Stealthy, I craned my neck forward and peeked inside.

My big amber eye stared back at me, magnified. I blinked, and the big eye blinked, too, ash flecks huge and fluffy on my inflated lashes. I tilted the glass, and there was my nose, even huger and sharper and more crooked than in real life.

I giggled. Soft metallic laughter rippled around the room in response, and warm invisible fingers tickled the back of my neck.

"Whoa." I squinted, suspicious, but the mirror remained silent.

Curiosity and envy scratched inside me like sandpaper. Such a pretty thing. And so peculiar. Ohh, couldn't I just . . . ?

The thought hung in the air like a seductive scent. Behind me, rushing water ceased. I hesitated, itching.

Stay here, Kane finds me going through his stuff and magicks me into a hellspawned newt. Or swipe the pretty shiny thing and run before he knows it's gone.

Common sense cleared its stern throat at me. *Ice, are you crazy? Kane paid Indigo to steal this, and Indigo doesn't work cheap. It's important, whatever it is. Kane'll come after you, and he'll make hellspawned newt seem like chocolate ice cream.*

I shivered, and started to put the hideous thing down.

—*Take me.*— That seductive whisper again, heady with the smell of iron.

I halted.

—*Take me, Ice. I'm only small. He'll never know. Be my friend?*— The glass winked at me, bright and precious in golden downlights, and irrational longing pierced my heart like a blade.

Just a shiny of no importance. *Kane can get his own. This one's mine.*

My heart warmed. After tonight, I'd earned it.

And what harm ever came from something shiny?

I squeezed, and the iron petals snapped shut, seamless. Already I mourned the lost shimmer of glass. I patted the sphere carefully and stuffed it into my bag. "Bye, squidgy. See you soon." And I ran, jumped, and skidded on bare feet across the mahogany floor toward the door.

The early morning tram to the city already teemed with commuters clutching briefcases and wheeled document cases and bags stuffed with gym clothing. The hot yellow sun climbed rapidly to bake storm-fresh streets, and as usual, the tram's air-con was cranked up to the max. I shivered and tried to find a seat to myself, but I ended up standing at the back, clutching the little plastic handles that hang from the ceiling.

My glamour is okay, but when you're flush up against some pasty office worker, it's hard to hide wings. Some fairies—like Blaze, of course, that gifted little shit can do everything, and no, I'm not jealous at all—some fairies can make humans forget what they see, so it doesn't matter. Others like Azure dazzle with their beauty. I'm not so lucky. People think it's easy, being fae, living in a shadow world. They should try a revolving door, or buying clothes that fit, or the dodge I have to do when some glamourblind guy slips his arm around me at the Court.

I also stank, and my glamour couldn't hide that. I was smeared in sweat and my own arousal before I even saw Kane. Now I was caked in it. Water, spit, vodka, demon come, you name it, adding up to a curious earthy reek that no one would mistake for the latest fragrance. I really needed a shower, and I almost regretted not giving Kane that last blow job.

So I stood and held the plastic handle like I needed it for balance, and tried not to stretch my aching wings too much. In my bag, my new not-mirror rolled and whispered, content. Home, shower, bed. No gypsy scam today. We'd scored big last night, and even though I'd spent most of my share on booze, we still had the loot to sell this afternoon. It wasn't half what we owed, but it might keep Sonny Valenti and his charming Mafia bloodsuckers off our backs for a while. Happy days.

A human girl bumped into me, tilting on patent leather heels. Damn it. I lurched back, but too late. Her flowery perfume hit my nostrils, and water molecules spread, tingling like a sneeze. My eyesight dimmed, images flooding like stormwater. Glitzy soirees in glossy Yarrabank apartments, luncheon at Flemington racetrack, expensive dinners in glassy rooftop restaurants. Days spent gossiping, flipping through magazines, sunbaking with cocktails by the pool, a glittering diamond ring, a warm and lucky boy who worships her.

She murmured an apology and sidled away, and my ears popped, the tram hovering back into focus. Envy stung my wings. Humans have everything.

It's a talent of mine I don't talk about, this witchy trick with human smells. I'm just thankful it doesn't work on my friends. I don't wanna know what they really think of me.

Across from me, a guy in a cheap black suit clutched a worn briefcase, white earphone buds dangling unused around his neck, dark hair artfully spiked. Smudges circled his eyes, his mouth tight and weary in his pale face. Even over my eau-de-slutgirl, I could smell boredom.

He slid a scornful glance over me, his lip twisting, and resentment soured my mouth at his disdain. Just some lousy office worker. Who did he think he was, looking at me like dirt? At least I had ambition, even if the object of my desire was unattainable. If I had any guts, I'd snark this guy raw.

I swallowed bitter indignation and looked away.

A cold metal whisper slithered into my mind. —*What an asshole. Why don't you tell him what you think of him?*—

I snorted. *Good idea, squidgy. Wish I had the courage. People with jobs they hate make me sick.*

He stared, incredulous. "What did you say?"

My cheeks sizzled. *Did I say that aloud?*

—*Might as well make the best of it,*— the squidgy whispered.

I shrugged, emboldened. "I said, who are you trying to impress, getting to work at six in the morning?"

"I'm sorry?"

"Didn't you get laid last night? Don't you have a better ass to kiss than your boss's?"

His brow creased, and my guts churned. I couldn't believe I said that. Guess I was still drunk. But that snarky mirror murmured glassy rebellion in my ear, and the jagged urge to taunt him chewed at me like teeth. I couldn't stop. "Advice, loser. You ain't never gonna get rich opening up. You really want to impress your boss, get under the desk and suck him off."

Another fat suit across from him muffled a laugh. My stomach hollowed. Now I'd done it. Lip like that'd get me punched in the face, or worse.

The loser gripped his case tightly and rose. "Yeah. I can see that approach has worked for you, career girl. Nice come stain, by the way. Very classy."

I clutched the bag closer, my palms slipping. The not-mirror cooed, comforting. *—He deserves it. You've taken enough shit from his sort over the years. Time to give some back.—*

He stalked off to find another seat, and the fat guy laughed again, greasy glasses twinkling in bright sun. "Baby, I like your style. You can work for me any time."

"Fuck off, gonzo." Embarrassment sizzled my fingerpads blue, and I turned to face the window before the squidgy made me say anything else. I squeezed the handle tightly, my insides hot and watery. Everyone was staring at me, I knew it, their disapproval tainting the air, and I squirmed, my glamour shifting in discomfort.

For all I knew, Loser had three kids and a 15 percent mortgage. I still resented his attitude. But what possessed me to attack him like that? First thing in the morning, in front of a tram full of strangers? He hadn't done anything to me, not really.

Gentle metal comfort clucked from the depths of my bag, and I scowled, unconvinced. Still wasted. That had to be it. Either that, or Kane really had screwed my brains out.

A giggle splurted up into my throat, and I had to plaster my hand over my mouth to keep it in.

The three stops until my transfer dragged for what felt like hours, and I slunk to the automatic doors with the fat guy's eyes glued to my grimy ass and my gaze fixed firmly on the floor.

Federation Square, where seagulls dipped and swerved, and sun shone brightly on the green metal-framed façade of the film museum. Workers grabbed early coffees from fragrant black cafés. A greasy black spriggan in a trench coat crab-walked between rubbish bins, picking out cigarette butts and half-eaten sandwiches with gnarled yellow claws. A grinning firefairy clung to a passing tram's roof, wings trailing flames in the breeze, cackling in delight as sparks rolled over her naked back.

My tram came, and I shambled on, half-asleep and headachy. I wanted my bed, warm and comforting and alone, where no one could hurt me or laugh at me.

The mirror burbled to me as we swayed along clicking tracks, my bag vibrating alarmingly under my palm. Secretly, I supposed it was kinda cool. I wanted to take it out, admire the glass shining in the sun, peek inside and see what I could see. But I didn't dare, not here, after what it maybe made me say.

But I remembered the disbelieving look on that guy's face, and a naughty smile flavored my lips. Yeah, that was kinda cool, too. I patted my bag absently. *Crafty, clever little squidgy. We'll be friends.*

—*Mmm,*— the mirror whispered, and I smiled to myself and daydreamed the rest of the way to my stop, of a new and delicious world where I said what I wanted and wasn't scared anymore.

Swanston Street, glass skyscrapers and retail cantilevers giving way to dirty office buildings and car parks, the university, my suburb with its bluestone gutters and cracked pavements and broken-down student houses. I drifted off the tram and flitted the last few blocks in a daze, blinking in the sunlight, my bare feet stinging on rough concrete.

I tumbled the squidgy over in my hands as I dawdled. Sunlight glinted on scratches in the rust, and underneath it showed all silvery and nice. I stroked it, and the thing inside purred. "So, squidgy, what exactly are you?"

—*I'm you. We're us. You're me.*— The voice chimed pleasantly, like bells or rushing water.

"Okay, so that didn't make sense. Who's in there? Are you a boy or a girl? How come you're telling me all these weird things to say? I mean, it's brave and cool and awesome of you. But—"

—*I want us to be happy.*— The squidgy rolled anxiously, caressing my fingers. —*Be my friend. Please. Don't break my heart.*—

"Okay, okay. Don't twist your knickers. Here's home. You like it?"

Our squat, a moldy white weatherboard, dirt where the lawn should be, a broken veranda with a dusty couch and a few dead potted plants, front window broken and boarded, magpies squawking on the rusty gutters.

We're not proud. We like it here. Why spend money on rent when you can party? Besides, we owe most of what we make to the Valenti clan. In the middle of an ongoing gang war, protection doesn't come cheap, even for a two-bit con like ours. Should've asked Kane to put in a good word for me with Sonny V.

Sure. Kane had probably already forgotten I existed. Probably did a different girl every night, trying to forget about his weird-ass girlfriend.

I flapped up onto the creaking porch, slipping the not-mirror back in my bag. Stale heat dried my lungs as I staggered into the lounge. No air-conditioning, and we swung from the ceiling fans and broke them long ago. Jewelry, crumpled cash, and broken glass littered the thin carpet, yesterday's spoils. Crusty yellow custard splashed the peeling green wallpaper and the TV screen, and our big orange beanbag was speckled with mashed jelly beans and popcorn. We'd had a bit of a party before we went out. No doubt Blaze would cheat at paper, scissors, rock and I'd end up cleaning again.

The mirror snorted. *—Tell him to clean up his own custard. Just 'cause you're a girl doesn't mean you do housework, right?—*

Yeah. Try telling Blaze that. He tries to be a New Age guy—he cleans his teeth and wears eye shadow and everything—but he's got that convenient boy gene that just doesn't see the mess, even when he put it there.

Ladylike snoring rattled from Azure's doorway, and I stuck my head in to see her tucked happily in bed, green hair brushed, wings clean and neatly folded under the quilt.

Affection warmed me. No doubt she'd made sweet, safe, sober

love to a clean, respectable fae boy in his nice clean house, slipped out of bed (*yeah, Ice,* bed—*not over the couch or up against the door*) despite his protests and showered before she came home. Before daylight. With all her clothes intact. By taxi, because she hadn't spent all her cash getting plastered. Without making a dickhead of herself, insulting some random guy on the way.

I looked down at my stained clothes, the blue bruises blotting my arms from harsh demon fingers, the stinky shimmer wafting from my skin. Weary envy tugged at my blood. *Some girls have class, Ice. You're not one of them.*

I tossed my bag into my doorway and passed Blaze's match-scented room without looking in. He wouldn't be there. If he got home before lunchtime, it'd be a first. So many besotted girls, so little time.

I stumbled into the stuffy gray bathroom and peeled off my clothes. Blaze had squirted shampoo all over the tiles again, and scarlet hair clogged the drain. I fumbled the tap on and leaned my head on my forearm, letting lukewarm water slide over me until I drifted asleep and woke up with a jerk. Water off, find a towel, make an effort at drying myself, stagger naked back to my room with an aching head and stinging eyes.

My room, torn lace curtains, silk flowers, and Kevin, my glass-eyed teddy bear, on the bedside table. My bed looked wonderful, the crumpled feather quilt inviting in its rainbow cover. I didn't even bother to shut the window to keep the magpie noise out. I fell into the quilt facefirst, the pillow soft and sugar-scented, dripping green hair cool on my back. Diamonds clinked gently on my wrists, comforting. The not-mirror rolled out of my bag, singing a sweet metal lullaby, and I cradled it in my hand as I dozed off.

My life. Take it or leave it. There's more than this, but I'll never see it. I'm just a silly fae girl. Not a person, with a job or a family or a life. A foolish, scared, useless fairy girl with aspirations beyond her means. Fancy that.

I fell asleep dreaming, of thieving a hellburnt demon's cave where the air stinks of pain and fire, my companion a deep blue shadow with warm copper claws. Dread thickens the air like hot fog, but I'm not scared. We creep hand in quivering hand over black blood-scorched earth, so stealthy past slumbering sharp-scaled hell-spawn, drifting over hidden trip wires and spike-riddled traps with a flutter of warm silver wings. The treasure chest is rusted, the lock trapped with poison. We steal the mirror in a shower of black sparks and flee. He wraps velvet blue arms around me, brushing his soft wings against mine, and the lips that burn my mouth taste of iron.

5

Feather-light kisses dusted the small of my back, and I groaned in deliciousness, rubbing my cheek into the soft pillow. I'm naked in his bed, and he'll kiss me all over with that sinful silver-blue mouth, kiss me until my wing tips curl and my nipples spring tight and my legs melt like hot caramel, and then he'll climb onto my back and slide inside me, deep and slow, and he'll crush my fingers on the sheet and lick between my wing joints while we make love.

Gentle pleasure built and broke in my belly, and I shuddered and groaned in delight.

Naughty fingers yanked knots into my hair. I snapped awake, warm honey sensation slipping away. Red sparks showered onto my pillow from a low giggle, and the smell of matches tickled my nose.

Did I just come in my sleep? Damn it. I sighed, burying my face in iron-scented warmth, but too late. Hot midday sunlight cracked between my eyelids, and the dream broke. "Get lost, Blaze. I'm asleep."

"I'm bored. Wake up." The mattress dipped, and curious claws scratched at my knuckles. "What's this?"

Warning clanged. *My squidgy. Mine.*

I jerked up and tugged the sweaty sheet around me, pulling the squidgy away. "Mine. You can't see it. Get your own."

He grinned, sleepy-eyed, scarlet hair sticky in the heat. Still dressed in skin-tight leather and pirate velvet, only he smelled of girly perfume, light and flowery. A fetching yellow bruise adorned his narrow chin, and he'd lost an earring.

—*He's cute,*— the squidgy observed helpfully.

I squinted. "Where you been, naughty boy?"

"Damned if I know. I woke up beside my clothes in an elevator, there's chocolate in my hair, and my dick hurts. Musta had a good night."

He ruffled his sparking hair, and the squidgy giggled. —*Ooh, he's really cute.*—

I giggled, too. Squidgy's a girl after all. "You're such a whore, Blaze."

"Someone's gotta do it. You stink. Where've you been?"

Nowhere. Doesn't matter. It's boring. You wouldn't be interested.

The cowardly words floated on my lips, but the sleepy mirror clicked its tongue at me. —*Why are you ashamed? Be proud. Tell the truth. You really care what people think?*—

Right. Yeah. Of course not. I fluffed my bedraggled hair, noble. "Why, with a demon lord, since you ask."

The squidgy laughed, and warm pleasure spread in my blood, unexpected. *So that's what truth feels like.*

Blaze laughed, and smacked a kiss on my cheek. "No shit. How was it?"

His lips felt strange, soft and sugary, not burnt like Kane's or rusted and mysterious like my dream lover's. I grinned. "Weird. Excruciating. I came about eight times. Wanna know how we did it?"

Blaze winked, and slunk crafty white fingers across my hip toward the mirror. "So was it twue wuv? Didya get his phone number?"

I squirmed away, and he followed, burrowing after me under the quilt in a flurry of crimson wings. He rubbed his head on my shoulder like a cat in our warm rainbow-stained shelter, and I giggled. "No. But I did get this."

I held it up and squeezed, and the petals sprang open. My mirror glinted at me, and I grinned back. "Hello, squidgy."

—*Well, hello.*— Slinky, like a hungry cat.

Blaze craned his neck and peered inside, and his dark eyes shimmered. "Oh, that's nice, Icy. Lemme see." His voice took on that seductive gleam that gives me shivers in all the wrong places, and he stretched out his hand.

I rolled away, teasing, cuddling the squidgy to my chest. "No. It's mine. You'll just break it."

"No, I won't. Give." He scrabbled for my rib cage and tickled, claws and all.

"Ah! Stop it!" My skin twitched all over, my wings jerking helplessly. I shrieked laughter and squirmed, but the quilt trapped me and I folded against his body, kicking and beating at him with my wings as I held the spiky mirror tighter to my breasts. He felt hard, supple, clever against my back. Good, in fact. Really good. His hot smell of woodflame licked me, creeping inside my mouth. My throat tightened. "Let go, you brute. Get off me. Damn, you smell fantastic."

Oops. That one just slipped out. A little too much truth. The mirror giggled, and I flushed, hot water burning through my skin. God, if I'd just flooded in his lap, I'd kill myself.

But he just laughed and rolled me over toward him, trapping my wings under me so I couldn't move. His sultry black gaze drifted over my chest, not at all innocent. "Yeah? Wanna taste me, too?"

The mirror laughed, sharp. —*Oh, yes. Yes, we do.*—

Oh, no, we don't.

With a fresh flush, I remembered I was naked. He'd seen me enough times, at the beach in winter, or between the shower and my bedroom, or that time when some fairy-hating scumbags wired me to a streetlamp and ripped my dress off. But this was different. Those were my breasts he was staring at, my skin all damp and blue with excitement. Naughty, horny little fae girl. I laughed uneasily and pushed at him, trying to pretend my nipples weren't scrunched so tight, they hurt. "Get your hand off it, Blaze. You're not serious."

"Why not? You were." He circled my wrists one by one and forced them over my head.

Okay, so I didn't exactly struggle. My back arched all by itself, straining toward him.

The mirror snickered, and spilled onto the sheet by my ear.

Images seared my vision, of his mouth on me, his bold hands exploring me, his tongue pleasuring me deep. I shuddered, lust ripping a ragged swath through my reason that filled rapidly with scorching embarrassment.

What was wrong with me? Was I still drunk? Blaze is hot boy-candy and we play flirty games, but I'd never seriously desired him before. Of course, I'd never lain under him naked with my wrists trapped in his double-jointed fingers and his hot thigh jammed hard between mine and that gorgeous red hair tickling my chest and . . . Oh.

He nuzzled my breast, lipping my twisted nipple. Sensation stabbed straight to my sex, and desire splashed my skin like hot oil. *Mmm. Pretty boy. Naked. Kissing.* "Blaze . . ."

"Uh-huh." He nibbled me again, harder. Yellow flame curled from his lips, licking deep warmth into my breast. My nipple stung and tightened, begging for his mouth.

—Don't fight it, Ice. You know we want him.—

I squirmed, burning. *Insane. Mad. Stupid. Tell him to stop it and get off me before something ugly happens.*

—How about, gosh, that feels good, make love to us right now?—

Just shut up, okay?

But careless glee sprinted in my head like a line of banshee blue, and hungry words scrambled in my mouth. I bit my tongue, but they slipped out. "Mmm, kiss me, that feels so good. Umm . . . I mean . . ."

"You mean you like it." Strange harshness edged his voice, and he flicked my swollen bud with his sharp tongue. "You taste horny, Icy-girl. Wanna fix that?"

He sucked my nipple hard into his mouth. Water sizzled under my skin. I whimpered. His sharp teeth grazed me, and when he bit me gently, my insides melted, it felt so good.

Decision time's passing, Ice. This is crazy. Get him off you. "But . . . don't we have this rule? . . ."

"Screw the rules. Come taste me. You want it." Ruby sparks ignited on his breath, entrancing me, showering my skin with stinging desire. He slid onto me, nudging my legs farther apart with his hips, and I didn't stop him. His svelte weight pressed down on me, and he would have forced his burning lips onto mine, only I strained forward and kissed him first.

Hard, needy, cruel. Mad. My lips bruised on his teeth. But I couldn't stop. I didn't care.

He tasted as I knew he would, of a winter bonfire, woody and aflame. He laughed into our kiss, and I did the same, reckless delight boiling inside me. I wrapped my leg around those slender hips, and he pressed my wrists harder into the pillow and slid his clever tongue into my mouth.

I swallowed, dragging more of him into me. My breasts hurt deep inside, my belly squirmed hot and empty, longing to be filled, aching with a deeper need than I wanted to acknowledge.

I wanted to feel him on me and inside me, enjoy his lustful flames licking my skin. I wanted to stop pretending he didn't turn me on. I wanted to stop caring what other people thought.

But more than anything, I wanted to stop being afraid.

Of other people, of men, of sex, of getting hurt. Of myself, of what I might do in a careless moment.

—*Yes,*— hissed the mirror, triumphant. —*We're us. Love you, Ice. Love you always.*—

"Ice." Blaze's whisper burned my mouth, his lips sliding on mine. "Fuck me. Do it. You know you wanna."

"Mmm. Yeah." His erection jammed hard against my pubic bone, tempting, and the twinge of delicious pain threaded a glimmer of reason through my crazed senses.

This isn't you, Ice. You're the sensible one. You don't want this. And even he's not usually this cruel. Why is he acting like this, after so many months of meaningless flirting? Something's wrong here.

The mirror buzzed, angry, and I broke off, breathless, too desperate to laugh anymore. "But what about Azure, she'll be jealous—"

"Screw Azure, too. I want you." He dragged my hands down to his waist, red flames reflecting in his eyes, and at the stickiness of his smooth hips under my fingerpads, my resistance simmered away. Selfishness tickled my spine like a warm feather. My body glowed with pleasure. For once I didn't care about consequences, and it felt fucking fantastic.

By my ear, that crafty squidgy cackled, and I grinned.

I scrabbled to get his pants open, and the truth spilled out, irresponsible, beautiful, no shame, no regret: "I've always wanted you."

A sweet, arrogant Blaze grin. "Yeah, I know. 'Bout time."

His mouth demanded mine again, hot and wet and laced with fire. At last I found the buckle and released it, and his skin burned my thighs. We didn't have a condom. I didn't care. I worked my fingers around his cock, and at the delicious throaty sigh he made into my mouth, lust unraveled in me like a coiled snake. I wanted to impale myself on him just to hear it again, to feel his desire slide down my throat. Flame licked his wings, singeing the quilt. The swollen flesh between my legs still hurt from so many times last night, but that only made this more enticing. I wanted to feel him where I'd felt Kane, erase the chilly feeling inside, and the nerves in my sex twitched hungrily. I shuddered, disbelieving and shamefully eager.

This is actually happening. I'm about to screw my best friend, and it's gonna feel really good.

"What're you lot doing in there, the laundry? Can't ya let a girl sleep?"

From the next room. Querulous. Infuriating. Predictable.

Okay, so that broke the mood. Guilt scrubbed me like a scouring pad, stinging and painful. What the hell was I doing?

"Forget her." Blaze rubbed himself between my legs, his lips still sizzling on mine.

Hot, hard, willing. My flesh ached with need. I squeezed my eyes shut in disbelief, my breath harsh and short. The words that came out weren't the ones I needed. "Oh, god . . . Please, just . . . Christ, get off me."

"You're kidding, right?" He pushed, and I wanted so much to push back that my bones hurt.

But I summoned the ragged scraps of my will and squirmed out of the way, shame boiling my skin. "We shouldn't be doing this," I whispered. "Quick. Before she finds out."

"Told you you're scared." He nipped the point of my ear, cruel and arousing.

"Not scared. Sensible." The happy, alien urge to crucify sensible clawed at my guts again, but I dragged my imagination to Az's reaction if she saw us. Not good, especially after I'd promised her . . . God, I'd actually promised her I wouldn't touch him. What was I thinking?

He sucked my earlobe with a sorrowful whimper. "Pity."

"Yeah. Get off me." I shoved him away and scrambled off the bed, hunting on the floor for some clothes, any clothes before she came in and saw us. I found a crumpled blue sundress and dragged it on, fumbling to tie the halter around my sweaty neck. Hastily I fluttered my sore wings to unwrinkle them, and water showered. I smelled of him, smoky with phosphorus and boy sweat. Surely she'd notice. Damn it.

By the time I turned, Blaze was up and decent, and I'd missed the curious spectacle of him stuffing that delicious hard-on inside those tight leather pants. I giggled and whispered, strange levity polishing my guilt. "How's that thing fit in there, anyway?"

He adjusted himself with a naughty wince. "You'd be surprised where it f—"

"Noisy pricks, aren't you? What's the party?" Azure fluttered in the doorway in her wispy white nightie, dragging a waterfall of green curls from her delicate neck. Sleepy glitter drifted from her wings to set her pale blue skin aglow.

Envy scratched my overwrought nerves, and I felt geeky and ugly and wished Blaze wasn't there. Even just out of bed and hungover after a night on the town, she's pretty as an angel.

Blaze winked slyly. "Icy's got a new toy."

My conscience stung. He's such a sweet liar. But his muscles shine with sweat, his lips are swollen, his wings tight and glowing, you can't miss the bulge in his pants or the stink of singed hair. Surely she'll notice, say something, hate me forever.

But poor innocent Az just blinked beautiful sleepy eyes, eager. "Ooh. I love toys. Show, Icyspice."

Great. Now we're both liars.

I shook my head loftily, eyeing that treacherous squidgy, who winked and teetered back and forth beside my pillow. "Nope. It's m— Oh no, you don't." Blaze dived for it. I dived after him. Az leapt on top of me, and we all hit the bed in a crunch of bones, snapping wings, and breathless laughter.

The mattress springs groaned. I gasped, my breath squashed away in a fairy sandwich. Blaze wriggled beneath me, and Azure flailed and yelled on top, waving her slender limbs. The squidgy giggled and rolled away, chased by three sets of grasping fingers—yellow, blue, and white.

Blaze came up with it first, his pale fingers smudging the glass as he held it in front of his face in yellow sunlight. "There's me. How ya doin, me? You're mighty fine. If you wasn't me, I'd take you home and— Oof!"

Azure elbowed him in the tummy, grabbing the mirror as he twisted away. "Nuff of that. I'm prettier than you. Look, there I am. Ugh. Wrinkles. No wonder he wanted the light off. That's it, I'm getting Botox— hey! No fair!"

I trapped her wrist with one hand and tickled her skinny rib cage until she let the mirror go in a squirming giggle fit. "Mine, I told you. Don't scare the poor little thing." I peeked inside, the pretty glass shimmering, and my heart tumbled happily, home. "There, there, squidgy. Don't let the scary fairy upset you. She's just jealous."

Azure wriggled and reached for it again. "Am not."

"Are too." I held it away, laughing and dodging, our limbs thrashing in tangles.

"Am not." Her voice took on an insistent, childish tone, and I decided not to press it.

"Are too," chimed in Blaze, pulling her hair.

Az shoved him away, hard, and he tumbled wailing to the floor. She scowled. "Am not, I said. What scumbag did Ice screw to get it, anyway?"

"What?" My heart stung, and I squirmed away and sat up, clutching the mirror in my lap. She sounded nasty, petulant. Like she meant it.

Blaze laughed and whacked me in the head with my pillow, dust flying up my nose. "A hot dirty demon lord, that's who."

Azure sniffed, haughty breeze lifting her hair. "That'd be right."

Ire seared away my restraint. I struggled to keep my voice even. "Lobster telephone! What's that supposed to mean?"

"You know what it means. You always get everything." Her eyes narrowed, her chin tight.

"Do not! Where the hell did that come from?" But I knew where it must have come from, and I swallowed again, desperate not to look at Blaze.

But Blaze laughed, nasty, and flung the pillow at Az's head. "Jeez, Az, why are you such a bitch? Didn't you get off last night?"

She batted the pillow away, and her face darkened, blue leaching deeper in her cheeks. "And what do you care, slut boy, off screwing everything with a pulse?"

A cruel grin twitched his lips. "Except you. That what this is about? You jealous?"

Her forehead crumpled, and tears blotted her lashes like green ink. He'd scraped too close to the truth.

My cheeks scorched, sour water flooding my mouth. "Let it be, Blaze. You don't have to rub it in—"

"Shut the fuck up, Ice." Azure rounded on me, green hair whipping her face. "You don't fool me. I know what you're doing. Always putting on that clumsy dopey-girl act to make people look at you, always trying to show me up. You're just jealous because I'm prettier than you."

"Yeah?" Her peach-scented wind lashed my hair, and I yanked the knots back, ire stinging my skin. The mirror hissed warmly in my hand, and spite gnawed my blood like a hungry rat. I let it chew. "Good thing you are, or no one would ever put up with your whiny-ass shit. At least I can still get laid after I've opened my mouth."

The silence scraped loud. We stared. Tears streaked her face like verdigris, her mouth quivering. Her wings drooped, and abruptly her breeze died.

My breath hurt, like I'd run too far, and my eyes stung hot. Not true, what I'd said. Nasty, thoughtless, an envious so-called friend. *Christ, what's wrong with me today?*

Blaze gave a shaky sigh and dragged sheepish claws through his hair, his wings curling. "Fuck. Sorry, ladies. I'm a bitch. Guess it was a rough night."

Remorse cramped in my belly. "Jeez. I can't believe I said that. I'm sorry, Az. I didn't mean it."

She wiped her nose, her voice indistinct. "Really?"

"Really. It's not true, what I said. I don't know why I . . ."

"Me, too." She sniffled. "I feel weird. Like someone made me. Please, can we forget it?" Her eyes shone, pleading.

Cool relief filtered my blood. I hugged her, and she hugged me back. Blaze whispered something in her ear, and she laughed and swatted him, and he winked at me over her head.

I smiled back, uneasy. I felt weird, too. I'd felt weird all day, edgy and careless and intoxicated, an uncomfortable emptiness inside like something I loved had been torn out. I couldn't possibly be drunk now, after so many hours.

Sharp metal edges nipped my palm. The mirror stared at me, its whisper rustling in my ears like wind from a distant storm. I squeezed it, and it protested with a shudder and a high-pitched whine. I squeezed harder. Grudgingly it snapped shut, and the whine silenced.

First the guy on the tram. Then throwing myself at Blaze. Then this stupid argument. Like I couldn't help myself, and just did whatever I wanted and screw the consequences. Like I wasn't afraid of anything.

All since this morning. All since I found the squidgy.

Hesitantly, I placed it down on the bedspread and snatched my hand away.

I looked up, and Blaze looked back at me, the memory of what we'd almost done lighting wary coals in his eyes. I swallowed, disappointment fresh and salty. *Shoulda known he'd never want me for real.* "You thinking what I'm thinking?"

He pointed at the rusty sphere, hesitant like it might bite him.

"What?" demanded Azure. "What is it?"

"The squidgy," I explained reluctantly. "I think it's . . . making us feel weird. I dunno. Maybe."

The squidgy sniffed. *—That's right. Blame me. Like you didn't want him, too.—*

"Shut up! Don't like you anymore." I swatted at it, and it rolled over sulkily and stayed silent.

Azure arched her fine brows at me, and I shrugged, sheepish. "There's someone in there. It talks to me. Can't you hear it?"

"No."

"Not even a little b—?"

"No," she insisted, tilting her chin away, but not before I saw a hint of sky-blue flush. So it talked to her, too. Interesting.

Jealousy burned my blood that the squidgy found another friend so soon, and I felt like smacking myself across the head for being so stupid. But it didn't make the jealousy go away.

Blaze wiggled bony fingers impatiently. "Where'd you say you found it?"

"In Kane's pocket. He had it at the club. I saw In . . . I mean, someone gave it to him. I saw."

Azure turned her stern mothering glare on me. "Whole truth, Slicey. Who?"

I shrugged, pretending it didn't matter, but my voice emerged small and scared like a mouse. "Indigo."

Blaze chuckled, scratching chocolate from his hair. "You're such a fangirl. You took it 'cause of him?"

"It was shiny," I protested feebly.

"Shiny Indy-score. Could be from anywhere." Blaze's eyes shone, his lips wet. Excited despite himself. Shiny rated highly with him, too. Another reason I liked him.

"The stinky caverns of hell," suggested Azure happily.

"Or under dung piles in a goblin's hideout."

"Or deep in the slime vaults of some demon's dungeon."

"Or the bottom of a manky cistern at Joey DiLuca's place."

"Or—"

"Okay, you two," I interrupted crossly. "I get it. I'm an idiot, all right? I screwed up. But we've gotta get rid of it somehow."

Az wrinkled her nose. "Can't you just drop it in the bin? Or dump it by the side of the road or something?"

"Leave it for some little kid to find? Don't think so."

"Break it?"

"No way! It might leap out at me, or get really angry or something."

"Back to Kane's?" Blaze fluttered his brows, like he knew what I'd say.

"Lick a spriggan's fingers. Are you crazy? I'm not going back in there. He'll bottle me and flush me down the toilet, or turn me into a glob of snot or something." Or touch me again. I shivered.

"Back to Indigo, then," Azure suggested, untangling her hair with a puff of air.

My spine tingled, longing and fear warring to see who could make me squirm the most. The erotic Indigo-flavored dreams I'd enjoyed so much this morning still scorched fresh in my mind, and the memory of Blaze's hot body on mine wasn't calming me down. In my current mood, I'd probably describe to Indigo every thrust and gasp and ask if he wanted to join me.

The idea flushed me violet. "Umm . . . Good idea. I'm kinda busy this afternoon, though, I just remembered, so if you guys could . . ."

Azure gave Blaze a crafty blue wink, and Blaze stifled a giggle.

Water boiled under my skin for the umpteenth time today, and I scowled, relief spreading. "Oh, fine. Make fun of my broken heart. Real nice friends you are."

"He's a stuck-up jackass," said Blaze, still giggling. "Dunno why you wreck yourself over him, Icy. Find yourself a real fairy."

"What, like you?" I spoke without thinking again, and hid a wince, my teeth aching lest Azure say something.

But Blaze just shrugged, his usually confident gaze slipping. "Like anyone who don't treat you like a fucking cockroach. You're worth better than that."

My nose fizzed, and I swallowed an embryonic tear. Blaze is selfish and vain and thinks with his dick most of the time, but he loves me, and I knew in my head he was right. Indigo sure gave me the insect treatment last night.

Bad luck for me I'm besotted with him.

"He's not a jackass," I protested, denial like sweet champagne in my heart. "He's just real busy a lot of the time, what with his profession and everything. He's a real focused dude, like nothing else ever bothers him, how cool is that? And he's gotta be careful who he hangs out with, because he could put them in danger, because he steals from demon lairs and goblin dungeons and Joey DiLuca's fucking cistern, okay?"

Blaze rolled his eyes. Azure poked her tongue out and mimed sticking her finger down her throat, and even I had to giggle at the excuses I made. "And, yeah, so he's got gorgeous silver wings, and that sexy metal hair, and he smells so good, I nearly pass out, and I want him want him want him and he's a total asshole about it every single time I ask him out." I sighed. "Yeah. Not a jackass at all. Thanks for clearing that up, Blaze. Really."

"He does have a pretty ass, though," Azure said brightly. "Blaze is right about that. All perky and tight and yummy."

Naked dream images ran fresh in my memory, not dissimilar to Azure's description. I glared. "Can we not talk about Indigo's ass? Please? If that's okay with you?"

"Just throwing bananas from the train. You know, trying to help—"

"We're going to Quang's this afternoon, right?" I cut in firmly. Quang was our fence, a smelly red spriggan with groping fingers and a potty mouth. "We'll sell him the squidgy along with everything else."

Blaze chewed his succulent lip. "But what if it's dangerous?"

Our gazes met, and I knew what he was thinking. One little look into that thing and we'd nearly made the horridest of mistakes. I chewed my thumbclaw, avoiding his eyes. "We're selling him stolen jewels, aren't we? He's used to a little danger."

"But still . . ."

My guts warmed. Blaze was right again. But desperation gnawed at me to get rid of it, to get things back the way they had been. I flicked my wings, insouciant. "We'll warn him not to look. Not our fault if he can't help himself. Right?"

6

Water splashes, and Indigo comes to with a start.

His forehead smacks against steam-coated glass, dizzying him. Black tangles scrape the mist, and he glimpses his own bedraggled reflection in the sepia-lit vanity mirror. For some reason, relief crackles his spine.

He sighs and rolls his neck under the spray, letting water flow over his aching limbs, through his hair, into his bitter-stained mouth. His dark skin stings, rust-scraped and raw, silvery scratches smarting.

Rough night.

Blackout. Dreams again, maybe. His wings hurt, inside to his bones, like he's flown too far. He doesn't remember getting home. Doesn't even recall taking a shower, and with weary distaste, he hopes there's no one in his bedroom.

He drenches his face. Dark water swirls down the drain, trailing grit on the tiles.

The rusted hellmirror. He remembers that. Evil thing, whispering at him like murder's ghost, sliding guilt-tainted needles into his veins.

He spits a coppery mouthful. Nasty thing. Kane's welcome to it.

And then Ice, the scrunchy yellow girl who teases his blood to quicksilver and his senses to golden warning. Scrambling off his lap like he'd cut her, the smell of her dusky wings crawling under his skin, so he slammed up his ice-walled attitude and pushed her away.

Hot regret splashes over his wings. Hasn't he done enough pushing away? She's nice, isn't she? An ordinary girl. Not dangerous. She wouldn't get weird with him. Wouldn't wheedle out his affection to use it against him. Would she?

Prickles on a pineapple. Damn right, she would. A petty scam artist like her? She's doing too good a besotted-fangirl impression not to be playing him. No doubt she's working for some thief-plagued master who owes Indigo a kick in the ass. Maybe even for Kane.

A tricksier girl than Ice once messed with his mind like that, and look where it got her.

Indigo snaps his teeth on bitter memories of auburn locks, a warm rich laugh, smooth red lips he'd kissed like her breath was air itself, now curving with delicious betrayal. An audacious theft twisted horribly wrong when she turned on him, tricked him, betrayed him once he'd led her to the loot. But then a demon's rotten snarl of triumph, sharp brass shackles searing Indigo's wrists, easily broken but too late, the ground quaking with the demon's indiscriminate rage. She flees with him, his false-hearted girl, broken and bleeding, scrambling up cracked stone tunnels toward the light, but he's too swift and she can't fly. She's not strong enough, he spits curses and shoves her away, but she falls. An accident. Not an accident. He isn't sure. But remorse rips his heart like poison fangs, and his claws tear her skin as he scrabbles to catch her, to hold her, fighting gravity's inescapable pull down a black spike-slashed hellpit. He can't. She falls, wide blue eyes rimmed with blood, her last spit-choked words a curse.

The rage and crushing sorrow are faded after so long, and all that's left is guilt, bitter regret, and the certainty he can never go there again. His heart's not for the taking. He won't fall for such pretty lies a second time.

But the image of Ice's awestruck gaze stirs his desire again, and he coughs and resists the need to touch himself. Kane's not welcome to her. Just because Indigo won't have her doesn't mean anyone else should be allowed.

Indigo's skin heats with honey-sweet memories he doesn't want, vague steamy images like he's watched through glass. Devoured the sight. Couldn't tear his eyes away. Kane claiming her, kissing those taut golden lips, sniffing her puckered breasts, spreading her pretty thighs on his filthy demon lap like she belonged to him, and in the shower Indigo slices his lip with sharp iron fangs, silvery blood washing onto his chest. The sting distracts him from his swelling hard-on, but it enhances it, too, and he gasps and indulges, stroking himself with light copper claws in the hot spray as he thinks of her.

Just a girl. An awkward, funny, sexy girl with fascinating flaws that tempt him and secret beauties that calm his raging blood. Normal. Ordinary. Imagine that. Ask her out, buy her dinner, take her to the fucking theater or whatever normal people do. Kiss her lips in the warm midnight breeze, take her somewhere fresh and clean and pleasure her, slide his body on hers and his tongue in her salty moisture and his cock deep into her willing body and let that be enough.

But he doesn't trust her. He doesn't trust himself, not anymore.

Current crackles across his wet skin like spiderweb. His cock strains in his hand, his balls tight, and he crunches aching teeth together and lets go. Guilt. Penance. Whatever. Just not her.

He twists the shower off and shakes himself, spraying rusty droplets on the glass. He rubs a towel in his hair and walks naked through the bedroom—empty, thankfully, bed still made—and his sparse blue lounge to the balcony, where the afternoon sun cooks the concrete and a light hot breeze cleans his skin in a sunbright view of shining apartment blocks and cerulean sky. A perfect day for views, for leaning off the dizzy-high roof with summer breeze lifting his wings, inhaling air washed clean of city filth. He likes it up there. But not today, not in this mood.

His shadow paints the floor, lean, wings carving like blades. He leans over to see the street six floors below, and his calves hurt, like he's climbed too many stairs. Images flash, obscure. Sprinting down a dark deserted street, his blood afire, laughing. Always laughing, this shadow self. Indigo doesn't remember the last time he laughed.

He turns his back to the breeze and stretches silvery wings. Water evaporates, cooling his blood, and the hot breeze lifts him, filling his membranes with the urge to fly.

Time he left this town. His soul is safe for now. His trade with Kane ensured that. Nothing here except bad memories and danger and a succulent yellow girl he can't have. Maybe Sydney, the north shore where the weather's cool, anonymity and salty sea breeze to comfort him. Maybe even across the sea, Jakarta or Colombo with their muddy monsoon gutters and warm typhoid rain, where the crumpled change in his pocket is a fortune and demons are poor and starving like everyone else, too busy gnawing at each other's throats in the dirt to hire a thief.

Yes, leaving. It's time.

He tosses the towel aside. Inside, he pulls on fresh jeans and buttons a sleeveless black shirt cut to fit around his wings. Cash, bankcards, slim silvery phone from the marble bench. That's it. His life. Portable, easy. No complications.

He glances around as he pulls the door shut. Dim, blue, cool. Empty. He won't miss this place, and no one will care he's gone. He'll just stop paying the rent and the bills, and the estate agent will lease it to someone else. Neat. Uncomplicated.

Cryptic images and the memory of roses suggest he has another place, darker and more sensual, that needs care. But the memory slips from his grasp, and he can't recall where or why. Doesn't matter. Maybe he dreamed it.

The cool white corridor lies deserted, and he glides into the bitter chromed elevator and presses *L* for lobby. There's an expectant finality about an elevator door. One world vanishes, crumbled to dust or scorched to hell, for all he knows. Another opens, fresh and ripe for pillage. Closure. Death. Rebirth.

But the doors clunk, inches short of closing. Jammed, on curled brown fingers with violet claws that rupture the metal like paper.

The stink of ash and roses scrapes his tongue raw.

His startled wings jerk into flight. Too late. Nowhere to go. Trapped.

Claws rake his hair, wrenching his head back, a rusty spike of agony in his spine. His knees slam into the steel floor, metal grating on metal, and smoky breath scorches his eyes, a burnt glimpse of wine-dark tresses and hell-green eyes swirling with sadistic delight.

Delilah, demon whore, brat princess of hell and pissed-off ex-mirror-owner.

Fuck.

She snakes her chocolate-skinned body closer, her torso encased in a black nylon sheath. She blinks dark lashes, and demonic compulsion slams into his guts, boiling his blood with false lust. "Indigo, you cheeky little shit."

Her husky voice caresses straight to his balls, and a rush of molten quicksilver hardens him instantly. Hatred twitches his skin. He's on his knees before her and he wants to drag her down with him, pull her plump brown mouth onto his cock and come down her throat.

Disgusting witch. His voice cuts his throat, salty like razors. "Fuck you."

He struggles to rise, wings gripping against steamy air, but Delilah's claws slash at his scalp and she holds him down effortlessly. The doors cruise shut, and the lifts sinks. She stabs the red emergency stop button, jerking the chrome cage to a halt. "In your dreams, you rusty little worm. Where's my mirror?"

Indigo bares hungry teeth, fighting an alien longing to bite her, chew her jutting nipples, sink his tongue into her weeping flesh. "Fuck. You. Hellslut."

Her emerald eyes flash scarlet, and she grabs his thrashing wing and crushes.

Agony crunches, metal teeth ripping down his shoulder. He throttles a screech and his vision blots black.

Delilah grins around needle teeth and squeezes harder. Sleek merlot curls quiver in glee on her shoulders. "No one steals from me. Least of all a sloppy blue iron-stinking maggot with a hard-on for blood like you. Where's my fucking mirror?"

Her voice filters through a ragged haze of memory, and shame and confusion scorch his heart. She's talking shit, but his blood sparks like shattered glass with deep delight, and he wants to scream, *No, you're a liar, I'm not like that, I didn't mean to let her fall.* "Gone," he gasps, his shoulder blades bending under excruciating pressure. Pain savages his twisting spine, and nausea crawls up his throat, choking. "Gave it away."

She laughs, black smoke curling from her nostrils. "Shoulda known. What did Kane pay you in, amnesty? Hell's in your blood now. Think you'll escape that easy?"

Indigo spits, and defiant silver-soaked saliva splatters her cheek.

Delilah howls. Electric rage crackles like green lightning along her arms. She lets his wing go and forces his jaw upward. Her claws slice his skin and choke off his breath. "Guess what, you thieving maggot? You just got yourself a new contract. Get me my mirror by week's end—in one piece, shithead—and I'll pay you by not nailing you to the wall in a screaming steel cell for a thousand years before I scrape your rotten blue skin off and eat it on toast. Get it?"

His wings curl with impotent rage, and his balls crunch tighter. Threats, pain, eternal torment. Same fucking shit as everyone else. Only she means it. His teeth judder, his mouth sweating inside, yearning to chew her apart, suck her, eat her. It's just a mirror. Not worth living that long for.

She smirks. "Yeah, I can see that's making a dent. Pity you're too fucking arrogant to have any friends or I'd nail them up next to you." She punches the red button again and leans in as the elevator drops, her lips a quiver from his, her damp breath smearing seductive ash on his tongue. "My mirror, or die screaming in your own shit. Your choice. You know where I live."

Her tongue flickers, hard and slick over his lips, a horrid, dominant kiss. Heat stabs into his guts, withering his resolve in an instant. He hisses and dives for her, but the doors whisper open and she's gone in a sweep of chocolate limbs and grape-dark hair, leaving only the stink of ash and bubbling red need.

Hatred seethes in his stomach, frustrated lust spiking into his balls like teeth. He screams and doubles in agony, and his copper claws rake deep scratches in the floor.

7

"No way, luv. I'm not taking it." Quang folded leathery red arms across his scrawny chest and eyed the squidgy with beady black suspicion. His pointy ears twitched, crusted with dirt and dead skin, and his potbelly poked at his stretched black T-shirt, which read MY ANGER MANAGEMENT CLASS PISSES ME OFF.

Dusty sunlight dribbled in from a wire-covered skylight. My pretty diamonds glinted on black velvet, beside pink pearl strings and a sky-blue opal choker. The squidgy jiggled next to them, littering rust flecks on the velvet. A scaly whisper slithered in my ears, threatening. *—Don't get rid of me. You'll be sorry.—*

I recalled the calming bell-chime voice it used when it liked me, and I shuddered. *Just leave me alone, okay?*

The squidgy muttered darkly. *—Nice friend you are. Fine. You're on your own. See how you like it.—*

And like a raindrop on the wind, the voice was gone.

My heart lightened, cautious. Good riddance. But unease jabbed my spine. I still wanted it out of my sight. I leaned on the dusty glass counter, offering Quang a nice view of my boobs swelling against my halter dress. "Five, then. Not a cent less."

Quang grinned and scratched coarse orange hair, a goaty stink wafting from his armpit. "It ain't the price. It's the smell. It's yucky. I'm not taking it."

I wrinkled my nose. He can talk. Quang's pawnshop is crammed in above a Vietnamese restaurant in downtown Brunswick, a dark den festering with dust and stuffed with moldy carpet rolls and crates of junk, and it stinks of stale cooking oil and spriggan sweat.

In the corner, Blaze rummaged through cardboard cartons, pulling out rusted bike chains, pistol parts, desiccated specimens in jars. Humming. Amusing himself. Ignoring us.

Could use your help here, dude. I scowled at him, but he didn't see me.

Azure smiled her prettiest smile, playing with her dress hem to innocently show off her thighs. "But the diamonds are nice. You like diamonds, Quang. And pearls. And the shimmery blue stuff."

Quang leered back, broken black teeth sliding up over his lip. "I'll take all those, darlin'. Just not the stinky round thing. Why'd I get the feeling you're conning me?"

The squidgy tilted and swerved on the glass, buzzing angrily. I grabbed it and jammed it back onto the velvet. *Behave.* "Why do I get the feeling you're ripping us off? Come on, Az. Let's take our business elsewhere."

"Fine with me." Quang tapped chewed yellow claws happily on the counter. "Come back when you don't get half as much, and we'll renegotiate."

He had us, and he knew it. Our scores are high-profile and dangerous, and besides, we're fairies. Most times no one else will touch us, and if we didn't get at least four grand for this little lot, our asses were toast. But we had one secret weapon remaining. I raised my voice. "Okay. Whaddaya say, Blaze? We go elsewhere?"

This time I got Blaze's attention. He glanced up, his hands full of broken crystal. "Can I have this? Sorry, what?"

"Quang don't want our squidgy," reported Azure, her tone thick with righteous indignation.

"That so?" Blaze dumped the crystal with a happy tinkle and sauntered up to the counter.

Quang cleared his throat, black eyes darting. "I's just sayin to the ladies—"

Blaze licked his ruby lips, a sight you gotta witness to truly understand, and it dried the words in Quang's mouth. "That a new haircut?"

"Um . . . What?" Quang's fingers smeared the glass, his flashy golden ring glinting in sunlight.

I stifled a smile. Quang's okay, for a skanky money-grubbing liar. He's just got this thing for pretty fae boys. Which makes him quivering jelly in Blaze's dirty-flirty hands.

You show weakness; we exploit it. That's what con artists do. Sometimes I feel bad for him, but not today. Today, I wanted him a trembling wreck.

Blaze leaned closer, and as if by accident, sparks twinkled from his claws, caressing Quang's crusty hand. "New haircut. Kinda cute. Anyway. It's a fine squidgy, Quangster. Very . . . umm . . . stimulating. Sure we can't come to some arrangement?"

Quang's leathery throat bobbed. "Well, I guess I could . . ."

"You guess you could what?" Blaze let his lips drift apart.

Quang squirmed, glancing from the squidgy to Blaze and back again. "Look, I can only take the jewels. It ain't the money. Just not my bag. Gives me the willies, okay? Sorry."

Despair weighed like stones in my heart. If even pretty Blaze couldn't talk Quang into it, we were lost. Stuck with this horrible thing. Damn it.

Disappointment built swiftly to careless anger, so abrupt, it scorched my senses and quivered my fingers with hate. I slammed my foot into the counter. Pain crunched into my toes, clawing up my ankle. "Ow! For fuck's sake." I kicked again, rage burning deep. The glass cracked like a starfish with a loud crunch, and this time the pain shocked me to silence.

I struggled to calm my breath, to hold my jerking fingers still. I don't kick things. I just get angry and hot and sulk for a while. But I couldn't help it. I wanted to crush something small and weak just to watch it hurt. If I'd had a weapon, I might have used it.

Fear crawled along my nerves like a cold centipede. This wasn't me. Was I going mad?

Squidgy, you still there?

Silence.

Scorn darkened Azure's frown. "Good one, Ice. Break everything. That'll help."

My blood seethed. I crunched my fingers tight until my claws bruised my palms, and rage bubbled and munched, leaving me hot and empty inside. Damn squidgy.

Quang backed off, lifting his hands. "Look, you guys need to leave—"

"Not so fast." Blaze fluttered over the dented counter and parked his cute butt, hooking Quang's thigh with a shapely ankle. "You never asked about my arrangement."

His voice seduced, a familiar sultry tone that crawled a shiver down my legs, quenching my rage.

He'd used that one on me this morning. *Fuck me, Ice. You know you wanna.*

My stomach coiled, discomfort jerking my wings tight. Surely he wouldn't really . . . Not just for that. He's got dignity, our Blaze. He screws anything that smells good, but on his terms.

Quang flushed a darker red and flicked a wary glance at us girls. "What, um, what'd ya have in mind?"

"I'll fix your counter," Blaze suggested coyly, and traced a delicate claw over one of the cracks I'd made. The edges glowed red with fire-fae heat, and glass fused with a steamy hiss, leaving a rippled ridge.

Quang stared, and swallowed, his imagination no doubt leading him to new and tempting places. "Should hope so."

Blaze beckoned, and when Quang leaned closer, Blaze whispered in his crooked ear, a smile curving his lips.

Quang's ears curled inward. He dampened his lips with a snaky black tongue. "Oh. Um. Okay." His voice was barely audible, and Blaze stared him sultry in the eyes without flinching.

I shifted, squirming. "Blaze, you can't be seri—"

"Don't tell me what I can and can't do." Blaze didn't drop his gaze. "Fuck it. See ya downstairs."

Az's face paled like dawn sky. "Blaze—"

"Save it, Az. You don't wanna see, leave." He twisted Quang's brittle orange hair in his fist, and when Quang dropped to his knees, I grabbed Azure's hand and dragged her toward the stairwell.

On the way down the creaking stairs, my guts writhed like I'd stuffed them with worms. I didn't want to hear, but I couldn't help straining my ears. I couldn't hear anything, and my nerves stretched even tighter.

Azure clomped behind me, her hand stiff and cold in mine, and as we squeezed onto the sunset-stained sidewalk, she ripped her hand away and rounded on me, big eyes glimmering emerald with tears. "You shoulda stopped him."

Her accusation bit me like a horsefly. Tears sprang to my own eyes, my vision glaring cyan in the sun. Blaze is a sweet guy beneath all that vanity. I don't give a damn whom he does—boys or girls, spriggans or banshees or humans, for all I care—but as far as I know, he's never prostituted himself before. "I tried to stop him, Az."

"Shoulda tried harder. He never listens to me. It's your fault, Ice."

"Is not!" People sidled past us on the skinny footpath, and I tucked my wings in and tried to keep my voice down below the traffic noise.

"It is too. You're the negotiator. You shoulda made Quang take our deal." That infuriating childish lilt crept into her voice.

Ire jabbed like she'd poked me with a pitchfork, but guilt pierced me sharper, all the way to my heart. It was my fault. I'd brought the squidgy home, and now to get rid of it, Blaze was . . . I didn't even want to think it. I didn't care if the mirror made him act this way, like he didn't care about consequences or conscience. It was my fault, and remorse cut my nasty tone to shreds. "Not like I held a pistol to his stupid fairy head. Just piss off, okay?"

Az stalked to the gutter and folded her arms, gazing out into the street with her chin in the air, an angry breeze fluttering her white dress.

I swore and kicked at the dirty concrete, my foot still sore, and for eternal minutes we stood there, waiting and avoiding each other. I cracked my knuckles. I tapped my foot. I hopped up and down. Pedestrians shuffled by. Cars passed. Traffic lights flicked from green to red and back to green. Damn it.

Light footsteps skipped down the stairs, and I whirled, my pulse cold.

Blaze emerged, blinking in the sun and scraping his hair back. Heat flushed his skin bright, and his chest heaved with light, short breaths. A drop of blood stained his thigh through his jeans, spreading.

I stumbled up to him, blue all over with embarrassment. "Blaze? You okay?"

He tossed a ragged green wad of cash at me, and I fumbled to catch it, sweat smearing my palms. A lot of money. All hundreds. I counted it swiftly. Five grand. The price of our jewels. Exactly what Quang offered us, no more. And the squidgy was gone.

I looked up, chill shrinking my skin.

Blaze cast me a cold, empty glance, still catching his ragged breath. "Fuck it. It felt good. What you staring at?"

My heart stung, and for once, I had nothing to say.

Midnight moonshine floods the neat grass courtyard behind Kane's town house with pale underwater light. The creamy façade looms tall, throwing black shadows onto the garden. Distant traffic smears the silence, and in the garden a fountain trickles, water over iron-bolted river stones and glassy blue ornaments, the rocks still smelling warm from the long-set sun.

In shadows above the porticoed entrance, Indigo floats, warm air supporting his wings, his dark hand resting lightly on the upper-story window ledge for balance. His reflection glints in distant headlamps, flashing in and out like a dim blue ghost. Beyond, inside, darkness stares back, the shadowy edges of a doorway in pale walls and the darker shape of empty carpet.

He sniffs the summer air, searching for the telltale ozone tinge of current, but only pollen and warm concrete greet him. He inhales deeper, the oxygen rush filling his blood. His nose twitches. Residue, the worn conduit of voltage past. If there's an alarm, it's off, or broken. Arrogance. Luck. Whatever. Saves him the trouble of shorting out the circuits.

He presses his palm against the top of the smooth window frame and grits his teeth in anticipation. Metaldark sweat springs out on his face, and the lock tumblers melt with a hiss and a puff of steam. Pain flares like acid. He yanks his singed palm away, the hot iron scent of his own burned flesh an unpleasant distraction.

He forces copper claws under the aluminum frame, a tiny grating sound he can't avoid. Molten steel squelches from the ruined lock to splash on the carpet inside. Smoke wisps upward into darkness. He waits a few seconds, his pulse elevated but controlled. No movement. No lights. Swiftly, silently, he raises the window sash and slips feet-first into Kane's upstairs bedroom.

His feet hit coarse wool. The room's empty, unused, the carpet bare of furniture. Not Kane's room, and no one else lives here. Air-conditioning taints his sweat with ash, and he slides the window closed behind him to halt the inward rush of warm air.

He closes his eyes, listening, breathing, searching for metal's innate pressure on his senses. His eardrums throb, painful. As always, it's deafening at first, and his sinuses whine in protest. Steel girders surrounding him, crushing inward like a claustrophobe's nightmare, wrapped in a tangle of dust and plastic-sheathed wires. White noise, garbage, hash on an empty channel, free to anyone who'll listen. Indigo's trick is to tune in. It makes him such a useful thief.

Right now it makes him impatient. He digs deeper, in that iron-free space between air molecules, and faint motes of life glitter in the emptiness like a lost fairy girl's diamond choker: A pin, dropped on the carpet and lost. The dim coil of a tap spring, a strip of bright chrome on a shower recess. Flickers of cheap gold on a circuit board, an intricate brass hinge, silvery flecks in the skin of a discarded photograph. A scatter of lead crystal, soft golden chains, a gold quartz watch, a platinum ring.

He swallows, dismissing it all. He's not interested in random plunder. He's here for only one thing, and he listens harder, scouring the fae-bright ether for the itching stink of a rusted round hellball.

He doesn't find it. Gritty sweat stings his burnt palm. Too much clutter. He'll have to look the old-fashioned way. Folding damp silvery wings, he pads lightly out into the dark corridor, ears pricked for movement even though he knows Kane's not here. If Kane were here, he'd be caught already.

Smooth off-white walls, an unused bathroom, the dry smell of vacuumed carpet leading to other rooms, empty, distant, stuffy with loneliness. Light spills up the curved white stairs, tall shadows angling, the rubble-flecked iron rail stabbing bright in his senses like a trail of fire. Down, on a draft of cool air that tingles beneath his wings, to mahogany floors lined with steel nails, receding like runway lights under the screaming tungsten filaments of halogen lamps.

The black television reflects him in a mosaic of glass and shimmering silicon transistors. The sick ache of overstimulation grips his skull. His stomach chews listlessly at what's left of the cobalt-laced fish he swallowed for dinner, and nausea climbs his guts to crouch in his throat like an oily toad. Metalsense makes him sick. He tries to focus on the cool blue titanium bangle shining around his wrist. Light, inert, comforting, it's the metalfae equivalent of a seasickness bracelet, but it's never enough. If he doesn't switch off soon, it'll get messy.

But he still can't smell the mirror. There's no rust here, not in this vapid façade of an apartment, almost as fake as Indigo's own.

Down a fresh-painted corridor, mercifully synthetic. He ghosts past a lead-spattered oil painting that glares in his eyes, and an old gilt-framed mirror backed with mercury sickens him with the stink of his own blood.

Kane's bedroom. Dim, cool, charcoal's acid tang drifting from neat white sheets. Metal clamors from the master bathroom, sharp chrome edges knifing his sinuses. No rust. No mirror. He swivels to leave, but gentle silver twinkles on his tongue like sherbet.

There, under the bed. Almost hidden by folded linen. He bends to slide one claw over knotted woolen carpet and hooks out a woman's shimmering diamond bracelet. Snapped, the silver wrenched apart, the clasp still holding.

He holds it to shadowed light, tiny rainbows prisming, and a faint fruity scent waters his mouth. Strawberries, tainted raw with alcohol.

His memory somersaults back to last night, Ice laughing on his lap with diamonds tumbling around her slender wrists. The same wrists that trailed those sweaty diamonds around Kane's neck and crushed them into his hair when she came.

Indigo drags the shimmering chain over his tongue, just to be sure. Sweetness flares like fruit juice from rough facets, delicious icing on the cake of fine silver. His blood sparkles. It's her.

Ice was here. The mirror's gone. Given her incorrigible jackdaw fingers, probably not a coincidence. Brave, quirky, cute little Ice. He wishes he'd been there to see it. He smiles darkly to think of her, and distrust of his own motives burns his bones.

He should leave her alone. No certainty she'll know anything. Kane could simply have the horrid thing with him. And for all he knows, she's working for Kane anyway.

But it's a place to start. A plan that doesn't involve picking a demon lord's pocket in public view.

Anticipation whets his metal-drenched senses. His headache swells, deafening, and he wraps the diamond chain around his finger, clenching his fist so tight, it cuts, and silvery blood slides over his knuckles.

He's still leaving. This is just for information. Ask his questions, use her blushing fangirl act against her. Find the mirror, return it to Delilah. Leave Ice alone and get out. That's all.

That's all.

Urgency twists his diaphragm, and he swirls on sweating wings and darts for the stairs. The motion sickens him further, and he barely makes it into the empty bedroom and out the window before gritty metal vomit explodes in his mouth. He spears into the air, giddy, and gasps warm fresh air through the acid remnants of his sensory feast and a faint, lingering lust for strawberries.

8

Afternoon sun glared in our shop window, spearing mercilessly through the purple tie-dyed drapes to roast us. The sign outside says CRYSTAL DREAMS, and we dress up like New Age gypsies and pretend to be fortune-tellers, dazzle them with glamour so we can steal their wallets and break into their houses if they look rich.

The air inside had been cooking all day like a dead pig. Hair stuck to my neck in trickles of persistent yellow sweat, and the scent of sandalwood candles stifled me, though we'd stopped burning them when it started to get hot.

Business was slow. Nonexistent, in fact. Our feathered dream catchers hung stagnant and damp. I sighed and gazed longingly outside, where light breeze ruffled café blinds and shopping bags, fingering lightly through people's hair like little dancing feet. The urge to flee swamped me like an ocean wave. I imagined the clean smell, sea breeze and pollen and freshly cooked pancakes from the café next door, and my head throbbed in sympathy.

In reality it'd be stinky with exhaust fumes and sweat and city dust. I didn't care. I wanted out to play, to let the wind ruffle my hair in the park and smell green grass's cool moisture, or drink in bright salty sea spray with a sugary sorbet and roll down the sand into warm waves at St. Kilda Beach.

I wriggled my legs on my wicker chair, the garish sequins on my top flashing in the sun. My silken skirts itched me, damp. Sweat trickled down my bare belly into my navel. Innate longing for cool water flooded my veins. "Can't we close up and go to the beach? I wanna swim and chase jellyfish and throw sand at little kids."

Azure glared up from her puzzle book, damp purple scarf tied loosely over her hair. Heat doesn't bedraggle her as it does me. It just polishes her beauty a little more. She puffed her wings, wafting cooling breeze over her face. "Be sensible for once, sensible one. How are we supposed to scam anyone if you piss off to the beach?"

"We don't need another one yet, Az. We just made four and a half grand, remember?"

"Yeah. Half of which you two already spent on booze and pills."

"It wasn't half—"

"And the diamond money we already owe to Sonny V," reminded Blaze, who was trying to fly upside down over the coffee table, his feet stuck up in the air and his dangling scarlet hair dripping sweat on the pinewood. He reveled in the heat, being firefae and all. I asked him once why he sweats, if he loves heat so much. He said because it makes him look sexy. I couldn't argue with that. "In fact, we owe Sonny a lot more than that. Five grand more by week's end. Fancy getting your wings ripped off by a hairy Italian gangster?"

"And your teeth pulled one by one," chimed in Az.

"And your claws torn out."

"And your ears sliced off."

"And a fat ugly cock up your— Ow!" Blaze banged his head on the table and tumbled to the floor, lithe denim-clad legs tangling over his head.

"Serves you right, idiot," I said crossly. "Stop doing that. Someone'll see."

Blaze unfolded himself and shook like a wet dog on his knees, wings crackling with green sparks. "Fuck 'em if they do. I don't care."

"Well, you should care. What's gotten into you lately?"

"Nothing. I'm just sick of other people's fucking rules, Other People." He glared at me, defiant orange flames flicking around his lashes.

I scowled back, his attitude scratching like a burr. "If Other People didn't watch out for your ass, you'd be crucified to cardboard in some human's butterfly collection by now."

"Uh-huh. You, watching out for my ass. I'll remember that next time we go to Quang's."

Discomfort swelled my blood. I still felt bad about that. But irrational ire twisted my tongue, and words spilled out, coated with uncensored truth. "Yeah, well, maybe you should just let Sonny Valenti suck you off instead of giving him the four grand, if you liked it so much."

I held my breath, blood hurtling too fast in my veins. *Uncalled for, Ice. Nasty. Say you're sorry.*

But Blaze just laughed at me, spite smoking from his claws. "Nah. We'd get more per hour for you, seeing as you're so keen on arrogant assholes with no manners. Is it true you come harder when you're crying?"

"Stop it, you two." Azure jumped up in a whirl of silken skirt, her nose twitching. "Someone's coming. Blaze, put your damn glamour back on."

I swallowed angry words and jerked up from my chair. Az always knew when business was coming. She could smell their intent on the air from down the street.

Fine. We'll do this one and then I'll get the hell out and go to the beach. Alone.

Stormy static zapped behind me as Blaze ignited his glamour. The doorbell tinkled, and a fat woman waddled in. Sweat sprayed from her rolling limbs and stained her stretched white dress, the colossal outlines of damp underwear clearly visible. White canvas bag with wooden handles, no separate purse. An easy one.

I wrinkled my nose at the sour stink, still smarting from the truth of Blaze's accusation. "Great. The incredible doughnut woman."

Oops. I said that kinda loud. Giggle.

"Shut up!" hissed Az between her teeth, and raised her voice, wafting her glamour-cloaked wings to puff a cool draft over the sweating woman. "Welcome, lady. Blessings of the stars upon you. How can we be of service?"

The woman shifted, uncertain, the floor creaking under her squashed rubber flip-flops. "I want to know the future."

Azure flashed her dazzling smile, and irritation crawled under my skin. "Of course. Sister Ice will consult the magic crystal. It never lies."

It never lies.

An epiphany washed over me, refreshing like lazy ocean swell, and a cool iron whisper of truth feathered my skin.

It never lies. How wonderful. How . . . liberating.

I snorted, fortified. "Don't need no stinkin' crystal to see your future, lady. An early heart attack and a triple byp—"

"Step this way," interrupted Azure loudly, pushing in front of me to usher the fat woman inside.

I gaped at myself for a moment, remorse stinging my cheeks. What a horrible thing to say. Stupid, too. We needed the cash. She didn't look flamboyantly rich like the last one, but the stones in her rings were large, and that was a Rolex digging into her flabby wrist. She could have treasure at home.

But alien mirth erupted in my chest, and I spurted laughter. Horrible, but funny. And true. I was sick of pretending. So, so sick.

Azure speared me a warning frown, her mouth tight.

I widened sarcastic eyes at her and flounced into my seat in front of the crystal ball. We found it in a dusty junk shop months ago, when we first came up with this scam. For all I know, it really is magic. "Okay, lady. What's the story?"

She lowered her sweating turnip-shaped body into the chair. "Well . . . I've met this wonderful man, you see. He says he loves me, and that we should get married. I must know if he really . . . If it'll work out."

Her tired blue eyes shone with hope, and I winced. Ten to one he was stinging her for her fortune. "Okay. Sure. Give me your hands. . . . What's your name?"

"Noelene," snapped Blaze, staring out the window. "Can't you smell it?"

I glared. He knew I couldn't sniff out names like he could. "You know what? Screw you, Blaze. Sorry, Noly-poly. Give me your hands—Okay, yuck. That's gross. Wipe 'em first, can't you?"

Bewilderment hurt Noelene's eyes, but she did as I asked.

Azure swiped frustrated claws through the air at me. But I ignored her, satisfaction lightening my heart for the first time since Quang's. It was sniggering, alien satisfaction, but I didn't care.

I wasn't on this earth to care what other people thought of me. Screw it, and screw them.

I dragged Noelene's clammy hands around the glass ball, and as her flabby arm lifted, a petroleum whiff of sweat and overworked deodorant dizzied me. "Shit." I coughed, but too late. My vision wobbled, and the images poured in.

Young, dark, boyish curls and swift cunning smile, silky black suit and a white tablecloth at some glassy restaurant that smells of patchouli. Eyes like hot chocolate, intent, she's mesmerized, her heart fluttering when he brushes his gold-ringed hand over hers. Lobster and champagne, lemon sorbet on an icy silver tray, she's paying, thrusting her brassy credit card forward, no, I insist, my pleasure. Driving her home in the sporty car she gave him, breeze tugging her lank hair, the smell of leather and designer aftershave and freedom. Kissing in the dark on the veranda of her rambling suburban mansion, her fat body wet and aching with need and loneliness, he tastes of Moët and heaven, he's pulling away too soon, we can wait, soon we'll be married and I'll make love to you in Paris. He leaves, too quickly, and she waddles into the dark house alone with her dreams.

I spluttered, shiny glass chaos raging against sensibility in my blood. So lonely, this poor woman, so in love with an untouchable prince who doesn't care. My heart hurt for her. I wanted to break it gently, warn her to leave before he broke her heart.

But the truth isn't my concern. Remember Sonny's trolls. We need her money. Keep her sitting here so Az can snatch her purse, get her address, her credit card numbers. Now's the time for a big fat lie. I'm good at those. *Yeah, sure he loves you. Congratulations. Go home and plan your wedding.*

I took a deep breath, and the words spilled out before I was ready. "Christ. Are you kidding? He didn't even have a hard-on."

"What?" Her damp forehead creased, confused, and behind her Az inched forward, crafty fingers reaching for the bag.

I stared into the blank glass, shaking. *Tell her he loves her, that he doesn't care about her riches. Tell her he's a nice Christian boy looking for a good woman.* But my poisoned pulse thudded in my ears, whipping me to careless truth, and before I'd even opened my mouth, I knew it was no good. "Lady, look at yourself. You think a guy like him wants to marry you? He doesn't even wanna fuck you. Tie the knot with him and you'll be over a cliff in your Audi by year's end."

Muscles clenched in her wobbly jaw, and she dragged her bag onto her lap in sweaty hands, out of Az's reach. "How dare you?"

I felt like crowing, or hiding under the table. Az waved her hands frantically, but pleasure chemicals thrust into my blood, hot and sexual. I couldn't keep my mouth shut, and it felt awesome. "Trust me, he's playing you. Dump his lying ass and find another boy toy. Here, our Blaze is free. He's cute, and he'll fuck anything for money."

Tears washed her eyes, and she clambered to her feet, sobs shaking her jowls. "You horrible little girl. You could at least have said it nicely." And she hove to, brushing Azure out of her path, and lumbered out, sniffing.

The bell tinkled, and the glass door slammed shut.

A grin splattered across my face like a custard bomb, and stuck there.

Azure rounded on me in a breezy storm, her face darkening to cobalt. "She didn't even pay. What the hell's wrong with you?"

"Nothing." I laughed, the expression on her face needling mirth between my ribs. God, it felt good not to give a shit.

"Plastic dogshit. You've got to be kidding me! You just broke that woman's heart!"

I folded my arms across my sequined chest, defiance steeling my spine. "So? It was the truth."

"I don't care! How about not getting my wings ripped off, Ice? How about not getting buttfucked to death by some warty troll?"

Blaze snickered, and she shoved him, fury bleeding her wings white. "Don't you start."

He fluttered back cheekily. "You gotta admit, the look on that fat chick's face was kinda cool."

"Have you both gone totally insane? We need the money, Blaze. Think she's gonna tell her friends good things about us? What are you gonna do, Ice? Sell yourself on the street? Get a real job? I don't think so." Az glared from Blaze to me and back again, and her pretty mouth dropped open in a gasp. "You're in this together, aren't you?"

"What?" I gave her a sarcastic frown.

"Razors on a waterslide. The two of you. You're doing things behind my back. Playing tricks on me." She lifted her tight little chin, greenish hurt flooding her face.

Blaze laughed, cruel. "What if we are?"

"That's ridiculous," I cut in, glaring at him. "We're doing no such thing."

But Azure wasn't listening. Tears trickled blue on her cheeks, and her throat caught in a clutch of sobs. "You're so mean to me! It's not fair!" And she yanked the door open and ran out in an indignant whirlwind, skirts trailing a whiff of lemon blossom.

I let my head fall back and sighed. "Real clever, Blaze. What'd ya do that for?"

"Do what?" He pressed his nose flat on the window, craning his neck to follow her exit, a curious little grin on his lips.

"Let her think we're throwing some big conspiracy party behind her back, of course."

"Well, aren't we?" He threw me a casual glance, but it fixed me in place like a corkboard pin.

I laughed, uneasy. "What are you talking about? I didn't tell her, if that's what you mean."

I tried to brush past him, but he slid bony fingers around my elbow. His hand shook, tense. No levity in his voice. No teasing smile on his lips. "I don't mean us nearly shagging. I mean this. She's jealous. You're careless. I'm . . . Well, I'm kinda twitchy, you know." He jerked his head, and vertebrae crackled. "Nothing's any fun anymore. Having a hard time keeping still. Don't ya think something's a bit wrong?"

I swallowed, and the echo of a soft metal whisper chilled my blood. Ice crystals crackled on my wings, and I tried to shake them off but they froze fast. "No, it's not possible. The mirror's gone. We got rid of it."

Blaze chewed his lip, and his bold black gaze flickered. "Did we? You sure?"

I remembered my delight at that woman's misfortune, the way I wanted to laugh at her and needle her and taunt and sneer and bait until the truth burned out of me like acid through a plastic cup.

I shuddered. I've always wanted to be brave. But not cruel.

My pulse gibbered at me, hot and seductive and in vehement disagreement.

I've always been terrified of consequences, mistakes, making an idiot of myself. Why's everything about me all of a sudden? What if Blaze was right? What if that spiteful squidgy cast a spell on us?

Stupid, right? I was a fairy, not some witchy magic chick. Hell, I didn't even believe in magic.

But what if it had?

Blaze brushed his finger under my chin, searing. "Think about it, Ice. Before it's too late."

My treacherous skin sparked alive at his touch. Discomfort scratched in my bones. I shook him off and pushed past him, his arm smooth and sweet on my fingerpads. "I don't wanna know, okay? I feel fine."

And I walked out, my body tingling with alien sensation and the dark whisper of denial.

9

Another midnight at the Court, the same as last and next, a carbon copy oblivion. Water throbbed in my ears to the beat, dizzying me pleasantly like alcohol, and starry lights dazzled my retinas in the primal smell of smoke and sweat.

But tonight colors swerved at me, objects jumping eagerly into my vision like magical apparitions of things I'd always craved but couldn't identify. Seductive tastes assaulted my mouth with every breath, flesh, ozone, fruity fairy glitter. My eyes rolled everywhere, covetous as I slunk through the undulating crowd, my gaze draping lustfully over figures and clothes and jewels, and half the time my fingers followed, earning me slaps and pokes and gleeful grins. If hell exists—and there's no denying it does, not in a sweltering black city ruled by demons—then there must be heaven, too, and surely fairy heaven's a nightclub, jammed with colors and sounds and sensory candy.

Wow. Look at that banshee's glassy earrings, that vampire girl's blue satin dress, that fire sprite's fabulous black wings. I wanted everything I saw, craved every smell, longed for every sweet vibration. And maybe it was just me, but there seemed to be an excess of screw-me-senseless gorgeous guys here tonight. Will you look at that green fae boy's butt? So tight, it'd burst like a cherry in your mouth, and the glowing green veins in those wings . . . Gosh.

My palms dripped, a greedy ache growing inside me. Mmm, sly vampire twins in identical white velvet suits, all long limbs and loose blond hair, tiny red jewels set into their teeth. And someone water me down, that fae-struck human boy was hot, dusky ruby-stained skin and double-jointed fingers and wet cocoa hair. Yeah. If there's heaven, it was definitely like this, anonymous and exciting and darkly beautiful. I just hoped the drinks were cheaper there.

At the bar, a tall, tanned human kid in black leathers and a ruby skull necklace stared at me, ultrablue eyes intense. My hungry gaze drifted over him, and I dragged it away. Luscious muscles, inked pretty with curls and arrows. Great ass. But human boys are trouble, clueless if they can't see us and nasty if they can. And besides, they just don't measure up, even big boys like this one. You want some serious anatomy, get yourself a fae boy.

I slid my last twenty across the glowing glass, my limbs still jittering. I'd walked the street for a while and headed home to work this madness off, but even washing the walls down from our custard-throwing party hadn't calmed me down or cheered me up. I kept thinking about how I tore that woman's heart out today, about what Blaze said, the way I leered with strange selfish eyes at everything.

The others hadn't come home, and our little house loomed lonely, shadows making me jump, every sound I made echoing in empty rooms. So in a fit of sulks, I'd pinned my hair up in a wild mango knot, squeezed boldly into what Azure calls my look-the-fuck-at-me-now outfit—it's a slinky silver Lycra number up to my ass with crisscross string straps over the back and more hole than dress at the front—and come here to the Court alone, to dance myself silly and drink this weird lust away. My skin itched, my fingers trembled, my body yearned for some elusive stimulant I couldn't name. I felt weird. It wasn't me. It wasn't right.

But it felt good.

I flicked the cute blond bar boy a wink and scratched my bare midriff, claws tinkling on my belly ring. "How drunk can I get for twenty bucks?"

"You really mean that?" He leant on tattooed forearms, buckled leather bracelets fragrant with his sweat.

My damp nose tingled, and I wanted to bend forward, sniff, run my tongue over the rough leather edges, tell him how nice it smelled. "Hell yes, I mean it."

"She's selling. She'll want more than your twenty, though." He gestured with his chin a few stools to my right, where a dusky earth sprite broke off a kiss with a pale-limbed vampire girl, their wet lips peeling apart like sticky tape. White flowers tumbled through her long caramel hair, her golden wings shedding bright dust. The vampire wobbled on her heels, thin black dreadlocks dangling, and the fairy spat something that looked like dark purple grape juice into a glass and handed it to her in exchange for a fifty.

Memory trade. Swap them something precious from your past and they'll use it to brew you a high you'll never forget, delirium or forgetfulness or plain oblivion. Whatever you like. Hot temptation licked my skin, and my dress stuck on my damp breasts as I shifted, but I wrinkled my nose and dragged my gaze away before I did something stupid.

I don't like people screwing with my mind, even if it does feel good. You never know what they'll erase, or insert. Besides, I didn't have enough cash. "No, thanks. I'll keep my memories. It's tonight I wanna get rid of. Gimme a vodka raspberry, babe, and keep tippin' it in 'till the money runs out."

"Comin' up." He poured, three shots and a splash for luck, and I drank, swallowing until it was all gone, vodka sliding down like cool syrup in my throat. The alcohol hit my stomach, and warmth slid into my blood like a slow needle. I didn't know if Blaze had paid Sonny Valenti his five grand or not. He could let Sonny suck his cock for all I cared. This was mine, the last of my stolen cash. Might as well get the most out of it.

I plonked the glass on the bar and burped, my sinuses already stretching. "That'll do it. Cheers, sweet pea."

He winked at me, and I headed for the dance floor, pleasantly unbalanced, warm comfort spreading inside. The crush tightened around me, slick limbs and sweat-fragrant bodies and the glittering flutter of wings, all pulsing like blood to the flooding sound. My heart skipped faster, and I wriggled in farther, my skin a tingling glory of contact. I didn't care if no one talked to me or tried to pick me up. I just wanted to dance, punish my disobedient body, thrash my eardrums ragged on this gorgeous noise, sweat out this madness and puddle it on the floor for someone else to drink.

I closed my eyes, letting the music fill me, caress me, seep into my burning blood. Damp throbbing air sizzled my senses, glorious, sparking my nerves in time with the beat. I stretched, writhed, jumped, twisting my arms and jerking my legs until I ached, wrapping my sensitive wing membranes over the glowing smell of hot living flesh. Water crept under my skin, drawing secret pleasure from within, filling me, drowning in the glory of motion. My sweat sprayed in droplets, clumping my flinging hair.

Light fingers, sliding hot over my bare waist. "Are you Kane's?"

Warm voice rough with smoke or whiskey, intriguing. A tempting caress on my hip. I cracked my eyes open. Blazing blue eyes, dark hair, ink, and black leather. That tasty human boy who'd stared at me at the bar. Trouble. I swallowed. "Look, I'm not interested, okay?"

Scarlet gemstones glowed in silver eye sockets along his necklace.

A skinny dark girl clung to his muscled arm, the same glaring blue eyes shining from her bruised face. He smiled, scary handsome, his fingers lingering on the curve of my waist. "Come with us. Show us."

I backed away into a squirming pair of banshees, their nails raking my wings. "No way. I am *so* not up for a threesome. Bugger off."

"You must show us." He bent to sniff my bare belly, tugging curiously at the ring there, and my skin squelched in alarm. Freakin' weirdo.

"Just leave me alone, okay?" I yanked free and squirmed through the crowd away from him, his sharp blue gaze scorching my back. I hid behind a tangle of sparkly fairy bodies and held my breath. He didn't follow.

After a moment, I sighed and let my eyes drift closed again, enjoying the rainbow smell of body moisture and the shuddering sway that the music thrust into my body.

I stretched my arms over my head in sultry smoke, content. I missed the warm tinkle of diamonds on my wrists, but that was okay. There'd always be more diamonds, and I never got to keep them anyway. I was just the messenger, a little fae insect in a gangsters' world. Diamonds were for Kane and Sonny Valenti and handsome blue assholes with no manners. But there'd always be more.

"That guy bothering you, sweet?"

"Only as much as y— Oh, it's you. Hi." I squinted in a jumping haze of strobe lights. Tumbling black-dyed hair, pencil-smeared lashes, a sapphire twinkle in his purple brow. Vampire lover boy, he of the delicious kiss and the collarbone fetish. I never did get his name.

He tickled a kiss over the back of my hand, deft fingers cold as his lips. He looked paler tonight, and his blue eyes gleamed glassy with starvation. "I dreamed about you."

"Great. Glad to be of service. Hope you enjoyed it." Hungry

vampire. Definitely not my type. Maybe if I pretended he wasn't there, he'd leave me alone.

But he spun me around and pulled me close, crushing my wings against his chest. Nice body, slim and lean, ripped jeans rough against my bare hip. His sharp chin dug into my shoulder as he nuzzled my wing out of the way. "I dreamed about tasting you."

Nice hard-on denting my ass, too. His breath moistened my neck in the hot smell of bourbon, and I shivered. Drunk, starving, horny vampire. Not good. "Baby, we had this conversation the other n— Hey, I never said you could put your hand there."

He stroked my half-covered breast, teasing gentle nails under the fabric, and his hot tongue slicked the ticklish point of my ear. "You didn't mind a bit of initiative last time."

"Well, I d— Mmm." His claw spiked my nipple, and shock crept tingling roots deep into my breast. My flesh hardened for his finger, and he pinched me, delightful. Recklessness flared in my blood. "Oops. Well, I suppose you can . . . Ooh." He swept kisses down my neck, cold lips but hot tongue, and nuzzled my dress strap aside to delve into the hollow behind my collarbone.

"Whoa." My knees melted, and slick warmth spread between my legs. His inky black hair rubbed on my shoulder, and shivers curled down my chest as he sucked that collarbone with a tiny sting of fang, just how I liked it. "Mmm. This kinda wasn't my plan, you know. . . ."

"Wasn't mine till I saw you." His voice grated, lustful vibrations tingling my ribs. "You look so fucking horny in this dress, and the way you dance makes me wanna slide into you right here."

"Uh-huh. Vampire sweet talk. You don't just mean your dick, do you?" I exhaled, delicate, aroused and disgusted at the same time. Fear piqued my pleasure. I knew I should push him off, get away before he hurt me. But . . . On tonight's special-crazy Icyspice scale of hot to scorching, he rated a definite *screw me now*. And flirting with danger was kinda fun, wasn't it? My heart raced, my skin shone damp and hot, and a needy ache brewed inside me that longed to be stroked. Couldn't hurt to have a little fun, could it?

"Honey, you can have everything I've got." He dragged me against him and crept his fingers over my hip and under my stretchy skirt.

Okay, so no underwear was a bad idea. Or a good one. My insides twitched in anticipation. What would it feel like, a vampire's bite? Good, maybe?

His fingertip brushed my exposed flesh. I shivered in delight, and he groaned and burrowed his finger deeper. "So wet."

Why, so I was. I giggled, mad. "Water sprite, genius. I'm always wet."

"Liar." He grazed my shoulder with hungry teeth as he stroked me, light as a whisper.

"Mmm. Maybe." Nerves tightened inside me, curious and pleasured. Tempted. The risk of infection was supposed to be small. And what else did I have to do tonight? Let's see. Nothing. Just like tomorrow night, and the night after, and the night after that.

My fear scratched at me like desperate claws, but I brushed it aside.

He snarled softly. "Don't tease me. You want it or not?"

"Why the hell not? Yeah. Wanna do it here? You can, if you want." I leaned back into him with a sigh, thrusting my hips forward to meet his hand. His body moved sensually against my back, and pleasure stirred in my guts. How would it feel, his fanged mouth on my sex?

He crushed me tighter, effortlessly strong. My pulse quivered, wary, but too late. Nerveless. Breathless. I couldn't pull away. I wriggled, but he tightened his arm to force me still. His razor tooth sliced along my collarbone, and the sting hurt more than I'd expected or wanted. Alarm jump-started my pulse with a jerk. Blood seeped, warm on my skin, and he laughed, his fingers curling between my legs. "Honey, I'll do it wherever the fuck I like."

And in one simultaneous movement, he pushed his finger deep inside me and forced hungry fangs into the skin of my neck.

Pleasure and pain, meeting in the middle. I gasped, delirious, as my vein popped and sticky warmth spilled, caught by his waiting mouth. My skin stretched, tore, ripped open under his tongue and teeth. A horrid cramp stabbed down the side of my neck, and my wing jerked, my shoulder convulsing in agony.

Yet inside me, flesh hardened as he stroked, pleasure flooding to my center. He found my nipple and pinched it, and my clit pulsed despite the ripping pain. He sucked, thrusting his finger inside me in time, and the sensation of blood dragging out of me as he forced inside started cramps of deep pleasure inside my sex that fought back the pain. I wanted to talk, to tell him not to stop, but my throat had seized with the ache and the shock, and all I could do was groan.

He sucked harder, dizzying, and pushed his fingers deeper into my willing flesh. My head swam, drunk. The thudding music faded, distant, hiding behind the inescapable thrust of my pulse. His body tensed against my back, mirroring my own reaction as my excitement grew. My wings twitched against him, tight and sore. His cock swelled, hard like glass in the cleft of my ass, and I wanted to purr. If he'd lifted my skirt and buried himself deep, I couldn't have cared less.

This monster was swallowing my blood. It hurt like poison. I didn't care. I just wanted the sensation, here and now. Not tomorrow or consequences or cost. Just now. Me and him, this rapturous agony that made me feel alive.

Abruptly, his teeth ripped from my flesh, stinging hard. Blood splashed my dress, shimmering silver in naked strobe lights. I blinked, groggy. "Huh? What?"

His hand slipped from me, leaving me hot and empty. "Fuck. Sorry, man. Didn't know she was one of yours. No disrespect." And he slurped and melted away from me.

Dizziness dissolved my thoughts to mush. I realized that bodies no longer crushed around me, that a distinct space separated me from the crowd on all sides. Either my dancing had scared everyone off, or . . .

Icy fingers fastened around my wrist, and too late I smelled storm clouds.

Hard demon body, cold against my back where the vampire had grown so wonderfully warm. Bumps tweaked my skin, and I shivered, dismayed. His hellweird voice quivered my eardrums, soft yet audible in the din. "You've something that belongs to me, strawberry girl."

Rust-stained glass flashed and jolted in my memory. I tried to yank away, knowing my strength was useless. But he let me go, and I spun around, off balance, jerking my wings to hold me upright. "What did you go and do that for? I mean, nice knowing you and everything, but—"

"You're welcome." Kane stared at me, beautiful and impassive as ever, and stretched out an elegant finger to wipe blue blood from the gash in my throat.

I squirmed under his black gaze. His cold finger on my raw flesh was more than I wanted of him. "I'm sorry, did I misunderstand? Didn't you just piss me off?"

"For keeping you alive." As if I hadn't spoken. "You don't really want to die, Ice. You're just bored."

"Whatever. Just leave me alone, okay?" Dizziness swirled pleasantly in my skull, and I laughed, light-headed. I felt glassy and bright inside, like I'd polished myself. Twenty bucks got me a better high than I'd anticipated.

He rubbed my blood between his fingertips, watching it sparkle in smoky rainbow lights, and smiled. "Looked into my glass, didn't you?"

"Dunno what you're on about." But hot anxious fingers scraped in my guts, and I wiped my bleeding neck. It wouldn't stop. I wiped it again, smearing my palm with warm inky wetness. So much blood. Not counting what had ended up in sweetheart's mouth.

My pulse cracked into a gallop, and my newfound courage fizzed away like snowflakes. Hot terror flooded my skin. Fuck. He drank my blood. My fucking blood. He could have infected me. I could have died. What the hell was I thinking? Nausea dripped down my throat, and I stumbled, my high heels scraping my ankles raw.

Kane caught me, freshly sharp claws cruel on my elbow. He dragged ash-coated lips to my ear, his voice grating like razors. "You took my mirror. Where is it?"

Blue sparks showered from his hair, and ash crackled hot on the tops of my breasts, smearing in blood and sweat. Smoke wisped. My skin wriggled in disgust. I wanted it off, but I didn't dare wipe it away. I gulped, my lungs tight. "Dunno. Got rid of it. Nasty thing."

"You can't get rid of my mirror, Ice. It gets rid of you."

My stomach sloshed with briny fear. Blaze was right. The squidgy had poisoned us.

All my fault.

I stopped struggling, and Kane's grip loosened to a caress. He didn't have to fight. He knew he had me.

Slowly, I swallowed, and rested my temple on his forehead, searching for some small comfort I didn't understand. My lips trembled. "What's happening to me?"

He didn't pull away. He didn't care enough to be unsympathetic. He smiled, his charcoal breath evil on my cheek. "My mirror magnifies desire. It lets you be who you really want to be." He sniffed my cheek delicately, and with a burning flush I remembered him licking me there, everywhere, pinning my wrists to the sheet, his body light and warm on me, inside me, making me come. Dark loathing crusted my heart like rust, but he wouldn't let go. "So many regrets because you're so afraid. All those delights you'll never taste, because you shouldn't. My mirror consumes *shouldn't*, Ice. Think about the potential. No more conscience, and your best effort is to have some grubby little insect suck out your life? Surely there's something you want more than that?"

I trembled against his searing lips, my vision shimmering blue with tears. Something I wanted more? I didn't want any of this. I'd fought with my friends, wrecked our con game, almost broken our most sacred rule. Not to mention those icky suicidal impulses from a moment ago.

Disgust and belated terror mixed a watery mess in my stomach. Christ, I'd be dead if not for Kane.

And demons won't even spit on you for free.

So now I owed him. Inevitability scoured my skin like sandpaper. I owed a demon. How the hell did that happen?

I shuddered in his half embrace, too afraid to look him in the eye. "What do you want from me?"

"I want my mirror back. Do that, and I'll cure you. Even though you deserve everything you've made, you little liar." His eyes grew distant, like I'd hurt him.

Shoulda known it wouldn't be that simple. But hope crawled in my bones, humiliating, and it was all I could do not to fall to my knees and beg for his help. "You can cure me? Really?"

He shrugged, his silken suit raw against my skin. "That's what I said."

He wasn't exactly filling me with confidence. "But . . . I gave it away. It could be anywhere by n—"

"Soon, strawberry girl. If you want to survive much longer." He brushed ashen lips on my cheek and wandered off. Calm, unfluttered. Infuriating.

Music exploded back into my ears, shudderingly loud. I shook myself frantically and rubbed my cheek, trying to shed any remnants of his touch, his beautiful scent, that feral ash that followed wherever he went. Around me, dancers forgot he'd been there and closed in, closer, closer until no space remained between them and me.

Fear smothered me like wet cotton wool, fighting the horrible alien exuberance that already bubbled again under my skin, threatening to betray me. My treacherous nerves tingled, and I tried to calm them with deep breaths, but my lungs hurt, my limbs quivering and jerking like an angry caged rat.

Hands brushed me, bodies pressed against me, hair and nails and fragrant sweat trailed over my skin, and my pulse dissolved in rapture. I loved it. I wanted to jump, twist, dance until I dropped, strip off my skimpy clothes and bathe naked in this wonderful sultry air, the warm wetness of random pleasure.

My hands shook, and tears rippled my vision, underwater blue. If I stayed here, I'd do something stupid. Attract the wrong guy and get wired to a streetlight and fairyslashed for my trouble. Pick a fight with a speed-crazed banshee or some gangster's human squeeze and get my ass kicked to mango pulp.

Give my blood to a vampire and die, just because it might feel good.

Terror stained my soul black, and I ran.

Tripping, stumbling against hard sweaty bodies, heedless of my wings, sliding on wobbly ankles until the dance floor was gone and I fumbled in green neon solitude, my sweat-drenched reflection flashing in a wall of spooky mirrors.

The warm dimness soothed my agitated pulse. Beside me a pale human boy with bruised wrists and a metal-spiked banshee in a white vinyl catsuit swooned against the glass, kissing, their bodies slicking together in a rain of sweaty pink hair, her long blue nails slicing delicate cuts into his skinny rib cage. Another death wish cousin. I swallowed tart sickness and turned away.

I looked strange in the glass, oddly shaped, not quite right. My reflection was still bleeding, the dark blue mess stark against my green-lit skin, the creature's teethmarks already bruising black. My hair clotted in it, rude orange locks stained dark, the rough pin-up job I did at home tumbling out in untidy hanks. A creeping ache still tore at my throat and clawed down into my back. What the hell was I thinking?

I pressed my hot cheek against the cool glass, and it sizzled. My fingerpads stuck, and my palm prints smeared blood and sweat, lustful moisture still sore in my lungs. My tears washed the glass blue, and I whimpered, my breath steaming in wisps. Guilty pulse thudded in my throat. Me and shiny things. Why'd I have to look? Why couldn't I just keep my stupid fingers to myself?

A tall shadow tinted the glass black, and my skin shivered at that metaldark scent. "Ice? Are you . . . Is everything okay?"

Wrapped in sultry shadow beneath the mezzanine, Akash watches Kane walk away from the yellow girl. Sensation crawls under his skin, unpleasant but compelling, and Akash labels it apprehension and savors it like fruity nectar. Delectable. His favorite so far is longing, that sweet hot pain deep inside that makes him shiver, but that one's fickle and hard to come by.

Kane spears a swift dark glance around as he leaves, and Akash ducks back into darkness, for all the good it'll do. Though if the demon can smell him, he's giving no sign.

He scrapes his dark hair back for the hundredth time, just to feel his stolen body move. The physical rewards are constant yet shifting, depending on fatigue, hunger, sensory arousal, and mood. The effects are countless. He's used to uniformity, predictability, sameness. Fascinating.

Fascinating, too, this yellow person Kane threatens. Akash remembers her from last night, on Kane's lap with pleasure sighing from her lips. Akash can't hear their present conversation, but a demon either threatens or seduces, and she doesn't look seduced, not this time; her face loses color and denial glazes her honey-gold eyes.

Akash knows honey. They have honey at home, and it's the color of her eyes, though they're flashed now with rainbow lights like starfire. He knows seduction, too, because he's watched it here, watched them play and tease and give each other pleasure, reluctant or eager or disgusted. He's getting better at copying their expressions, figuring out what they mean. Seduction looks like color and warm sweat and hot breath, and this yellow person exhibits none of those.

"She looks afraid." Beside him, Indra strokes a finger along her thigh, watching the skin bumps rise. She's still wearing the short leather skirt. She likes it.

So does Akash. He's never thought about what she's wearing before.

"Yes. Well done." His eyes swivel back to the yellow one, and he's oddly pleased by the way his gaze lingers on her. She means something to Kane, even if it's only as a minion. He fingers his necklace, the skulls pleasantly warm and angular on his fingertips.

"And sad. The water on her face means sad. Or angry."

"Yes." Indra does well. She's already begun their collection as he ordered. He needs to examine these creatures, figure out how Kane exerts such power over them. They have a warehouse a few city blocks away to hold their specimens for interrogation and experiment. Separate boxes to keep them clean, one of each if possible. He wonders if the colors matter. "That one knows about Kane. She could be useful. Do we have a yellow one, Indra?"

"Not yet." Indra licks her finger. "Salt."

That tickles his interest. "Really?"

She offers it to him, with a passable happy smile. Lips curled, eyes bright, brows slightly raised. She, too, has practiced facial expressions. "Try it."

Something inside his body tightens, like he's tied with invisible cord. He takes her wrist and slides her fingertip between his lips. Her skin glides across his teeth. Vibration tingles his mouth. Interesting sensation. He licks her finger. Her skin is smooth, and bright salty tang tweaks the very tip of his tongue. Delicious. He lets his lips close around her painted fingernail, and on impulse he pulls with his tongue and her finger slides into his mouth up to the knuckle.

His tongue stings, aroused, and hot sensation stabs deep into his blood.

Swiftly she pulls away, her face changing color. "Don't. It is not permitted."

Akash swallows, licking the raw spot on his lips where her finger passed. He shifts, compelled, and movement is uncomfortable. Her human taste still fires in his mouth, the rapid hot delight of it making him wonder if he's broken some hidden rule. He tries to speak and finds his throat dry. "What is not permitted?"

"It." Indra looks away and sticks her finger out to let it dry.

Akash stares into the crowd, but he's not seeing anything. He concentrates on his body, memorizing every last flush and tingle of this new sensation. He wonders if they all feel like this, so wild and uncertain and eager. It would be easy to forget purpose, feeling like this. Easy to discard higher things and wallow in wet sensory gluttony.

Understanding washes him, warm, and he laughs, the smoky air and rippling muscles pleasant inside his chest.

Sensation is the key to Kane's power.

Feed them with heat and sex and substances until their minds weaken. Clever, this sneaky demon lord. Far cleverer than Akash's masters supposed. Shadow told Akash this would be an easy victory. Shadow was mistaken.

It doesn't seem possible. But it's true. Shadow was wrong. Akash must adapt.

But how to fight Kane, when he lures their souls so powerfully? How to defeat an enemy who gives the creatures exactly what they want?

"There she goes. Look." Indra nudges him, cautious.

"What?" He blinks, distracted. The yellow woman wobbles past him, blind with tears and rage.

"Unhappy." Indra confirms her diagnosis.

"Kane did not please her."

"Why not? He is a demon. The prince of lies. Is it possible—?"

"—That he failed to convince her?" Akash frowns.

"Possible. Not likely."

"Then it is she who refuses to please him." Akash thinks hard, the electricity pumping in his brain tickling. "She disobeys him. This may be a weakness. We shall find out. Come." He takes Indra's hand, the contact a pleasant flush of warmth, and together they follow.

10

Ice? Are you . . . Is everything okay?"

So improbable that for several seconds I refused to recognize that velvet-steel voice.

So riveting, my heart clogged in my chest, thick and silent.

So fucking typical, I had to laugh, my forehead still smearing the glass.

Bleeding, crying, half drunk, and terrified. Could I possibly be any more unattractive? . . . Hang on. . . . Nope. Don't think so.

Not that I cared, of course. I'm over him, remember? I sighed. "Yeah, I'm just great, Indigo. Thanks for asking."

"My pleasure." His voice dripped over me like a molten shower, and his iron-drenched shadow swallowed me, teasing dark shivers from my skin. I swallowed, edgy. I forget how big he is, not just taller than me but also solid and unfragile, like a fairy rarely is. Indestructible. An uneasy metalfae anomaly.

I craned my neck sideways. There he stood, shoulder leaning lightly on the glass, his reflection a dark blue shimmer in a halo of silver. His glamour flickered, a neon-lit ghost, and for an instant, I glimpsed his overlay, bland, unassuming, smaller and plainer than he really is, his rich cobalt tones blanched to ordinary chocolate human skin, his blue-black hair muted. *Look away,* whispered his glamour, *don't see me,* and for a moment my gaze obeyed and slid lazily off him like oil. I blinked, and the effect dissolved.

Awkwardness crunched in my mouth like popcorn. *Why does he do that? Fairies don't glamour-whip fairies. It's not fair.*

I sniffed, sticky. God, he was such a show-off in those clothes. Anyone else might look a bit girly in slashed-off sleeves and metal jewelry, but there was nothing girly about Indigo. Not even with those perfect lips that looked carved from silver. Inky skin, bare arms strong and light, rainbow titanium bracelet wrapping his left forearm, steel-gray shirt just tight enough to show me curves I'd dreamed about licking. Straight muscle-hugging jeans—god, that fairy's thighs could kill you. And those wings, sharp like silvery glass and as dangerous.

He said nothing. Just stood there and smelled good, warm steel and fire.

Sure. I was over him, all right.

I turned my face away, sick. He already thought me just a silly girl. Now I looked like a whore, covered in blood and bruises and stinking of some other guy's spit. He'd never take me seriously. "What you want?"

"Now, or ten seconds ago before I saw you crying?"

Like I wanted to discuss it with anyone, let alone him. If he wanted to brush me off, fine. I wouldn't share with him now.

I tried to wipe my nose, but only smeared snot everywhere, and in exasperation I pushed away from the glass to face him. "It's nothing, okay?"

"Nothing doesn't usually bleed all over your dress." His gaze flicked to the mess on my throat, followed the bloodstain downward, and lingered.

I swallowed, my hand fluttering to my chest. That wasn't just sympathy in his expression. Was it? "Don't, okay? It's nothing."

He licked silvery lips. "Mmm. I was just wondering . . . has everything been okay for you lately?"

"Indigo, I'm fine. I told you."

"Right. So nothing weird's happened?"

"Of course not." Suspicion tickled my palms. Did he know something?

He eyed me coolly, close even from a million miles away. "You sure? Nothing like . . . Oh, I don't know. Voices in your head? Bad moods? Crazy impulses?"

My guts heated. How did he know? "No, I told you! Don't be ridiculous. Why d'ya keep asking me?"

"Because I have something that belongs to you." He leaned closer, warm and enticing, and unfolded long three-jointed fingers. A string of silver-set diamonds coiled in his dark palm.

I gasped. My pulse swelled, thumping in my chest, and a happy little ache flowered in my belly.

I'd thought I'd lost some pretties at Kane's, but I'd been too sheepish to tell the others when we needed the money so bad. Now I might get to keep them for once. My mouth watered. Sparkle, sparkle. Mmm. I wanted to squirm, to press my legs together.

I stretched out a greedy hand. "Never seen it before."

"You sure?" He trailed the bracelet over my fingers, tempting me. The jewels burned hot, and they glinted green like emeralds in smoky neon.

"Uh-huh." I grabbed, but he twitched the shinies away, and I overbalanced, fluttering to keep upright.

He clicked his tongue, metallic. "Not so fast, Ice. Questions first."

The tiny lisp my name made in his mouth made me quiver. I stared, transfixed by the glitter, and shifted itching wings. "Where'd you get that?"

He sniffed the jewels lightly and flashed me a teasing glimpse of silver teeth. "Nice try. But you know where I got it."

Great. Now he really thought I was a whore. I sighed, and gave up. "This is about that rusty ball of Kane's, isn't it?"

"Clever girl." He slithered my bracelet casually around his nimble fingers.

My eyeballs swiveled to follow it. Prick. He knew my weakness. I tore my gaze away and lifted my chin, dignified. "Well, you can't have it. It's gone. I gave it away."

Static crackled across his knuckles like fireworks, and his steely irises glowed molten. "You what?"

"I—I got rid of it. It's nasty. It . . . talks to me, or someth—"

"Where is it, Ice? Tell me." His voice cracked like rusted roof iron, and he wrapped hot fingers around my wrist and pulled me closer.

God, he smelled even better close up. His hip brushed my belly, those hard thighs so close to mine, and I flushed, trying to keep my mind on the issues. I couldn't tell him, could I? He'd only go and take it and I'd be screwed. "Why? Whadda you care?"

"I care. So should you. It's Kane's mirror. He wants it back."

"Shoulda taken better care of it, then."

"Yeah, that's what I said to him. It's your own fault, dickhead, get your own fucking mirror back."

"Really?" Admiration breathed on my skin for his courage.

"No, of course not really. Just tell me where it is." Glowing metal rippled white in his eyes. His fingers tightened, and my bones grated together.

"Ow! Will you get off me? Not telling if you're gonna be nasty." Pain flared, but my disappointment hurt worse. I wriggled, dismay slithering in my guts like a snake. I'd thought better of him than this. *Tell me he's not like all the rest. Tell me he isn't going to hit me.*

But he shivered like I'd tickled him, blinked curiously at me, and let me go, hiding his hand swiftly behind his back. His eyes shone clear and cobalt, sorrowful. "I'm sorry, Lady Ice. I didn't mean it. Forgive me?" And he knelt at my feet like some weird blue angel, steely black hair sifting over his forehead, neon shimmering silver and green on his wings.

I laughed, disturbed. "Hey, don't get all weird on m—"

He pressed burning silver lips to the inside of my wrist.

"Oh. Gosh." His kiss scorched me like sunburn, but I didn't care. My pulse danced against his tongue, and though my wrist still cried out where he'd crushed me, the pain dissolved into seductive glory. His lips teased my skin, caressed me, drew my pulse quicker. His tongue stroked me, delicate and fresh, until my sex ached with anticipation. I wanted him to do that forever, to slide his mouth up the inside of my arm, kiss the crook of my elbow, my shoulder, my collarbone. Wrap that clever tongue on my breasts, around my wing joints, between my legs.

He finished with one last sensual lick, and when he pulled away, I whimpered, bereft, that spot on my wrist suddenly chilled. But a tiny stripe of heat still seared my skin, and when I looked down, diamonds glittered back at me from cooling silver. He'd melted the bracelet around my wrist.

Cautiously I fingered the warm gemstones. They sparkled back at me, and the ache in my belly sharpened. My very own diamonds. Imagine that.

He gazed up at me, intent, and though his eyes still burned bright, new softness glowed inside. Like he'd suddenly been struck by this amazing new idea to be nice to me for a change.

Goofy affection swelled my heart, and I sat on it firmly. I didn't get him: rude, sweet, frost, hellfire, inconstant like oil on a pond.

Like there were two of him, constantly changing places to confuse me. Like I was a game he invented to amuse himself.

I sniffed, pretending I wasn't still shivering all over from his kiss. "Like that's supposed to make it better."

He fluttered to his feet, warm glittery breeze ruffling my hair. "No? What kind of apology will you accept, then?"

Anger prickled my skin. So he assumed I'd forgive him for nearly tearing my arm off, did he? Not to mention acting like such an asshole every time we met. I opened my mouth to give him a stinging retort.

But he leaned over to whisper into my ear, his hair springing on my cheek, and my breath reduced to a remnant, dissolved in his heady molten scent. I swear his body shook, so tense those scant few inches away. "I'm sorry, Ice. I haven't been myself for a long time. I'm scared . . . God, I'm terrified I've given you the wrong impression. Can you forgive me? If I'm sweet for you from now on?"

Confusion addled my senses. His body heat condensed on my lips. I licked tempting copper, drunk. I'd never known him to be like this. On edge, yes, but not nervous. Not vulnerable.

My heart melted. I wanted to hold him, stroke him, quench his trouble in my arms. I wanted to kiss him until we both ached. I wanted to throw him off me and run, and I knew my old boring self would flee, make some excuse, some foolish mistake that let me off the hook, avoiding decision and danger.

Screw that.

Daring, I tilted my face a fraction toward his. "Umm . . . What kind of sweet do ya have in mind?"

"Whatever you like." He twined smooth fingers between my knuckles and squeezed, and his hot iron breath flowed over my wounded neck in a rush. "You smell so fresh."

Surprise and guilty pleasure stiffened my spine. His sharp claws stung the back of my hand, but I almost didn't notice in the lost delight of his touch. His bangle zapped me, static creeping up my arm. My left arm. Funny. Could have sworn he wore that on his left wrist. Pay attention.

His cheekbone slicked on mine, and stayed there. I bit my lip to stifle a gasp, and words it seemed I'd always wanted to say flooded my mouth like glorious faestruck wine. "I love it when you touch me."

He rubbed that glorious metal-spun hair on my cheek, and I felt every steely strand. "Mirror, Ice. It's for your own good. Tell me and we can get on with this."

Still inches of air between us. Still only his hand crushing mine. Imagine if he actually touched me, if his body slid on mine. Unbelievable. He never looked at me right, never touched me, never tempted me like this. My heart quivered, afraid, and I realized that part of the reason I persisted with him was that I knew he'd never say yes. I never thought I'd have to face the consequences. But now . . .

Desire shuddered my muscles, overheating me. Deep inside my skull a warm alien whisper dared me to take my chance, just this once, and though I hated the scaly serpent sound of that voice, I couldn't resist.

I tilted my head back, and hot water trickled down my neck and between my breasts, soaking my dress again. Waterfae, dripping and disheveled with desire like a beach model. I knew it looked hot. I stretched, tempting him. "Kiss me and I'll tell you."

"Tell me and I'll kiss you." He drifted closer, and I closed my eyes, breathless. Static crackled over my nipples, shivered in my hair, tingled my skin. The metal studs on my dress zapped and clicked onto him. My belly ring yanked toward him, pulling my skin taut, and I wanted so much to follow, my guts ached.

But my own chaos crippled me, and my muscles stiffened like glass. He frightened me. I frightened me. I didn't dare.

But his lips hovered so close to my throat, and his finger traced my ragged wound where the blood still flowed, and his body trembled hot like a fever. Like he'd given in to some crazy impulse he couldn't resist.

A loose pin jerked from my hair and snapped tight to his shoulder. My lips quivered, words itching to spill out. Maybe he was drunk, or sparkly. I didn't care. I wanted Kane's cure. But I wanted this more. "I fenced it. Quang's in Brunswick. He might still have it—"

"Enough." His breath raised bumps on my neck, heat washing all the way down to my sex. He sniffed a hot trail up over my chin until his mouth drifted over mine. My flesh tingled. God, I wanted him to kiss me. I could already taste him, already feel his tongue on mine. I inhaled, dizzy with anticipation.

A hot finger poked my shoulder, startling me backwards, and warm breeze ruffled my hair with the scent of matches.

My eyes snapped open, and Blaze grinned at me under a spray of bloodred hair. "Ice, darlin', there y'are. Come have a drink with me. . . . Well, bugger me. Look at that." He bit his knobbly knuckle in mock surprise. "Indigo. Guess I didn't see you. How about you get your rusty-ass hands off my friend before I break your fuckin' teeth?"

My pulse screamed in denial. *Blaze, you idiot.*

Indigo hissed, current crackling between his fingers. "Try it, prettyfae."

Blaze rested a possessive forearm on my shoulder, his eyes flaming scarlet as he stared Indigo down. Gutsy, from a six-inch height deficit. "If I find out you put that blood there, I'll melt your damn wings together and chew 'em off. Okay?"

Indigo's hand hardened in mine like tempering steel. Sparks sizzled along his wings, threatening.

Blaze snarled, angry scarlet flame licking around his wrists.

Alarm hitched my breath tight. Blaze had guts and a nasty

rat-fighting streak, but Indigo could probably tear him in half and munch up the pieces. Reluctantly I pulled my hand from Indigo's, his dark metal warmth still lingering on my palm. "It's okay, Blaze. Calm down. It's nothing."

"Don't look like nothing." Blaze's stare didn't falter.

"It's okay. Let it be." I looked over my shoulder at Indigo as I dragged Blaze away. "Talk to you later, okay?"

Indigo just stared at me, his eyes glowing orange, ragged black hair slicked to his face with static.

I shivered and looked away, my skin prickling.

I stumbled with my arm around Blaze's shoulder, and a warm hand arrested my fall.

The dark kid in bike leathers again. Thorny tattoos, tarnished silver necklace with ruby skulls, drug-stunned girl on his arm. He clutched my forearm tightly. "Show us."

I flushed in a strange scent of flowers, and my control snapped. I pushed him in the chest, anger vibrating in my blood. "Are you following me? Huh? What the fuck you looking at, stalkerboy?"

He caught himself on shining mirrors, palms smearing. His girlfriend scowled and stepped forward, and I flexed irate claws, my heart galloping, ready for a scrap. But Stalkerboy rested a cooling hand on her shoulder and smiled at me, his eyes glowing sapphire blue.

Blaze tugged me away and spat wet golden flame onto the ribbed metal under our feet as we reached the dance floor. He wore pale jeans and a tight green rubber tank top that steamed on his superheated skin, and his crimson wings quivered in anger. "You okay?"

I yanked him to a stop, lustful blood cooking my body wet like a sauna. The echo of Indigo's electricity still tingled through me, and my traitorous skin clamored for more. "What'd you do that for?" I demanded for maybe the tenth time tonight. "What is it with you people? I can take care of myself."

"Yeah, sure looks like it." He wiped blood from my throat and evaporated it on his fingertip, sizzling.

"Indigo didn't do that, okay? Some other asshole did that. I'm over it. I was doing fine, thanks."

"Oh." Blaze bit the inside of his lip, flushing guiltily like a kid who knows he's done wrong. "Sorry. I thought—"

"So you should be. What's your problem with him anyway?"

"Don't care how hot he is. Bet he wanted something."

Warm embarrassment splashed my cheeks. Damn it. I mean, I knew that now, but hearing Blaze say it squirmed sordid disappointment through my limbs. How were these things obvious to everyone but me? "Yeah, okay. You're right. Don't rub it in."

Blaze slipped both elbows onto my shoulders and heated himself a few degrees in sympathy, wrapping me in flickering warmth as he stroked my hair. "Hey. Don't be upset. Let's have a good time. Come dance with me."

I scowled. "No."

"Pretty sparkles say yes." That wheedling tone glossed his voice, and he slipped crafty fingers into his pocket and came up with a shiny glass vial. Emerald fairy sparkle glittered inside like a magic potion. He tilted it before my eyes with a tempting little smile, and the glimmering liquid swirled, mesmerizing, bubbles jumping in the strobe lights.

I eyed it suspiciously. "What is it?"

"Just a little bliss. I got it for you. Pleeease?" He flashed me his pretty black eyes under a rakish scarlet sweep of hair.

I sighed, a reluctant smile twisting my lips, and plucked the vial from his fingers. It was hard staying angry with Blaze when he turned on the charm. He meant well, bless him. Probably better nothing happened between me and Indigo anyway, no matter the tender underskin he'd at last shown me. The two-faced bastard would only have hardened up afterwards and broken my heart.

For the so-called sensible one, I'd sure fallen for an untouchable metal prince. Stupid, faefoolish me.

I ripped the cork out and snorted. Sugary bliss burned a hole through my sinuses. Water misted my eyes, sun and grass and violets glaring like rainbows. My muscles flushed with warmth, and slow pleasure stroked my sex, sly and breathless like a gentle blow job. My wings swelled, quivering in violet delight. If I were a boy, I'd have a hard-on. My head swirled, candy tanging fresh in my mouth. I felt warm, safe, uncomplicated. Life was easy. Everyone was my friend. Nothing mattered. Not mirrors, not sexy coldhearted blue fairies. Just this.

I smiled, lazy, and held the vial to Blaze's nose. "Love ya to bits, ya know that?"

He inhaled, sucking up the last green waft of sparkle, and his eyes shimmered wet, his pupils blossoming scarlet. He grinned with drunken cunning and tossed the vial aside to smash on the floor, flames ribboning from his fingers. "Likewise, sweetie. Come here and dance with me, and I'll keep all those horny boy sluts off you."

Colors assaulted me from space, swirling. My limbs quivered, blood flowing fresh, burning for contact and sensation. I slid my hands around his narrow-muscled ribs, tickling him with my claws, and his lit-phosphorous scent tasted like home and safety as well as like challenge. "Who'll keep you off me, then?"

"Guess you'll have to." He sniffed my hair, poking his nose in beside my ear, and his lips curved in a grin against my cheek. "You stink of copper. See if we can't sweat that off, huh?"

I giggled. Sweet, dirty Blaze. "Can I trust you?"

"Nope. You care?"

"Never." I rested my head on his shoulder, our bodies snug and warm together, his hot blood soothing my still-racing heart.

11

In a mirrored corner, Ebony grins and stretches against warm glass, relishing the warm, clean desire flowering inside. Oh, now he understands Indigo's trouble—yes, he does. She's very tasty, this Icygirl. So fresh and clean and sweet like plums he could eat all day and not get sick. And the madness sniggering in her veins calls to him like nothing else. She's seen the mirror. She'd know him. She'd understand.

But that was close. He giggles, hiding his face with cheeky hands. They nearly spotted him, Indigo and his succulent death wish girl. She caught him unawares, her pretty tears warming his heart. The bright candy taste of her confusion drenched him with impulsive desire, and he showed himself before it was time. Lucky the snarky faeboy had interrupted.

Lucky, and maddening. She's glorious, and Eb nearly stole her from Indigo in one sneaky little switch. Now he'll have to try again.

He straightens, stretching out the sweet cramp in his loins. Beyond time Indigo got laid. Eb hasn't time for such squalid things. He has a queen to worship. Queen Icygirl, mirror lady of chaos.

Beyond the comforting shadows, Ice and her friend walk away, and Ebony smiles and watches the muscles in her legs move, tight and tasty under the thin golden membrane of her skin. He can feel that movement on his palms, as if he's sliding them up over her thighs, pulling her down onto him to kiss and bite and love her despair away. . . .

Mmm. Naughty. No way to think about your queen.

But Indigo played his tricks on her, the svelte gold-brushed pretty, turning her on, making her breath shorten and her juicy nipples tighten and her body ache, and Ebony couldn't help but enjoy it. The berry scent of her sex still tingles his nose.

And now this other thing, festering inside him like greasy black cancer, sucking away his life and his energy. She wants Indigo, though that blue metal freak swats her away like a mosquito, and the stumbling hot shimmer of emotion wasting between them boils Ebony's blood like a furnace. Jealousy, pure and savage, spoiling his fresh desire.

If she were his, Ebony would treat her like the queen she is. Hold her, keep her, kiss her softly, as Indigo never will. Beg to drink away her misery, open that salty conduit to heaven with his claw and let her sorrow bleed away. She deserves no less.

Ebony scrapes back sparking hair, and it cuts his fingers, sharp like wire. Blood oozes. He licks dripping knuckles. Next time, he won't let Indigo misuse her so. He won't hide, not anymore.

Now, she's half-buried in the crowd, gold-dusted tendons curving in her naked limbs as she cuddles her handsome firefae boy. Her breasts press into his chest, soft flesh swelling to escape her tight dress. Her friend sneaks his fingers into her fruity hair, and she smiles, sharp white teeth gleaming.

Ebony watches, discomfort scraping his nerves like a wire brush, that writhing envycancer growing inside him until his guts hurt. She's very pretty. His balls still ache from the episode with Indigo, and watching her dance lithe and slow against hot flamefae flesh isn't helping. So fresh, so clean. Even Indigo said so.

Ebony licks salty lips, transfixed. Indigo wants to have her, taste her, love her, slide himself inside her and feel her soft wetness on his metalbright skin. It might be nice. Ebony wonders if she'd like that with him, and dryness tickles his throat until he coughs it away, flushing.

Indigo's always done those sordid, empty things for him. Eb finds no delight in them, not anymore.

But such thoughts about his queen are unworthy. Disgusting. He bangs his head back into the glass as punishment. Metal crunches, and glass shards spike his scalp, deliciously painful. But his greedy gaze slides back to her, and he stares intent as her luscious golden lips open for sly firefairy kisses.

Foul sweat crusts him, burning, and he wants to scrape it off with wild hands, wash himself all over until this horrid lust is gone. They aren't clean, the things he'd like to do with her. They aren't nice. They don't mean anything. And he knows where they lead.

He'd like to take that dirty firefae and rip his pretty head from his neck, too. But Ice looks happy. Eb's got no cause.

A whiff of cold fairy blood brightens his nose like berries. It's her. Stolen. He rips his gaze away to follow her scent, glad to have something else to do. There it goes, a splash of her, staining some thin white vampire's breath. Some filthy tricksy animal that's tasted her, drunk from her, knows her touch and her smile and her damp golden flesh. It won't do. She shouldn't be treated like that. Her smell belongs to Ebony.

Rage fires his frustration, and he jerks himself upright to follow, muscles twitching hard.

Around the corner, where the strobes don't stab and the green neon fades in smoke-throttled distance, he slides eager fingers over the thieving vampire's shoulder, pulling him to a halt. "I like how you smell."

A lie. He stinks, this thoughtless murderer, stinks of meat and rude lust, and the only nice thing about him is Ice's faint stolen flavor. Ebony savors his rage, swallows it, lets it spread until he's quivering with bright fury. He'll lick that berry delight off before he's done. He'll scrape it off with his nails if he has to, stick his tongue down the boy's dying throat and suck it out.

"Sure you do." The boy shrugs him off, coal-dyed hair falling, but his penciled blue eyes jerk a swift double take, and he hesitates, the hunger that whitens his thin cheeks no doubt weakening his resolve. "I mean, thanks. You, um, looking for someone?"

Ebony tightens his grip, cold vampire veins pulsing under his palm. Bones shift, only a suggestion of his strength. A promise. "I'd like to show you something."

Sapphire glints in a purple splash of eyebrow, and the boy's lip curves in a shadow of lust. "Look, I don't normally do guys—"

"—but you'll make an exception for me." Ebony lets the vampire taste the iron-rich scents on his breath. "I'm . . . jaded, you see. Bored. Over it. Looking for something special. Something . . . delicious."

The boy's drugged eyes glaze. "Umm . . ."

Ebony wets his ear with a seductive sigh. "You can swallow. I won't struggle. Or I will. Whatever you want. I promise you'll like it."

The vampire licks ruby lips, fresh spit dripping on hungry teeth. "Okay. I'm in. Can we . . . umm . . . make it quick?"

"Oh, it won't take long." Ebony slides his palm over the boy's throat, testing the skin with brittle claws, and tugs the boy closer until those raw red lips quiver under his. "Do you know death, beautiful boy? Have you tasted it?"

"Oh, yeah. Tastes like hell." Spit flecks dance in the vampire's snarl, strawberry-rich with Ice's blood.

Ebony attacks with an angry kiss, sucking that stolen bliss from cold, rotten lips. His pulse quickens at last on the sultry scent of surrender, and he grins. "Then come show me."

I don't have all night, Joey. Whatta ya got?" Delilah slouches her elbows back on the warm glass bar, whiskey and salty skin thick on her demon tongue. Lights glow around her in drifts of nightclub smoke, the damp air slicking pleasantly on the dark brown skin of her human form. The noise grates sweetly in her ears, a pleasant change from silence and black despair.

She shifts her shoulders, enjoying the tactile pleasure of her copper-mesh dress and the slide of wine-dark hair on her back. Too long she's been away, too long skulking in hellblack holes with the worms, only emerging when the stink of the demon court's wrath ebbs. No longer. Kane is old and stale. She's young. Time for a change.

Beside her, Joey DiLuca swallows white aniseed liquor, glossy green eyes unblinking. The drink he offered her sits untouched beside him on the bar. His ravenous banshee would-be lover croons protectively at his side, her vicious blue hair slashing over the shoulder of his pewter-gray suit. Her perfume is pure rage, tainted with corruptible devotion. Joey, on the other hand, smells dry and dusty, of leather and an empty conscience.

Joey jerks his pale chin forward, snakelike under his gray fedora, and the black creature living inside him roils darkly under his skin. "That yellow one? She took your mirror. From Kane, no less. Must be quite a thief. Told you this wouldn't be easy."

Joey drags lightly on his cigarette, ash glowing, and as he releases the smoke, his white fingers relax on the filter and shiny black webs show, glinting wet.

Delilah's nipples tweak inside her meshed metal dress, and she scowls. DiLuca scum. The snake thing is a turn-on. But it's not enough.

She'd wanted Dante, their charmingly insane vampire prince, pretty and ruthless and mad like some ancient imperial despot. But he got himself murdered, and this Joey's a gutter-slinking gunrunner with no imagination. If he's the best the DiLuca clan can do, she's half a mind to leave them to bloody ruin at the hands of their Valenti enemies. But Valenti are Kane's, and any enemy of Kane's is an asset to be used.

She follows his gaze, her shoulders slipping into a lying shrug. "Don't give a fuck. Okay? We've had this discussion."

Joey shrugs, too, unruffled. "Just thought you might need some help. Now you're on your own, so to speak."

"I don't need your help, little man." Irritation rains snowy ash from her hair. Kane is already weak. She tastes it on the strong summer air, that toxic tingle of freedom and opportunity that fires her black demon blood. She smells it in the sickly stench of honey that drifts like a foul oily coating on the fresh water of willing souls. The old enemy from the sky has returned. Kane is under attack. The demon court can go fuck themselves, with their rules and protocols and dusty lore that must be obeyed.

Joey leans back on the bar and shows his unnerving toothy smile. "You're not supposed to be here. Not in Kane's town without an invitation. You know that."

She stretches her arms to the light, laughter frothing in her chest as she spins in a joyful circle. "That just makes the air taste better. The demon court can suck my dick. Whatta they done for me lately?"

"Besides throw you out on your ass?" Joey tosses the empty filter away and lights another one, smoke puffing, a lock of soft blond hair slipping incongruous from beneath his hat.

Steam hisses from Delilah's teeth before she can stop it. "How'd you know that?"

Joey laughs, charming. "I know stuff about things, rosebud, and that includes you and your demon pals. Just because Kane acts like a spoiled brat with Asperger's doesn't make him stupid or slow. Don't underestimate him. Look where it got Dante."

Anger still boils brimstone-rich in her blood. "Dante was a fucking idiot," she snaps, enjoying the banshee's yowl of protest. "A walking vampire hard-on, all ego and no thought. Couldn't keep his dick in his pants."

"I don't have that problem." Joey snakes out his free hand for her wrist, and suddenly his lips are inches from hers, his emerald eyes glinting with promise. "Tell me what you want. Anything. I'll get it for you."

Delilah inhales reptilian breath, the cold smell of scales and venom, and her skin shivers. Curiosity cools her fury, and she slides a freckled brown arm across his shoulder, pressing closer. "And in return you'd expect what?"

Joey shrugs faintly. "We can be good for each other. I have people, money, resources. If you've got ambitions in this town, you need me."

"I asked what's in it for you." She licks plump lips, tempting him. The banshee's neon hair quivers, a growl rumbling in her chest.

Joey grins, and stretches his neck to whisper, bones popping. His voice slithers in Delilah's ear, reptilian sibilants hissing. "I want Ange Valenti'sss head on a ssstick. And Sssonny. And Fabian, and LaFaro and their whole ssstinking crew." He withdraws, resting his hand lazily on her hip, smoke drifting from his cigarette. "I assume that's in the offing."

"Mmm. Now you're getting interesting." She slides long fingers into his lap and clicks her tongue in mock disappointment. "Why, Joseph, such feeble ambition. Your dick's not even hard."

"That's because you're about as sexy as a dogshit sandwich. Don't doubt my ambition because you don't turn me on."

Delilah chuckles, challenge twinkling fresh in her jaded blood. One blink of spell-sparked lashes and he'd be drooling on his knees. Perhaps another time. She flicks a provocative glance to the snarling blue banshee and back again. "What, I'm too powerful for you? Not delicate and breakable enough?"

Joey's forked tongue flickers along his lips. "Something like that."

Delilah smiles and sways away from him. "I was wrong about you, Joey DiLuca. You're not quite the sniveling wormeater I had you pegged for. Perhaps we'll have a little game, see if we play nice together."

Joey crushes his cigarette out on the bar and rests his cane on his thigh to dust off his hands. "Whatever you say. What'll we play for?"

"Why, your famous mirror, of course." She reaches at last for the drink he bought her, and aniseed burns her tongue. "I chase it; you chase it. Whoever gets there first wins."

"And what do we win?"

"Well, that depends. If you win, you get me being nice to you for a while. If I win . . ." She swallows the rest, and stretches happily with a warm belly. "I get to eat your skin, of course."

"Done." Joey tilts his hat with the top of his cane, ironic.

Delilah crinkles her nose at him in a smile. "Oh, and it's not just the mirror. I want the metalshit scum who stole it, too. Sound fair?" She stalks away, the banshee's jealous screech ringing out behind her.

The crowd filters around her, unaware, and she inhales, pleasured. Her tall heels work her calf muscles pleasantly. She likes this place, this Unseelie Court, with its seductive sounds and heavy air, rich with the stink of mortality and soulfood. But it isn't the feast of souls or even Joey that lured her here from her plotting tonight. It's that blue metal shitworm over by the glass, the one who stole her mirror.

Her glossy violet nails spring to ragged claws, and she swallows a greedy mouthful of flaming saliva. The mirror is incidental, though amusing. It's the feeling of being thieved, the creature's blind arrogance that fires her ire beyond reason. Mere slaughter is too painless for him, an eternity in hell too quick. But the shame cracking his eyes in that elevator told her everything. He'll return the mirror to save his friends, and when he does, she'll savage their regard for him one agonizing fiber at a time and send them all screaming to hell. When he gets there, they'll be waiting for him. That's what hell is.

And then, she'll eat Joey's skin. Or not.

Speaking of which, there's Joey's golden thief, wrapped in skimpy silver cloth and cowardice. Delilah bristles, black charcoal shards springing from her hair. She doesn't care if the fairytart stole the mirror or not. She's Indigo's simpering sunflower girlfriend, bright and soft and vulnerable. Delilah stalked them together in the dark, smelled the raw attraction, the fear, the vivid ozone reaction of fresh lust. Bait for a predator, tasty with childlike fae naïveté.

Delilah licks plump lips and watches the golden one, wrapping herself like wet plastic on a candy firechild, dirty sparkle watering those mad fairy eyes.

He's fine, her fairy squeeze, his body knotted and succulent, flame dancing along shining crimson wings and flickering in fire-bright hair. Ripe for a rape and a fairyslashing, rip those arrogant wings off and watch his vanity bleed into the dust. Delilah can arrange that. But the air he exhales crawls with crafty deceit, and she hangs back at the bar, pleasured, to watch him weave his lies around her.

Now they're kissing, hesitant at first like guilty friends and then the full who-gives-a-fuck, tongues mixing and bodies yearning and his fingers wrapping in her sticky hair.

Delilah grins. Indigo's girl, sliding sexgreedy hands over some other guy's ass. Is he watching? She flickers out soft tentacles, searching the dark air swiftly for iron-laced sweat, but he's not there. Pity.

A rattling sniff beside her pricks her attention. Blue airfae girl, white dress, flowing green hair tied up in a knot, lime tears shimmering on her cheeks. Pretty thing. Delilah inhales, and tangy jealousy tingles her nose like a sneeze. She follows the girl's gaze to the dance floor, and delight squirms under her skin at the potential for mayhem.

She leans forward, scraping brown elbows on the bright bar. "Is that yours?"

The blue girl wipes her nose, oddly inelegant compared with her figure. "Huh?"

"Kissing that skinny yellow girl. Is he your boyfriend?"

The fairy tries to smile, starting a fresh wash of tears. "Yeah. Just doesn't know it yet, I guess."

"You poor darling. You're much prettier than she is. I'm sure he'll see sense." Delilah exhales and her breath darkens the air, an oily ghost of false trust.

The girl inhales and looks up, her eyes wide. "You're kind."

Delilah shapes a smile and paints it with demonic persuasion. "We girls have to stick tog—"

"She's supposed to be my friend, you know." The girl hiccups and slurps her sky-blue drink. "She's meant to be my best friend forever, and she goes and steals him. She always gets everything." A pretty scowl, dark with indignation and jealousy, but something else sizzles the air on her disenchantment, too, something that pricks Delilah's fingertips with delight.

The rusty hellstink of a stolen iron ball, mixed with the insane sheen of petulant demon-haunted glass. Another of Indigo's pitiful friends, poisoned by the mirror. It doesn't get much better than this.

Pleasure wrings Delilah's belly. Soulfood. Jealousy tastes so good, like skin or a mouthful of hard flesh. And the mirror magnifies jealousy so well. She purrs, vibrations stirring deep in her throat, and leans closer to light sly fingers on the fairy's slender hand. "Come, dear. Tell me everything."

12

I must have been dreaming again. This felt too good to be real.

My head swam, wet and warm with fire and drink and sparkling light, and flames tickled my nose, not dark molten iron like last time but zinging fresh and alive like the kind of rich perfume I could never afford. Dark bass still thudded in my ears, and under it a cold metal whisper scabby with rust and desire, rippling my body with distant tension. I savored it, breathing deeply in humid air like water, and chaos reveled under my skin, hot urgency bursting free with my sweat.

The cold spring of steel against my cheek, my pleasure-swollen breasts flat against some rippled wall that grazed my skin. The same skimpy dress I wore tonight, the same pins falling from my hair like lost diamonds to plink unheard on the floor.

Deft boy hands traced my hips, and I pressed backwards, searching for his body, my wings shuddering with need. Teeth grazed me, teasing me, sharp down my wing's edge to my neck, sinking in, nibbling my spine like a playful predator. I shivered, desire watering my limbs weak. His hips ground into my bottom, and he felt deliciously hard. I squirmed back to press against him, my skirt crumpling upward, sultry air teasing bare skin at the top of my thighs. He spread my wings apart and licked a burning trail down my vertebrae, his voice pebbled with lust. "Say you want me."

"I want you. So much. Please." My wet hair plastered to the steel. His breath sizzled my skin like fire, and I didn't care where we were or who was watching. I was losing my mind, and it was every drug and every drink and every pretty boy I ever had melted into one.

"Tell me you don't care."

His tongue flickered over the knuckle where my wing met my shoulder, and hot delight shivered down my spine. I groaned, lost. My favorite words, burning in my throat. "I don't care. Please."

He pressed himself against my bare bottom, and his hard cock slipped wet against my skin. I squeezed my eyes shut, desire stopping my throat and stabbing a delicious ache through my sex. I hadn't undressed him or opened his pants, but his fiery skin rubbed sweet delight into mine and he pulled my thighs apart onto him. He pressed himself between my soft cheeks, and for a moment I groaned and shivered because I thought he'd slide it in then and there, but he didn't. He rubbed himself in my wet flesh, so slick, the moisture slid down my thighs. "Say yes, sweetie."

My blood sizzled bright with mirror-wrought compulsion, and wild abandon possessed me. Muscles jerked inside me, yearning for him. My voice cracked, desperate on disappearing breath. "Yes, god, yes."

He crunched his teeth into my shoulder with a groan and pushed deep inside me.

I was tight, and the friction seared me. He pulled back and pushed harder, deeper, as far as he could go. Delight flooded me, dripping off my fingertips to stain the steel wall. I laughed, and it stretched into a deep groan as he moved in me, stroking me, slow and intense and delicious. This was happening. He was inside me, and he felt as good as they all said. His wet hair dragged on my wings, his breath sparking my shivering skin. He sucked my wing joint, hot and hard, and my eyes watered. I gasped, pleasure tightening rapidly deep inside me. "Shit, I'm gonna come."

"Say my name." He slid his arm around my waist, pulling me harder onto him, shifting the friction just right. "So you know. Say it."

Damn, he's good. My muscles squeezed him tighter, rippling, and I hardened and twisted and gritted my teeth and melted all over him in a breathless shuddering splash. "Blaze. You're beautiful."

I jerked awake, panting, my eyes squeezed shut.

Warm linen stroked the front of my body, comforting, and I sighed in bed, catching my breath, relief and regret flushing my skin. My pulse still bubbled, and my nipples hurt like I'd pinched them in my sleep. Hell of a dream. Hot dirty Blaze-sex. Worse ways to spend the night. I giggled, pleasured, and a distant headache flared in my scoured sinuses, remnants of sparkle and too much vodka.

Heavy soreness weighed my limbs. I wriggled sticky thighs, and beneath me something slim and hard wriggled back.

Confusion tightened my skin. I cracked one eye open in diluted shadow. Torn cloth blinds pulled over the window, a streak of sunshine on ripped carpet. Singed merlot sheets, a pillow stuffed under my crooked arm, a crusty whiff of burned hair.

Definitely not my room.

Dismay sprayed cold bullets in my guts, and slowly I lifted my head.

Crimson hair, splashing on the pillow in the fresh scent of matches.

Dread clotted my pulse. I jerked up, and my legs tangled with his, his translucent white skin sliding under me. He was naked. I was naked. Not a good sign. I glanced around swiftly. Fingerpainted wallpaper, comic books, a broken game console, crayons mashed into the carpet. His door lay half-open, glass shards littering the rug. No one could see us. I poked his ribs, keeping my voice to a whisper. "Blaze."

He pulled the pillow over his face, rolling away into a ball, limp wings fluttering. "Sleeping now."

"Blaze, wake up." I dragged the pillow off and poked him harder, crusty mango hair falling over my shoulder.

He uncurled with a groan and flopped onto his back. "What for? I set the house on fire?"

"Be serious!" I hissed, glancing around again.

Blaze squinted at me, bleary-eyed, and quirked a sleepy smile. "Oh. Mornin', sweetie."

I flushed, and shifted my hips on the sheet, trying to keep my gaze above his waist. Pretty naked boy. Waking up. Hard-on. Mmm. "Hi. Um. Did we, uh . . . Did we have sex?"

He lifted his head to peer down at himself, naked, flushed and sticky with sweat and whatever else, and looked up at me, grinning. "Well, I dunno. Whadda you think?"

"It's not funny, okay?" I tried to scowl, to fan my anger. But a secret rusty voice whispered warm rebellion in my heart, and I could only remember what I'd said to him in that sexy not-dream. *I want you. I don't care. Please.*

He scratched himself, sighing. "Nope. Not funny. Hot, though. Fucking excellent. Haven't come so hard in months. Don't you remember?"

"No." I yanked my face away, burning with shame. I remembered enough. Az would never forgive me. I'd never forgive me. I'd never look at him the same way again. I shifted, and the fragrant mess between my thighs suggested we'd done it without condoms. Even better.

"Yeah, you do." He twisted up with a strong flick of wings, and all of a sudden I was on my back under him in a shower of hot sparks with his thigh slinking between mine, his naughty lips teasing my ear with licks of flame. “Remember? Against the wall out back at the club? You were so hot. You came on me and I lost it. And then when we got home, you did me again, you sexy thing.”

My pulse quailed, even as my flesh squirmed in pleasure at his touch and his words. My wings strained beneath me, swelling. “You mean . . . We did it at the club? In front of everyone?”

“Yeah. Why not?”

My retort hissed too loud. “Because she could’ve seen us! Are you out of your fucking m—?”

He stopped me with a kiss, and for a moment I fought him before my resolve melted and I sucked his tongue in deep.

Not *I promised her* or *I love you too much* or even *I don’t like getting naked in public, thanks very much.*

Because she could’ve seen us.

Because we might have been caught doing something bad. Something fun. Something selfish.

My desire flared, insatiable and careless, and horror slashed me with jagged claws even as the need savaged me deep to say fuck it all and do what I liked for a change. I swallowed, and kissed him harder, my blood searing with hot metal foolishness. Our teeth smashed together, his blood like cherries tingling my tongue.

He broke off, laughing softly, and pulled my thigh around him, hot claws stinging. Flame rippled along his dark wing veins, sunshine-bright with desire. “Whiskey chocolate, Ice. Why didn’t we do this a long time ago?”

His hard-on pressed into my wet flesh, and I twitched there, eager. I strained against him, my nipples rubbing on his narrow fae-muscled chest, tweaking tension deep into my breasts. I wanted him. I wanted to slap him. I wanted to crawl away and cry. “Because we’re not supposed to. Azure’s in love with you—you do know that?”

"Sure. You care?" He rocked his hips, his lips poised to catch my cries.

Nerves squirmed deep inside me, and I groaned into his mouth. I couldn't come up with an answer I wasn't ashamed of, and what he was doing between my legs wasn't helping. "Because you're a crazy whore who doesn't give a shit and you'll dump me first chance you get?"

He slipped lower to press against my entrance, and bit his lip, gasping. "You care? 'Cause I don't. Not since you and that dirty little mirror. I don't give a fuck about anything. You know what I wanna do?"

"Uh-huh." My breath shuddered. I knew what I wanted to do. I squeezed my hand between us, guiding him.

He pushed inside me, hot and twisted with hard fae flesh, and folded smoking fingers in my hair. "Mmm. I wanna break things, Icygirl. I wanna kill and crush and shatter. Makes me feel good."

Excitement burned away my reason. I knew exactly what he meant. I wrapped my thigh around him, light-headed, my body sighing in pleasure as he filled me. He dipped his lips to my breast, and I flattened my wings and pushed my nipple into his mouth for him to chew.

"Damn it, Blaze, can't you keep it d—? You bitch!"

Oh, bugger.

Hot delight at being watched tingled my limbs, but my guts wrenched with sick shame. My back arched itself in sensual abandon, and I tore my attention away from the luscious feel of him inside me and forced my sex-sleepy eyes open.

Azure stared in the doorway, appleskin hair unkempt and beautiful, lime horror splashing her face. Her wings drooped in dismay. Her pretty mouth quivered, and inky tears spilled. "You bitch. How could you? You promised!"

"Oops," murmured Blaze with a breathless smile, but he didn't flitter off me or pull away. He stretched his wings and pushed harder, his thigh muscles quivering under my calf.

Treacherous pleasure swamped me, my deepest muscles reacting to his caress, and I gritted my teeth on a sigh of delight. Tears swelled my eyelids. I stared back at her, shame burning in my blood, but that feral metal parasite squirmed deep in my heart, rebelling, drugging my senses with selfish rage. I opened my mouth to fight it, to scream and writhe and get him off me so I could explain. But all that came out was a helpless giggle.

"Go ahead, laugh." Azure's face crumpled in wet green despair. "I thought you were my friend. You *promised.* I *hate* you!" And she flapped her wings in a puff of angry dust and skittered away.

"Az . . ." I squirmed around to watch her go, stretching my arm out helplessly, but the creature inside me laughed cruelly, and the lure of Blaze's body was too strong. My flesh quivered in the faint beginnings of orgasm. I whimpered, miserable and hot and struggling against brutal pleasure, and dug my fingers into his hips, unsure whether I was pushing him off or pulling him closer. "Like this is all my fault. She hates me."

"Yeah, that'll do it." Blaze crunched his teeth on my collarbone, flame spilling from his gasp. "Sorry, sweetie. I've gotta come. I can't . . . Shit."

He was getting off on her misery. Too cruel. I wriggled and pushed him. "Stop it. No, Blaze. Get off me."

"Fuck." He squeezed his eyes shut and jerked away, doubling over.

For a moment, I felt sorry for him. I don't normally do that. But he didn't deserve my courtesy. I scrambled up, frustration and disgust worming together inside me. Last night's dress crumpled in a stained heap on the carpet, unwearable. I yanked the sheet from the bed's end, tugged it around me, and stumbled into the lounge. "Az?"

Not there. I poked my head into her room, but it lay empty but for her sugared-apple scent, the bedcovers thrown back and still seeping her damp warmth.

I jittered to the bathroom, where the splintered door sat wonkily shut, her sobs faint but distinct. I rapped with two knuckles, those guilty worms in my tummy chewing harder now. "Azure?"

"Mushroom stew, Ice. Go away. I hate you." Sniffles, a wet cough.

I rested my forehead on the splintered paint, my eyes blurring. "I'm so sorry."

"Fuck off. You promised. You always get everything." A clink, like she hit her head on the tiles.

"Please, Az. I didn't mean it—"

The door yanked open, and I stumbled in, catching myself on the towel rail. She glared wet-eyed, her face smeared with snotty green tears, and angry breeze blasted me in the face like a gale. "Then what did you mean? Huh? I saw you last night, rubbing yourself all over him right in front of me."

I hadn't even noticed she was there. "I'm sorry! It was an accident."

Fury flushed her pale wings scarlet to the tips, and she leaned over me, poking her green-smeared nose into my face. "Then what was that just now? Déjà vu?"

Her stretched voice scraped my nerves. "No, I told you, I—"

"Once is an accident, Ice. Twice is a dirty lying bitch who can't keep her hands to herself. You've probably been doing him all along, right? Laughing at me."

"No! That's not true, okay? It was just last night, and then . . ." Guilty tears scorched my throat, and I clenched my fists in frustration. "I couldn't help it! It's that damn mirror. It makes me."

"Right. Sure. I believe you. Nothing to do with you being a cheap horny slut, then."

My heart stung like she'd stabbed me, and for a moment I

couldn't breathe. This was happening. She hated me. We were breaking up, and it was my fault. My mind gibbered, denial scrabbling in my throat like a half-squashed fly, and I grasped for the mirror's confident metal voice, but it had deserted me. I stammered, bereft. "Blame me, why don't you? What about him? It was his idea."

"He never promised. You did. Get lost, Ice. I don't like you anymore." She shoved me in the chest, claws scraping like poison.

I staggered back, my wings crushing on cold tiles. She pushed past me, and as her footsteps faded, despair splintered my heart like glass. I banged my head back against the ceramic. My skull clanged, but the pain didn't make me feel better, and when tears tumbled hot on my cheeks, I whimpered and let them fall.

My lungs ached, swollen from too much hasty breath. My eyes stung, my lips tingled raw from illicit kissing, and no matter how much my body sang with happy chaos, I knew I couldn't do this anymore. Not this selfish pleasure fixation, no matter how good it made me feel. Not after seeing her eyes, haunted and broken and so disappointed in me, she broke my heart.

And that cursed mirror was to blame.

I sniffed. Okay, so was Blaze and so most definitely was I, but the mirror started it. It sucked away my control, made me weak by giving me what I thought I craved.

I'd always wanted to be brave and carefree and self-reliant. Well, now I was, and look where it got me.

Azure hated me. We'd all be dead by week's end because we owed Sonny money we couldn't possibly raise. And how could I ever look Blaze in the eye again?

I had to get the rotten thing back, return it to Kane, and plead with him to reverse this insanity. I had to.

Blindly, I pushed myself upright, the Blaze-fragrant sheet tangling around my sticky body. I yanked the sheet free, determined.

Shower, wash my hair, get his damn smell off me. Go to Quang's and beg the mirror back again. Any price. Any game. If I had to give him a repeat of Blaze's favor and let him touch me, I'd do it. If I had to sneak after some greedy power-twisted gangster and get my wings torn off stealing the cursed thing back again, I would.

And then I'd spend the rest of my stupid little life begging Azure to forgive me.

Until Sonny Valenti and his goons raped me to death and munched what was left into little bits, that is.

If I didn't do something stupid and get myself killed another way first. Like steal a demon lord's toys, or seduce a hungry vampire, for instance.

Of course, I'd already told Indigo exactly where the mirror could be found. I'd have told him anything to extort that kiss he promised me, but I couldn't even get that right. I swallowed on sour selfishness, and the worms in my stomach only slithered harder.

I couldn't believe I'd done that. Told him everything for the hope of a single kiss. He was probably tricking me all along, using my crush on him to get what he wanted. He'd probably stolen the damn thing back already. I was screwed.

I leaned both hands on the sink and stared down my reflection in the spotted vanity glass, daring myself to look away. Brown circles around my eyes, lashes clogged with makeup and tears, dark blue bruises mottling my throat where the vampire bit me, the teethmarks almost healed over but still scabbed with blood.

What a careless, selfish idiot I'd been.

Blaze stuck his head round the doorframe, scratching lazily at knotted crimson locks. "She a bitch, or what?"

"Don't even talk to me." I slammed the door on him, weak wood splintering, and wrenched the shower on, urgency dribbling hot in my blood.

13

Akash inhales in early morning sun, the warm smell of cooking wheat and sugar mixing with sour traffic effluent and last night's spilled beer. His nose twinkles with sensation. Invigorating. Dangerous. Even the air is a temptation in this place. Clever, sneaky demon. At home, they never told Akash about this.

Eyes open. Dazzle. Water. Blink. Smeared pavement, folding kitchen windows open to warm breeze. The street is quiet, only a few cars and one or two cafés opening for breakfast. Beside him, Indra sniffs the crisp white blossom on a potted shrub, her fingers smearing in dusty pollen as she fondles each petal one by one.

Akash breathes and watches her, the dusky fall of her hair, her skirt lifting as she bends, the shimmer of her thigh in sunlight. She's getting dirty, street dust and fingermarks and her stolen body's sweat. Perhaps he should wash her. The idea pleases him. Water, running on her pretty arms, his fingertips gliding on her skin. Yes.

He squints happily, enjoying stinging tears. A new thing, this hot glare, the malice of an unkind sun. No wonder Kane thrives here. The air burns, heat shimmering over rude black tarmac, and the stink is unrelenting. The very light is from hell, stark and hot and inexorable, and colors burn brighter than any rainbow.

Akash is starting to like it here, and distantly he wonders if something's wrong with him.

If Shadow knew that, and if that's why Shadow sent him here, on this strange, impossible mission . . .

But to what end?

He glances at the sky, but the sky blinks back and doesn't answer.

A twitch against his palm. He blinks, distracted. He's holding something. A wrist, pale skin inked with a thorny red rose. "What?"

A banshee in a swimsuit and sarong points a painted fingernail across the sunlit street. She scowls, a passing tram's breeze ruffling her rose-pink ponytail. "That's the place. Quang's. Above the takeaway. Okay? Can I go now?"

Akash moves his lips into his best smile. "That's a lovely song you have."

"Whatever. Get off me, you freak." She pushes back her sunglasses, threat swelling dark and melodic in her throat.

He just squeezes her wrist tighter. She struggles, but he drags her with him, off the street into a greasy alcove, where a big rusted blue trash bin hides behind a dented metal gate. Such a dirty place, greasy with fish stink and grime. Delicious.

The banshee yowls for help. He crushes her jaw shut. "Quiet, pretty."

Silken sarong threads catch on splintered brick as he tosses her against the wall. Her delicate jaw bruises red under his fingers. His inked forearm quivers as blood and adrenaline swell his veins. He's kept his strength, and in this chemical-rich body, it feels even better.

"Mmm phm!" Her thin face whitens, and her wide eyes turn to Indra for help.

But Indra ducks around the gate, sniffing for observers. "Quickly, Akash. Someone will see."

"Quickly," he agrees, and squeezes the banshee's mouth open for a kiss.

Fresh youth, and the bloody taste of fear. Her struggles force more strength from his muscles, more chemicals, more pleasure. Inside her mouth, it's smooth and cool, the remnants of some fizzy drink tingling his tongue. He pulls her jaw open to thrust his tongue deeper. She writhes and scratches at his face with curved pink nails, her magical voice strangled in absent air. Too easy to fight her off.

He grabs her tongue with his, searching. She screams down his throat. Vibration sizzles. He swallows. It's agonizing, his throat stretching, the thorny magic ripping his flesh as it goes down.

He retches, warm pleasure flooding his guts, but he keeps it down. The banshee sighs one last sad melody and slumps, her eyes rolling back.

Akash lets her body slide and turns away, catching bloody breath. The banshee's stolen song purrs and thrashes inside him.

Indra slides her warm hand into his. He laughs, a fresh musical edge on his voice. "Good."

"Good," agrees Indra, and stretches up to kiss his cheek.

Warmth sparkles from her lips, spiking a shock down his hormone-swelled spine. It's the homage he deserves from an underling, and he's never thought about liking it before. Impulsively, he kisses her in return, his bloody lip print staining her face.

Indra jerks back, genuine alarm widening her eyes, and slicks her hand from his grip. "No. Not right. Don't."

Tension pulls Akash's muscles, awkward. He wants her mouth, her tongue, like the banshee but nicer. "Don't be afraid. They can't see."

"They see everything." She rubs the spot, smearing the corner of her mouth red.

"Not here, they don't."

She shakes her head rapidly. "They do."

He tries to touch her face, but she ducks away, and something deep in his chest hurts.

Wounded, he glances at the sky. Nothing.

They cross the street without holding hands, slipping between jerking vehicles in single file. Akash frowns at the empty space beside him. It doesn't feel right to have her behind him. Maybe later he'll cheer her up. Play a game with her. She used to like his games. But first, an item to collect.

They step over the paper clogging the gutter, and Akash surveys the dirty glass door with satisfaction. "This is the place."

"Here?" Indra eyes the narrow stairs, her eyebrows contracting. Very good. She's improving her facial expressions.

"Quang's in Brunswick. Kane's mirror is here." Confidently Akash strides forward and wrenches the metal handle off with a wristy snap. The lock clunks free, and the broken handle clatters on the concrete. Indra scrambles to catch up, sliding her timid hand into his as they climb the creaking stairs.

He lets her. She's afraid, and it's his place to comfort her. By rights, he should punish her for disobedience, but the idea of disciplining her with silence in this place sends a warm shiver along his bones. They're isolated here. The sky is silent. Without her, he's alone. Maybe there's some other way to put her in her place.

The stairs curve into warm shadow, the air moist and thick with food's oily stink. Carpet torn to strings, dust and broken glass, carpet rolls and shelves and boxes of hidden smooth-smelling objects. A cracked glass bench, dust-smeared. Unseen feet thump closer beyond a broken doorway, and a crumpled red person squeezes out, scratching his crooked nose. He squints at them through sleep-crusted lashes, sweat dribbling on his scrawny red rib cage. "We're closed. Whaddaya want?"

Akash halts before the counter, and Indra scrambles up. "Spriggan," she identifies hopefully.

Akash doesn't look at her. He's still upset with her, and they've already got a red one anyway. "Quang's. In Brunswick."

The spriggan stares, insolent, and scratches wiry orange hair, pulling short glossy pants up with his other hand. "Yeah, I'm Quang. Who the fuck are you?"

Akash leans his knuckles on the counter and gives the Quang his nicest smile, prickly banshee persuasion crooning in his throat. Her stolen song tastes like peaches. "I am Akash, from the sky, and you have something I require."

The Quang blinks, glassy. "Mmkay. I'll trade ya. Whaddaya got?"

Sunlight stabs, and Indigo jerks awake, shielding his eyes with an aching blue forearm. His knees scrape on concrete, broken metal digging sharp and bitter into his bones. Blood sparks accusation in his mouth, and cold dread creeps under his skin.

He straightens, wincing as his muscles protest with a crackle of current. Sensation needles his wings, swollen veins stretching under pressure. He flutters, and distant pain shivers his bones. Silence, only the distant scrape of traffic, the dark alley smell of grease and cigarettes. He stretches cramped thighs, and something heavy rolls off his lap, thudding onto the concrete.

A head.

Attached to a body.

Indigo's pulse splinters. He scrambles backwards, crablike.

A body. A boy, slim, dark T-shirt and jeans. Dusty black-dyed hair tumbles lifeless over a purple-stained eyebrow, drained blue eyes, slack lips over sharp vampire teeth. Limbs fold, helpless and white and unnatural. Spit trickles. Scarlet blood seeps, slow and clotted. Dry. Dead. Empty.

Indigo swallows, nothing in his mouth but dust and copper. Blood crusts his jeans, his shirt, his aching arms. Blood splatters the warming concrete, puddles against the cracked brick wall, splashes the rainbow-sprayed garbage bin like rust. Blood. Copper-laced, delicious, revolting vampire blood.

Bile froths in his throat, and he chokes a metal-stinking mouthful onto the concrete. Pain spears his skull, the harsh iron slither of alien laughter.

He scrabbles to his feet and crouches against the wall in the dark, scrubbing hard at crusted arms. No one here. No one saw him. He can leave now, run, fly away into blinding sun, and no one will ever know. The world won't miss one more scrap of vampire flotsam, any more than it'd miss Indigo were he bled dry on the concrete like a squashed insect. Yes. Fly away, across the sea to poverty and glorious freedom in some muddy tropical paradise. . . .

"Not a chance." Indigo slams his skull back into the wall, and the malicious metal voice shuts up for the moment. But the mirror's vile seduction still burns ruts in his veins, dragging pleasure from his blood, tempting him to rashness and murder.

He's killed, dark and silent like poison in the night, and no one stopped him.

Urgency rips his pulse raw. He claws his hair with sticky fingers, trying to slow his breath, to scrape his memory for the last clear thing he recalls. Ice and her diamond bracelet, the mango scent of her hair, the unexpected warmth of her cheek on his. Poor foolish fairy trembled at his touch like she might actually care for him. Whispered like she might actually want his answer. *Not telling if you're gonna be nasty*, she said, and everything after that's a blank.

Indigo grits his teeth, and stray flesh sticks, greasy with guilt. He spits in disgust, and meaty strands splat the concrete. He can't deny this ghastly truth anymore. When this sorry kid died, Indigo wasn't there. He was someone else. Some seductive shadow self, darker, warmer, more dangerous.

Terror leaches thick into his blood. Since he first peeked into that cursed mirror—the night Natasha fell—he's suffered blackouts. How many times? How long has he been like this without knowing, before this latest brush with the mirror thrust his secret face into the light?

No doubt the vampire kid was an asshole, but it makes no difference. He can't pretend this isn't happening, can't ward off the inevitable with sparkle or caffeine or determination. Eventually his mind will wander, he'll lose concentration or fall asleep, and that rotten metal voice will whisper again and next time it could be Ice's blood running down his arms and her pineapple-sweet skin sticky between his teeth. Hell, maybe he'll give her that kiss he owes her first. . . .

"I said, not a fucking chance." He crunches dirty claws into his palms to stay with it, and grimaces at copper's stinging slice. He'll never hurt her, such a simple innocent girl. Delilah must never find out Ice means even a pleasant dream to him. He'll prove the hellslut's threats empty if his final breath scrapes to nothing doing it and he screams away the next thousand years in some rust-spiked hellpit.

If he can keep Ice safe—retrieve this cursed mirror and break the spell—it might make up for all this death.

But where to look? She must have told him. She must. He forces his eyes shut against guilt's screaming glare and drives himself to remember.

Cold lights, a wall of mirrors, bright blue blood on golden skin. A kiss, that membrane-thin skin warm and seductive, the strawberry scent of her wrist making him imagine licking her all over, the crease of her elbow, inside her thigh, the sweet folds of her sex. He could smell the curved steel piercing her navel, and wanted to suck it into his mouth.

Dread and desire stir molten in his blood, and silently he begs it not to be true. *Tell me I didn't say any of that. Tell me I didn't kiss her wrist like a lover.*

—But you did.— The whisper caresses Indigo's thoughts like velvet. *—A flash of diamonds, mango hair tickling your cheek, her breath like sugar on your tongue. Kiss me and I'll tell you, she whispered, and you would've, only you didn't need to. Quang's place, on Brunswick Street. She told you. She told* me.—

Copper claws steal slyly for Indigo's will, and he snaps his eyes open, fighting to stay in the light. Sunshine dazzles, comforting, and a soft dark laugh slips away like a raindrop on glass.

Weird. But no time to assimilate it now. Damage control. Cover-up time.

Indigo locks out the screeching metal netherworld and focuses, his attention fierce and bright like a pinpoint.

Coldly he surveys the gruesome scene, trying to ignore his pulse's horrid scream, the cold iron sweat soaking his skin, the scaly nausea crawling inside. The body can stay. No one will care. He drags it upright, the cold limbs strangely light now they're drained of blood, and heaves it over the metal lip into the bin. Garbage crunches, bones clanging on iron.

See ya, pretty. Have a good sleep. Sorry I fucked you up, you parasite.

Swiftly he strips his shirt off in a squelch of clotted blood and wipes the stains from his skin before tossing the sticky fabric after the corpse. Now he's at least presentable. No point trying to clean the place up. From the state of the dead kid's hair and clothes, shadow Indigo's fluids are all over the fucking place.

Indigo's cock twitches in shady memory. His balls ache like an echo, and his mouth fills with sly, lustful spit.

He slashes a sharp claw across his knuckles, the pain bright and distracting. The evidence doesn't matter. Banshees turn up in landfills, spriggans wash up rotting on the beach, gangsters and fairies murder each other with abandon in Kane's black city, and no one tweaks an eyebrow. No one will come looking for him. Not another random fae killer.

Anyway, Indigo's shadow self is a ghost. Crafty. Brilliant.

—*They won't catch me. They didn't last night, or the night before.*—

"You're wasting your time." As if there's someone Indigo can reason with about this.

He laughs, helplessness bubbling bright. Too late for reason. Only action. Find this mirror. Leave. Keep Ice safe from this ghastly ghost inside him. And then . . . Well, maybe the mirror can cure what it sickened.

—*You won't destroy me.*— The whisper threatens, silky, and sharp metal clangs deafening in Indigo's head. —*We'll find this mirror. For her. To keep her safe from your ugly demon woman. And then we'll do what we must to scratch our itch. Don't think you can silence me now.*—

Indigo's brain swells, a sharp pain ripping at his skull. His muscles jerk, and he yanks his hair, desperate to get his claws inside his skull and scrape this monster away. "Christ, you make me spew, acting so noble. You're just another fucking thrill killer."

Smirk. —*Well, so are you, Indigo. You killed Natasha. Dropped her slender body in a spiky pit. Watched her bleed to death and liked it. Where d'ya think I got the idea?*—

Dizzy sickness clamps his guts. His blood lurches, pain shooting through his limbs. The clamor brightens, tearing his ears like thunder, and Indigo bites off a scream and blacks out.

Too easy.

Ebony scrapes a last smear of vampire blood from his hands and flitters away into rising sunlight.

14

Quang? You there?" My voice echoed, empty.

I halted at the top of the stairs, wiping damp palms on my skirt. Nearly noon. Normally even Quang was up by now. But I'd found the door handle ripped off, the lock broken, and now I couldn't see anyone.

The spriggan's workshop lay deserted. A single bulb burned over the glass counter, dust motes circling. Blaze's half-mended cracks glittered under sticky tape in a stray ray of sun. A fly buzzed, solitary. Cruel moisture laced the air, prickling my wing membranes with a strange sad smell of loss.

I edged inside, nervousness trickling in my bowels. Shelves loomed, lined with boxes and layered with dust, broken jars and metal fragments, and tangles of wire. The usual. But wrongness prickled my spine like nagging teeth. Something out of place. Something odd.

My flip-flops crunched on broken glass, sharp edges pressing the soles of my feet. "Quang, it's me. Ice. I wanna talk to you about that round thing you got from us."

No answer. Maybe at the markets today. His cousin Tran had a stall there, selling dodgy phones and thief tech. But that didn't explain the broken door.

I delved farther into the gloom, shoving boxes aside with my foot. Dust smeared the counter's edge, like someone swiped it clear with a shirtsleeve. More flies buzzed, and I caught my first whiff of blood.

Nausea twinged, and I teetered forward on furtive wings to peer over the counter.

A bent red toe, poking out on the floor.

I swallowed. Toe, attached to crusted foot, attached to scrawny spriggan leg, and on the carpet an oily green splash of blood.

Glass tinkled behind me. I whirled, my pulse scuttling for cover. No one. Just a mouse, and the drone of flies.

Cold water slicked my palms, and my wings jerked nervously. I wanted to dive out of here, but if I didn't find that mirror, I was screwed.

Let him just be hungover, or stoned on too much dodgy weed.

I know he isn't. But please.

I sidled around the counter. My chin jerked stiffly, reluctant to drop and let me see. I forced my gaze downward, the breath squeezing from my throat.

Ugh. Sticky pool of blood. Red spriggan in Batman boxer shorts, cartoons that read BAM! and BIF! and ZOT! Ragged hole in his throat, eyes wide and vacant. Scrawny limbs twisted rigid, muddy green stain on his chest still sticky.

My nose fizzed hot, and tears misted my vision blue. Worse than I'd hoped. Better than I'd feared. At least they hadn't torn his hair out or ripped his claws off or cracked his toes apart one by one just for fun. They'd just slashed his throat, and he'd bled to death on stinking carpet like an insect.

My throat ached. Poor Quang. I squatted and fingered his eyelids closed one by one, masking his dulled black eyes. I hadn't known him well. I didn't buy him drinks or hang out with him or call him my friend. But anger and sorrow still squeezed tight around my heart. Rotten fae-murdering pricks.

I fisted my eyes to dry them. Coulda been rival gangsters, of course. Some DiLuca moron with a grudge. Quang's attitude pissed people off far and wide, and anyone who collected the sort of money Quang handled from day to day made themselves a target.

All of which made no never mind to the vicious asshole who owned Quang, the ubiquitous Sonny Valenti. If his self-righteous goons showed up and saw me here, my sweet fairy butt would be chewing gum.

And I still hadn't found the mirror. Here's hoping whoever killed Quang hadn't taken it.

Urgency wriggled, slick with slimy guilt. This was all my fault. If I hadn't brought the squidgy here, Quang might still live.

I straightened, determined, my teary eyes still stinging. Yeah. And if I'd never been born, custard companies would be poorer. There was nothing I could do now except find the damn mirror and get out before Sonny realized Quang wasn't answering his phone and sent Cousin Fabian here to stuff my wings down my throat.

I dragged my gaze from Quang's pitiful corpse and surveyed the shadowy shelves with a shaky sigh. "Come out, squidgy, wherever you are. I won't hurt you."

But for once, when I needed so much to hear its nasty voice, the horrid metal thing was silent.

My vertebrae crackled, nerves pulling my muscles out of whack. *Typical. Guess I'll hafta look on my own.*

I flexed uneasy wings and knelt on the carpet beside the dark green slime of spriggan lifeblood to sort through the mess.

Ebony crouches panting in the dark and watches Ice rummage through junk, her form partly hidden by the counter. Beside him,

Quang's safe crackles, iron ringing in his metal-sensitive ears. Ebony can't see inside, not such a small space enclosed by metal. He was about to crack it open when she turned up, and now he can't move lest she notice him.

But part of him wants her to notice him, to see him and smile, that berry blush staining her cheeks. He watches, strange peace warming his heart. She's so pretty and innocent. Fruity hair tumbles across her brow, unheeded, tangled ends dragging on her bare shoulders. She's concentrating, a drop of water hanging from her nose, her pretty silken wings folded back. Hunting for the mirror.

She won't find it.

Satisfaction tickles his nose, and he suppresses a sneeze, his eyes stinging. He's already searched through everything, glass and wires and bent metal and pretty things that any other day he might want to keep. The spiteful thing isn't here, unless it's in the safe. Indigo teased her desire for him to find it—a cruel and heart-shy beast, that Indigo—nasty Indigo tortured her to find the mirror, and now in a flush of silvery rage Ebony knows why.

Indigo wants Ebony gone.

Wants rid of him, and foolish enough to think the mirror might oblige. Wants everything boring and lifeless, without reckless impulse to light the way. Wants pretty Ice all to himself, wants to trick and tempt and possess her and scrape away with his rough iron will all the chaos that makes her so beautiful.

Wants to leave her lost and shivering, alone in her prison of fear.

Ebony grits metal teeth, disgust sharp on his tongue like poison. If she were his, he'd not ruin her so. He'd keep her, wild and challenged and mirrorcrazy, and if she must bleed to death in his arms to preserve that perfection, then so be it.

Fury boils his blood molten, and he makes up his mind. She's his,

Ebony's, in all her insane beauty, and Indigo can't have her. Can't ruin her. Not ever.

And here she comes. Copper-tainted love swells Ebony's rusty heart, tempering his anger to sweetness, and he looks down, checking himself for mess. Blood on his shirt again, thick and green and already drying, and awkwardness prickles his palms with sweat. An accident. He didn't mean it. The spriggan just caught him by surprise. But black is such a lying color. She'll never see, not if he distracts her properly. He rises, sweaty palms leaving a dark smear on his jeans.

I whirled, my wings jerking tight, and sighed. "Christ, you scared the piss outta me."

Indigo wiped dark hands on his jeans, wings glittering in a shaft of golden sun. "Sorry. Didn't mean it. You okay?"

My pulse didn't quiet, and I flexed my shoulders, jittery, trying to calm my flight impulse. How long had he been hiding there, watching me? "What you doing here?"

He fiddled with the bangle on his right wrist, rocking on his toes with a silvery flutter. Awkward, like last night. "Same as you. Came for the mirror. Found him." He nodded at Quang's body, and guilt sharpened my blood that I hadn't covered the poor guy up.

Then again, neither had Indigo.

Self-consciousness numbed my skin, and I fingered the pretty diamond bracelet he'd welded for me. "Did you know him?"

"A little bit. Sold him a few trinkets. Peeled his hands off my ass a few times. I'll miss him."

"Me, too." The image of little red Quang grabbing Indigo's ass—on his tiptoes, presumably—frothed hysterical giggles up in my throat, and I swallowed them before I made an idiot of myself. My wing membranes tingled, and it wasn't just because Indigo smelled fantastic, that warm mix of skin and iron that never failed to make me ache.

Unease prickled my fingerpads. No doubt he'd gotten his price from Kane. What did Indigo even want the mirror for? He'd hinted last night that he knew something. He wasn't being honest with me.

Not that I'd come clean about what I wanted it for either. Too embarrassing.

Silence lengthened. I squirmed, not knowing what to say. Warmth had flowered between us last night. Today was a whole new game.

Indigo folded his wings down along his back with a self-conscious shrug. His gaze slid about, not sticking to anything in particular. He wrapped a black lock of hair around one nervous claw, and his wings flitted loose again. "Look. Um. About last night."

Metal-fragrant breeze ruffled my damp hair. Warm memory whispered in my blood, and again his strange softness cast a seductive velvet spell, tempting me to respond in kind, tell him it was okay he'd lied to me, that he'd used my desire for him to get what he wanted.

But my heart still tripped, my breath too heavy in my lungs to laugh, and I was too angry that he'd caught me off guard yet again to be nice to him. "That is so typical of a boy, you know that? You've hardly said a civil word to me for months, and now we're standing here with a dead body five seconds after you just scared the tripe out of me, and you want to talk about last night?"

He shrugged, weirdly gentle. "Don't you?"

My cheeks sizzled. No, I didn't want to talk about it. I wanted to do it again. Brush my cheek on his and slide my fingers into his hair and pull his mouth down to mine like I should've done last night.

Stretch my naked body beneath his and purr, like I'd done in my dream, make love to him in the smell of hot metal and sea breeze, a warm updraft caressing my skin, his fingers tangled in my hair. Forget about this damn mirror, and live.

I eyed Quang's corpse, disquiet rubbery in my belly. "Look, this ain't the time—"

"I'm sorry, that's all. About your firefae friend. I shouldn't have hissed at him. If you two are . . . I mean, I guess it's probably better . . ."

"I don't wanna talk about it, okay?" Before he could say, *It's probably better that nothing happened*. I'd be expected to agree, and then it'd be over between us forever and ever—and I didn't want that. But I did want it, too. On-again, off-again Indigo wore me out. I couldn't trust him. I didn't know what I wanted from him anymore.

"Okay." He lifted his hands as if to ward me off, and his silvery eyes glimmered golden, so brief, I almost missed it before he looked away.

Dismay crushed my heart tight. If I didn't know better, I'd think I hurt him.

I shifted, awkward, and searched for something else to talk about. "How come you hid when I came in?"

He blinked at me, confused. He darted his gaze left and right, at the walls, the skylight, the floor, and checked the clock, like he'd forgotten where he was or how long he'd been here. And then he looked at me, curiosity blossoming his pupils black, like he'd forgotten I was there. "Sorry, what?"

I swallowed, my awkwardness swelling to unease. "When I came in. What, you trying to scare me?"

He snorted, and the old bulletproof Indigo was back. "Wouldn't waste my time. Tried the safe yet?"

Warm dismay flooded my cheeks. A twinge of sympathy, a

glimmer of softness so I think I've got a chance, and then he smashes me flat again. Conversation over. Inscrutable, infuriating boy. Frustration itched my skin. "What?"

"The safe. I've checked the rest. It's not here." Slow, simple. Like I was some stupid child.

My wings bristled, and I plonked one hand on my hip, damp hair spilling over my shoulder. "And I should take your word for that why?"

"Think I'd still be standing around in a pool of spriggan blood if I'd found it?"

Good point. I glanced again at Quang's body and swallowed. "Who d'ya think did it? Gangsters? Boyfriend?"

"Walls of glass, Ice. I'd look a little closer to home if I were you."

My throat stung. "What's that supposed to mean?"

An arrogant Indigo shrug, so different from the shy one a minute ago. "Mirror one day, dead the next. Doesn't seem like rocket science to me."

Guilt razored my skin, and I hugged myself, exposed. "You saying it's my fault?"

"Are you?" He flicked me a dark question, just long enough to make me squirm before he resumed surveying the room, his stormy gaze sharp and short. "Bit tidy in here, isn't it?"

Bristle. "Tidy? You kidding? There's crap everywhere."

"Yeah, but where Quang left it, last time I looked. If you were hunting something you were desperate enough to kill for . . ."

"I'd make more of a mess." Curiosity needled my palms. Right, as usual. Nothing overturned, nothing broken. "Maybe it wasn't thieves after all."

Indigo squatted by the body, wings folding lengthwise like a locust's, and fingered Quang's dead hand, which still sported its flashy golden ring. "Yeah. Or Quang handed it over before they killed him."

"Or they already knew where to look," I added, inspired. "Maybe a gang puke, someone who hangs out here."

Or, someone who could find the mirror without looking. Someone who could close their eyes and search the air for a little metal ball.

Someone like Indigo.

Blood had clotted on Quang's scrawny forearm, and Indigo slid his middle finger through it, delicate, watching the mess smear and collect on his claw. Absent, like his mind wandered elsewhere. Abruptly he looked up, his silvery mouth tight. "I'm sorry. Did you say something?"

I shivered. "Never mind."

He brushed past me, his wing edge tingling silvery dust onto my shoulder. "Look, it's still whole."

Dumb, I followed, around the counter into Quang's dim office. Plastic chair piled with computer parts, flies crawling on an empty pizza box, an electric motor in dusty pieces on the cracked laminate bench. Oil, spriggan sweat, and beer twisted the air sour. I wrinkled my nose. "Eww."

Indigo poked at a rusty gray shelf near the floor, copper claws clattering on steel. Floor to ceiling with boxes, old televisions, broken computer monitors, and DVD players.

I peered over his shoulder. A scratched gray safe bolted to the floor, bronze combination rings holding fast, the numbers worn off by greasy spriggan fingers.

He tapped at the mechanism, sounding its thickness. "Want a go?"

My belly warmed, and my fingers itched to try, even as I shivered at the thought of actually working in front of him. "Can I? You mean that?"

"Hell, no. Think we've got all day?"

My heart crushed flat. I bit my lip, yet another flush wetting my cheeks. He flashed me a little grin, and now I didn't know if he meant it or not.

I sniffed, hurt, trying to pretend I wasn't watching like a hunting vampire, already straining my ears for the telltale clinks of tumblers. "Fine. Be like that. I'm not so shabby, you know. See if you can impress me. I'm ready."

"I'm sure you are." He clamped his left hand over the door's edge, and the metal sizzled and melted.

He hissed and yanked back his hand, his bangle jangling. Molten iron dripped on the carpet in a lick of blue flame, and the door fell open, its ragged edge smoking red.

I gaped. I couldn't do that. Blaze probably couldn't even do that, not in such a hurry. "That's cheating!"

"Sue me." He tugged the door aside, a fine sheen of sweat glistening on his arms, and gave the contents the barest glance. "It's not here. We should be leaving."

I barely heard him. Prismed light dazzled me, twinkling like tumbling stars, and my pulse stuttered alive. A tangle of bright jewels, still fragrant with my sweat and a faint ashen stink. My sparklies. Ooh, yes. Mine.

I thrust my hand inside, and diamonds and silver tumbled over my wrist, mixing with my new bracelet and shining in vestiges of sun. My heart flooded with pleasure. One was lovely, but more was better. And Quang didn't need them anymore. "These are mine, remember? You said they suited me. Which was a real nice thing to say, by the way, if you don't mind . . ."

But Indigo stood and sniffed the air, ignoring me. "Iron blades downstairs. Steel earrings. Something round and tinny with a screw. Someone's coming."

He tugged me up by my elbow with sharp blue fingers. I yelped and stumbled, clutching my diamonds to my chest. "But what about the mirror? We haven't looked—"

"It's made of iron and lead, Ice. I know what it smells like. Trust me. It's not here." He sniffed again, a dark sheen of sweat on his cheek, and his eyes burned red. "Not tin. Brass. That's Joey DiLuca's cane. Time to go."

"Wh—" Now I heard it, too: sly footsteps creaking on the stairwell. Fear hacked at my nerves. I dropped my voice to a whisper. "DiLuca? What's he doing here?"

"Same as you. Same as me. Time to go."

"But what—?"

"The mirror's Kane's. Joey wants it. Simple enough for you?"

"But we don't have it!"

"Think he'll care?"

My blood curdled with dismay. That damn mirror again. If it really was Snakeboy DiLuca slithering up those stairs, he had cast-iron balls even coming to this neighborhood, where we all paid the Valentis protection.

And Joey didn't exactly have a reputation for patience. Which meant he'd be in a fine wing-ripping mood when he found the mirror missing.

My stomach shriveled. Not good.

Indigo skipped over the counter with a sharp wingbeat and landed in a crouch on the floor. Dust danced around him, streaked with sunlight from the thin chicken-wired skylights above. "Any exit back there? I don't taste anything."

At last my muscles jerked into action. I stuffed my diamonds in my bag and flung my head about, hair flying in my face, looking for a loft, a trapdoor, a crack—any way we could get out.

No windows. Shelves, unbroken carpet, brick pillars and a heating pipe, ceiling fading into darkness. I scrabbled at the edge of a patch of linoleum and uncovered only concrete. My heart jittered. "Nope, there's nothing."

But he'd already launched himself at the ceiling with a slam of silvery wings. He gripped the window's edge with steely fingers and slammed his palm into the ragged chicken wire. Zap. Static flickered. The wire glowed, dripping, burning to nothing under his fingers, and he smashed his elbow through the skylight with a grimace, showering the floor with dusty glass shards and a few drops of silvery blood. "Come on."

Urgency flickered in my veins, yelling at me to move. But infatuation tugged my mouth into a dopey grin, my heart sloshing with delight. Gosh. I felt like Lois Lane. He really was the coolest guy I knew.

"Ice, will you just get up here?" He swung on the jagged window frame from one bulging night-blue arm, scissoring his wings lightly to take his weight, and reached down for me, quicksilver sliding down his muscled forearm.

My heart sighed, fascinated. I could look at him all day when he was like this, all purpose and orders and rampant boy energy. I hopped over the counter and fluttered upward, reaching into the sun for his bloody hand.

"Give me my mirror, you fairy shitsmear."

A shiver ripped up my spine at that cold, smooth voice, and unwilling I looked down.

Slate-gray suit, narrow pale face, hat tilted over shiny snake-green eyes. Joey flashed me white teeth, and pointed at me with his brass-topped black cane. "And give me your skanky girlfriend, too. I like her."

Rude fucking gangsters. Anger fired beneath my skin, mirror-bright and dangerous. I battled the raw urge to swoop down there and chew his pointy little nose off, and fluttered higher.

But a high-pitched screech tore at my ears, and sharp fingers snaked around my ankle and yanked.

Air jammed beneath my wings, stalling. I squealed, and kicked at the grinning blue-haired banshee who clung to my ankle with painted nails. My flip-flops flew off and thudded into the shelving, and my toe connected with her cheek, claws ripping in.

She just yowled and grabbed her other hand higher on my calf. Climbing. Dragging me slowly downward, out of Indigo's reach.

"Ice, come on!" Indigo's fingertips stretched for mine, and I scrabbled for his hand, but it slipped away.

My heart squelched dread into my throat, and my stolen metal courage failed.

I thrashed my weak wings harder and flailed my legs to get her off me, my pulse racing. But she just pulled harder, her magical shriek chilling my bones.

"I can't reach!" Desperation thrust fresh sparks into my muscles, and I strained with aching wings and stretched with all my strength toward Indigo's searching hand. I willed my bones to lengthen, but I couldn't reach.

"Ice!" Indigo let go of the window and dived for me, but too late.

My wing joints hyperextended with a sick crunch. Agony speared my shoulder blades, and with a final sick judder, my wings buckled and I fell.

My knees thudded into the carpet, burning. Shock jarred through my bones, rattling my skull, and my jaw cracked together, my teeth crunching millimeters from my tongue. I yelped with my mouth shut, strangled, and Indigo darted up and away, cursing in a rain of rusty glitter.

Chill stabbed into my veins. Suddenly, I felt wretchedly alone.

The banshee crowed like a rooster, and rubbed her lavender-scented hair in mine, sniffing me like prey. "Here she is, boss."

"Thank you, Mina." Joey strode forward, tossing his cane from hand to narrow hand and stared at me, snake-green eyes glinting cold. He didn't blink. Not at all.

I swallowed, too-familiar dread icing my blood. I'd heard bad things about this Joey. Nasty, fairyslashing things.

I forced my eyes to stay open, water spilling onto my cheeks. Deep inside I burned to snark at him, spit in his face, but childish terror squeezed my throat closed, and all I could think was, *Please, don't let him slash me. I can cope with nasty tricks or beatings or even a rape, especially from a human-sized guy like him when it won't kill me. Just don't let him cut my wings off.*

"Pretty one, aren't you?" Joey licked thin lips and reached for my face.

I recoiled, flapping my sore wings to jerk myself away. But Mina jammed her knee into my back, jolting me upright. She yanked twin handfuls of my hair and forced me rigid, and I flung my head back and forth until my scalp stung and tore, but I couldn't get away.

My eyes crossed as Joey's hand came closer. Alarm punched hard into my diaphragm, and I nearly retched. He'd rip my tongue out. Break my teeth. Tear my nose open. Scratch my eyeballs until they bled. Make me suck him off.

But Joey just touched a cold fingertip to my lips, as if he hushed me. Unwilling, I inhaled the stink of rotting leather and cigarettes.

Indigo hissed, clinging to the ceiling like a spider, his blood plinking faster onto the carpet. "Get your grubby hands off her. Last chance."

I hadn't realized he was still there, and foolish gratitude wiped my skin with wet warmth. He could have been miles away by now. Still, no way would he risk himself for me. I was still screwed.

"Taken. Now come the fuck down and give me my mirror, if you don't wanna see this." Joey grinned, and at that surreal sight, icy terror crackled up my spine. I struggled, but I could do nothing.

Wet black webs squelched out between his fingers and slithered over my lips.

Disgust wormed under my skin. Joey forced a blackened finger between my lips, dragging scaly skin over my gums, scratching at my teeth with his horrible salty claw, forcing between them to find my tongue. Cold, smooth like a snake's skin, the sickening tang of salt and moldering meat.

Sour bile burned my throat, bubbling up into my mouth. I choked and tried to bite, but Mina purred and yanked my head back, forcing my jaw open. Joey shoved his fingers in harder. His webs stretched my lips until they tore, my own mango-sweet blood sliding into my mouth. His scales scraped my palate, scrabbling for my tonsils, and I gagged a flood of saliva and bile, helpless tears scorching my eyes.

He didn't laugh or smile. He wasn't enjoying my misery. Just doing what was necessary, cold and determined and without hesitation. I almost preferred rape to this. He was just a man, even if he was some kind of weird lizard underneath, and men were satiable. I'd swallow his hard-on and he'd like it and in a few minutes it'd all be over.

But this? This could last a very long time.

Hot downdraft rushed, parting my hair, and suddenly my mouth stung empty and the world gleamed cobalt with the shadow of iron and blood.

Claws dragged over my jaw. My skin ripped, pain sparkling like frost. Copper tingled my tongue. Joey hissed and stumbled, the cane flipping from his hand.

I tried to scramble up, Mina's fingers still ripping my hair. My belly ring and the zip on my dress yanked taut in abrupt magnetic flux, and Mina screeched like a wounded bird, blood splattering from her face. Suddenly I was free, spitting and choking on bile like I'd just vomited something very yucky.

A burning wet hand grasped my forearm and yanked me aloft.

Gratitude and worship washed me in equally warm measure, beautiful like a custard shake in a bubble bath. Embarrassing, to be rescued like a silly girl. But wonderful. My fingers didn't make it all the way around Indigo's wrist, but I held on so hard, my claws dug in practically to the bone. His rainbow metal bangle cut into my palm, and incongruous oddness struck me. Wasn't that on his other arm before? You notice the stupidest things in a crisis. Instinctively I flew, my overstretched wings aching.

Below, blades scissored. Razor steel zinged. A dark shape whispered wickedly past my wing tip.

I jerked away, singed. The knife thumped hilt-first into the ceiling and bounced uselessly to the floor. *Hah. Too slow, banshee. We win.*

Curses fired up at us like poisoned artillery, and we ducked past still-melting chicken wire and the skylight's jagged edge into warm, bright, welcoming sun.

Fuck." Joey DiLuca snakes to his feet in fury and swipes his cane up from the carpet, glowing green venom splattering from his claws.

Mina retches on her knees. Broken glass crunches under her palms, her pretty nails torn. Blood streams from her torn eyebrow, her lip, her ripped earlobe. "Sorry. I missed. Let me after them—"

She's already stumbling to her feet, fetching her fallen knives, dragging back bloody blue hair, heading for the stairs. Joey grabs her elbow, fighting his voice calm even though rage and frustration blacken his heart. "No. They're gone. You won't find them. It's okay. We'll make another ambush. Peace, Mina."

She curses, blood and spit flecking. Blood trickles into her eye, from her nose, down the corner of her mouth. Damn magnet-ass fairy ripped her fucking piercings out.

Angry black spines erupt from Joey's forehead. He lets her go and squelches them back inside with an effort, jamming his hat back on so she won't see.

There's one, fallen, a tiny iron ring caked in dust and blood. Joey plucks it from glass shards, and his cold blood pulses warm at the sight, the ragged rosy edges of her skin.

Once he was Dante's foil, his protector, the one who cleaned up all the blood and bodies and dragged Dante back from the brink of chaos when things got out of hand. Now Dante's dead because Joey wasn't there, and he's got Mina. Pretty Mina, who worships him with those lying ruby eyes.

Whose candy scent waters his mouth slyly when he's not expecting it.

Whose lovely bleeding face swells his veins with cold-burning rage.

Suddenly he wants to slip the ring into his mouth, suck it clean for her, taste her insides on the warm iron. Bright self-hatred sweetens his fury. Like she'd want it back after he'd done that.

"Here." Joey tosses the ring at her and stalks over to the dead spriggan, snapping his webs in and out in frustration. Good thing he already hates that thieving ironfairy. It means he can enjoy this ice-fresh loathing without it having anything to do with her.

The smug blue bastard stole Joey's mirror. No other reason Joey'd want to rip those soft gray eyeballs out and swallow them whole. Certainly not a few bruises on his girl's face.

Not that she's his girl.

He squats, leaning on his cane. The body's not stiff yet, and one scrawny red arm tumbles to the carpet. Joey flares his nostrils at foul spriggan sweat and stale beer. "One good thing from this. A dead Valenti rat."

Mina folds herself beside him, her slender thighs smooth in tight leather. She scrapes up some blood and sniffs it, her torn nostril dripping. "Thought you said that blue prick was a thief."

Lick that sugary banshee blood from her lip. Swallow her kiss. Taste her sweat.

Joey tightens his lips and concentrates on the corpse's slashed throat. "He is."

"So why not come at night when no one's around, master? Why'd he do this?"

Stab wound, short and sharp, a single neat slash right to left. Blood mostly on the carpet, a fat green stain, only residual splashing on the corpse. Curiosity thickens Joey's aroused senses. "Didn't die in a fight."

"What?"

"He was already on the floor, Mina. Did you hear what the fairy slut said, as we came up the stairs?"

"Some shit." She shrugs. Her magical hearing is better than his. She just doesn't listen.

"Some shit like 'we don't have the mirror'?" Joey drops his cane and crawls forward to sniff the corpse's throat. Blood, spit, a trace of oil. That's all. The evidence is too distant for his human senses, and his sinuses sparkle, itching to flower.

He doesn't dare glance at Mina. Just slides his neck out and lets the scales sprout.

Let her look. It's the truth, after all.

Vertebrae mutate in his neck, and his muscles stretch with a splurt of adrenaline. Keratin plates burst from his skin, warm black pigment spreading like blood. His vision dims. Colors die. Sounds fade, blotted out by a sparkling new world of scent and vibration. Electric cycles buzzing the air with static, tiny rhythmic shudders deep in the building's steel-webbed foundations, the flicker of insects and dust in myriad starlight shades. His lips scale over, his mouth dries, his tongue sprouts forks between serrated fangs that slide from his gums like blades. Venom swells his palate.

The scales itch to slide down his body, to cover him. Heat flushes his balls, twitching his cock to hardness, and he grits shrinking teeth and resists, his skin crawling with need beneath nuisance clothes. Grunt. Slither. Swallow. But not all the way. Not everything, not in front of her.

He gasps with the effort of holding back, and slithers forward on misshapen serpent elbows to the body. His fins scrape on the carpet, and his skin vibrates, tingling. The spriggan's skin is rough and cool on his scales, and he rubs his neck along the corpse's chest with delight. His mouth opens, and he inhales, his tongue forks flickering right and left.

Sensory juices tingle his palate. A kernel of heat, slowly dying in the spriggan's heart. The rapid cycle of the lightbulb above, the breeze as Mina shifts her fragrant hips, some distant footsteps vibrating the floor. The rich stink of dead spriggan blood, acrid with shock.

Joey slithers over sharp ribs, a curved collarbone, ripe spriggan muscles sharp with sweat and bristles. Wrist tendons, a cold slimy palm wet with blood. And underneath, almost too faint to detect, the sweet dusty taste of flowers.

Memory stabs bright into Joey's quivering sinuses, and he grins with mobile jaws, his control stretching. Kane's aberration. Akash, he called himself, dressed in a handsome human body but, like Joey, something quite different underneath. Kane was too angry to realize anyone watched, not the least a wicked snakeshifter with an enhanced sense of taste.

Triumph swells his warming veins, and he wants to slide naked on dead skin, warm his scales slowly with friction and failing body heat, pretend Dante's still alive and Mina's just a naughty knifegirl with whipcord thighs and everything's how it was before.

But not with Mina watching.

With a hiss and a sigh he withdraws, and once he's pulled back inside his clammy, tight human skin, he's left with only a parched mouth, a raging thirst in his throat, and an aching hard-on.

And Mina staring at him, her bloody lips quivering in disgust or loathing. Or interest.

Tingles erupt in starved arteries, and Joey grips his cane and stalks to his bloodless feet. "Get up. We've an angel to chase."

15

Alley walls loomed tall on either side of us. At the far end, cars cruised by in the street, their sour exhaust rising under my wings and spiking pain into my skull. My breath tore my lungs ragged. My jaw still stung where Joey's claws ripped me, and my mouth felt coarse and raw inside. I fluttered limply to dusty concrete, my abused wingbones protesting, and leaned my hands on my knees to recover my breath.

I sweated. I hurt. I stung. Damn it, this sucked. All except the part about holding Indigo's hand, which I wasn't anymore, because he'd dropped me from ten feet above the ground and now my feet hurt.

I'm not too good with flying at the best of times. Blaze can dart about like a dragonfly on heat, and Azure likes to swing from glowing streetlights and chase the moths, her hair fluttering in her own breeze. But not me.

Like usual, I barely scrape by compared with those two. And having my wings bent back by a mad knife-sporting banshee wasn't helping.

I panted and squinted in the hot afternoon sun, the bricks knobbly and solid against my bare shoulder. Quang's was a couple of blocks away. Any farther than that, and someone would notice us. "Are they following us?"

Indigo lighted beside me, luminous wings weightless in the sunshine. "Nope. They can't fly, remember? Though neither can you, by the look."

Ah, now I knew why he hadn't abandoned me. He needed someone to taunt. My hero.

I scowled, still catching my breath, and scratched my stinging chin as I straightened. The cuts swelled under my fingerpads, inflamed. "Like I've never heard that before. I'm more of a ladylike flutterer, okay?"

Indigo giggled. Yeah, really. Not a giggly guy, my Indigo, but my efforts at flying sure raised a juicy one. Just when I think he's a coldhearted centipede, he goes and does something like that.

I shook my wings at him in frustration, soaking him in droplets. "Water fairy, look. Water is my element. Air just gives me the shivers. Throw me in the ocean and see how I go then." I love the ocean, diving under cool salty water, my hair streaming back in the gurgle of distant whale voices, jellyfish brushing over my skin. I fold my wings back and kick like a mermaid, and under I go. But my skin still shrivels like a prune if I stay in for too long, and I have to come up for air like everyone else or I'll drown.

There's always a catch, see. Azure will rip and suffocate in a windstorm just like a human, and if Blaze gets too close to the fire, he'll burn.

Our own elements, killing us. Welcome to life as a fairy.

"Okay," Indigo said, shaking my drips from his hair, the ghost of that cute giggle still teasing his lips. "Next puddle we see, you're going in."

I scowled again, in case he missed the first one. "And don't even talk to me about heights. In case you were going to, ya know, in which case you can just shut up right now."

"I wasn't." Silvery blood rinsed down his forearm in my water, and his skin sparkled in the sun. Static crackled blue, outlining wet muscles.

Metal boy. Shiny. Wet. *Mmm.*

Titanium rainbowed like oil as water dripped over his wrist. Definitely his left arm. Must have imagined things before, right?

His claws dripped, and current arced blue between his fingers. My skin tingled in sympathy. What would that feel like, if he touched me?

His gaze caught mine, burning, and swiftly I looked away, lightheaded. "Okay, then."

"Sure."

"Fine." Damn, my chin really itched like a bastard. I scraped it with my claws.

"Show me your face."

"What?" I scratched again, harder, and blisters burst, spreading the itch.

He lifted my jaw with his finger, ducking his head to look, and clicked his tongue. "Joey really got you a good one. Already swollen. Wash it out."

"What?" I say that a lot around him. *Gotta get some vocab, Ice.*

He touched a cut. It stung, and my skin stuck to his finger when he pulled it away. He waved his fingertip before my eyes, showing me a blob of evil green goo. "Venom. Wash it out or your skin'll rot." He licked his finger clean and spat, wrinkling his nose. "Nice."

Alarm tumbled my pulse downhill. "Venom?"

"Yeah. You know. Like a snake."

"But he had his hand in my mouth. I coulda swallowed some!"

Already my chin swelled, my flesh tight and hot. I swallowed, and it hurt. Frantic, I shoved my claws down my throat, scrabbling for my tonsils to make myself throw up.

Indigo grabbed my wrist and gently forced my fingers away. "Stop it. Calm down. It's venom, not poison. Drink as much of it as you want. It won't hurt you."

I swatted at the scratches on my chin, panic tumbling in my pulse. "But what about these? I've gotta get to a shower—"

"No time. Wash it out."

"What? How?"

"Water fairy, right? Before it sinks in, Ice. Now." Urgency sparked his eyes rusty red, and panic tightened around my lungs like a rubber band.

"I . . . I can't." I flushed, not from effort but embarrassment, and water seeped on my skin like light sweat, not enough.

"What?" His turn for monosyllables, a whisper that didn't engage my confidence.

I shuddered, my skin cold and horribly dry. I jerked my wings, but I'd already shaken off the water. My stomach flipped, cold, and I jumped up and down in frustration. "I can't do it on purpose! I don't know how."

He swallowed, and his wing tips rippled coppery. "Shit. Okay. Calm down. We'll fix you up. Come here." He slid his hand around my neck and pulled me close, ignoring my jitters.

His powerful steely scent slid deep into my sinuses, and my head swam, light, either from the venom or from him. I flapped ineffective hands. "What are you doing?"

"Just stand there and take it, okay?" And before I could react, he nudged my chin up and opened his hot mouth onto my throat.

His lips burned me, gentle yet unyielding. My breath slid away in a hot rush of surprise that quickly melted into delicious pleasure. My skin sparkled under his kiss, all the way down. I closed my eyes. He kissed my throat, my jaw, the delicate place where my pulse trembled, wet openmouthed kisses that poured molten delight down along my collarbone and tugged my nipples tight.

Heat shivered down my spine to tingle between my legs. I tilted my head back, and water dripped over my chin, not just sweat now but the real hot water of desire.

His tongue stroked my slashed skin, stinging yet delicious. My veins constricted under the pressure, my pulse beating harder. So he was a taste fetishist. Just like I'd imagined. *Baby, you can taste me all you want.* His brittle claws teased my scalp and crunched in the dripping hair at the back of my neck, and I couldn't suppress a whimper of delight.

And then he sucked, noisily, and I realized belatedly what he was really doing.

Not kissing me. Not licking my throat for the pleasure of it. Sucking out the poison. Making me wet all over, just to wash the venom out.

He released me and spat a mouthful of blue-tinged green slime onto the concrete. "Yuck. Gross." He worked his mouth to get more saliva, and spat again, cleaner this time.

I licked my lips, still breathless and trembling, and my voice shrank somewhere on its way from my swollen throat to my mouth. "Thanks. I think."

He glanced up at me halfway through wiping his mouth and halted, completing the remainder of the movement carefully. "Sorry. I didn't mean *you* were—"

"I know. I agree. Pretty stank, huh?" I tugged my diamond-stuffed bag tight on my shoulder. The scratches still hurt. The bruise he'd so sweetly made there hurt, too. But it hurt worse, deep in my heart, that he'd said that. That I'd wanted him to touch me even though he'd done nothing but insult me all morning, and that even when he had his mouth on my throat and my pulse trembling under his tongue, the rest of me hadn't tempted him for even a moment.

Just like Blaze said. Indigo wanted something. Only reason he was still here.

Water still trickled over me, warm and painfully obvious. Embarrassment curdled my guts, and I stuck my hand on my hip, trying to look pissed off instead of bewildered and aroused. "So, what do we do now? Run away? Hide? Jump in front of a tram?"

He fingered his bottom lip with one claw, mesmerizing. "I'm thinking strawberry, rather than chocolate."

Infuriating boy. "Look, sorry if I'm a bit slow, but what the fuck?"

"Strawberry ice cream. That's your favorite, right? You look like you could use one. It's on me."

I waved my arms in frustration. "You pick now to ask me out? And how the hell do you know what flavor I like?"

He shrugged, sensual. "You want some or not?"

"You wanna go for ice cream? Are you crazy? I mean, hey, I'm flattered, but did you forget that we've got Snake-Ass DiLuca and his bondage princess chasing us?"

Indigo caught my wrists and gently forced me to relax. "Which is why we're going for ice cream. At Valentino's. Think Joey'll dare show his scaly butt in Angelo's place?"

My wits flittered about like autumn leaves, and his hot grip on my wrists—I've always wanted him to hold me down and ravish me—wasn't helping. My gaze stuck itself like wet leaves to his silvery mouth, and I peeled it off with a squelch.

Valentino's. Ange Valenti's café. Ange would probably be there himself, and even if Sonny was around, I still had a day or two's grace. Grudging respect for Indigo's wits soothed my irritated nerves, and I stopped wriggling. My fingerpads itched to touch him back, but I stilled them. "Good point."

"Yeah. I thought so."

"Indigo."

"What?"

"You're still holding me."

"Oh. Yeah. Sorry." He let me go, and hid his hands shyly behind his back.

Frustration jammed my nerves, and my wings quivered tight. Maddening, impossible boy.

I straightened, tugging my bag over my shoulder, and side by side we walked over smeared concrete toward the sun.

I stole a glance at him, so close beside me. This was either my lucky day, or some weird nightmare. Sunlight glinted on his silver-foil wings, almost too bright to watch. His lips shone, still silvery wet, and I remembered their warmth on my inflamed throat and wondered if he'd ever kiss me again.

His hand brushed mine, accidental, and he cleared his throat and tucked his hands behind his back again.

A warm hollow emptied inside. I felt like a blushing schoolgirl. Not that I ever went to school much.

A dragonfly zipped by, and he lifted a coppery claw and let the insect land. It preened itself in the sun, wings flickering. He sighed, short. "Look. Ice cream's not like the diamonds, okay?"

I couldn't help but glance down at my wrist, where my shinies danced in sunlight. My belly warmed. *So pretty. Mine.* I got a kiss with them and everything. But at what cost? "Whatcha mean?"

"I did what I did back there with the venom without asking. This isn't an apology. But we need to talk, Ice."

My skin dampened at the memory of his mouth on my skin. *Sure, let's talk. About doing it again, only without the venom.* "Umm."

"About this mirror, and what we're going to do." He flicked his finger, and the dragonfly darted away.

"Oh. Yeah. That."

A fleeting glance, delicious. "Besides, I've been waiting for the chance to take you out."

My stomach hit my kneecaps, and giggles ripped in to take its place. Yeah, this must be a dream. A psychedelic one, like when you snort too much banshee blue and pass out. I snickered. "Oh, you're such a liar. I've only asked you about a million times and you always brush me off."

"You always want to go for pizza. I hate pizza."

Giddy warmth spilled in my heart. He hates pizza. Who knew?

Afternoon sun burns ocher through cracked warehouse windows, dragging long shadows from machinery draped with the dirt and cobwebs of disuse. Dust motes spar in crisscrossed shafts of light, a cruel cage of silent accusation, and below stands Akash, his lips locked in a flame-tickled kiss with a slender silvery fairy.

His throat bulges with the fat throb of stolen magic. The fairy's wings judder and crackle, but it can't escape, trapped in the cruel strength of Akash's arms.

Akash swallows one final time and pulls away. The fairy's body slumps to the concrete, its dulled pearlescent wings crushing beneath its weight. Its pretty head hits the floor at a strange angle, and dust filters slowly into long black hair. Glassy eyes stare, blank, extinguished like its pretty flames.

Now those flames are Akash's. Yellow fire ribbons from his fingers to flicker out a few inches from the floor. His nails glitter, drenched in fairyshine, and he smells gunpowder.

Just like the banshee's song. Pretty. Pointless. No help against Kane.

Akash slams himself onto his ripped plastic stool and fidgets, unable to keep still or dodge the unfeeling sun's glare. Strange stolen powers gibber and struggle inside him, bickering and gnawing at each other like an ornery crowd. He's eaten firefae, banshee, black spriggan, green spriggan, earthfae, absorbed their fickle powers into his own, and he still doesn't understand how Kane tempts them, or how to stop it. About him, nailed into crude wooden crates, more creatures wail and protest and scream, waiting their turn, and the air stings with sour fear.

On the desk, the Quang's rusty sphere rolls and giggles, sly laughter that echoes in Akash's heart.

Akash swallows, and his guts fight him, struggling to explode. Something's not right. His nerves quiver, and he slams his palms on his knees, the light pain a welcome solace, but only for a second or two. Evil yearning fires his blood, new and excruciating, and even though the sunset-drenched sky will not speak, he knows somehow it's his own fault.

This is not what Shadow sent him here for. He was supposed to claim this broken city back, purge it of wicked temptation. Not drink it up and long for more.

Silence. Screeching heat. Horrid water impregnating the air like maggots. Surely this place is hell itself. But his body craves it, hungers for bone-shattering sensation, more and again and rougher and harder until he screams.

But he doesn't scream, not now, not with Indra watching. This, too, is a new sensation, this hiding, the cunning delight of lies, and it coils tight and delicious inside him like a venomous snake.

He scrapes his teeth together and grates his elbows back and forth on the torn wooden desk until the ruts char and smoke, but it doesn't help. The boxed creatures snarl and curse. His fingers shake, the fine hair on his arms ripples in some invisible sensory breeze, and with a disgusted snarl he jerks up and paces, raking his hair with sparking hands that alternate hot and cold. He doesn't know what to do. If Shadow finds out he's changing . . .

The sphere wobbles, seasick.

Akash snatches it up, and metal fins scythe open. The mirror glints at him, inscrutable. His eye reflects back at him, bloodshot blue. "Show me Kane again."

The mirror snickers, and shows him.

A black cavern, blood-soaked earth and burning oil, puddles of flame shimmering green and blue. The image pans, dizzy through screeching brass doors carved with teeth and tongues. Silver wings sparkle in firelight, a sneaky blue hand snaking out to steal. Flashes of storm-gray eyes and reddish metal claws, a fall of auburn hair, straining blue wrists in cruel chains, rich splatters of blood and a scream so deep, it hurts Akash's lungs just to listen. A name, howled raw and broken to an uncaring heaven. Natasha. Akash doesn't know her.

He squeezes, edges slicing his palms scarlet. "Not that. More."

Fast-forward, noise and images tumbling, past a chocolate-skinned demon mistress with flaming purple hair, through acres of blackness and curling hellflame to the nightclub, dark and alive with sound and wrath and neon-lit smoke. Flash of diamonds, sharp demon teeth, the slick heat of a kiss, yellow claws scraping on linen and the horrid death-pleasure of losing your breath.

The mirror sighs and lingers, a slow, languorous image of the yellow girl twisted in soaked white sheets with Kane. Limbs entwined, wet hair tangling her throat, lips sliding swollen together.

Akash growls, the banshee's angry magic festering in his throat. She's very pretty. Such slim legs, her thighs dusted with gold as they wrap around the demon's hard body. Her wings are delicate, so fine, they crumple like silk, her arms long and graceful even embracing such a foul creature. And Kane, earth's golden child—so beautiful, he's frightening—Kane keeps his eyes closed, like he's pretending nothing's happening. Like it's all beyond his control.

Akash murmurs, his fingers fidgeting with possibilities. Maybe this means Kane is in her power. The power to seduce Kane is one worth having. But how is it done? "Show me more."

The mirror sighs and obliges. Fast-forward, a scrabble through sun-parched city streets to a weathered house, withered plants and paint peeling in strips. Crisp yellow flame on crimson wings, a flash of bold black eyes, white fairy skin translucent in burning sun, the sharp citrus flavor of guilt. A tumble of apple-green hair, luminous blue eyes pooled with tears . . .

Frustrated, Akash shakes his head, fairysparks spitting. "That's not what I meant. Back. Show me Kane's yellow girl."

The mirror grumbles in protest. Twitching red spriggan ears, grasping leathery fingers, a meaty tongue scraping on glass.

Akash yowls, vibrant with stolen banshee compulsion, and the mirror recoils and does as it's told. Yellow girl, laughing against broken bricks with sunshine in her eyes, the rich metal kiss of her lover.

Acid floods his veins, bitter on his tongue, and his bones ache. He rejoices. Jealousy. Not just unease or apprehension or vague happiness. A real, raw emotion from hell.

Urgency hastens his pulse. This yellow girl is surely the key. He must find her, examine her, suck out her secrets. He peels his hungry gaze away and snaps the mirror shut. "Indra!"

Akash studies her with fresh glass-warped cynicism. Still wearing the same dusty clothes, her dark hair clumped from lack of combing. He still hasn't forgiven her, and she's worried. She doesn't want to be alone. *Please him,* she's thinking. *Make him remember he needs me. Give him everything he wants, and maybe he'll take pity on me.*

He's thought like that himself on so many occasions, prostrated himself under an unfeeling sky with silence for reward. Punished so many times for asking too many questions, for staring too long at the stars, for asking the insects where the sun goes at night. He knows now to call that emptiness pain.

He knows now that the sky lies. Shadow lies. Kane is not weak but near invincible. Pain is not evil, rather food for the soul. The world is not steeped in suffering, but immersed in sensory pleasure. And rather than condemning the creatures to torment, all that emotion and sensation make them happy.

The sky is false, and Akash is alone. Abandoned. Expendable. He was never meant to succeed. This mission was punishment, just like everything else, for too many questions, for always asking the wrong things of the wrong people. Something is most surely wrong with him. It's called curiosity, and he won't ever give it up. No matter how they brainwash him.

He owes Shadow nothing. He need no longer obey.

So why fight Kane? Why not just stay here and drown in sweet reality?

In his mind, the earth shudders and opens up to suck him away.

Indra blinks, her pretty mouth trembling. "Yes, Akash?"

His heart softens. He is her sky, her watcher, her protector. He'll not be so cruel. He'll not lie to keep her obedience. She doesn't deserve this treachery.

He reaches out to her, and shyly she slides dusty fingers into his palm. He smiles gently, covering the rage that squeezes his heart like a vise. He'll still search for Kane. Kane has answers, can show him how to survive in this delicious place. But a demon won't give his secrets up willingly, not to an ancient enemy. "We must seek out this yellow girl Kane chose."

Indra nods eagerly. "We shall."

He points to the stinking, yelling crates. "First, we shall examine our creatures. Then, I shall wash you. Then we can begin our search."

He bends for her kiss, and this time when he kisses her in return, she doesn't protest. Her soft lips squash a little under his, warming the seductive taste of rebellion. —*Bite,*— whispers the mirror slyly, —*lick, swallow,*— and a rush of burning blood melts his resolve's cold shell.

Her fingers shake in his flame-rippled grip, and she fidgets. "Must you wash me, Akash?"

"I like to look at you. I wish to make you even prettier. Don't you want me to?"

She blinks shyly. "If you wish it."

She still doesn't understand. She has her own wishes now. He squeezes her little hands together. "But do you wish it, Indra?"

Confusion clouds her face. He kisses the crease between her brows, and that rebellious taste flares stronger. He smiles, free at last, and tilts her chin up to bring her lips to his.

A shocked moment, and then her warm lips spark alive into a feverish kiss. Akash trembles against her, his body awash with strange needy sensation. She doesn't taste of flowers and breeze and raindrops, the bright comforting taste of home. She tastes of flesh, hot and glorious, her lips smooth and supple on his, her tongue emerging shyly to rub against his. He sighs into her, sharing their breath, and the little sound she makes in her throat tastes of bewilderment and fresh desire.

But she breaks off, her breath heaving and scarlet flooding high in her cheeks, and avoids his eyes.

He knows now what wanting involves. So easily fed, this need. He reaches for her, his body burning.

But she shakes him off with all her strength. "No, Akash. It is not right. I do not wish it." Her flushed face tightens in disapproval, and she runs, her footsteps disappearing into the gloom.

"Indra. Return." He clenches shaking hands and calls out to her, the fairy's stolen sparks fingering his skin. But she doesn't turn. She won't obey him. Something is broken. He hurries after her, out into the dirty alley where broken glass glints orange in fresh sunlight. Hot summer breeze caresses his face as he searches left and right. She's gone. Hiding. From him.

Akash licks stinging lips, still wet from kissing her. Her taste lingers in his mouth like an accusation. His newfound pride hurts, bruised by her rejection. He could find her, punish her, twist her naughty body to his will, make her hurt and cry and bleed to wash his dignity clean.

The fact that he even thinks that forces a strangled scream of fury from his throat. He whirls and grabs the mirror, ripping it open with a vicious squeeze. The glass glints at him, uncaring, and steals silent black fingers toward his misbegotten soul.

A sly caress inside him, soft and dark like midnight feathers. His will wilts, parched by her absence. What is there, without that perfidious sky? Without her? He is alone. Alone, and lonely.

The mirror cackles, triumphant.

The sound coats his courage in fresh steel. He is not alone. He still has purpose. He will stay in this painbright world that fires his blood, and nothing Shadow can do will stop him. Kane has answers, and Akash will have them. He must.

He wills his stare stronger, his eyes blazing back at him from the glass like sapphire frost. "No. Obey me. I am stronger here. Obey."

The mirror squirms in the clutches of his death-blue gaze and relents with a petulant snivel.

Impish thing. Defeated, or just giving in for now? Akash frowns. He knows capitulation. He's been there himself so many times, the reluctant smile, the modest lowering of eyes, the whispered acquiescence in return for freedom.

But no matter. Purpose served.

Akash smiles at his new servant, and flame flickers from his teeth. "Good. Never mind the other creatures for now. Find me the yellow girl."

The mirror whimpers and obeys.

16

Vine leaves ruffled on the pine pergola, dappling the afternoon sun pleasantly on my face. The air swarmed with deliciousness, my nose orgasming in a wash of melted butter and coffee and peppery tomato bruschetta. Valentino's was half-empty, too late for lunch and too early for dinner, and a caramel-eyed waiter winked at me as he glided by between empty linen-draped tables, his tray laden with scones and iced chocolate drinks in tall glasses.

I kicked my feet against the wooden legs of my chair, enjoying sultry summer warmth, and dipped my spoon in the berry ice cream mountain on my plate. Chocolate sauce dribbled down pink slopes, loaded with colored sprinkles, and I caught it with my tongue, dark cocoa sweetness melting into my mouth. *Mmm.* Valentino's has the best fudge sauce in the whole world.

Across from me, a fat green spriggan with an armload of shopping bags slurped a latte, bubbles frothing out her nose. In the corner, a pair of black-suited trolls muttered and gulped espressos, tusks gleaming and sharp yellow claws digging into the little cups, and next to them a giggling blue air sprite swiveled golden wings and poked his nose into a plate of whipped cream.

Next to me, Indigo reclined in his chair, long denim-clad legs stretched out. The crisp black ends of his hair stuck to his dark cheeks in the heat, and sweat slicked his arms with copper as he scooped up an icy pink blob. His bangle rainbowed in the sun, green and blue swirls flashing. Left arm. Definitely the left.

Summer, ice cream, cute waiters, a date with Indigo. Doesn't get much better than this.

Except maybe not being chased by gangsters or going insane. But you can't have everything.

I chewed on a marshmallow, soft sugar popping between my teeth. "So . . . what's the story on you and this mirror, anyway? You did for Kane already. Whadda you care?"

"You first." Indigo sucked ice cream from his spoon, his lips gleaming a surreal pink.

Nerves squiggled my blood. I didn't want to tell him my stupidity. "Why do I have to go first?"

"I asked first." An errant strawberry blob dribbled down his fingers, and I watched to see what he'd do. The ice cream test. Waste it? Wipe it? Would he be swift and thoughtless, or deliberate?

He ducked and licked the drips up. Slow, sensual, savoring, his dark tongue sliding lovingly over his knuckles and his claws. Not a drop spilt. I squirmed, my damp thighs sticking on the cane. Sweet and dead sexy at the same time. *Great. I'm turned on just watching him eat ice cream.*

I swallowed my next mouthful too fast, and my freezing throat ached. "I asked last night. You first."

He shrugged, crushing chocolate shavings into the plate with his spoon. "Told you. Kane wants it back. You're lucky he's not coming after you, magpie girl."

"Yeah. Guess so." I recalled Kane's strange, absent touch and shivered. Indigo picked at a stain on the tablecloth, determined to look at it instead of at me. Did he care that I'd slept with Kane? A little bit jealous, even?

At last his gaze met mine, soft warm gray like rain clouds. "So what's your story, Ice? Why fence it one day and scrabble after it the next?"

I stuffed more ice cream into my mouth, my teeth protesting with a cold spike into my gums. My voice squelched through a freezing mouthful. "No reason. I realized I got ripped off, that's all. Quang's a sneaky little shitball."

Indigo laughed, silver teeth sharp. "Right. You looked into the glass."

"Nope." I gurgled as I swallowed, my throat sore. How did he know? Had he looked, too?

"Did so."

"Did not."

"Did so. How'd you know it's a mirror, if you didn't open it?"

"Did n— Oh." He had me there. I sighed. "It's shiny, okay? You should understand that. I saw a pretty shiny thing and I took it. But it wasn't as much fun as I thought, so I got rid of it."

"Don't believe you. What happened, Ice?"

His gaze didn't falter, and my spine prickled under his scrutiny. I bristled, mirrorspiked words bubbling up in my throat. "Nothing, okay? Just this stupid guy on the tram, and then I messed up our fortune-telling con because I couldn't lie, and then there was this vampire and I wanted him to drink me and Kane said he'd make me better if I gave the mirror back and then you came along and pulled that switch on me like you do, nasty one minute and nice the next, and what the hell is it with that anyway, and then Blaze hissed at you and I went with him and we had sex. Three times. In front of Azure. And now she hates me and he avoids me and we owe the Valentis five grand by Friday and Quang's dead and the DiLucas are chasing me and I've ruined my life over a piece of fucking glass. Okay?"

My stomach tied in bulging knots, and sickness threatened to swamp me. Surely he'd despise me more than ever now. Tears slashed at my eyes like acid, and I fumbled them away, dreading the look I'd get from him, that little upturned lip of disgust.

But he just chewed his claw, silvery teeth flashing. "So . . . Kane will cure you if you give it back?"

My strangled heart relaxed, just a little. He wasn't judging me. I sniffed, stupid gratitude tearing me up all over again. "Yeah. Lucky for me we're both taking it to the same place, right?"

"Lucky. And Blaze . . . isn't your boyfriend, then?" He scratched at the tablecloth, like he wasn't really interested in my answer.

I scraped my face clean with my palm, my throat tight. "No, he's not my damn boyfriend. He's not even my friend anymore. Dead grandmothers and incest. Don't wanna talk about it. Okay?"

I rummaged in my bag for something, anything to do that didn't involve thinking or looking at him. Diamonds spilled over my sticky fingers. My phone tumbled out, the screen flashing neon with a new text message. I ignored it. Probably Blaze, giving me shit. I wasn't in the mood.

Coins rolled onto the tablecloth, a couple of bucks at most. Good thing this woolly mammoth–sized sundae was on Indigo. Tissues. A squashed green jelly bean. Can opener. Lipstick, color orange. And amongst the rabid gleam of diamonds, a flash of scarlet-spiked silver.

I stared, and scrabbled the diamonds aside.

Tarnished silver skulls glinted up at me, ruby eyeballs flashing, threaded on a fat spiked chain.

My stalking biker boy's necklace. Tangled in the diamonds from Quang's safe.

I recalled the kid's weird blue eyes, the way he'd smiled at me when I hit him. Like he expected me. Like he'd been listening. Excitement tightened my throat. "Look at this!"

Indigo wrinkled his nose. "Yuck. Bit morbid, isn't it?"

"It was in my diamonds. I saw a guy wearing it at the Court last night."

"So?" He dipped up some ice cream and flicked it at me.

Chill stung my cheek. I wiped it off and glared at him. "So, sometime between last night and this morning, he's swapped it to Quang. How much you reckon it's worth?"

Water flooded his eyes, and he sniffed, wiping his nose. "Chromium. Stinks like rotten apples. So they're real rubies. So what? Wanna put all that back in your bag before someone rolls you for it?"

Caution. Boring. Anticipation thinned my pulse, and I bounced up and down in my seat, water droplets spraying. "But what if that guy swapped it for the mirror?"

"Maybe. Coulda swapped it for a couple hundred bucks and a blow job, too. Mosquitoes and chopsticks, Ice. You're grabbing at anything."

I scowled, my enthusiasm dented. "Sure, go all superior on me. You got any better ideas?"

Indigo glanced at the coffee-chugging trolls and casually pushed the diamonds toward me without looking. "Cactus up your nose, Ice, will you stop attracting attention?"

My wings bristled. "Why've you gotta—?"

A thick hand slammed onto my shoulder. "Nice diamonds, fairy girl. I think they're mine."

I gulped at those sharp European consonants. My voice shriveled to a husk. "Sonny . . . I mean, Mr. Valenti. Hi. I was just looking for y—"

"Good of you to bring 'em by." Sonny loomed over me, his hulking leather-clad shoulders blocking out the sun. Dark, hard-eyed, his mouth thin and stained from too many cigarettes. A bit like his cousin Angelo, without the teeth or the old-world manners. With a permanent case of fire ants up his ass because his self-absorbed and glaringly gay cousin Nino had to die raped in some sordid hotel apartment before Ange would give Sonny Nino's place as second in charge. Jealous as a shithouse dog because Ange still prefers lizard-ass faeborn confidants to him. And in an eternal bad mood because Ange still won't give him the other thing he wants, that hellcursed blood infection that makes you last forever.

All of which makes Sonny V one big, ugly, bad-tempered Italian dude.

My excitement bubbled forlornly, lost in smothering dismay. I never get to keep them.

I stole my hand out, but Indigo wrapped his arm around me to hold me back. His whisper warmed my cheek. "Too late. Leave it."

The fact that he'd warned me only stung my despair harder. I wriggled, helpless. Why'd I have to flash them around like that? At Valentino's, of all places?

Sonny lifted a fistful of shinies twinkling to the sun, his broad forehead creasing. "Very nice. How much you and your pals owe me again?"

I hate it when they ask questions they already know the answers to. Never bodes well. I swallowed, dry, and firmly pushed Indigo's arm away. "Five thousand."

"These'll be nice, then. Good girl." That condescending smirk I hated.

I managed a weak smile, faint brightness struggling in my heart even though rage lathered my blood at this forced meekness. At least something good might come of this. He'd leave us alone, at least for a while. "So we're square, then?"

Sonny stuffed my lost jewels into his pocket and turned away. "Sorry. I can only accept payment in cash. End of the week, darlin'. As before."

I gaped at his wide black-clad back, indignant. "But that's not fair!"

Sonny halted.

Indigo's arm tensed on the table, muscles twisting. Sharp unease sliced my nerves. *Oops.*

Sonny turned and pounced on me.

I yelped and jerked backwards, but he was quicker than he looked. He wrapped his fat fingers around my shoulder, his dirty teeth shining an inch from my nose. "Life isn't fair, fairy girl. Wanna talk about it?"

My shoulder screeched, pain warm and horrid like his coffee-soaked breath. His fingers crushed into my collarbone, and anger flared hotter than the hurt. My rage boiled over, and I swatted at him, claws raking. "Ow! Get off me, you dirty fairy-beating asshole."

"Umm. Yeah. We were just leaving." Indigo folded his long hand over mine and squeezed, hard, and the twin pressures made me gasp at my foolishness.

But Sonny shoved me, and I tumbled, ice cream splashing. I scrabbled for Indigo's hand, but my fingers slipped, and my bony butt bounced on the hard floor, crumpling my wing tips under me. My palms skidded and ripped on sandpapery tiles. "Ow! That hurt! Stupid prick."

Sonny wiped the hand he'd hurt me with on his pants, and his flat gray eyes gleamed disgusted as he loomed over me. Behind him, the two trolls lumbered up, their suits too tight, big green foreheads shining dully in the sun. They fixed beady little eyes on me and grunted, thudding their scaly fists together.

My skin shrank. I scrambled back a few inches like a frightened crab, banging my head into the latte-swilling spriggan's chair. Surely they wouldn't. Not in front of everyone.

But the cream-nose fairy had already crawled away under the

tables, and the shop-till-you-drop spriggan sidled from her seat, hairy ears pinned back like a scared dog's. She scrabbled for her shopping bags and ran out, toeclaws clicking.

Now Valentino's was empty.

Sonny grinned. "Say you're sorry."

At the sight of that supercilious smile, rage lit me up like a flashbulb.

Memories erupted over my skin like lava. All the times some brainless gangster had threatened me, all the times I'd ever dredged up a false smile and fluttered my lashes when I felt like raking my claws down their smug faces. Every guy who tried to force me, every fae-dissing idiot who ever hit me or teased me or threatened me, pushed me against a wall as they passed or pretended I wasn't there. Even when I was a little girl, all the times I'd stared wide-eyed at humans, their safe families, their careers, their rich carefree lives, and someone said, *No, darlin', you can't ever have that. You're different. You're trash. You're just a silly fae girl. Get back in the dirt where you belong.*

My skin swelled with angry vapor, and mirrorstolen courage ignited my blood like wet phosphorous.

Say I'm sorry?

You've got to be fucking kidding me.

I scrambled to my feet and strode closer, my fists squeezing tight. Indigo hissed a warning and slid knobbed fingers around my wrist, but I shook him off. Years of bottled-up angry words burned like sunfire on my tongue, demanding release. "Damned if I'm sorry. You're a lousy prick, Sonny, and your ass-licking friends, too. What, too afraid to fight a man? Get a hard-on picking on little girls half your size? Huh? Gonna go home and jerk off?"

Sonny's smile dissolved. Crimson flushed his face. Behind him, the trolls grumbled and rolled threatening shoulders.

Giddy defiance drowned the last fragments of my fear. I laughed, delight sliding like a drug into my blood. "Yeah, I bet you will. Go ahead and hit me if it makes you feel good. Wanna watch me tremble?" I stretched my eyes wide and chewed my claws, knocking my knees together in a pretend shiver of terror.

Sonny licked his lips, deliberate, and with a thick flex of biceps, he flipped a pistol from his holster and leveled it at me. "I said, say you're sorry, you sour little fairy cunt."

I recoiled, my charade melted. His crude insult stung me, but I barely noticed. For the first time ever, I stared at the scary end of a firearm.

Stinky oiled brass invaded my nostrils and crawled down my throat, only to return, dragging cold fear wriggling like a frog into my mouth. My chest hollowed, and my courage ducked for cover, leaving me with shaking muscles and a sick stomach and nerves that twisted and writhed in every limb.

He'd shoot me. He'd really shoot me, just for calling him names. And Blaze and Azure would still owe him five grand.

My skin quailed, bumps stinging like needles.

Tell him you're sorry, Ice. Simper and grovel and make him believe it, or you're dead.

But ugly recklessness swamped me like hot quicksand, and I opened my mouth in a shimmering fugue of glory to tell him to get fucked.

"Take that back or I'll make you a fucking lightning rod." Indigo arced onto all fours between me and Sonny, angry scarlet static crackling between his fingers. He flared his wings, silver flashing in the sun. Heat haze shimmered over his taut muscles like an angry aura, and he snarled like a panther, spitting iron sparks.

Girlish admiration sparkled in my veins, but fear watered my guts, too. Sonny would shoot him, too, and it'd be my fault. Common sense burned in, lucid like sunlight through snow, and I stumbled forward aghast at what my idiocy had wrought. "Indigo, don't—"

Sonny yanked back the slide and released it with a steely click, and swiveled to aim at Indigo's eyeballs.

My brain gibbered, lost, and time slowed.

Sonny grinned in slow motion, his voice stretched. "Shut it, maggot—"

Indigo dived like a striking wasp, streaking in a heartstopping flash of silver for Sonny's throat.

Long blue fingers wrapped around the pistol barrel. Sonny's finger whitened on the trigger. White voltage blazed like an arcweld, blinding me, and ripe electricity tore the air like thunder.

Sonny screamed and jerked, smoke sizzling, and the pistol fired.

Splinters exploded, torn vine leaves scattering. My right ear ripped open inside, burning. Indigo tumbled to his feet in a shower of sparks. The pistol clunked to the tiles, still crackling with static. Sonny flailed, flapping at blue flames licking his clothes, and the troll twins growled and slapped their fat hands on his burning body.

Indigo dragged me off my feet. "Scramble, Ice, for fuck's sake."

His cracked voice zoomed away, distant and dull like I floated underwater. His glamour zapped, a prickly cocoon shimmering around both of us. I stumbled after him, blood pounding in my torn ear, my wits reeling and my legs floppy like custard. My head throbbed. My throat stung with ozone. The air stank of dusty thunder.

Mad giggles throttled me. I'd never felt so good.

Or so wrong. Indigo had saved my ass again. Or, he'd saved himself and dragged me along for the ride. It didn't matter. We were alive, and together, and it seemed a precious, wonderful thing—and no thanks whatsoever to me.

We staggered out hand in hand into blinding sun, and as traffic slowed and pedestrians teetered back in alarm, I squinted through blue-watering eyes and let him drag me up and away.

Indigo flits up a rusty drainpipe one-handed, straining for balance with steely wings as he drags her below him. She's shaking, poor girl, her hand sweating a river in his. More than once her fingers slip and he has to dive for her wrist, delicate bones crunching in his grip with a sharp jab of memory. Over a concrete lip onto roof tiles, dry and brittle in hot evening sun, spicy with traces of tin. Lest his silhouette reveal their flight, he clenches his jaw and ignites his secondary glamour, the one that makes him dim. Wobble, flicker, disappear. The air spits and shimmers, pregnant with fat fae lies: *Don't see me. I'm not here. Look away.*

He skips lightly over tiled ridges, glowing metal corners, gutters, glass, the air a warm stagnant breath that stinks of city iron and imminent rain. Behind him, she trips, her inflamed wing joints still weak from the beating she got at Quang's. His arm aches from holding her, and his pistol-scorched palm screams in hers like she's made of coals. But it's dull compared with the steely blade of deception that spikes his throat and slashes his every breath ragged.

She's not working for Kane, not laying some lie-spiked trap. Kane promised her a cure. All she wants is to be free of this nasty mirror that's fanned her courage to a fiercer blaze than she can control.

—*Exquisite, isn't it?*— The sultry whisper teases him, and he pretends it's not there, but his blood responds with a heady flush of wonder and desire that doesn't lie.

Is it possible that she's not deceiving him? That she means every word? That the catch in her breath, the warm throb in her pulse when he kissed her tempting throat was real?

The idea dizzies him, rich like whiskey, and his knees smack the rusty roof, metal on screeching metal. He catches himself, and twitches her after him before she falls, but her tiny hand burns in his like an accusation. He struggles to think straight, to plan, to see more than a few feet in front of him.

Imagine that. Not to step in shadow, always waiting for the cruel knife in a wing joint or the bullet in the back of the head. To sleep in peace, without one ear pricked for treacherous footsteps. To wake each morning without wondering if today she'll be gone.

Since that horrid day in hell when Natasha savaged his sense with her lies, he's never been certain of anything. Pity that this time, it's him doing the lying. Ice humbled him with her honesty, but he didn't say a word about Delilah. They can't give this mirror to two different demons. If Ice finds out, she'll never forgive him. And if he gives Ice what she wants—the cure—then Delilah will come after him. What's left of his life won't be worth the rusty grit under his claws, and he'll spend eternity in agony in a locked iron room. Perfect.

Just fucking perfect.

Unless, of course, Ice is lying. Unless she's invented that crystal-shine story about Kane to trick him. She is a con artist, after all, wide-eyed and innocent and smiling pretty lies.

But how can he ever know? He's already tempted himself too much with the berry nectar of her skin and the shy, lithe brush of her limbs next to his. How can he be sure without risking his mind and his senses, not to mention his heart?

—*Coward*. His shadow self swirls, scorching his blood with scorn. *She'll never be yours if you don't take a chance. Story of your life, Indigo. One little bruise and you cry.*—

Fear slashes at his skin that he'll hurt her, and Indigo shakes his head, stubborn, as he dives past flitting eucalyptus leaves and black power lines that glow copper-bright like fire. *Not a chance. Leave her alone.*

But bright fairy longing consumes him, and his body aches with all the need and pent-up isolation he longs to pour into her. She makes him feel clean and shiny, like he's not felt since that stormy day in hell when his heart shattered. He has to know if she's for real, before he does something stupid and tells her the truth.

That he likes her, as he likes chocolate or summer rain or sunflowers. That her awkward wit and clumsy charm lighten his heart, that her wide amber eyes bewitch him, that he can't get her beautiful fruity taste out of his mouth. That when he's with her, he feels clean and hot and on a razor's edge like he's drunk too much heady fairy wine, and that his need to touch her isn't just loneliness or lust, but . . . something else.

If he steals her cure, she'll surely hate him. Eternity in a screaming iron cell might hurt less than her disappointment.

—*So tell her,*—dares his shadow,—*tell her or I will. She's wonderful just the way she is. She doesn't need a cure.*—

Bitter spite stings his mouth. He grits his teeth, swallows, resists. No way. Not her and Ebony. Never. He must talk to her. Show her he cares. Get her away from Ebony before she has to find out the hard way. Before it's too late.

Sharp pain stabs his skull, and his stomach wraps itself tight around a soapy kernel of sick hunger. He hasn't eaten in too long, and there's no metal in ice cream. Should have asked for mineral water, oysters on the shell, a tomato sandwich, a rare steak. Iron house frames loom like a screaming white maze below him, dizzying him to the point of faintness, and he flutters weakly to his feet in a deserted residential street, struggling to keep the flame of reason in his head alight.

17

Over sunset-splashed rooftops we dived, fluttered, dipped, only his warm hold stopping me from falling. Bricks hit my ankles, scraping my skin away. Dizziness swirled my brain to sickness, and glass and roof iron and colored concrete tiles scattered in my vision like an upended slide show.

His glamour rattled the wind with static. Warm drafts pressed my wings, up and down and sideways until I didn't know which way was which, and my inner ears sloshed. I felt sick. I felt wonderful. And when we finally skidded to a halt on cracked black tar, a solitary streetlight burning above, I collapsed on my butt on the median strip and let my hands sink gratefully into rough gravel.

Sharp pebbles poked my bottom and stung my bare feet. A car cruised by, oblivious. Some dim suburban neighborhood, dull gray houses and dead gardens, no trams or traffic or people. Dry air crumbled in the smell of dirt and hot concrete. Somewhere far away, lightning flashed, and a few seconds later thunder rolled in like a distant ocean wave. Tension zinged excitement into my skin. A storm on the way.

Indigo wobbled down next to me, catching his breath and wiping sweaty hands on his ass.

I grinned weakly, my cheeks sore like a bride's. "Here, let me do that."

His dark skin looked damp and drawn, his face tight. He plopped down in the dirt beside me, leaning his forearms on his raised knees, and wrinkled his nose in a little smile as he swallowed a few times. "Guess you're okay, then."

My popped ear gurgled like a plughole. I wiggled my finger in it. "Oh, sure. Never better. You?"

He turned his hands over, showing his dark blue palm burned raw and silvery with blood. "Been worse."

I winced. "Ouch. That looks sore. But . . . hang on. Wasn't it your right hand you burned on that pistol?"

He shrugged, holding up his scorched left palm, titanium wrapping his wrist. "Guess not. Sizzle, steam, ouch."

The same old suspicion gnawed me, and urgency nibbled my toes like bugs. I fidgeted, unsure. "No. I saw. And that bangle was definitely on your right wrist the other night. Doesn't look like it comes off in a hurry. What's up with that?"

He swallowed again, and looked away.

I swallowed. Must be something in it. But I wasn't sure. All I knew was that mirrors switched things from left to right, and that he wasn't being honest with me. "Okay. Fine. Aren't you going to scold me?"

He picked ripped skin from his palm, frowning. "What for?"

"Well, y'know. Giving lip to an insane Italian murderer. Making you burn your hands to pulp. Nearly getting us killed. That sort of thing."

His brow wrinkled. "Why would I scold you for that?"

"Well, if ya don't mind me saying, you're a scolding kinda guy. And it's dangerous, right?"

"I guess. But you were amazing." He ducked his head shyly to rub crisp hair on my cheek, his dark iron gaze flickering to mine.

The sharp sensation dazzled me. I shifted, nervous. What was he playing at? "Yeah? I mean, yeah, sure. Thanks."

He wouldn't look away. "I mean it, Ice. You're brave and strong and smart like . . . like a little tigress. Only prettier."

Delight shocked me rigid, and I ached deep inside with longing. Left hand, right hand, whatever. What did I care, if it softened him up like this? I shrugged, trying to keep it casual, trying not to show that the merest brush of his gaze on my skin made me hot. "Thought you'd never notice."

"Oh, I notice." He shuffled his butt closer. Now his hard thigh pressed against mine, tempting.

My voice lost itself somewhere in my throat. "Yeah?"

"All the time." He dropped his chin on my shoulder, tension in his whisper that made me shiver. "Truth, Ice. You've waited all your life to say those things. I know how hard it is to let go of fear. Don't you feel . . . free?"

Giddy hormones jumped and giggled in my brain. His shadow covered me, dark and exciting, and the sheer size of him awakened dark tingles of desire in my belly. Daring, I rested my head lightly against his. His fine metal hair sliced into mine, sharp ends teasing my scalp. My insides warmed. "Yeah. God, yeah. It felt great. But what if—?"

"What if nothing. We're still alive, Ice. We got away. You shed your fear, and the sky didn't crumble. Did it?"

"Guess not." Cautious hope shone. We'd escaped, after all. Sonny hadn't killed us. Maybe this madness would be okay.

Especially if Indigo understood.

Not that he would. He didn't have a nasty magic mirror chewing his ass, making him say weird things. Did he?

I snuggled closer, his warm metal scent wrapping me in delight and lazy desire. I wanted to purr. I wanted to throw him onto his back and kiss him, make him wild with desire for me. Yeah. I'd even slide down his body and peel his clothes away, drink in that coppery blue skin, smell his sweet metal arousal. Go down on him, taste his hardened flesh in my mouth, lick him and swallow him and make him remember me.

Or not.

He sniffed at a stray wisp of my hair, and sparks danced between us like fairylight. "And you know the best part?"

I caught a spark on my tongue, and it sizzled. Tingles swept my mouth, shivering warm all the way to my fingerpads. "Mmm. I'm liking this part right here, but go on."

"The best part was, you laughed. And not at yourself. You should do that more, Ice. You glowed. You looked so beautiful, and you sounded happy."

He said I was beautiful.

The world suddenly glowed, the air scintillating with strange new wonder.

A nervous smile parted my lips. Snarking at slash-happy gangsters, no problem. Indigo kinda sorta maybe hitting on me? Shiver. But I didn't want to move away. I didn't want this to end. "Hey. Umm . . . Thanks for the ice cream."

Indigo shrugged, fiddling with a tangle in my hair. My scalp tingled. His claw caught, tugged gently, stroked the hair smooth. "No worries. Went well, doncha think?"

"Oh, sure. It was okay for a first date. Let's do it again sometime." Daring, I dusted dirt from his arm with one finger. His skin stuck to my fingerpad, slick and sultry, muscles curving hard. I wanted to lick my finger. Better still, slide my tongue along that ridge of muscle, taste him, swallow his metal sweat. "We should figure out the rules, though. Home by ten, no shagging in the first five minutes, that kind of stuff."

He caught my hand, teasing my claws with his. "Sure. I do rules. Whatcha have in mind?"

I stared, mesmerized. He played with my knuckles, static flickering, and I felt it all the way inside. "Well . . . what about for a first ice cream date where gangsters threaten to beat us senseless? Do I get a kiss good night?"

"Do you want one?" His gaze flickered silver, unsure all over again.

I sighed, my body alight with frustrated desire. I was sick of figuring him out, of waiting for him to make the moves because I was too scared. Screw that. "Is that a serious question? I mean, are you actually wondering if I want you to kiss me? Honestly, you must be the dumbest fucking fairy in M—"

He didn't wait for me to finish. He just slid lithe blue fingers into my hair and pulled my mouth onto his.

Hot, bright, shocking. Surprise sweetened my desire for an instant, before it burned away under fierce delight. His lips caressed mine, his claws stung my scalp, his thumb teased that soft place under my ear where tingles spread like hot honey all the way down to my toes. He curled his tongue over mine, delicious, smooth metal and flesh. He tasted of strawberry ice cream and warm iron, dark and earthy and wonderful.

My pulse swelled, heat spreading though my veins. I tightened my fingers around his arm, his muscles taut under my palm. I opened my mouth to kiss him deeper, but he shifted back a fraction. "It's true, then," he whispered, his delicious iron taste a temptation. "Sky didn't crumble after all."

I gasped, bereft, my mouth still alive with that intoxicating flavor. *Tell me it's not over already.* "What? Did I do something wrong?"

He laughed, breathless, and leaned his forehead on mine, caressing my hair in shaking fingers. "God, no. I just . . . I've wanted this for so long. I just never thought you did, too."

Urgency rippled my muscles tight. I licked my lips, willing him to kiss me again. "Are you kidding? I've asked enough times."

"I know. I never thought you meant it." His eyes burned molten, reddish lashes curling sharp, his inky hair shining scarlet in the last gasp of a fading sun. So close, his lips an inch away, his dark male body just a stretched arm from mine, radiating secret iron warmth I longed to drown in.

Unbelievable. Confusion and delight addled my senses, toying with my lust until my skin wept. This couldn't be happening. He was untouchable. He'd never want me.

But I was here, and he was here, and I might never get this chance again.

I slid my wrist over his shoulder and wriggled closer. His delectable scent flooded my senses with desire. My voice disappeared, leaving a jagged whisper. "Well, I mean it now. Kiss me again. I want all of you."

He gave a blood-tingling groan and reached for me, and this time I didn't waste precious seconds wondering. My eyes slid closed, and I let him open my mouth, seeking his tongue, enjoying the razor sting of his teeth. He swallowed on me, teasing my tongue with his, caressing my lust from me, filling me with slow fire, deliberate like he had all the time in the world. I shivered, burning, and my insides melted, moisture dripping everywhere like hot fudge sauce. Sensual, just like the way he licked that strawberry ice cream. A man who took his time. If he made love to me, I'd probably die of pleasure before he finished.

His strong arm cradled me, and when the world tilted, I let him hold me, do what he wanted with me. He eased me onto my back, leaning on one elbow above me, his wings shedding rusty sparkles over us. I stared, transfixed, my body trembling and wet. My nipples stung. My hands shook. I couldn't breathe. My sex hurt, swollen, longing for him, and distant fear twinged my skin.

I'd wanted men before, wanted them so bad, my head spun from dehydration and my flesh swelled so much, I bled. But this was different. I'd dreamt of him too long. I couldn't pretend this away. I couldn't avert my face, forget myself, lose myself in sensation so I wouldn't get embarrassed by my lust.

I couldn't even close my eyes. His face, so perfect, the midnight curve of his cheekbone more beautiful than I could bear. His silvery lips, wet with our kiss, his hair gleaming copper in fast-fading sunlight. His eyes, gosh—I was drunk on them, tilted at the corners in a sweep of coppery lashes and smoldering with molten intent. People said he was cold, my Indigo, cold and slow to ignite, but not now; now he stared at me, hungry, besotted like he couldn't get enough.

So beautiful. So perfect. So far beyond my sad little horizon, it hurt.

Reality scraped my soul, sharp like broken glass. Too beautiful, too clever, too talented for me. If he broke my heart, I might not bounce back.

His gaze flicked to mine for an instant and dragged back to my mouth. He swallowed, those amazing eyes gleaming golden all for me. "Ice. You're so sweet and beautiful. I'm sorry I've been cruel to you. I'm just . . . it's hard for me to let anyone close. Can you forgive me?"

He said the *beautiful* part again. I grinned, foolish, my eyes leaking. The streetlight glared in my eyes. My wings scraped in the dirt. My shoulder blades hurt. I didn't care. I just wrapped my fingers in his wire-sharp hair and pulled him back down to me.

Gosh. Even better than before. His teeth caught on mine, sharp and metallic, and I laughed, breathless. "Say something else nice about me."

He slid closer. The length of his body pressed into mine, lean and steely yet fairy-light, and when his cock pressed into my thigh, it felt the same. Well, how about that? He was hard from kissing me. Muscles tightened deep within me, and I imagined how he'd feel there, inside me, stroking me smooth and hot and slow. Maybe soon I'd find out.

He smiled, like he knew what I was thinking, and punctuated his words with more kissing, his lips caressing my chin, my cheekbone, the corner of my mouth. "You, Ice, are the bravest, wittiest, loveliest, maddest, most terrifying woman I know."

I giggled, dazzled. Here I was thinking him a straight-up vanilla fairy. "Those are all good things, right?"

"You have no idea how good. Do I get one back?"

"One what?"

"Something nice, of course."

Never thought his ego would need a kick. "Oh. Well. Same things all the girls say, I guess. It's a no-brainer that you're gorgeous. I mean, who wouldn't cream herself over a six-foot-three metal fairy? Especially with that tasty blue skin and those lick-me thighs and your eyes, they're . . ."

I swallowed. Crazy fairy whore. Waffling. Focus. "Yeah. Okay. And you're funny, in a dead clever kinda way, even if you're mostly picking on me. And you're . . . Well . . . You're just great. You don't take shit from stupid humans or gangsters or anyone. You always know what to say. You're never afraid—gosh, if I had half your courage . . . And you're, like, the cleverest dirty scumbag thief I know. I just so want to be you. And . . ."

"And?" He prompted me with another dazzling kiss.

I sighed into him, and words slipped out between kissing. "And most of the time you're all steel and glass and unbreakable-like, but sometimes you show me this gentle streak. If you don't mind me saying, being such a tough guy and all. You split open for me, and you're all warm and tender inside that metal shell. And it just makes me want to eat you up like a . . . like a passionfruit."

He stared at me, his lips shining silver, and I blanched. *Now I've done it.*

But he just dipped his mouth to mine again, and this time he twisted his claws in my hair and held me there, his coppery groan slipping into my mouth. He slid on top of me, his thigh easing between mine where I ached. Our tongues melted together, his warm iron flavor flowing inside me, and when he broke off, we were both gasping. His breath burned my lips, and he traced a lingering hot claw over the pulse in my throat. "This is insane. You'd better not be lying."

Pleasure squirmed inside me at the intensity of his kiss, but in a chilling flash I saw ash-streaked blond hair, golden limbs, hard black eyes that burned azure. *Tell me if you like it,* Kane said. *Maybe she lied.*

I kicked the images firmly aside. Kane had no place here. I grabbed Indigo's hand and pressed it to my breast, above my somersaulting heart. His palm grazed my nipple through my flimsy top, and the shock of needy sensation made me groan all over again. I wanted his tongue there, his teeth, the slide of his naked flesh. "Feel that. It doesn't lie."

"Sometimes it can." He spoke softly, pained, even as he caressed my hard nipple so sweetly, it hurt.

Sorrow whittled chunks from my desire. I wondered distantly who'd lied to him, what happened to make him say that, but it didn't matter. Dismay simmered beneath my pleasure. He didn't trust me. He thought I was making it up. "You're outta your mind, you know that?"

"Yeah, I think I am. For you." He scraped my hair back with his forearm, cradling my head close to his, his warm body pressing lightly on mine. I inhaled iron, coppery sweat, a tinge of rust—god, I couldn't get enough of his smell. Daring, I slipped my hand over his hip, feeling the sharp bone, a flash of naked skin above his jeans, the tight curve of his ass.

He pressed against me with a pleasured murmur, and ducked to whisper in my ear. "You're amazing. Please don't forget this. No matter what happens. I like you, Ice—you're fresh and clean and perfect, you set me free and I've been locked up so long, I don't know what to do about you. I want to preserve you forever in glass. I want you in my bed. I want . . . other things. And I'm afraid, Ice. I'm afraid that I'll . . . that someone will steal you away. That you'll vanish if I close my eyes. I don't want that."

The longest speech I've ever heard from him, and he made no sense. He scared me with all this thinking. I didn't want to think about this. I just wanted the easy oblivion of his mouth on mine. I licked my bottom lip, quivering with need. "Jelly on a blanket. I'm not going anywhere. Can't we just—?"

"Shh." He crushed a kiss on my lips, heady and hot and just long enough to leave me gasping. He glanced up at the distant looming skyscrapers, breeze ruffling his inky hair. He fluttered eager wings, and his eyes twinkled with silvery mischief. "Come on. Let's do something nice. Walk with me. You like views?"

Tension rippled my blood. If we moved, this moment might vanish. I ran my thumb over his shining silver lips, letting him catch it with his tongue. "I like the view right here just fine."

But he dazzled me with that sultry silver smile, and delight bubbled in my veins, washing away my fear. If he was crazy, then so was I, and I wanted to drown in it with him. I'd regret this, sure as I'm yellow and funny-looking. But for the first time in my sorry little life, I truly didn't care.

I grinned back, anticipation burning me up inside. "Okay. Where we going?"

"Wait and see." Indigo pulls her up, her pretty hand so small and warm in his, and it's all he can do not to wrap her in his metal embrace, crush her lithe body to his and fly far away. The shift of her fingers on his palm is hypnotic. She's so light, like she's made of sunshine, and for an instant, her smile paralyzes him.

For once, he told the truth. It didn't hurt like he imagined it would. And she didn't run away. She's still here, not only shifting shyly in front of him but hot and vital in his blood, too, her taste lingering in his mouth, the precious feel of her still sparkling on his lips and fingers.

Insane, to have waited so long.

It's amazing just to walk with her, unafraid, watching her skip and laugh and splash happily through puddles as they thread their way through gritty black streets toward the city. Shadows loom tall, split like razors with neon-bright iron light poles. Humidity thickens, distant thunder growing closer. Indigo's metalsense flickers, tormenting him, and that black ache whispers cruelly in his skull, but he doesn't care. He can't take his eyes off her.

Memorize her. Drink her in. Consume her, before she vanishes like breath on a mirror.

Ahead of him, Ice twirls like a tipsy ballerina, wings fluttering crookedly, her fruity hair trailing shimmering droplets behind her. Her crystal laughter shines in the air like starlight. The lacy frills of her skirt tease her slim golden thighs, mesmerizing. She's chattering, telling him something, her enthusiasm bubbling like a waterfall, and he longs to listen, to let her voice wash the dirt from his skin.

But Ebony-ache blurs his vision, and the sneering black velvet whisper deafens him.—*You're weak, Indigo. Cold and crunched up inside like tinfoil. You heard what she said. It's me she really covets. The part you despise. Don't dare think you can do this without me.*—

I can, he wants to scream. *I can, and I will.* But pain crunches his teeth, slashing bright blood into his mouth. His muscles spasm, and he staggers in a metalbright blur, his wings scrabbling at the air to keep him upright. She's ahead, dancing crookedly in a puddle, and she doesn't see. He rakes stinging claws through his hair, fighting the horrid impulse to claw his own eyeballs out.

Determination stings his bones. Ebony can't have her, not now. Taking her to this view, high above the city to his favorite solitary place, is insane. He should leave her, push her away like he's always done, keep her safe in case Ebony returns.

But his smitten heart wails at the thought. He wants to show her. Can't leave her now, just when he's getting it right. He swallows on iron bile, fighting a rush of warm quicksilver mischief. *Not now, Ebony. Not ever.*

Ice halts and turns, her precious amber eyes bright with concern. "You okay?"

"Uh-huh." Rich black giggles slide in Indigo's blood, but he forces them silent, and when she wiggles her delicate yellow fingers, he ignores the warning throbbing in his skull and takes her hand.

The elevator crunched and hummed, sweeping us upward in the soft lemon scent of detergent. Cool air-conditioned air fanned me, drying my sweat. I giggled, my eyelids itching under his warm hand. "Can I open them yet?"

"Nope." He pressed against my back, hard fae muscles shifting like curved metal parts as he moved, and I could feel him sniffing my hair, scenting me, inhaling my perfume.

Not that I was wearing any. I hadn't anticipated this. At least tonight I didn't stink like a whore. At least, not yet. "How about now?"

"Nope." He teased my wings with crisp metal hair.

I rubbed back, and he rewarded me with a lick, spreading hot shivers all the way up to the tip. I giggled. "Now?"

"Nope nope. Keep 'em closed."

"Where we going?"

"Somewhere special. It's a surprise. You'll like it."

The elevator pinged, and slid to a halt. I squirmed in pleasure and excitement. A surprise. Goody good. Maybe he'd brought me to his place. Even better.

His hand slipped from my eyes, and I squeezed them shut, enjoying the game. Elevator door, sliding closed behind us, another lock clicking open. More cold air, my wings stinging dry, the lost warmth of his body a seductive echo. Slippery warm tiles under my bare feet. His knobbly fingers strong and slick in mine, leading me on. The warm smoothness of metal around his wrist, brushing my arm. A door whispered aside, heated air rushing on glass, and we flittered up a few steps onto sun-warmed concrete.

Summernight breeze whipped my face, the smell of rain and nighttime and warm city streets. Distant traffic noise whispered. Sparse raindrops stung pleasantly cool on my cheeks, and I opened my mouth, letting the fresh bitterness catch my tongue. Happiness flushed me. I wanted to run and twirl and jump until I was soaked. I laughed, stretching out my arms blindly. "Rain, rain, I love the rain. We there yet?"

"Just a bit farther." He guided me forward, rough concrete scraping my toes.

"Where we going?"

"Stop right there." He pulled me to a halt. My feet slicked on smooth steel. Breeze lifted my hair, spiraled warm fingers around my bare legs, dragged my skirt against my thighs. He slipped his arms around my neck from behind and covered my eyes again. His close whisper warmed my ear. "Do you trust me?"

My body started to ache all over again, longing for him to touch me the way he had in my dreams. "Gosh, you feel so nice. Sure I trust you. Can I look now?"

"No, I mean d'ya really trust me?"

"Umm . . . I guess. Sure. Some reason I shouldn't?"

A soft coppery chuckle. "Well, you did just let on that I'm your weakness, Ice. Apart from sparkle and fat juicy diamonds, that is."

Disquiet crept in on insect feet, worrying my high. "Uh-huh. Guess I did."

"And you did just admit we're in competition. For the shiny, I mean."

"Guess we are." His body against mine made me shiver, for more reasons than one.

"And there's the whole left–right bangle thing. That gives you the creeps."

"Uh-huh." The wind rose, threatening, whipping my hair in my face. Worry caressed my lungs with silent black fingers. So there was something to that bangle business after all. Which wrist was it on now? And this was just a balcony, right? In some skyscraper apartment? Alarm sparked, and I strained to open my eyes.

But he clenched his fingers tighter, his claws digging into my temple. My pulse skipped. He rubbed his crisp hair in mine, that cute little gesture I'd liked so much. Now, it seemed a wicked tease. He slid his open mouth across my cheek in a possessive kiss I wasn't sure

I enjoyed, even if pleasure did shiver all the way down inside me. "And you did just tell me who owns that ruby necklace."

My heart thudded, too fast for comfort. "Uh-huh. Indigo, you're creeping me out now—"

"So the fact is, Lady Ice, you shouldn't trust me, because . . ." I felt his lips curve in a smile against my ear, and he whipped his hand away from my eyes.

I teetered, and looked down.

Empty space lurched at my feet. My toes curled on the steel edge of a rooftop, a hundred floors of nothing looming below.

Shock jerked my limbs, and I overbalanced.

The air gripped me like sucking octopus tentacles, dragging me inexorably over the edge. Sour terror splurted into my mouth, and I screamed.

My wings pulled against swirling air, useless. My arms flailed in circles, reaching for anything to hold me back, my only solace Indigo's warm hand in the small of my back. *He knows I can't fly. He'll catch me.* "Indigo, help me!"

A sly metallic laugh, mocking. "Because I don't need you anymore," he finished coolly, and gently but firmly he pushed me off.

18

For an instant, I didn't fall.

Anyone who's seen the cartoons where the scrawny coyote skids over a cliff will know what I mean. Until you believe you're falling, you're suspended in the rare sweet air of denial.

I'm not falling. He didn't just push me. I'm not about to die.

And then you look down, and you can't lie to yourself anymore.

The ground loomed up at me, glowing city lights impossibly far away. Terror chewed my guts to pulp. I whirled my arms, my feet tripping in space. I strained my wings wide to catch myself, but pain speared my joints, my membranes stretched to breaking in a whirling gust of wind, and I knew I couldn't hold my weight.

My struggles drove me facedownward, and I fell.

Air howled in my ears, the screeching discord of madness. Water streamed from my eyes, blinding. I couldn't hear. I couldn't see. I couldn't think.

I screamed, and fell faster, and faster, my pulse a sprinting squeal of panic. The breath ripped from my lungs. Raindrops knifed my skin. My wings dragged behind me, wind tangling them uselessly together, and I struggled to free them, to force them out into the rushing air to break my fall. But my joints dislocated with an ugly jolt that resonated in my skull like a gunshot, and I just tumbled over and over, a tangle of wings and limbs and gut-melting terror.

Hellflash scorched before my eyes. *This is how I die. Thrown from a skyscraper by the maniac who's stolen my heart. A blind, foolish, lovesick fairy girl who can't even fly.*

The irony didn't cheer me up.

And then something thudded into my chest and dragged me sideways.

My limbs whiplashed, pain ripping into my joints. My chin smacked into my chest. Hair slashed at my face. My unjointed wings lurched taut in suddenly swirling wind, and my shoulder blades screamed with selfish agony. And then I gusted upward in a steely embrace, floating on glittery twitches of wings far stronger than mine.

My ripped ear ached. I opened my eyes in a blue-blotted haze. Windows, city lights in prismed reflection, a flash of silverfoil wings. The dark alcoves of apartments, green vines crawling on lattice, lounge lights and televisions in muted glow. In and over a glass railing with a polished white edge, and my burning feet splatted on something blessedly solid.

I reeled, my pulse galloping, and sucked in a breath for the first time in ages. Oxygen swarmed in my panicked blood, and relief swamped me, dizzying. Solid ground. Tiles. A room. *I'm not dead.*

No bloody thanks to him.

A rich chuckle rumbled my back, and he pressed his cheek on the top of my head and slid strong arms around my waist. "Gotcha."

Crazy fucker still had a hard-on. I could feel him, hot and tempting against my hip. Rage juddered my muscles. I struggled in his embrace, wrath drowning my gratitude. "Get off me, you fucking freak!"

"Okay, okay." He let go, still laughing.

Asshole. I straightened, tossing my giddy head. "Fine. I'm f—

Oops." My limbs buckled like wet paper, and I crumpled onto my butt, my bones jarring. Mortified, I scrabbled to get up, but my strength melted in the aftermath of terror and the stupid relief of being alive. My abused wings hurt like poison. My pulse wouldn't slow. My skin wouldn't cool. I just lay there and flopped in a puddle of my own water like a grounded fish.

A very, very angry fish.

He leaned one elbow on the balcony rail, coppery sweat gleaming on silver-swelled muscles. Tension quivered along his thighs, and he was still breathing hard, his excitement uncontained. His blackmetal hair gleamed, tousled by the wind. He shot me that sultry silver-fanged smile, and I couldn't peel my eyes away.

Fury slashed through my blood like lust. "How the fuck is this funny? You just threw me off a bloody skyscraper!"

"Should see yourself now." He let his gaze drape over me, white hot, and his tongue flicked his teeth, mesmerizing. "Knew it'd get you hot."

"Are you out of your mind? I can't believe you did that! You know I can't fly!"

"I was never gonna let you fall." Molten metal swirled in his iron-gray eyes, a fiery glimmer of hurt or apology. "I'd never hurt you, Lady Ice. You know that."

So sincere. My anger softened, a little. Maybe he hadn't meant anything by it. I scowled, still shaking and hot under his gaze. "Whatever, okay? You scared the shit outta me."

He poked at my naked toes with his foot, teasing me, and a naughty little grin tweaked his silvery mouth. "No fun for you if you're not scared out of your mind."

I still wanted to leap up and strangle him. But the treacherous mirror giggled and groaned in my head, fueling my anger with excitement and raw desire. Moisture trickled over my legs, soaking my skirt. Anger throbbed harder in my veins, stinging my flesh sharp like desire. I squirmed my hips, but the water wouldn't stop. Now embarrassment as well as rage flooded my cheeks. I hated it. My will struggled against the very idea of it. But my breath fought harder in my lungs, my wetness splashed the floor, and struggle as I might, I couldn't deny that being alive right now, in this instant, fired my blood like nothing ever had before. My sex throbbed. My nipples ached. God, I wanted him to touch me.

Deep in my body, the mirror giggled and stroked me, rich and seductive like a lover. It felt so good, I swallowed a gasp. *Damn it.* I kicked at his thighs, frustration lending me strength. "Fun? That's your idea of fun? Are you fucking insane?"

He laughed, dark and intense, his eyes glowing. "Yeah. I am. Insane. Petrified. Alive. God, you turn me on like this." He grabbed my flailing ankle and tugged.

My butt skidded over slick tiles, and my skirt raked upward. I kicked harder, but he fought for my other ankle and suddenly he was on his knees. My legs curled over his shoulders, silky skirt ruffles falling in my lap, and he pulled my knees apart and licked a hot wet swath of trembling lust up the inside of my thigh.

Breath rushed from my lungs. My skin sizzled, hot like sunburn from my breasts to my sex to the sensitive tendon at the top of my thigh where his teeth scraped me, raw and needy. He bit me there, swift and crafty, and sensation jolted straight to my clit. A groan forced from my lips, unwilling, those lustful hormones dancing through my blood. Adrenaline rush be damned. This was a life rush, an unbreaking wave of sheer joy and crippling tension from which I couldn't surface. My pulse hammered in every vein, painful. My breath jerked and shuddered. My wits sloshed, drowning in lustful liquid. Surely it was the mirror, tormenting me. I didn't care. I couldn't calm down. I needed release.

He pushed my thighs farther apart, and I let out another helpless groan. He pressed me onto my back and pulled my thigh up onto his shoulder, and all by itself my knee crooked around him, desperate.

He sniffed me and slicked his tongue under the edge of my panties, deliciously hot and agonizingly close.

My tight flesh thrummed, and slick moisture slid from me. He gripped me tight around the hips, and I wriggled, helpless frustration cramping my legs with blood-sweet pain. No fair. He'd done this on purpose. I wanted it too much. "Damn it, don't fuck around, can you just—? Oh, shit."

He slashed my panties away with stinging claws and fastened his tongue hard on my pulsing clit. Sensation juddered through my legs. Not pleasure. Too extreme for that. Raw nerve damage, intense and razor-bright and exhilarating, pouring hot delight through my whole body. I think I screamed. I certainly didn't push him away.

I was burning, but his molten mouth still scorched me. He delved his tongue deeper into my folds, and my flesh slid and swelled between his lips, aching for him to take me. At last he thrust his long curled tongue in, claiming me, caressing me deep inside until I wanted to scream for release. He licked me, kissed me, teased me with his teeth, every stroke dragging me closer to what I craved. Still impatience wrenched my muscles taut like whipstrings. I squeezed my eyes shut. The tension inside me twisted, harder, tighter, more unbearable. I sobbed, my teeth aching. I couldn't take this. I dragged desperate hands through his sharp hair to pull him into me. "Harder. Please, harder."

Great. I was begging. Now the bastard would take me even slower.

But he sucked my clit hard into his mouth, flashing sparks before my eyes. And now it did feel good, my desire flowering like a volcano, spilling delicious burning sensation inside me like lava. When he thrust his long finger inside me, searching for my deepest pleasure, I split apart.

Water crashed in my ears. Sensation rushed all the way to my fingertips, my scalp, my toes. My muscles spasmed, and the tension shattered like dropped glass, draining me. I groaned. Blessed, erotic, wonderful relief. God, that felt amazing.

I melted, limp, and if he hadn't been holding my legs, I'd have collapsed to the floor.

He caressed my ankle and kissed me softly between my legs like he kissed my mouth, slow and deep, but I barely felt it. I was numb.

I lay there, dazed, my wings crumpled beneath me. Lights swirled in my eyes, dazzling me. My muscles wouldn't move. My brain glugged like sun-warmed custard. Where am I again? What just happened?

Oh, yeah. Indigo just gave me a blow job.

Correction. Indigo pushed me off an eighty-story skyscraper, and then gave me a blow job.

That doesn't seem strange at all. Does it?

Mirrorsparkled mirth frothed in my chest, and I laughed, fresh and full like a rose bouquet. Life was good.

He swept me up, and next thing I knew we were inside in the dark. His warm arms cradled me, his rusty breeze fanning my face. Shadows of furniture, faint rosy sweetness on the cool air. Sensation prickled back into my limbs, and I wobbled my head up, wet locks sticking to my cheeks. "Where's this?"

"My place. One of them." He nudged a switch, and gentle light blossomed. Steel-gray carpet, rosy walls, a black marble kitchen top. Masses of dark roses drying in crystal vases, petal edges crisp and curled. Stuff everywhere, books with ripped covers and half-read magazines and silver DVDs missing their cases. A one-room place, shiny black bath in the corner and his bed in a loft up a light ladder. Couch looked comfortable, too, a splay of warm ocher cushions. I'm not fussy. Right now, I'd have him on a pile of broken glass.

I giggled, dazed. "Pink. Not what I expected."

"I told you, I've made the wrong impression. What did you expect?"

"I dunno. Bars on the windows. Mirrors. Guns in the fridge."

He flitted up the ladder, his chest warm against my thighs. He dropped me facedown on the crumpled quilt, heedless of the moist mess I made.

Excitement clenched my thighs tight. I inhaled delicious copper, the velvety smoothness of the quilt slipping on my cheek. Shadows streaked the bed. He slid his body onto my back, light and hard-muscled, fragrant rust flecks showering. "Knives, not guns."

He nuzzled between my shoulder blades, teasing a slow tingle down my spine with one crafty claw. Static arced tenderly over my skin. My ribs thrilled. His thigh wrapped around mine, pressing me into the bed. My wings quivered with fresh desire. I yearned back against him, my breasts aching, my skin wet for him, the flesh between my legs still slick and hot and swollen. I'd had my release. Now I wanted him all over me, under me, inside me. Long, slow, lazy love that lasted all night, lots of deep kissing and sighs and *oh my gods*. "What did you say?"

He slid his arm under my belly and flipped me over, folding my wings under me with a deft swipe of his hand. Now his body pressed into mine, torturing my breasts, making me ache and yearn. He licked a damp trickle from my shoulder, his hair dragging like a hot whisper over my throat. "I don't do guns. No intimacy in a bullet."

My body yearned for his touch, but my brain staggered a few seconds behind, and when it caught up, unease fluttered wildly in my heart. My wings stretched, ready to jerk me away, but he lay on top of me, trapping my body with his. Sudden awareness shivered through me of how strong he was compared with me. Sex is often like that. It's one thing that gets me hot. But . . .

He traced lazy fingers over my hip, and my breath caught, my claws digging into the quilt. "You know, that's a really freaky thing to say."

He stroked my hand to relax it, unhooked my claws, spread hot wet kisses in my palm. "Hardly. Would you rather die of indifference? Or of love?"

He kissed inside my wrist, and I shivered. I couldn't see him. I didn't know if he was laughing at me or not. After all this time, I'd finally made it to his bed, and I wasn't sure I wanted to stay. I swallowed, nerves clawing my throat. "Are those my only choices?"

He laughed, steel on crystal, and the vibration tingled my bones. "That was funny. I like you, Ice. Very much. Don't be afraid. You can check my fridge for weapons later, okay?"

He licked in the corner of my elbow, and pleasure sparkled to my fingertips. Damn, but staying was tempting. I stretched my arm above my head, searching for the bedpost so I could push against it, press my body harder against his, wrap my thigh around his to feel him where I ached. His hips crushed into mine, his delicious hardness making me groan. He'd already ripped my underwear away, and my skirt didn't cover me. I could feel every tight muscle, every engorged twist, every quiver.

I groaned in desperation, yearning for contact, sensation, affection. I gave in. *Make love to me, just once. Even if none of those wonderful things you said about me were true, just let me pretend for a little bit longer. It'll give me something nice to think about when I'm alone again. And again, and again.* "Please. I want you. I won't ask anything. Can't we just—?"

Click.

Cold metal sizzled tight around my wrist.

My pulse gibbered. Another click. I tugged my arm. It wouldn't move. I tugged again. Hard edges dug into my wrist, and metal clanked on metal.

He'd cuffed me to the bed. Without asking.

My guts twisted, the old fear scratching wildly in my chest, that shackled madwoman jerking awake. Unpleasant memory savaged my desire, the times they'd hurt me, taunted me, used their strength against me.

I jerked up, tipping him off me. The short chain wrenched me sideways, twisting my bones, and I tumbled onto my hip, my heart somersaulting. "No. Not that. I don't like it."

He lifted his palm to placate me. "It's okay."

My cursed pulse wouldn't agree. No matter how his eyes mesmerized me, or my body longed for the caress of his naked flesh. No matter how I wanted him to love me, fear caged my heart in jagged steel. I scrambled to my knees and shook my trapped wrist, panic prickling my skin with nasty claws. "Take it off. Sorry. I can't—"

"It's okay, Ice. Don't be afraid. You'll be safe here." Swiftly, he climbed off the bed, shaking his hair into place like a wet dog. Electricity singed his curls, the hot scent of burnt metal wafting.

I gaped. "What are you doing?"

"Don't you understand? You're in danger. He'll never let you stay like this. If you're cured, you'll be lost. I have to find the shiny before he does. Before it's too late." He wiped quivering hands on his jeans, rainbow metal shimmering on his right wrist. "You'll be safe here. I'll be back before he comes."

"Are you outta your mind?" Realization thrummed through me like seasickness, jolting my stomach. Left, right. Hot, cold. Soft, steely. Whether he admitted it or not, the mirror had affected him, too. Made him jumpy, changeable, bipolar or something. Not quite right in the head.

I rattled in my shackle, frustration stabbing deep in my body. He still wanted me. I felt it, and not just because of that lovely hard-on. In the way his breath caught, his kiss burned me, his fingers lingered on my skin in the places that made me moan.

"I can't let you hurt yourself. I'll be back soon." Static arced between his silver wing tips. Sweat and my water still shone on his arms. His molten red gaze gleamed, licking over me like warm fudge.

My sex hurt me in response, my pulse too tight for my tender flesh. He wanted me, all right. But crazyfae was actually turning away from me, with some weird idea he was saving me from myself.

And I could do nothing, except watch him leave.

The apartment door clicks shut behind him, and Ebony smacks his head back against it, metal clanging on wood. His skin grates, his head aches, his claws shudder, and quicksilver blood pounds in his flesh like poison. His burning hard cock demands things of him, gives naughty breathless orders, and it's all he can do to walk away from her. He's used to voices in his head, but not like this.

Oh, but she's an unexpected delight. Her fruity scent still burns his sinuses. The glorious salty taste of her orgasm still sparkles in his mouth. He can still feel her under him, her skin fresh under his tongue, her body pressing into his, seeking him out, finding his pleasure, teasing it out until he didn't know where to begin with her.

She's thrashing around in there, thumping at the walls, and his needy flesh screams at him to go back inside, crush her naked body under his, push his cock inside her and finish what he started. First he'd wanted her blood, her bright life flowing over his hands. But that fleeting connection wasn't enough. His eyes wouldn't leave her body alone, his lips itched to drape themselves on her skin and pleasure her, his hungry tongue kept sweeping the soaked air for her scent.

He can still smell her delicious woman-smell, strawberries and ash, and as he forces himself to walk stiffly away, a nasty metal ache brewing in his balls, he wonders if that scent will ever go away.

He wonders if he wants it to. The delight of her chaos floods his blood with desperate calm he's not felt since . . . well, since Indigo dropped his beautiful, treacherous lover in a spiky pit and blacked out for the first time. Accident or not, Ebony was born that day, and Indigo's never been the same, so closed off and cold, he can't connect with anyone, let alone fall in love. Since then, Ebony's wandered the earth, searching, yearning for something he can't find. Maybe now, he's found it. Empathy. Acceptance. A twin spirit, reveling in her own madness.

Indigo never accepted him, never understood. But she's got her own itches, this strawberry liquor girl. She'll understand blood's rich lure, the anticipation, but also the disappointment, the delight that lasts only for a second or two before it's false. She'll know why he does what he does, over and over again.

Affection, yes. Love, yes. She'll surrender to him. Only a matter of time.

Crazy, wonderful, precious girl. Indigo mustn't have her, mustn't prune her spirit off like a weed. She thinks she wants that. She thinks she wants *him*. She doesn't understand.

If Ebony must, he'll save her from herself.

Shunning the elevator, he pushes the weighted fire door open and skips down the concrete stairs, his body still a rampant jungle of lust and yearning blood. The rough galvanized railing glows, the salty zinc spoiling his Ice-drenched palate.

He needs that mirror, before Indigo comes back and ruins everything. Already the whispers scratch in his head, the hammering, the horrid sense of his wits leaching away. He grits his teeth, savoring her taste on his tongue, using it to bolster his strength. This is for her. But he'll need help.

The iron skull necklace is one thing. Finding its previous owner is another, and he doesn't have time for his usual thief tricks, the questions, the bribes, the kisses and sweet promises.

He's leading Indigo straight to the prize, of course. Can't be helped. Just keep the prick at bay for a little longer.

He leans hard on the door at the bottom, the steel handle sparking under impatient palms. The door scrapes open, and he ducks between underground car park traffic into the street, his glamour zapping fresh and deceptive in ozone-laden air. The sky burns orange, gathering clouds reflecting the sparkling rainbow lights of Melbourne. It's still raining, the warm drops splatting on his wings, and in the distance, lightning flashes, ever closer. Trees rustle in wire cages on the black-tarred verge between glassy towers that clutch toward heaven, and summer-dead leaves dance at his feet in the warm night breeze.

Melbourne in the summer rain. There's no sweeter place, no place tasting more like his heart. If Indigo wants to go to Colombo, he can go alone.

In an inspired flash, Ebony wonders if the mirror can sunder what it splits, and the crafty seed of a plan worms to life in his rust-black heart.

Skipping toward the city, he slips out his little silver phone and dials.

Three rings, and Kane picks up. Ebony swallows, straining not to spit out the foulness sliming his gums. Kane made love to Ice. Ebony and Kane have an unpleasant connection. It doesn't taste nice, that jealousy.

As always, the demon's voice is pleasant, calm. "Ebony. I wondered when you'd call."

Somehow, Kane always knows whether it's Indigo or Ebony. Some hellmagic trick? Or recognizing his own?

No matter. Hell can't be worse than this. Your mind eaten from within. Your happy heart crushed by your own weakness. The girl you love diluted, washed away like a watercolor in the rain.

Ebony licks eager metal teeth, anticipation working a sensual shiver up his spine. "About your little shiny. I think I know where it is. But now I need to find someone."

In a grimy backstreet, Kane listens, and his claws crunch splinters into the handset. "I know this filthy thing. Akash. I sent it away."

Beside him, Angelo motions for silence and bends to scent around the corner, nose twitching. Angry sparks rainbow from Kane's hair onto spray-painted brick. He doesn't have time to deal with Akash now. Angelo's about to pull off a juicy triple hit on some DiLuca maggots. Their boss is dead. Crunch their bones to juice while they're down. Fun.

Ebony giggles, fairy-light. "Whatever you say. But he's still here, and he's got your shiny. Any clues?"

Wrath springs Kane's teeth an inch longer, and with a vicious blink he spears his winged shade skyward like a bat. Swoop on warm upcurrents over jeweled city lights, rain and dust and thunder, and under it all the spreading wet stink of flowers. Zoom closer, homing on the stench, a warehouse in Carlton with a rusted iron rooftop and jagged windows.

His shade hovers, quivering. Akash. Still there. It disobeyed. Nasty, horrid thing, spreading petty dissent through his city like a cancer. It won't do. Melbourne belongs to Kane. If the liars upstairs wanted it, they shouldn't have let it fester alone in the dark for a century and a half. Fucking hypocrites.

Kane sucks his shade back in with a nasty crunch of leathery wings and jerks away from the wall to pace. Frost crackles the concrete under his feet. He gave the foolish thing its chance. Once Angelo's done, he'll cut out this festering wound and munch on the stinking flesh.

But for the moment, he has Ebony.

Steamy flames hiss from his needle grin. "Oh, yes. I'll tell you exactly where it is. And you'll find out what the worm is up to. Bring my mirror back to me, Ebony. Now."

19

The door snapped shut like a magnet, and he was gone.

I kicked in frustration, leaving a smear on the sheet. Alone in his rose-drenched apartment. Chained to the bed. With no underwear on, and a shivering ache gnawing through my body like an underfed rat.

I'd imagined a lot of things about Indigo, but I'd never imagined he'd do something like this.

At least he'd left through the door and hadn't jumped out the window or ripped a hole in the ceiling or anything. Crazy metalfae.

My skin crinkled, uncomfortable. This was all my fault. I'd let him seduce me with his chaos, let him build my sick mirrorfever to a raging fire, when what I really needed to do was calm down, think, relax.

But I couldn't. He'd lied to me about not looking into the mirror. He'd pretended to help me even though he clearly had his own agenda. He'd deceived me after all, and I was so livid with myself for falling for it that my teeth stung.

I rattled my chain, furious, and had to force my hands still. Fine. Let him go off on his crazy quest to save me. I didn't need him. I could do this on my own.

First, get out of here. Then worry about finding Stalkerboy, he of the frightening angel-blue eyes and weird threesome aspirations. I didn't know what he'd really wanted with me that night at the Court, and I didn't care. He'd traded his skulls for the mirror, and he was my only lead.

I sucked in a calming breath and crawled up onto shaking knees to peer at the shackle in dim mood lights. Chain only a few inches long. Ratchet type, no keyhole, already too tight from my struggles. *Good one, Ice. Teach you to flip out.*

The other end locked tight to a strip of wood as thick as my arm. Unless I took the whole bed with me, I wasn't shifting it. And he'd snapped the cuff on before I knew what he was doing. No time to spread my fingers, tense my muscles, make my forearm as big as possible to get a bit more wriggle room. When you've been tied up as much as I have, you learn these things.

Still, cuffs don't work too well on double-jointed fairy hands. They're designed for humans, with their inflexible knuckles and tough skin. I grabbed my thumb and pulled.

Doonk.

The joint popped out with only a feeble complaint. Wobble, wobble. Now my thumb was all floppy.

I pushed it into my palm and eased the cuff over my welted wristbones. Still too thick.

I pulled my little finger backwards until the joint slipped out.

Ouch. That one hurt. Moisture popped out in beads on my skin, slicking my hand like oil. I squeezed it, discomfort wrapping my arm. Now my hand was all skinny and slippery like an eel.

I grabbed the metal bracelet and pulled. The cuff inched upward. Again, another inch, bones crunching together. Again, and my hand slurped free, like a little yellow baby being born. Aww.

I tossed the horrid wet cuff away, steel clanking on wood, and yanked sore knuckles back into their sockets. It bothered me that Indigo's fingers bend backwards, too. He knew I'd get away. Maybe he just liked chaining me up. Or maybe a few minutes' head start was all he needed.

I clambered off the bed and pulled my skirt down to cover me. My top was all twisted, too, and I tugged it back around, the thin cotton scraping my tortured nipples. My battered wings protested. I shifted them gingerly, the joints still raw from the fall and his mouth. No ladylike fluttering for me. Still, they didn't seem badly damaged. I craned my head around, chasing my own wing tails in a few stumbling circles, but I couldn't see any rips. My heart lightened. A bit of good news, amongst all this other trash.

I clambered down the ladder, and as his hot copper smell faded a little, my brain started working again. I had to find Stalkerboy, find out what he'd done with the mirror. I cast around for my bag, checking the floor, the couch, the kitchen bench. Nowhere to be seen. I stuck my head out the glass balcony door. Nothing. I must have dropped it on the way down.

I sighed. Great. I'd already lost the diamonds and the ruby skulls to Sonny at Valentino's. Now I'd lost my purse and my phone and everything else that remembered who I was. If I died and they found my body, they'd never know my name.

I flipped the kitchen tap on full and thrust my wrists under. Water splashed up my arms, blessedly cool, calming my jerking blood. I had no clue who Stalkerboy was, but he seemed to know me. Back to the Court, then, see if I can sneak in without paying, make a spectacle of myself some more and he'd find me. Easy peasy.

I splashed my face, letting the drips run down my fevered neck onto my chest, and took a few deep breaths. But unease still shimmered in my stomach. I swallowed, faintly sick, and snapped the water off. Swimming through quicksand. It wasn't a very good plan. But I didn't know what else to do. Might as well make the best of it.

I shook myself dry, splashing drips onto spotless marble, skipped over to the door, and flipped it open.

Blue eyes, so bright, I blinked. Tanned shoulders scrawled with ink, rain-soaked dark hair, tiny steel spikes glinting through his skin.

Stalkerboy.

My pulse ripped into a sprint. I gulped, my fairy senses awash. Danger. Fight. Fly. But treacherous muscles seized my limbs tight, and I couldn't move.

He clenched a silver-ringed hand, and in it, cruel iron petals snapped closed.

The mirror. Stalking me. The squidgy had shown him where I was. I'd wondered what weird plans he had for me. Now I was about to find out.

Fear sparked my nerves to life, and I scrambled to slam the door in his face.

But he slammed it aside one-handed. It hit the fuchsia-dark wall, and splinters flew.

I backed off, my limbs trembling and my wings uselessly tensed for flight. Nowhere to fly to. "Leave me alone. What you want?"

He didn't say anything. He just screamed.

Unearthly noise shattered inside my skull, spiking glassy agony into my ears. High, piercing, banshee-bright. I doubled over, clutching insides suddenly rippling with sick vibration.

Stupid indignation hacked my nerves as I staggered. *No fair. That's a banshee's scream. Not supposed to be able to do that.*

Dimly, I felt his fingers stroke my hair, and in a haze of pain I tried to turn, run, fly. But air ripped to evil shreds in my lungs, and my limbs shook to water in the awful scarlet noise, and before I could even scream, my brain swelled to mush and everything swirled to black.

Blaze leaps, sharp wings drawn back, and launches himself like a flame-drenched spear at the polished shop window.

His feet crash into the glass. Splinters explode, tinkling in a shower of sparks on teddy bears and painted dollhouses and frilly patchwork things now swimming in a jagged sea of broken glass. No alarm. No flashing lights. Idiots probably don't even have insurance.

He darts away with stinging ankles, desperation burning empty holes in his heart. Not enough. Never enough. This urge to destroy won't ease. Broken glass always soothed his anger, calmed his questing heart, but not anymore. Not since Ice and her cursed squidgy. Now he's always jittery and always horny and always sick to his guts with rage, feverish, sweaty, and juddering, a full-body hard-on that just won't go away.

He squirms through the hole and grabs a yellow-furred bear. Yellow and green, like Ice, his no-longer best friend. His heart stings hot. He just wanted to make her love him back, just for a few minutes. Wanted to hurt her like he hurts, hollow and burning.

The bear stares at him, splinters dusting its glassy eyes, and in a burst of inconsolable anger, he ignites it. Flames lick and catch, green plastic bows melting. He tosses it away, and crawls outside, disconsolate. The place might catch fire. He doesn't care.

The street is quiet, streetlights buzzing alone, only a few cars and no people. If anyone sees him, they're keeping quiet about it. Good move. He's in no mood for hiding, and his glamour pops, negligent. He skips along the footpath under dusty cantilevers, flitting upward at intervals to smash the lights one by one with his fist, leaving a trail of darkness and bloodstained broken glass behind him.

A drunken spriggan slumps nude on a piss-drenched doorstep, sucking on a beer bottle with ragged lips, stunted blue legs waving weakly like an upturned possum's. She gives a bucktoothed smile, spit dribbling. "Nice one, mate. Fuck 'em."

Nice one, yourself. A garbage bin snickers at him as he passes, and he leaps and kicks it over with both feet, refuse and rats spilling into the gutter. He takes aim at a rat with one incendiary claw and fries it dead in its tracks with a sharp ribbon of yellow flame. Steam rises from the charred corpse. Giggle. Shrug. Still no fun.

Despair seeps into his heart like thick dark wine, and he lets it overflow.

Storm-drenched moonlight wets black pavement, and scudding clouds pick up speed. He turns a corner at random, another, another. Shadows flicker by on dark alley walls, dust, moonshine, his own silhouette, lithe and poised and dangerous, the flames dripping unchecked from his wings lighting his way in eerie scarlet gloom.

Broken windows gleam above a garbage compactor, rusty and blue, leaning drunkenly against a warehouse wall. His heart lightens. Maybe a wino inside, or a homeless kid to torment. He skips up, ready to alight on the lid and scare the fuck out of them.

Sob. Whimper. Sniffle.

Blaze halts in a swift crouch on the ground, sweaty hair flopping in his eyes, claws crunching in the dirt. He sniffs into the shadows. A girl, hiding, bruised and lonely. The scent of her name floats on the air, sky and rain and flowers. Indra. It's Hindi, or some fucking thing. Always he can smell their names, even when he couldn't care less. His blood burns at the fresh meaty smell of her sorrow, and careless of breaking his glamour, he sweeps out a fevered wing and showers the wall with orange sparks to reveal her.

Dark hair straggles on skinny white shoulders. Black leather skirt crumpled in her lap, showing bruised legs. White arms wrapped around her addict-thin body. Tears streaking dust on her china doll face. Purple rose tattoo flashing on her strap-wrapped ankle. She gazes up at him, sly fear glazing her blue eyes.

With a hot flush of interest he recognizes her, the little pouty-mouthed waif in the biker kid's shadow. Ice's stalkergirl, the one Ice nearly ripped a chunk out of at the Court after Blaze dragged her away from that metal-skinned loser. Childlike. Flowery innocence under a worldly façade. Not killmebeautiful, but prettysexy, like Ice. Wounded. Teaseable.

His fingers tingle with unnamable need. The old mischief ignites in his heart, tempering the rage just for a moment. He withdraws his glowing wing and edges closer, offering his hand. "Come out, Indra. I won't hurt you." *Much.*

She huddles tighter, licking ripped lips. There's blood there, the marks of teeth. He inhales, and feels her. Shock. Disbelief. Disgust. Hunger. Her eyes cast about dully, unfocused, and her honeyflower scent hits him again. Enchanting. His blood tingles fresh like a garden, filling his desire, throbbing his pulse tight, making him rapidly, scorchingly hard. *Something to break. Goody.*

Sweat trickles down his neck. He wipes his nose, uneasy in the raw light of strange flowery sympathy, and gestures at that syrupy blood on her mouth. "Who you hiding from? Did your boyfriend do that?"

Because I'd like to. Give me your mouth, your hands, your sweet flesh, those pretty bruised legs around me. In the club I'd tempt you with sparks, seduce you, dance against you with flame on my fingertips until your body weeps for me and we can spend an hour or two forgetting this shitty life. Easy enough. So why do I feel sorry for you? What's this damn affection you're making me feel?

She sniffles, artful, her tears brimming. "He tried to show me. I didn't want to."

He inhales again, that sly rosy magic, and his heart bleeds for her even as his mirrorwarped desire freshens. "Well, that sucks. Get yourself a better boy, darlin'." He helps her up. Her wrist cools his burning palm, and his cock responds, smarting like sunburn. Would she feel like that inside, cool and smooth and soothing on his aching flesh? Desire strikes in his balls like a handful of matches. A bleeding, weeping little human girl. He swallows dry guilt and backs away. "Look, I'd better—"

"Can you show me?"

The smell of flowers dizzies him speechless. Surely he's imagined that, the sudden pleading in her eyes. "What?"

Her fingers curl around his, gentle but sure, and suddenly her body's against his, so cool and tiny, her little breasts plump on his chest. "Show me how I can please him. I don't know what to do."

Her lips brush his, so girlish and soft, and in an instant they're kissing, his greedy flame licking her face. Sparks erupt stinging from his wings, and shuddering he folds her in his arms. She groans, and opens her little mouth to him. Her tongue fits soft and shy on his. Such a little girl. His blood overheats. He tries to keep the kiss gentle, caressing her lips like they're precious, teaching her with long sure licks what she's meant to do. She responds with another groan, letting him taste her. He slides a careful hand to her breast, and her nipple flowers eagerly, swelling hard in his fingers. His desire burns hot and fast like oil, and before he knows anything about it, he's on top of her on the dirty concrete under a sheet of flickering flame, sliding hungry fingers up her thigh.

She moans and claws at his hair, the rose petal scent of her desire dizzying him. He pushes her leather skirt aside, trying to be gentle, trying not to leave claw marks, but fuck it's hard when she's wild and innocent and hot for it at the same time. She's cool between her thighs on his sweating hand, and when he touches her for the first time, she gasps and jerks like he's shaken her awake.

She's fresh and wet, her flesh soft. Carefully, he traces her little clit, so plump and ready for his mouth. He slides a finger into her, and a shudder rips his muscles tight. God, she's lovely, so smooth and muscular, more like a fairy girl than like a human. But there's no dimple there, no soft little ridge, no bump in the delicate skin. She's not a virgin, and for the first time he wonders if she's tricking him and why.

But it's too late. Her powdery scent intoxicates him, and in a few seconds he's nudged her thighs apart and he's pushing inside her. He should go slowly—she's small, just a human girl—but he can't. She's so tight around him. So good. So blessedly cool and moist. Delicious flame bursts from his pores, threatening to push him over the edge. Just the feel of this witch could make him come. "God, you feel great."

She whimpers, tense. "It hurts."

"It won't for long." He bends to kiss her body as he moves inside her, licking her breasts, sucking her tight nipples, and before long she relaxes with a pleasured shudder.

She gasps and rocks under him, pushes him deeper like she knows what she's doing. "Yes," she whispers. "Show me. Help us. Promise me."

He groans and thrusts, unwilling but compelled. Something weird. Something wrong. But still the words slip out on a ragged sigh as her muscles drag pleasure from deep in his balls. "I promise."

"Promise on your soul." She moves against him, sultry, her eyes glazed with deep pleasure.

"Yeah. On my soul." Bewitched. Tricked. But he can't stop. His cock swells inside her, ready to explode, and he thrusts faster, harder, using her as she uses him until orgasm slashes through him like broken glass, tearing screaming sensation deep into his flesh. Flames scorch over his back, scarlet flashing from his wings like neon against the dirty wall. "Ah. God, you little bitch, you feel good."

Liquid slides around him inside her, sticky and caustic like over-sugared icing. His breath scorches. His cock still hurts, his rage barely satisfied. Did she come? He didn't notice. He doesn't care. She tricked him, for who knows what weird-ass reason. He should get off her, spit on her, and leave her in the dirt. But he can't. He can't get up. He can't move.

She slides beneath him, a satisfied smile shaping her lips. "Now you're mine. Come tell Akash what you did."

A flash of flowery compulsion wilts his nerves, and when she nudges him up and bids him follow her, he can't help but obey.

20

Slimy awareness slicked my senses like river water, and I fought to wake.

My head hurt, like I'd dragged my brain through broken glass. My wing joints ached. Thunder rumbled, distant but threatening, and on some unseen metal roof, raindrops pattered like insect feet. I inhaled, the dusty stink of an airless space baked in the sun. Rusty light pierced my crunched lids. I opened, and my eyeballs gritted like sandpaper.

A lightbulb, gently swinging left to right, shedding that sphere of reddish light. Beyond it, darkness and dust and the smell of rain. A smooth surface soothed my shoulders, my wings, my backside. I wriggled, and the smoothness didn't move with me. I lifted my hand to feel my face, and it wouldn't come. I tried my other hand. It wouldn't come either. Furious, I kicked, and my ankles hit something rough and tight that slammed them back down.

Reason filtered through woolly haze: *Lightbulb is up. I'm on my back. Correction—tied on my back. I can't move my arms. I can't move my legs. I'm helpless.*

Panic scrabbled through my body, shredding my nerves to useless flesh. My pulse yabbered stupidly at me to flee, and I fought jerking limbs. I sucked in a breath and looked down—at least I could still move my head—and trepidation chewed at my nerves like a hyena with a bone. Rope around my ankles, rope around my wrists. A white surface like a tabletop. *Christ, I hate being tied up. But all my bits are still there. I'm still dressed. Don't see any blood.*

Rustle.

My skin broke out in a cold wash. My head whipped around, my cheek slapping into the table.

Stalkerboy smiled, unnerving. He sat a few feet away on a tall stool, pretty dark hair tumbling damp around his shoulders. Watching me. Waiting for me to wake up.

Presumably so I wouldn't miss whatever was about to happen to me.

He glided over to me, his balance uncanny and beautiful for a muscled-up biker hooligan. I couldn't see a weapon. I couldn't see the mirror. Maybe he just wanted to hurt me. Panic bubbled in my blood, but instead of lying here gibbering, that old Icyspice attitude came lurching out. "What's going on, Stalkerboy? Where am I? Why am I tied up? What are you—?"

He lighted a warm finger on my lips, shushing me, and something weird rippled beneath my skin at his touch. I moved my lips, resisting the urge to spit. His finger tasted of daisies. He smiled again, and took his finger away. "Not Stalkerboy. Akash, from the sky. Kane is my enemy."

The names sounded glassy and alien in his mouth, and harmonics pealed in his voice, beautiful and unnerving like a charmed-up banshee. I remembered his hateful scream at Indigo's with a shudder. He's just a human kid. How did he do that? And if that freaky white-toothed smile was meant to calm me, he was kidding himself. Those sky-blue eyes shone with rampant hunger. He looked like he wanted to eat me whole. I shivered. *Weird* didn't begin to describe this.

Fear slid hot needles into my blood, and I raged against it, my heart aflame with disgust. Yeah, I was afraid. But damned if I was helpless. Screw that.

Surreptitiously I squirmed, testing the knots. "Good for you, Akash from the sky. You gonna let me go, or do I hafta kick your ass?"

He bent closer and sniffed my cheek. I tried not to look away, not to show him my fear. Sweat gleamed on his dark-stubbled jaw, beaded on his studded brow, twinkled on the tiny ruby ring in his nose. Long tilted cheekbones, straight nose, supple lips, velvety lashes. I'd even say good-looking, if he didn't have me tied me to a table. Prick.

He leant on his elbows next to my head, his flowery smell unpleasantly close. "No kicking. No going. Tell me about Kane."

I shifted some more, trying to work my ankles loose. "Who? Don't know who you're on about."

Scarlet flame rippled over his knuckles, wispy like a fairy's, and he leaned closer, impatient. His hip pressed into the table's edge, and something hard and metallic clunked against the plastic. Distant giggles whispered in my head. I risked a glance downward. A taut round shape swelled in his jeans pocket.

The mirror.

He clicked his tongue, impatient. "You lie. You know Kane. You kissed Kane. He gave you pleasure. Tell me how it felt."

My stomach wobbled, the scent of flowers cloying. Christ. He'd watched us? And what was with that flame thing? Humans couldn't do that. "Look, you've got the wrong girl."

"No. Ice. Yellow. Honey eyes. Berries. You are the one. Tell me how it felt." He sniffed me again, his mouth alarmingly close to mine, and I wriggled, anticipating a forced kiss.

He just stared, sky-blue, two inches away.

I fought not to blink or recoil. His intensity made me squirm, like he could see right inside my head. I wouldn't get anywhere by lying to this fruitcake. Better to let him think he was getting what he wanted, and work on getting the hell out of here. "Okay, okay. You got me. Tell you how what felt?"

"He gave you pleasure." Akash's gaze slid down to my mouth, and back up to my eyes. Shiver.

I laughed, forced. "Hey, that's kind of a personal qu—"

"You touched him. He did not fight. How is this?"

Confusion tumbled in my head, and I kicked my feet harder. The damn rope wouldn't loosen. "What? You're not making sense."

He frowned and sniffed my hair. His own dark locks trailed over my cheek, soft, damp, smelling of rain. His throat looked smooth and tanned, and I saw deep clawmarks, partially healed to scar tissue. I licked my lips. He smelled kind of nice, a faint twang of flowery blood tingling my nose.

I swallowed, recklessness rippling my nerves. *No, I didn't just wonder what he'd taste like.* This guy was a freak, and I'd had my share of freakadelics today. *Get a grip, Ice.*

He straightened, a frown still denting his brow. "You defied him, and he did not punish you. How is this?"

The twinge of mirror-rich desire that awakened in my body only made me angry. I jerked against my ropes, cutting my skin. "Enough with the stupid questions, okay? Something's wrong with you, you know that?"

"Yes!" Excitement flushed his cheeks, and he knelt beside me and rested his chin eagerly on the table's edge. "I knew you'd understand. Explain this . . . thing wrong with me. I must know!"

"Look, I've got no clue what you're on about, but if you want me to say anything that doesn't begin with *fuck* and end in *off*, you'd better untie me right now."

"I cannot. You will try to escape. The others did."

Dread spiked my joints, spoiling my snarky façade. "What others?"

"The others. They were useless to me." He waved his silver-ringed hand at the darkness. His fingernails were spotless and white, and that incongruous fairy flame flickered again between his knuckles.

I lifted my head and strained to see. Vague outlines of boxes, wooden from the nailheads glinting in the ever-swinging light. Splintered edges, broken or torn in half. For the first time, I noticed the groans, the wails, the scratching. And on the ground, a dark shape, muddled like a heap of cloth, something silvery gleaming. . . .

I gulped. Wings. A body. *Holy shit.*

"I asked the fairy. He told me this." Fire licked lovingly around Akash's forearm, and nothing burned. He smiled, shattering and cruel. "Now I'm asking you."

Icy chill seeped from my pores. He'd stolen it all. Sucked up their power like a leech. The banshee's voice. The fairy's flame. Who knew what else? And what did he want from me? I couldn't sing a lover or spark a fire or do anything particularly cool. I just leaked. He couldn't want that. Could he?

I squirmed. My ropes weren't loosening, not with him watching. Time to play nicey-Ice. "No need for unpleasantness. Just tell me what you want and I'll play nice and we can all go home."

"You have power over Kane, my enemy. I must learn that. Show me."

Understanding glittered, and helpless laughter bounced from my lips. "You so have the wrong end of the cactus, loverboy. I don't have power over Kane. He had a hard-on for his ex-girlfriend. I helped him out. That's it."

"Girlfriend." Akash's eyes blazed whiter, and savage compulsion spelled my heart like a poisoned thorn.

My vision bubbled, and fear scraped in my teeth. Discomfort

thickened my tongue with the urge to speak, and my words slurred in a rush. "Yeah. Y'know. Lover. Chicky. Arm candy. She dumped him. Look, why am I even telling you this—?"

"Kane has a lover?"

"Sure. I mean, I don't know him very well. But he's just like an ordinary g— Hyypf!"

Akash grabbed my throat, nails slashing. My tongue crushed, strangling my words and my breath, and black flecks dizzied my vision. My lungs jerked instinctively, longing for air. He thrust his face within an inch of mine, and his breath left a warm damp spot on my lips. "I am Akash from the sky. Kane is my enemy. You will tell me everything, or I will drink it from you as I did the others. Do you understand, yellow girl?"

My bones shuddered in trepidation and rage. I'd kill the bastard for this. But drinking didn't sound good. The others certainly hadn't fared well out of it. Compulsively I swallowed, bile scorching my membranes. I forced a nod, as much as I could manage in his grip.

He loosened just a little, and I dragged in delicious flower-tainted air. Relief cooled my skin. I gulped, and swallowed, and gulped again, my composure ripped ragged. "You're an asshole, Akash from the sky. Beating up on fairies for fun. Hope you're proud of yourself."

He ignored me. "Tell me how you seduced Kane."

"Oh, so now with the personal questions, you fucking fr—"

"Tell or drink, Ice." He licked his lips, a hungry gleam in his eye, and caressed my throat, warm fingers running lovingly over my collarbone.

I shivered. "I didn't, okay? He seduced me."

"Why?" He slid his hand to my chest, fingering my skin.

"Hell, I don't know. Because he thought I was easy. Can you please not do that?"

"No. What power of yours did he wish for?" He peered closer, lifting my cotton top's neckline to examine me.

My nipples jerked tight under his scrutiny, and ire tangled with my frustration like sprung wire ripping at my nerves. I banged my fists against the table, maddened. "None! I told you! I don't have powers. I'm just a stupid little fairy girl."

He sniffed my breast, curious, and followed a scent trail down to my exposed belly. His breath tickled me, warm and peculiar. "You're a very pretty fairy girl."

My stomach roiled. "Oh, please. I mean, I'm flattered, but can you not—?"

"If you have no power, then why did Kane pleasure you? In return for what?"

"Jesus. You really are from the sky if you're asking me that."

"Yes." He flicked me his cosmos-blue gaze. So clear, so empty of pain or experience or life. Like he'd seen nothing, felt nothing. Never loved or hated or hurt. He just hungered. For knowledge, sensation, emotion, anything he could get.

Curiosity gnawed at my bones, and I wriggled and kicked, but it wouldn't let go. Danger clanged in my head, warning me, but I itched and I yearned and I couldn't help it. I strained my twitching nose forward and inhaled.

His flowery scent slammed into my sinuses like hot water, drowning me. My vision flickered, and images whirled and tumbled like a sandstorm.

The sun, dazzling in empty blue sky, the blinding white sweep of feathered wings. Disembodied whispers a bright comfort in his head. A cool white hand slides in his, soothing. Endless hours of reading, thinking, brooding in silence, a long sunlit room full of identical blond others dressed in white. He can draw beautifully, flowers and birds and waterfalls and dragonflies and the sun, always the sun. Now he sketches himself, the strangest thing, standing in a dark starlit garden alone. And then a cell, cool white walls only a few feet wide, a door that won't open no matter how abjectly he begs, the oppressive weight of silence like poison in his ears. Tears, cold on his cheeks and painful in his throat. He knows what it's like to cry. The cold blue eyes of his master, burning with rage beneath feathery white wings like an angel's. Jagged lightning flashes, blinding. Screaming in free fall, wind scorching his face. And then he's on his knees in black city dust, where a new hellcrimson sun burns his skin and the air stinks of shit and blood. He can't fly anymore, and he stares shell-shocked at the silent sky and doesn't know what to do.

The pictures shattered and swept away. I choked. *Holy shit.* Akash-from-the-sky was an angel? Did that mean heaven existed after all? What was it like? Were there fairies there, or was it just for humans, like everything else?

Thirst for answers parched my heart, before another, nastier thought struck me. Maybe heaven existed, and They didn't like us very much, having all that fun and selling our souls to demons and all. Maybe the folks upstairs really had come for Kane.

And They'd sent Akash, who for all his strength and wiles and pretty inked muscles didn't even understand why people slept with strangers sometimes.

They were so screwed.

I almost felt sorry for him, even if he had killed the guy who really owned that body, as well as the poor fairy on the floor and who knew how many others. I swallowed. "Look. It's not always an exchange, okay? Sometimes people just do it for fun. Because it feels good. Having someone you don't know . . . Well, that's part of the point. You can really let yourself go. No regrets, no after. Just now. Get it?"

His eyes brightened as he studied my hipbones. "So . . . Your power is that Kane did not know you?"

"I guess. Kind of."

He poked at my skirt, dubious. "I do not know you. Show me."

Dread crept beneath my skin like a prickly rash. "You what?"

"Show me how you tricked him."

Horrid light dawned. I swallowed cold nausea. "You want me to . . . ?"

He grabbed my hand and kissed it, his lips a warm tingle on my knuckles. "Touch me like you did him. Trick me so I know how it's done. I must know."

I tried to yank away, but the rope savaged my wrist and his lips lingered, tasting me, his tongue curling sweetly around my thumb. I struggled, anger flaring. "That's got to be the worst line I've ever heard. Custard mountain, loverboy. In your dreams. No way."

He did something swift and hard under the table, and my wrist ropes jerked free.

My wings sprang tight and ready before I realized what was happening. I had only a second of freedom, and I wasted it stunned.

He grabbed my hands and jammed them down beside my head, pinning me harder than the ropes and just as effective. My wrists knobbled on the table, bruising in his smooth fingers. His strong chest crushed my breasts, squeezing away my breath. His full mauve lips hovered close to mine. His eyes dazzled me, and that crooning banshee voice twinkled with persuasion. "Obey. Obey, or I drink. I'll have your secret one way or the other."

My blood boiled, searing my veins with electric fury. Heaven-sent or not, he was just another bully, using brute strength to get his way. If I defied him, he'd drink me, whatever that meant, but it couldn't be good.

Sacrifice my dignity for safety. Humiliation or pain. Story of my sorry life.

But safety wasn't all it was cracked up to be. If Indigo gave me one thing tonight, he gave me that. And pain didn't scare me anymore.

Satisfaction licked in my veins like deepest pleasure, and my anger filled me, sexual, stroking me inside like a lover. I jerked my head forward, pressed my forehead into his and grinned at him, defiance blazing in my heart. "Fuck you, Akash from the sky. Show me what you got."

He grinned back, sharp like a spike in my heart, and mashed his lips onto mine.

Blood, salt, dust. Hard lips dragging on mine, impossibly strong. I couldn't wrench my head away. His tongue squirmed between my lips, forcing into the gaps between my teeth, levering my mouth open. I clenched my teeth, but he forced my jaw apart, and the jagged edges of his teeth jammed in mine and I couldn't close my mouth.

Oh, this was worse than Joey's slimy webbed fingers. My face hurt. My lips sliced open on his teeth, and blood ran into my mouth and down my chin. His tongue raped me, hot muscle scouring my mouth, invading, tasting, searching. I squirmed my throat muscles to avoid him, but he wrapped his tongue around mine and pulled, hard.

The skin inside my mouth stretched horribly, like a sock pulled inside out. Pain seized my throat. I yanked my wrists, but he crunched his fingers tighter, and my bones grated, hot spikes thudding in. Sickness clenched a fireball in my stomach. Perversely I willed it to explode, to splash up into his mouth and taste really bad. *Drink this, asshole.*

He sucked, a banshee growl rumbling deep in his throat. Suction yanked my tonsils taut, and at last my stomach heaved, the horrid cramp a ferocious delight.

But it wasn't vomit that came up.

It was something fat and spiky like a hot rambutan, scraping inside my chest with angry claws as he dragged it out of me. It fought, this spiky thing, wriggling like a trapped rat, and ghastly terror watered my guts.

He was drinking me. Whatever fairy strangeness I had, he'd swallow it whole and throw the wrapper away.

A scream swelled my larynx. I fought his awful grip, thrashing my head and my arms and everything else I could move. But he just held me down and forced his tongue in harder.

My desperate cry smothered in his mouth. My jaw wrenched tight. The spiky ball ripped up inside my neck, tearing my throat to stinging shreds. My muscles weakened like melting jelly, and I tried to struggle, but my strength was gone. I couldn't breathe. I couldn't see. The sound of my own death screeched like claws on a blackboard in my ears, sharp with cruel mirth and glassy shards of mirror.

But my last desperate rageflame flickered bright. He wouldn't get me like this. Not without a fight. Mirrorbright courage flashed my muscles with one last defiant spark, and I sucked in a shuddering flower-scented breath through my nose.

Confusion, disbelief, the oppressive silence of his beloved sky. Loneliness, the raw disgust in some dark-haired waif's blue eyes tearing at his heart. Desperate yearning for squalid sensation he doesn't recognize or understand. The awestruck realization of helplessness with a demon's claws embedded in his throat. Solitude. Lust. Fear. Despair.

I exulted, blood rushing fatally from my brain. *Just like a stupid little fairy girl, Akash from the sky. Just like the rest of us you despise so eagerly from up there. You've fallen to earth, and you're one of us now. You'll never win.*

For an instant, his grip froze, and he faltered.

And then he flew off me, his teeth jolting away from mine like I'd smacked him upside the head.

Cool air flooded my bruised mouth, the bloodstained taste of freedom. The spiky magicball sprang free with a thrash and a cheeky giggle, and dissolved bubbling in my stomach. I gasped for air. Fresh, delightful dust roughened my torn throat.

Relief washed me with warm droplets. I flopped my aching head to the side, an exhausted smile stinging my torn lips, and that warm relief crackled to ice on my skin.

Akash sprawled panting on his back in the dust, spit and my blood dripping from his lips. A bleeding blue-haired banshee knelt astride his throat, one shiny black-clad knee jammed into his larynx. Her pretty lips stretched in a vicious snarl. A familiar spiked blade shone wickedly in her hand.

My skin quailed. Mina. Joey DiLuca's girl.

Joey stalked forward into the light, his brass-topped black cane tapping on the concrete. He kicked Akash in the ribs, eliciting a soggy sigh. "Mirror, shithead. Now."

I snapped my head back around, tension stopping my breath in my lungs like a cork. Joey stood with his back to me. Mina was distracted by her prey. Maybe they wouldn't see me.

I flexed my limbs, testing. Akash had untied my wrist ropes. Only ankles to go. Quietly, I pushed myself up.

Pop.

My wing joints, crackling as the pressure came off them.

I snapped still like an icicle. My heart squeezed tight, waiting for Joey to spin around and chew my skin off.

But he was too busy kicking Akash in the guts to notice me. He jammed his sharp cane into Akash's knee and twisted, fabric and skin tearing. "Mirror. Give."

Akash just stared up at him with a bloody grin.

Cautious relief calmed my nerves. *Heh. You're an idiot, DiLuca. Pain's not gonna convince this guy. Too much like what he's after.*

Inch by inch I stretched forward, keeping my sore wings flat to raise no shadow.

"Mirror or you die." Joey's voice slithered, reptilian, and Mina crooned happily, toying with her knife's edge at the metal studs in Akash's eyebrow. Her own were torn ragged, missing, her lip and nose scabbed. Indigo did that at Quang's. I couldn't bring myself to care.

My spine flexed, thankfully smooth and silent now, and I stretched forward, making myself as small and low as I could. My breasts slid down my thighs and squashed into my kneecaps, and I slid out a stealthy arm and curled it under the table. Prickly rope brushed my fingerpads.

Akash squirmed on the ground with a smooth, sexual groan that gave me shivers. "You can't kill me, hellspawn. But I'd like your body. I'd peel the skin from it and let the snake out."

I strained forward, searching for the knot. There, knobbly and damp, the rope fat with my water. I picked at it with urgent claws, my pores sweating cold despair. Damn thing wouldn't come undone.

"Just slash the fucker," Joey ordered. Metal scythed. Blood spattered, that distinctive runny ketchup sound. Mina giggled, and Akash howled, a horrid mix of laughter and tears.

I wiggled my claws in tighter, working the knot loose. The rope inched aside, agonizingly slow.

"Last chance, pretty boy. Mirror." Shadows dipped as Joey knelt.

Akash spluttered wet laughter. "Come take it."

At last, I wormed my claw in and dragged the knot apart. The rope slackened, and I slid silently off the table onto the floor, my heart pounding a hole in my rib cage.

The table's shadow shrouded dark, and for a few seconds I lay there, blinded, my ragged breath frighteningly loud in my ears. Free, wings and spiky magic gutball intact. But Joey and Stalkerboy would fight it out and keep the mirror, and I'd be back where I started. Unless . . . What was that?

I squinted. My eyes adjusted, and shapes slowly emerged on the floor in front of my nose. Pebbles, a discarded nail, dusty tumbleweeds collecting under the table. And beside them, a shadowy, glinting steel ball.

Mirror. Tumbled from Akash's pocket when he fell. Hiding under the table for me to find.

I stared, my pulse skipping. The mirror rolled a few inches to the right and wobbled, beckoning.

Breathless, I snaked out a swift arm. The metal crooned softly in my hand, a warm and satisfied noise I now knew only I could hear.

—*Knew you'd be back,*— it whispered, smugness dripping like acid.

The urge for revenge itched my sticky palms. Anger shook my forearm. I burned to throw the ugly thing against the wall and watch it shatter. *Teach you to screw with my mind, squidgy.*

I crunched my teeth, swallowing raging violence like vomit. I folded my wings in tight and wriggled like an earthworm toward the light's edge and safety, the mirror burbling with satisfaction in my hand.

Darkness only a few feet away. The table stood between Joey and me. With luck, he wouldn't see me before I made it out.

Grit scratched my elbows and scraped on my grounded belly. I kept crawling toward the darkness and safety. Behind me, the wet smack of flesh on flesh, a reptilian hiss. I didn't care who'd hit whom. I glared at the mirror in my fist, my mouth tightening as I wormed along. *Kane's welcome to you, nasty thing. You'll get yours. Just get me out of here alive.*

Akash sang, his unearthly voice grating with hatred like glassy shards. My ears curled in protest, hurting deep inside. I jammed breath into my lungs so I wouldn't pant and give myself away, and kept crawling.

Finally, my nose poked into darkness. Then my chin. Then my wing tips. I scrambled to my feet in the dark at last, fresh relief spreading comfort through my aching limbs. I'd made it.

The thing lurking in the shadows grabbed my elbow.

Shock iced my lungs. My skin screamed shivery warning. I yanked free, my heart walloping, and stumbled backwards into the light.

A banshee shriek rose, warbled with shock. "Fairy's getting away!"

I skidded, fluttering mad wings for balance, and my arms waved wildly. The rust-flecked mirror glinted bright for everyone to see, and in the shadows, a dark metal chuckle rang out.

Too late, hot iron scorched my nose. Familiar heat slithered over my skin. Indigo?

Joey dropped Akash with a soggy thud, green and scarlet splashing from his hands. Black scales sprang out on his forehead, spreading to cover his face like fast-motion fungus. The pale skin on his hands rippled and blackened to shiny taloned fins. His eyes glowed like green neon, and like a snake on the strike, he launched himself at me across the table.

I shrieked, unbalanced. Black fins scythed an inch from my nose. Neon venom splashed my face, and that familiar slimy stink electrified me.

Drops seared my skin like acid, rotten leather-stink churning my stomach. I jerked away with a panicked flutter, and my hands flew up to ward him off. But he didn't attack me again. He just slithered a steely black flipper around my wrist and twisted, hard.

Agony razored up my forearm. I screamed and struggled, fury crunching in my throat, but I couldn't break his unearthly grip. He wrenched harder, and my bones protested with a sick crunch. Despair clotted in my heart. I clutched feebly at the mirror, but my numb fingers wouldn't respond, and Joey reached out glossy black talons and plucked it away.

Easy as you please. Stupid, weak, useless fairy girl.

Frustration whipped my skin raw. I squealed and kicked at him, trying to pull my arm from his weird grip. "Get your rubbery hands off me, creep."

He flipped the giggling mirror away into his jacket and yanked me forward by the shoulders. The scales on his face retracted beneath fresh, pale human skin, and he threw a lickerish grin at the shadows behind me. "Pretty thing. So breakable. Perhaps we'll finish our game." And his forked tongue slipped out, and he wrapped it quivering across my lips.

Wet. Cold. Wriggly like a worm. The stink of cold spit, laced with meat.

My skin caterpillared. Bile swamped my mouth, choking me. He grunted, and licked me again. I squeezed my lips together and struggled madly.

And then Mina screamed. A horrid, gurgling, desperate scream that chilled my bones.

A rich metal whisper split the air like a warm blade. "Game's on, snakeboy. Think again."

Joey whipped around, one hand slipping off my shoulder. With a furious wriggle and a jerk of wings, I yanked free.

Indigo clamped his sharp blue chin on Mina's shoulder, one arm folded around her waist, ultralong blue fingers plastered over her mouth and nose. His wings stretched tight above his head, poised on an icy edge to flit backwards, and rusty glitter sparkled the air.

Mina's eyes bloomed huge and bright like garnets. Her feet scrabbled and kicked, but he evaded her easily. Her chest heaved as she tried to sing, to make any sound at all, but all that came out was a muffled *mmph!* as her lungs searched for air.

Joey cursed, and swiped for me, but I leapt away, circling the table toward Indigo and Mina. My limbs shook, tense. My mind squirted in little circles, and common sense slashed at my courage with stinging claws, demanding my attention. *Don't be stupid. You're not safe. Run away before it's too late. Lock your heart away.*

Yeah. Because that plan's done well for me so far. Screw that.

I circled closer, wary of Joey's greenvenom glare. On the ground, Akash flopped like a beached seal, scarlet bruises ripped open on his handsome face. He giggled, bloody froth running. Weirdo.

I sidled around his flailing hands, indignation splashing back to me like a water bomb. *Rotten bully. Hope those bruises scar, asshole.*

Mina struggled, her scarred face purpling under a wild tumble of shimmering blue hair. Joey gripped his cane in black-finned hands and hissed at Indigo, his slimy tongue flickering. "You got a death wish, fairy?"

Indigo wrapped his free fingers around Mina's jerking throat, and pressed one delicate copper claw against the place where her pulse throbbed. A cruel smile tainted his silvery lips, and his eyes glowed warm blue. "She'll bleed pretty, Joey," he suggested, sniffing at the tiny bead of blood swelling under his claw. "So clean and warm. She wants it. They all want it, in the end. Let me show you."

Warmth spidered along my limbs. He'd touched me like that, tracing his claw over my pulse while we kissed. Now, icy violence glinted in that velvet bedroom voice. Even I was convinced he was a psycho who'd stop at nothing. But I still needed him to get out of here.

Joey's fangs gleamed. He spat slimy green spit and tossed his cane away, wicked black webs crackling. "What did Delilah promise you, fairy? I'll rip it from your bleeding hands while you die. This is my score. Let her go."

Confusion clouded my vision. Delilah? I'd heard talk of her on the street, some renegade demon bitch sniffing around DiLuca. Indigo was beholden to Kane, not Delilah. Gangsters were so dumb.

I smirked and waited for Indigo to laugh, to tell Joey he didn't know shit from ice cream.

But Indigo just smiled, chilling. "Your guts in a cream pie. We'll eat it together, Delilah and I, once I've returned her little glass. Hand it over, or your pretty bleeds."

Hollow nausea rippled my intestines, and I choked. He'd lied to me. Told me what I longed so much to hear. Blinded the stupid little fairy girl with false kisses so she'd tell him what he wanted to know.

And now he'd give my mirror away to the enemy—for money, no doubt—and abandon me to madness.

Foolish emotion swamped my heart, strangling me, and tears scorched my eyes. *I'm so fucking stupid. I thought I interested him. I thought he wanted me. I even thought he liked me.*

As if a cold, calculating, loveless metal thief could care about a stupid, ugly, lonely girl like me.

Right.

I blinked, forcing myself to swallow whatever blubbering noise I'd been about to make. Fine. So it hurt. I was used to that, right? I could deal. Salvage some dignity here.

He might be a lying metal prick with a cowpat for a conscience. But I still voted him least likely to kill me out of this lot.

I shook my eyes clear, trying to comprehend the situation. Indigo still held Mina before him like a shield. If Joey struck, Indigo need move only a little and she'd cop the venom. Smart. Nasty. Sickening.

Mina thrashed, weaker this time, her pretty eyes bulging. Indigo sniffed her hair fondly, spit-dripping fingers still fixed over her nose and mouth. "Better make up your mind, Joey. She smells tired."

Joey screeched, the grating wail of a reptile in pain, and coiled his flexible body tight. "Get your handsss off my girl."

Indigo chuckled, dark. "Too late. Look, she's already giving in. Mirror, DiLuca, or she dies for my curiosity. What a waste."

Joey writhed, green venom frothing from his teeth to stain his suit. Shining fangs clashed together in fury, and he ripped the mirror from his pocket and flung it.

Hard. High. Venom splashing the floor. The ball curved glinting through the air, into the empty space between me and Indigo.

Too high. Too fast. Out of reach.

The mirror razored open, screaming like stretching glass as it flew, and overhead, the lightbulb flickered and dimmed in terror.

My pulse hammered my flesh to putty. Crazy impulse clutched at me to let it fall just to spite them all. Indigo needed that mirror in one piece, to give to his lousy demon mistress. So did Joey.

But so did I. Without it, I had no cure. If it smashed, we were all screwed.

And I couldn't catch worth a damn.

Caution melted in a hot flush of terror, and blind reflex jerked me into a run.

My legs stretched and strove. I careered closer, thrusting my wings against warm air for extra speed. The mirror flexed in the air like a gymnast at the top of its curve and started to fall.

I bunched my thigh muscles and launched into the air.

Indigo's hand flashed out, and he leapt.

Mina tumbled to the dust, screeching for breath. Joey streaked to her side in a scrape of rippling scales.

I stretched my arm for the mirror, wings straining to hold me. It bobbled sharp on my fingerpads. Triumph splashed warm fudge over my heart, and I tumbled back to complete the catch.

But ozone burst fresh in my nose, and cold static snapped the air. My hair sprang taut. My teeth zinged, and harsh magnetic field yanked at my earrings, my belly ring, the zip on my dress.

The mirror careered away like a planet smashed out of orbit, and landed with a metallic crack in Indigo's outstretched palm.

Below us, Akash dived on Joey, cackling like a mad thing with his bloody teeth bared. Joey snarled and fought back, snaky body squirming.

Ten feet above the ground, Indigo and I collided.

Breath thudded from my lungs in a hot metal haze, and I fell.

Rough concrete slammed into my shoulder, crushing my ribs together. My wings ripped, agonizing. I rolled over, groaning, and strong blue fingers snaked around my wrist, dragging me to unwilling feet.

I stumbled as he tugged me away into the dark, conflicting emotions blurring my eyes again. I wanted to slap his lying face. I wanted to cling to him and let him take care of me, recover that wonderful mix of freedom and safety I'd felt in his arms. I wanted him to kiss me. I never wanted him to touch me again.

I sucked in air, fatigue already spiking my chest, and together we ran.

21

Joey slams Akash's skull into the concrete one more time. Blood sprays, and at last the stubborn fucker shudders between Joey's clamped thighs and falls limp.

Panting, Joey climbs off and crawls over in a rainbow blood slick to retrieve his cane. He doesn't bother looking around for the fairies. He knows they're gone, heard their mincing footsteps pissing off into the dark. The mirror gone with them. Again.

Frustration seethes under his black-mottled skin, and he heaves to his feet with an angry hiss. Pain stabs his injured knee, and he forces the joint to shift, stretching snakethin and back again to shut it the fuck up. Bones click together, and the pressure eases.

Around him in the dark, trapped creatures screech and moan. He should set them free. In the light, Mina sprawls, bloody, her breath dragging in ragged gasps bereft of music. Smooth pale thigh shows through her ripped leather pants. Her lovely blue hair is ragged, torn by razor copper claws.

Rage thrusts icy needles into his blood. He slithers scales and fins away with a wet squelch and stalks up to her, leaning on his cane to offer her his bloody hand. "Get up."

Her jeweled eyes shine bloodshot, her face bruised, but her lips spread in a smile and she makes a weak laugh. "You let him take it . . . for me. To save me."

"Yeah." The stupidity ripples his skin. But her hand slides warm and delicate in his, her nails jagged. Their blood mingles. She's so warm. So fragrant. He pulls her to her feet. She winces at torn muscles and stumbles on her heels, but doesn't recoil.

He steadies her. Her curving waist feels good, the damp leather tasty, a fleeting brush of exposed skin.

"Thank you." Shyly, she lifts her chin, offers herself, baring a seductive glimpse of throat.

He can't help it. Another kiss, and this time their lips melt together, gentle and searching, and his cold blood ignites. Her hot candy lips move under his so delicately. Her tongue so soft, her taste so delicate and clean. Her wrist so fine and slender in his palm. Her small breasts perfect against his chest. The fresh feminine smell of her skin. His pulse quickens; he's dangerously hard. The snake writhes and seethes with venom, only a whisper's width beneath his skin.

But he can't. He'll break her, or himself. He'll forget what's important.

The family is everything. Power is everything. His own obsession—call it what it is—is insignificant. Mina is nothing.

He drifts back, just an inch. Already his lips cool. She whimpers and presses for more, but he grips that fine wrist and forces her away. "Don't thank me, Mina. You were careless. I paid for it. Don't ever put me in that position again."

And before he can see her expression, he limps away, leaning on his cane. His pulse thudding a warning. His flesh burning to change.

He doesn't need to listen for her shuffle to know she'll follow.

. . .

Joey's crippled footsteps fade, and Akash flicks his eyes open.

He giggles, fresh with blood. He's not so easily dealt with. The little snake man is too confident.

Pain caresses his limbs as he staggers to his feet. He can't breathe through his mangled nose. A steel pin in his lip dangles loose, and he rips it out and tosses it aside in a scarlet spray. His pretty inked skin oozes with venombright cuts. He wipes the mess away. His left arm bends awkwardly, bones scraping.

He laughs again. Such sweet sensation. He enjoyed the blood rush, the pain, the power. Fighting is fun. He'll do it more.

He enjoyed that dark blue fairy, too. He'd like those magnets for himself. Soon he'll get that blue fairy and drink it.

Pure warm covetousness spreads inside him. Yes. This is what earth means. Wanting. Satisfying urges, one after another. He'll like it here.

More laughter pleasures his bruised lungs, and he reaches inside for his healing energy. His split skin ripples, mending, but inside his shattered arm, it sputters short.

He wobbles the arm. Pain still flares, the bones not knitted. Pity. He likes this body. He enjoyed the yellow girl's reaction to it. Thinking of her makes him warm inside. Her wonderful spiky magic just beyond reach under his tongue, her spicy kiss, her tough lithe body. If he had the shiny glass, he could find her.

He doesn't.

"Akash?" Shy footsteps sidle up behind him, honey-sweet.

He sighs, dissatisfied, and turns.

Indra bows her head, hands clasped in front of her, her sly gaze darting upward. "I've brought you a gift."

Her skin looks flushed, her mouth curling with satisfaction. Curiosity pierces him like a dart. What has she done? "Show me."

She tugs a gleaming figure into the light. Firefairy, slim and pretty, flame dripping like sunlight off its wings. Baffled glaze in its eyes.

Indra smiles hopefully.

Akash frowns. "I've got one. Do better."

Indra slips her little hand in his, grating his broken arm, stopping him from turning away. "But he showed me. I understand now. I want to please you." Her faces shines up at him, glowing with hope.

Her lips are bruised and bitten. Her face flushed. Faint teethmarks on her throat. The smell of charcoal spoiling her honey.

Jealousy stabs harder than the pain. She's touched the thing. Kissed it. Let it touch her. Had it inside her body like a dirty human.

Rich anger spikes Akash's blood like a drug. She's ruined. Rotten. Poisoned. Just like everything else in this hellburnt city. He knows what to do with poison. Oh, yes.

Tenderly, he fingers her wounded neck. "Thank you, Indra. Now we must find the yellow girl's mirror."

She beams up at him, and nausea slides cold in his stomach. But he knows what must be done.

He kisses her cheek, but her taste is pale, faded. Dirty. Not like home. She tries to kiss him back, but he averts his face. "It's time for you to go now."

"Home?" She brightens, pleased.

"Not home."

Her face drains. "No. Please, Akash, not that."

"Yes, Indra." He fondles her hair for a moment. She meant something once. But she's a resource. He must use her.

Her lips tremble. "Wait, Akash. Let me—"

He wraps his fingers around her throat and squeezes.

She chokes, her eyes goggling, and he slams his mouth onto hers and swallows. Rich, smooth, helpless, the candy taste of blood.

All too soon, it's done. He lets her lifeless body drop. Her energy flows inside him, sparking his muscles afresh. He flexes, and with an electric snap, his broken arm heals. His nose squelches back into shape. His split lips knit smooth. The scratches on his ink fade and sink back into smooth skin.

He scrapes back bloodstained hair and laughs, rich with flame and warm banshee music.

The firefairy stares, its mouth dropping open. "Holy shit. Whatever she did, it wasn't with me, okay?"

Akash eyes it, uninterested. He should just crush it. It makes no sense, and it ruined Indra. And he's already got one, already stolen its flames. But a worm of warm desire coils in his blood. It's nice to look at. Maybe he could play with it. Fight with it. Maybe it can teach him. He walks up to it. "You're very pretty."

"Well, thanks, darlin'. You're . . . umm . . . kinda interesting yourself." The thing licks its red-stained lips, a golden flicker of interest over unease in its eyes.

Intriguing. Akash lifts its chin with a speculative finger, curiosity aching his flesh. "It doesn't . . . pain you that I drank her?"

A bold black stare, encouraging. "That's your business. Look, I like your style, Akash. I saw you stirring shit up at the club. I don't know what you're up to, but I want in."

It knows his name. Fascinating. "Why?"

"Damage. Breaking things. Cool stuff like that. What I see, you're the champion." Inviting flames finger its pretty red hair.

Smug warmth coats Akash's blood. Flattery. Pleasant. He leans closer, sniffs the thing's mouth for scent. Fire, ash, a hint of Indra's lost honey, an earthy taste, not hellish but exciting. Delicious. His body reacts, stormlike, a careless blood rush. He shouldn't get distracted like this, but it feels good. "No. It's not possible."

It bites its lip, sultry. "You mentioned a yellow girl's mirror. I can help you, if you'll let me go."

Even more interesting. Akash licks its cheek, and sweet cherry blood pleasures his tongue. "How?"

"I know her. I can take you to it. Or bring it to you."

He brings it nearer, and its body feels tight and feverish, warming his newly healed skin. He wants to play with it, make it talk, learn its secrets. Akash grips its throat, holding it away. "Later. First, show me what you did."

22

Blackness engulfed us. My footsteps thudded unevenly as I scrambled to keep up with Indigo's loping insect strides. He tugged me behind him as we ran in darkness, enveloped in shimmering static. "Closer," he panted. "Glamour. They can't see."

Shapes loomed out of the gloom, and I swerved, stumbling. He yanked my wrist, dragging me along. My temper flared with the breath searing my lungs, and I forced out a ragged whisper. "I can't fucking see, okay? It's pitch-black in here!"

"Shh. Metal. I can see just fine. Duck."

A broken steel girder flashed by above my head, and we were out.

Moonlight scattered on black pavement littered with broken glass. High alley walls on either side, shadows lurching. Behind us, Akash's warehouse loomed, tall and gray, broken windows glinting as clouds scudded away from the moon. Lightning split the sky, chased a second later by growling thunder. The air stank of imminent rain, humidity thick and metallic on my skin. Normally I loved storms. But now the smell recalled touching Indigo, and I felt sick.

We rounded the corner under a flickering yellow streetlight. Cars growled past, raindrops splashing dusty on their paint. Neon signs glowed in rainbows, cafés and takeaways and pawnbrokers. Civilization. Good.

"Let me go, okay?" I yanked my hand free. Awareness still prickled electric along my fingers, and I propped on my knees to catch my breath and tried to ignore it. Sweat dripped down my elbows, and water trickled onto my shoulders from my stress-sodden hair. I scowled at him, and sorrow wore my voice thin. "You've got your mirror. You can go now. Off you flutter, back to your skanky demon mistress. I'm sure she'll show you a good time."

But he'd already backed me up against a window.

My pulse swelled, treacherous, and my aching body sparked at his touch. I trembled, furious. "What are you doing?"

His hair flashed jagged in lightning silhouette. His eyes glowed violet. He pressed his body against mine, curving his wings to shield me, his hot fingers alive in my hair. Lightning stabbed again, closer, and static cracked alight on his dark skin in sympathy. Electricity crawled over his wings like tiny green fairylights.

He bruised my face with kisses, his lips hot and urgent on my cheeks, my forehead, my eyelids. "Lady Ice. My precious queen. You okay? He hurt you? Christ, I hope Joey kicks the living crap outta him. And then dies a horrible spiky death. Both of them, I mean. God, I can't talk, let me just . . ." And he captured my mouth with his, and every angry, indignant, bitter word I wanted to scream at him dissolved like icicles in the sun.

His lips melted with mine like warm metal, and desire rippled down my spine, pleasure knifing deep and swift like a poisoned dagger.

I fought it; yes, I did. My common sense squirmed like a chopped rat. I didn't want him. I couldn't.

But god, his mouth felt so good on mine. So slick and warm, so perfect. And his lean body next to mine, so rich and fragrant, it sprang my every nerve alive. Tiny raindrops spattered on my face, the tinkle of rain dull in my ears beneath our twin heartbeats. I couldn't think. I couldn't resist. I just plastered wet palms against the glass and kissed him back.

No fair.

His kiss tortured me, deep, hard, desperate. I sighed into him, heat dripping down to fill my breasts, harden my nipples, make my belly and my sex ache. He held my chin with gentle fingers and eased my mouth open farther, and I drew his long curled tongue onto mine and reveled in the dark metal taste of him, the slick tartness of his mouth, the sharp steely edges of his teeth.

He murmured darkly and obliged me, claiming my mouth with his tongue, letting my taste slide over him. A deep shiver spread inside me, filling me like steaming water. When Akash opened me like that, I wanted to spew. Now I wanted to swallow, consume him, make this beautiful fairy mine forever. Forget that he'd deceived me and lie down under him, peel his clothes away, give him everything.

But he had deceived me. My mind raced, rebelled, fought, even as my body reacted with fierce desire to his caress. My hands lost themselves on his chest, palming his curving metal shapes, sliding around to his back, the curve of his shoulder, the smooth chill of his wings. He groaned into my mouth and pushed closer. Not subtle, this time, not slow or careful but ravaging, hungry, crushing his hard thighs into mine, his trembling cock into my hip. He slid one hand down over my breast, squeezing me, searching with hungry claws for my nipple.

I didn't want him touching my breasts. He'd lied to me. But he found my aching nipple and twisted, and pleasure stabbed deep. He'd used me. I didn't want this. My claws ripped into his shoulders, my hands wrenching with need. Moisture flooded me, so abrupt my muscles hurt and my skin stretched painfully. Rain and water ran down the glass to soak my back, my wings, my clothes. My sex swelled too tight, too hard. My hands itched to make him feel the same. I wanted to caress those hard fae muscles, trace my claws along the ridges, slide my fingers along his cock and make him shiver.

And I wanted to rake my claws down his face and scream at him for betraying me.

He nudged my chin upward and trailed burning kisses down my neck, his teeth lingering lovingly on my collarbone. I shivered, swallowing a desperate groan of pleasure and need. Damn it. Only he did this to me. Only he could make me want so hard when I wanted not to so much.

Anger swilled acid into my desire, and I jammed my palms against his tempting hips—oh, god, how I wanted to drop to my knees and suck those slender bones into my mouth, rip his clothes away and slide his cock deep into my throat and swallow him—I sank fury-tense claws into his hips and shoved him away.

His mouth slipped from my skin, his gasp a soft accusation. I wanted to tear my hair, smash the glass, scrape my claws on the concrete. I'd never kiss him like that again, and it relieved me and terrified me at the same time.

He stared, his taut lips shining, jagged blackmetal hair falling wild in his glowing eyes. His static-bright wings quivered. His chest heaved, coppery sweat staining his black shirt, a tempting flash of skin showing where I'd torn the cloth. He blinked at me, confusion shadowing his eyes, and pressed the back of his hand to his lips, shaking his head like he was lost.

Switch. Just like at Quang's. Like he flicked over from someplace else.

Is he sparkled up, or what? Who was I just talking to? Who just kissed me like he meant the living hell out of it? And where was that fairy now? Damn metalfae. Crazy as a snake missing its ass.

He touched his lips again, caressing the wetness I'd left there. "Ice? Where are we? What just happened?"

"You're such an asshole, you know that?" I yanked my top straight where our unexpected passion had tugged it awry. The cotton glued to my damp skin, the friction an unwelcome distraction. My breasts still hurt, my nipples demanding his touch, his mouth. My wings strained for contact, shared flight, the rasp of silver. My sex still flowed with slick moisture, glands aching under pressure. My flesh was swollen, my most tender parts pressing against each other uncomfortably. Every movement was a torture, and staring from two feet away at this beautiful copper-and-midnight fairy boy with my spit on his lips didn't help. Scrunched-up hair, wet shirt sticking to his rippled fae chest, silver wings afire with electric lust. My pulse throbbed. God, he looked sexy. Whoever the hell he was.

He reached out to touch me, but I waved my arm to ward him off, and he clenched his fist and pulled it away, his forearm muscles tense. "Please. Humor me. I'm . . . My memory's not so good these days. What happened?"

I folded my arms, trying to tear my gaze away, but it kept bouncing back on invisible rubber bands. "Don't pull this moody trick on me again, okay? It isn't funny."

"No, it isn't. We got the mirror, right?"

"Oh, so you don't remember frightening the crap out of me in that warehouse? Strangling that girl half to death?"

A flush tainted his dark cheeks silver. "Okay. And the shiny—?"

"It's in your back pocket! What the hell's wrong with you?"

"Nothing. It's okay. You have to go. Now." He scrabbled the mirror from his pocket and pressed it into my hands. "Take it. Leave. Before it's too late."

"What? No! Indigo, what's going on?" I backed off along the

window, frustration searing my nerves to crisps. "Why'd you kiss me, if you're just gonna push me away?"

He released his breath in a rush, his firedark gaze intent on mine. Coppery sweat slicked his cheeks. "I'm sorry. I shouldn't have done that, okay? Just get out of here before he comes back. There's not much time." He grabbed my hand and wrapped my fingers around the steel, forcing my grip tight. "Take it. Go to Kane. Get your cure and don't come back."

The metal stung cold and lonely in my palm, but it soothed compared with the empty chill in my heart. "No way. I don't buy it. What's really going on? Why'd you spend all this time hunting for this thing and half getting yourself killed about a dozen times because of me, just to hand it over? And what about the demon bitch? What did she promise you? Money? Power? Or just the fucking fun of it?" Cold fury ripped my voice to shreds. I shoved away from the window, resentment seething in my blood along with embarrassment that I'd let him kiss me like that, responded like that when I knew he'd betrayed me. I couldn't believe I'd fallen for his sweet tricks. He'd used me, and now he pretended none of it mattered.

He sighed, exasperation sparking scarlet on his breath. "Don't be like that. You're not the only one who gets threatened around here, okay? I'll get away from her somehow."

Disbelief nailed my lungs tight. He wasn't tricking me for kicks? "She's chasing you? Like, you'll go to hell?"

"I don't care about that. I care about you. Get out of here."

My heart juddered. The wind rose, swirling cool raindrops onto my burning face, and thunder clashed like iron. My nerves exalted, mirrortoxic excitement flooding my veins. My nose sparkled, and I slapped my wings together to stop them fluttering. "You what?"

He eyed me steadily, hair ruffling in ozone-fresh breeze. "It's yours. Take it. I don't want it anymore."

Horror chewed at my skin like hungry ants. He'd chance a demon's wrath for me. So I could be cured, of a glorious blood-burning madness that half the time I wasn't sure I didn't want anyway.

He'd go to hell for my cowardice.

Helpless admiration washed warm currents over my heart. That was so romantic.

And so maddening, I could punch his fine-angled midnight face. I shook my head and thrust the mirror out to him, straining my arm so he'd take it. "Oh, no, you don't. I'm not sending you to hell so I can feel good about myself. That's not fair."

"And I'm not letting you die for my bad decisions." His breath struggled, his eyes wild like he fought inside with some unseen beast, but he wouldn't drop his gaze. Wouldn't take the damn mirror from my hand. I shook it, terror rippling my muscles, but he wouldn't move.

I wanted to roll on the ground and kick my legs and scream. I wanted to grab him and run, anywhere we could hide and pretend this wasn't happening. I stuck my hand on my hip, trying to look pissed off and in control, but my voice trembled around a stupid lump in my throat. My eyes watered. I wiped them roughly, streaking my face. *Damn it.* "Like you care what I want. You just don't want it to be your fault."

Blue lightning arced from his wing tips to spike the wet ground, and hissing steam whipped away in the rising wind. His eyes flashed a dangerous violet, lashes sparking. "I never want it to be my fault again."

"What do you mean?"

His gaze slipped. "Doesn't matter."

I jumped up and down, frustration jerking my calves, my skirt flopping. "It does matter! You can't just lay that out there and then clam up. That is so your problem, you know that? All that strong and silent shit really fucks you up."

He closed his eyes and sighed, slow and weary. "Fine."

"Yeah, fine. Go ahead. Shut me out ag—"

"Wanna hear the story or not?" His jaw tensed, tendons sharp, and his teeth made a little metal shriek.

Truth at last? I swallowed, nerves tingling. "Oh. Okay. Sure. Go ahead."

He slumped against the glass beside me and rubbed his eyes with thumb and forefinger, coppery lashes springing. "I knew someone once. A human woman, Natasha. I loved her so much, it hurt my eyes to look at her. We roamed together. We thieved together, and one night she . . . We were climbing from a pit, running away, and she couldn't fly. She fell, and I didn't catch her." Silver tears slipped onto his cheeks, scattered by raindrops.

My heart squeezed tight, and tears stung my eyeballs. I tried to imagine how I'd feel if Blaze or Azure died in front of me. If Sonny had shot Indigo while I stood there. "I'm sure it wasn't your f—"

"I tried, but . . . I was angry with her, you see. She'd pretended to love me so I'd help her to the treasure." He raked his wet hair flat and ruffled it again, frustrated. "The mirror, Ice, okay? We were stealing the mirror from Kane's temple in hell, all spiketraps and burning pits and trip wires like it is, and when we got there, she . . . Well, she'd meant to trick me all along. She trapped me there for Kane to find so she could have the mirror for herself. She broke my heart and I hated her for it. I . . . I don't remember the things I hissed at her, but they were awful. If I'd just let her leave me, she'd have been safe. But I had to fight with her, didn't I, I had to scream insults at her, and Kane found us both. We . . . I broke the chains and fled, and she followed me, it was steep and rocky and without wings she couldn't climb fast enough. She begged me to help her. . . ." Indigo squeezed his eyes shut, wetness filling his lashes.

I swallowed. "It's okay—"

"No, it isn't, Ice. I was so angry with her for lying to me. I shoved her away and she . . . she fell. I tried to catch her. I really did. I held on so tight. But my fingers were bloody, and . . . and her little hand was so small. I couldn't hold her. She died because of me, Ice. I can't let you die because of me, too. They're my consequences. I won't let you suffer them."

Icy shards ripped deep into my heart. Jesus. No wonder he was so afraid of girls. Of liking a girl. Was that why he'd acted like such an ice-walled prick for so long? Because he feared he might like me?

I'd finally gotten him to admit it, and now one of us had to die?

I slid timid fingers onto his arm, but gently he brushed them away.

His gaze settled on me again, silver sparkling on his lashes, and the determination glowing there made me shiver. "There's more, Ice. Please. Just listen. I looked into the mirror that day, to see what was so damn important that I'd lost her. Ever since then, I . . . well, it's like I'm split in two. There's this shadow half of me locked away, the part that could love her . . . but it's the part that hated her, too, and it's dark and angry and dangerous and . . . and I can't control it, Ice. I black out and I wake up somewhere else, and I don't know where I've been or what I've done."

His molten gaze shifted, just for an instant, and my throat hurt. That rainbow titanium bangle, so snug now on his left wrist. I was right. It didn't come off. It swapped, whenever he felt like it. He was two fairies, and at least one of him had known it all along.

Two fairies. Indigo's kindness, flashing in and out like neon. No accident. The way he kissed me, so hot and passionate and full of desperate emotion. But whose? How was I supposed to tell? None of it was real.

My throat burned tight. "So everything you've said to me is a lie, is that it?"

"No!" His jaw tightened, pulse shifting. "No, Ice. You make me forget it all. You make me want to be whole again, and I . . . I don't know what to do. I'm crippled. I don't know how to give you what you need. I'm sorry. Just take the mirror and go."

Lightning crackled, deafening. I rubbed my arms, chill aching my bones though the stormy air stuck hot and thick to my skin. "So what, I'm just supposed to let some demon bitch tear you apart?"

He shrugged, casual, though unease leaked dark blue ink into his eyes. "I'll get rid of her somehow."

Anger skewered my nerves. "That is such boy bullshit, you know that? She's a fucking demon. You don't get rid of demons."

He eyed me steadily, calm, ineluctable, unmovable. "Ice, there's no other way."

"There must another way!" Tears slashed at my eyes, and words rushed unstoppable from my tongue. "Don't you see, I can't do this! I can't let you do it. It's not so bad, all right? I'm not so nuts. It's just this . . . this urge to do stupid things and live on the edge and say every idiot thing that slips into my head and when you threw me off that skyscraper I was scared shitless but I've never felt so fucking good in my entire life and . . . and I want to be brave and crazy and reckless but I don't know if I can do it alone, and you helped me see that for once in my sorry little life I'm *not* alone, and if I have to do it without you I think I'll die right now and get it over with because I'm in love with you and if you push me away one more time I'll break into a million screeching bleeding little pieces and make a big mess and Christ I can't believe I said that."

Hair whipped my cheeks in the rising wind, and I left it there, tears fresh on my face. For once I didn't care if he laughed at me.

He swallowed, dragging hair from his cheeks with unsteady fingers. "Ice—"

The rain pelted harder, drowning out his voice in the battering sound of water on iron roofs and tiles and concrete. Fat raindrops drilled the pavement like bullets, splashing huge on my skin. My hair plastered to my face, warm and glorious, and my wings soaked transparent with sweet-smelling droplets. My watery senses lit like searchlights, and I wanted to dance, splash, lie down with him and roll in the puddles, run and whirl and jump until we were soaked.

Indigo slid his fingers into mine and tugged me around the corner for shelter, an alley under a slim line of eaves. Rain still soaked my clothes, splashed over his silvery wings, slid in shiny rivulets through his hair. Sapphire static crackled over him, arcing in random slices through the sheeting rain. So beautiful. My fingers zapped where he held me, and miniature lightning crackled up my forearm.

Storm water rushed around our ankles, overflowing, the noise swelling ever louder. He pushed me against the wall, curving his wings overhead to form an electrically charged silver cocoon. Static crawled in my hair, lifting the soaked strands, and magnetism tugged the jewel in my belly taut, teasing me like caressing fingers.

He planted his hands either side of my head, leaning over so I could hear him above the din, and his voice came out low and strained and full of unexpected pain. "I'm so sorry. I can't bear that you're unhappy because of me. Tell me what to do."

He smelled fantastic wet, warm iron mixing with rust. My mouth watered. His dripping hair slicked on my cheek, his breath tickling the point of my ear. My fingers tightened around the mirror, and my voice shook. "Just be honest with me. That's all I want."

He dropped his head, water spilling from his hair, his gaze for once level with mine. His eyes shone blue at me through the rain, copper lashes rimmed with wet diamonds. "You're so precious and wonderful and innocent. You clean me, Ice. You wash my guilt away. I can't . . . I don't know if I want to live with you hating me."

Light welled from some lost cavern deep in my soul and showered me with glittering delight that melted the tension inside me to glowing honey. Laughter bubbled from my mouth, and I let it flow.

He stared at me, wounded, and backed off, his wings folding sheepishly in sheets of water. "What?"

"Nothing." I laughed more, old shackles cracking open at last in my chest. We were drenched. My skin would shrivel up like a rotten orange. He'd probably rust. I didn't care. The cowering specter of my fear rubbed its scrawny arms, shook itself in wonder, and scampered away giggling. I'd been afraid for nothing. He actually cared about me.

He hadn't said as much. I mean, he didn't say, *Ice, I love you more than a million diamonds, be with me forever*, or anything silly like that. But I meant something to him, even if only for a moment while we stood here yelling at each other to be heard in this glorious rain. He had ice around his heart, this one, his affection frozen deep by a horrible mistake. But warmth still burned in there, and for one diamond-precious moment, he'd let me in. If that's the best he could offer, it was good enough for me.

And if I hadn't lost my mind—if I hadn't been so pissed off at his coldness that I went home with Kane and stumbled across this ugly mirror—none of it would have happened.

Maybe some things are just fate, and you shouldn't rage against the chaos or squeeze your eyes shut to pretend they aren't happening. Sometimes you just have to leap off a skyscraper and trust you'll be caught.

I stepped slowly up to him, my limbs shaking. He just stood

there, staring at me, rain-jewels glittering on his lashes and dripping through his hair. I placed my hand on his chest, where he was warm and slick under my palm. His heartbeat quickened, and I struggled to keep my voice calm. "Delilah . . . If you don't take her the mirror, she'll never stop chasing you."

He covered my hand in his. Pressed my palm to his chest. Tucked his copper claws under mine. His irises swirled like molten metal, blue and green darkening to hot maroon. "And if I do, you'll never stop haunting me."

I stared, mesmerized by the rain, transfixed by his eerie beauty. He drifted closer on an electric flicker of wings, clasping my hand close against his chest, and softly his body brushed mine. His long blue fingers wrapped mine completely.

He laid his forehead on mine and closed his eyes. His hair splashed my face, his silver lips sparkling with raindrops. "I need you, Ice. You're all I have that's good. I don't want you to leave me. But . . ."

My heart overflowed, and the fine mesh that remained of my defenses washed away like glitter on a moonlit beach. Shuddering, I fluttered up on my tiptoes and pressed my lips on his.

His shock flickered static between our mouths for one bright second. My teeth tingled, alive. And then he tightened his fingers around mine and kissed me back.

We'd kissed a couple minutes ago, hot and lustful and unforgiving. But this was different. Gentle, shy, a single soft kiss, then another, and another, longer but still hesitant, like we feared something would break. His lips melted into mine, so soft and yet steely, so tender and yet full of anguish and pain and desperate loss.

My chest ached. This was insane. It wouldn't solve anything. But warmth spilled into me like hot chocolate, dark and rich and delicious, making me want more of him, more of this glorious sharp-sweet world where he let me love him. His dark metal taste stung my tongue, thrilling me, and the care in our kiss only made me want him harder.

I pressed closer, searching for more. He let me lead him, caress his mouth with mine, part his lips so I could taste him. I tempted his tongue with mine, drawing him out until he hissed deep inside his chest and crushed his arm around my waist, lifting me and pulling me flush with his body as we kissed. The warm smell of metal enveloped me, the steely muscles of his arm, his hard body, the crunch of his bangle into the small of my back. Rainwater spilled in the echo of thunder, and static crackled across my skin like hungry fingers, creeping under my wet clothes, into my hair.

He deepened the kiss, crushing me against him in a velvet metal embrace like he never wanted to let me go. My fingers clenched around the mirror, frustrated. I wanted my hand free to touch him, undress him, feel his skin under my fingerpads. I wanted to throw the damn thing to the ground and hear it scream and shatter.

"Here." He slipped the sphere from my hand and fumbled it back into his pocket. Rain ran into our kiss, warm, the dusty taste mingling with the glorious sting of iron. My watery senses overloaded, my whole body thrumming with sensation. I grabbed his sodden hair and held him there, swallowing, his tongue alive and insistent in my mouth. His hair bloodied my knuckles, stinging like paper cuts, but I didn't care. I loved the metal slide of his teeth, the molten slickness of his lips.

Our wet bodies plastered together, and the sleek hardness of those delectable fairy muscles slid slowly against me as he moved, a full-body caress that ignited my nerves like matches. The steely twist of his cock pressed into my belly, coated in soaked cloth but scorching me. Mirror or no mirror, I burned for him, this strange metal maniac who'd driven me so efficiently out of my mind.

Urgency chewed like a plague of insects. I wrapped my thigh

around him, but he was too tall for what I wanted, and with a slick crunch I popped my hip joint so I could reach, curling my calf around his waist. My muscles protested, but it was worth it just to feel him at last. He slid his dripping hand up my thigh and pulled me onto him, and when I remembered my underwear was already gone and his claws were digging into my bare bottom, my last wispy inhibition evaporated. I wanted him. Here. Now. Before this dissolved in a sweet dream like it always had before.

He slid his kiss to the corner of my mouth, my jawline, nudged my chin up to kiss a trail of hot desire down to my throat, his lips lingering on the vein, tasting the throbbing pulse of my excitement. Cuts still stung there, and he traced them with his tongue, murmuring. Tension stirred, tugged, awakened inside me. My breasts ached for him. I gripped his hair and pulled him downward.

He nuzzled the wet cloth of my halter, nipping at me with sharp metal teeth. His tongue wrapped over one nipple through the thin cotton. Gentle sensation flared deep, warming my whole body. He sucked me slowly, gently, drawing my pleasure out until I moaned.

My muscles weakened, and my head fell back. My eyes slid closed. Such care. Men have always taken me quickly, carelessly, hot and breathless but empty. I'd never been anywhere like this before.

Gently he tugged at the knot of my halter, and it slipped free.

The old fear whetted my desire sharp, and I slipped my hand up to clutch the cloth in place. "Someone might see."

"I want to see." He kissed my collarbone, biting me softly, his fingers tracing my breast, drawing me on.

The ache between my legs blossomed and grew, and I shivered. "Please. Not here. Can't we go somewhere else?"

He kissed my fingers where I held the cloth, and slipped his arm tighter around my waist. His whisper burned my throat. "Hold on."

And with a flit of silvery wings and a shower of raindrops, he leapt into the air.

We darted upward, and I clutched my legs around his hips and pressed my cheek on his chest. His heartbeat echoed in my ear, swift and strong, rain and his coppery sweat tingling sharp and delightful in my nose. His body felt wonderfully warm and safe, his steely embrace unbreakable as with wings and one strong arm he flitted up a drainpipe, copper claws snicking on brick. For an instant he lurched backwards under dripping iron eaves, flaring his wings wide to keep aloft, and then we were on the roof, his feet lighting almost soundlessly on sloping water-rippled iron.

Clouds rumbled, steel and silver, close and warm like I could touch them, and the rain fell unfettered, spilling over my shoulders, into my mouth, running sweet tingles down my back. Lightning cracked, deafening. He flipped me around and crushed my back to his chest. He leant over to lick hot shivers into my ear, and his teeth nipped me, exquisite. "There. Now no one can see us."

A breathless smile parted my lips. God, I loved the rain. I curled backwards against him, and at the touch of my wings, he murmured and rubbed his cheek against the springy edge. He kissed my neck, my throat, my shoulders, wrapping me in hot ribbons of sensation, and when his fingers crept once again to my halter, I let him peel the wet cloth from my breasts. My nipples stung hard in the warm trickling rain, and gently he laid me on my back on the smooth iron.

Inch-deep water gushed, spilling down past me toward the gutter. Tingles swept my skin as the water drenched my wings, slid between my toes, around my clutching fingers, into my hair. I blissed out, desire melting deep into my guts. My own water splashed out to be lost in the deluge. I felt the rush in my mouth, my lungs, my blood, a rich drawing-out of current that teased my flesh into hot delight.

He hovered over me, an inch away, his body brushing mine with the lightest of touches, and his mouth sought mine with sweet reverence that sparked my desire hotter. He spread his wings over us in a glittering silver shelter, deflecting the raindrops in electric blue sizzles as he dragged his sharp wet hair over my throat, my chest, my breasts.

"No," I murmured into his mouth, sliding his lips on mine, our breath mingling hot and sticky. "Don't. I want to be drenched. Let me— Oh."

He flashed back his wings and wrapped his tongue over my nipple. Tasting me, pleasuring me. Sensation stabbed straight to my sex. I groaned, the contact too much to bear and at the same time not enough. He sucked, and I arched my back, straining toward him. "Please. Touch me. I want to feel you. Please."

A soft dark laugh sizzled my breast, and he shifted to my other nipple, kissing and licking and sucking it with the same slow torture as the first. Still his body barely touched mine. Avoided me as I wriggled to reach him, easily evaded my strength as I locked my hands behind his back and tried to pull him down onto me.

I shivered, afire. I was right. He'd take his time, and it might kill me.

He kissed his way down my body, trailing hot tingling bumps. Metal fangs grazed my hipbone, nibbled at my belly. His breath sizzled my wet skin. Anticipation clenched my inner muscles tight. God, I wanted his tongue inside me again. The flesh between my legs was slick and sore, begging for contact. My clit ached. I gave up trying to pull him onto me and just held him there, wrapping his sharp hair around my knuckles and urging him downward.

He lifted my sodden skirt and licked up the inside of my thigh, scenting me as he went. He parted my legs and sniffed me to drink in my flavour, and gave a fiery little groan that inflamed me. "You smell like sunshine. I've dreamed of your smell." And he slid his tongue up my slit in one hot, loving stroke, and fastened his lips on my clit.

My knuckles ripped bloody in his hair, and I cried out. God, he felt so good. Last time was instinct, my flesh yearning for release. This was pure pleasure. He teased me with his lips, sucking, coaxing the hard little bit of flesh out of hiding, and when he tongued that sensitive exposed tip, I choked back a scream, the pleasure struck me so deep. I felt it all the way through my body to my fingertips, like that very first wash of orgasm—only it wouldn't break, wouldn't stop, wouldn't let me go. My nerves thrummed with excruciating delight. My skin crackled with his sparks, and the water gushing over my skin only made it feel better.

I squirmed my head from side to side, hair sticking to my cheeks in the rain. My heart shone, so drugged with pleasure that I glowed, the water around me shining blue. Maybe I was foolish. Maybe I only imagined myself in love with him. But my body responded to him like I'd always imagined it would, every kiss and caress and lick of his tongue inflamed hotter and brighter not only because he treated me with honesty and delicacy and skill, but also because it was him doing it. I'd never felt anything like this. He deserved to know that. I tried to talk, but my words came out in a tortured groan. "Stop it. I want to make love with you. Please."

He just pressed harder, sweeter, slipping his tongue over me in tiny circles and swirls that dragged my pleasure to an even tighter peak. My bones shuddered, and I think I screamed, and then he sucked me deep into his mouth one more time and I was gone, over the edge, crashing like a waterfall to splash into delicious heaven. Hot ripples of pleasure slammed into me like a shock wave again and again, spilling out from his mouth on my sex to my spinal cord to explode on my skin in fevered shivers. He prolonged it with his tongue, exquisite, not letting me go until every last spasm wrung from my muscles and I fell limp.

I gasped for breath, my body shaking. Christ in a cream cheese sauce. That wasn't an orgasm. That was the apocalypse. The world had ended. I was dead.

But I wasn't. If I were dead, the kisses he was lavishing on my taut wet flesh wouldn't feel so good. He liked doing that, kissing me there like it was my mouth, caressing me with his lips, delving his tongue between my folds. He licked me once again, and my swollen clit protested, too sensitive. I jerked, helpless, and with a final reluctant kiss he let me go.

He climbed up my body, sliding at last over me, his weight light and metal-strong. I fumbled to undo his shirt and scraped the sodden black fabric away so I could feel his smooth flesh on mine, and when our bodies touched, skin at last on naked skin, delicious fire scorched my blood. He kissed me, deep and hard, our tongues mixing, the pollen taste of my fluid like roses in his mouth. I didn't usually like that, the taste of my own arousal. On him, it intoxicated me.

I slid my hands over the taut curve of his ass and wrapped my thighs around his hips, popping my joints to pull him closer. My skirt was rumpled and I pressed my bare flesh against him, still so sensitive, it hurt. His cock felt smooth and steely, and desperately I wormed my hands between us to search for the buttons on his rain-soaked jeans. They popped open one by one, and his cock sprang into my hand, hot and hard and slick already from the rain.

My flesh jerked in anticipation. Gosh. So taut, so swollen in my palm. So real and heated, that grating metal sound he made in his throat when I stroked him.

I wanted. I needed him now. Trembling, I stretched my thighs higher around him and guided him, slid him over me, panted as I pressed him against my aching clit—oh, god, again, just a little more—and then my swollen wet folds and finally searching deeper, to push him into me where he belonged.

He gasped, and stopped me with his hand on mine. "Ice . . . wait . . . you still don't understand."

Shit. Now he wants to talk. My body ached with frustration. The tip of his cock brushed me lightly, right where it felt so good, and I shuddered. My entrance clenched, searching hungrily for him, wanting to suck that hard twist of flesh deep inside, and it was all I could do not to force myself onto him. The world's first female fairy rapist. Classy.

"What is it?" I buried my face in his metal hair, glorying in the sting, and slid a desperate kiss up to his sleek pointed ear, nibbling on the tip. His cock swelled even tighter in my hand, and he groaned, jerking, slipping just that little farther into me. *Oh, yeah.* "You nervous? Me, too. It's okay." I chewed his earlobe, eliciting a sweet gasp and a shudder. "Or you like boys? I won't tell. If you're gonna come too soon . . ." I swallowed raindrops from his taut blue neck, the rich steely taste of him running down my throat. Tingling swept my tight flesh, wrenching me closer to the edge, hot hungry teeth gnawing deep inside me. I gasped, tortured. My wetness slid so, so easily over him. God, I wanted him inside me. "Doubt it. I'm sure we can—"

"Sometimes I'm not myself." He clenched his hand tighter on mine, forcing me to wait. "I might hurt you."

Fever just burned brighter in my veins, and the rainwater glowed neon blue. An inch from fucking me senseless, and he actually cares if he hurts me. How hopelessly romantic is that?

My muscles clenched with longing even as hot tears stung my eyes yet again, washed away by the slashing rain. I'm moved by such pitiful things. But I can't help it. He overflows me. He's too much for me.

I twisted my hand in his grip, fumbling to get him inside me. My breath quickened, harsh, raindrops stinging on my tongue. "Then hurt me. I don't care. I can take it. I just want to be yours."

"No. This is for you." And he swept us a few feet into the air with a silver flash of wings, his arm around my waist gently turning me over and laying me facedown in the sloshing runoff.

Water caressed my face, rich with iron and dust, just like him. He lighted onto my back, his hips pressing into mine, his cock slipping hard against my bottom and sliding between my thighs. Anticipation shivered my wing bones. I'd had a dream like this, and I'd come in my sleep without a touch. Would he do it like that? God, I hoped so. I parted my lips to let glorious water run into my mouth. "Kiss me. Please, kiss me."

He laid his palms on the iron either side of my head so he wouldn't squash me, and dipped his hot lips to my shoulder. Warm delight shivered down my back. He licked me, caressing me with molten kisses down my spine, between my trembling wing joints. The taut skin there yearned erect and quivered for his tongue, hard like my nipples. He found my wetness with his cock, slid over me, pressed against me right where I wanted him so bad, it hurt. My flesh constricted, tight. I gripped his wrists, one smooth, one metal-clad, and pressed my burning cheek to the iron roof.

He wrapped his tongue around the sensitive place where wing met shoulder. I gasped, shuddering. It felt so good, so gentle, so sweet. My thighs trembled, tingling. And then he sucked the joint right into his mouth and pushed into me.

Hot. Hard. Deep. Perfect. I whimpered at the sensation, his sigh of pleasure burning my shoulder, the warm iron roof pressing into my breasts, his smooth cock sliding into me, pushing my wet walls apart. Deliciously hard. I was so tight and swollen it hurt, glorious, unwilling muscles stretching. He pulled out a little and drove back in, harder, deeper, stifling a groan. Pain stabbed, the constriction in my muscles too much. But delight flamed more intensely than the pain. I bit my lip on a cry, blood stinging my tongue.

He flitted his wings softly, silver shimmering in reflection on the sheeting water. The shape of him filling me, rubbing his cock against secret sweet places inside me, spiked shivering delight deep into my bones. He brushed his cheek on my shoulder, his breath tight. "You okay with this?"

"I'm so much better than okay." My voice trembled. My muscles clenched inside, rippling over him. *God, I'm gonna come just lying here.*

He rocked against me, moving inside me, and with every movement he caressed me with his lips and tongue, right where it made my skin shiver. My eyes slid closed, and the world dissolved into a shimmering wet haze of delight. A pleasured sigh escaped me, and I let my head stretch back, hair dripping, my face exposed to the rain. He bit me softly, sucking, teasing his sharp teeth over my sensitive flesh until I moaned and wriggled, my pleasure rising too fast. He used the entire length of his cock to pleasure me, pushing into my deepest center and then pulling back until he was barely inside me at all. And then he'd enter me all over again, parting me and pushing deep inside. God, I loved that part, the moment when it goes in. How did he know that?

He groaned against me, slicking his cheek against my sodden wing. He eased into me, luxuriant, deep, and my flesh tingled and tensed. Static rippled across my back, and his wet hair tumbled on my cheek as his teeth grazed my shoulder. He gasped, and his cock swelled inside me, our fairy flesh melting together in hot delight.

Pleasure dazzled me breathless. He felt so good, so right. We fit so well. Sensation took root and flowered all over my body, so beautiful, I whimpered, unable to stop what was happening to me. "God, I love you."

He groaned and thrust deeper, quivering against my back in his pleasure, and as he seated himself fully, his hot iron breath exploded in a rush on my shoulder. "And I love you, beautiful girl."

That was enough. My hardened flesh spasmed, and orgasm tore me from inside like a blade. Harder, faster than the last, like hot wires sparking with his static deep under my skin, dragging pleasure from my center until I couldn't breathe. He moved with my body, pressed me tight to him, let me come on him, my muscles clamping on the hard twist of his cock. My claws dug into his wrists, drawing silvery blood. His arm muscles juddered, and he gasped with the effort of holding himself back.

I pushed my hips back onto him, helpless, my pleasure not done. Already another spasm built inside me. He licked my ear, brushed his lips down my cheekbone, sought my mouth over my shoulder to kiss me. His mouth tasted of iron and rain. His whisper sizzled my cheek, molten, laced with urgent coppery desire. "I can't do this much longer. I want to kiss you. I want to see your face."

Swiftly he slipped himself from me and rolled me over, flicking rusty water from his wings. After his body, the rain-soaked iron chilled my back. I gazed up at him, enraptured. So beautiful, the midnight curves of his slender fae chest, his narrow blue hips, the lovely intricate fae shape of his cock, still slick with my juices. Lightning crashed, illuminating his jagged dark hair with a halo of gold.

I swallowed. Even for a few seconds, the loss of him inside me was unbearable. I reached for him and pulled him down to me, and he gripped my thighs in both hands and slid back inside with a deep metal sigh.

I cried out as he took me, my breath forcing out in a rush. God, he felt so good. As if I'd forgotten already what he felt like, and it was the first time all over again. Sensation spread, delicious, sparkling in my belly like hot diamonds. I groaned, overcome. He worked me again, his cock so smooth and hard like steel and fitting me perfectly deep inside, my curves and ripples hugging him. He took me hard, urgent. My nipples rubbed against his chest, friction hardening them to stinging pebbles, and I gasped, moisture splashing from me to soak him all over again. "Yes. Like that."

Metal screeched as he crunched his copper claws into the roof iron either side of my head. His chameleon eyes glinted silver and violet, and he pushed into me harder, deeper. I sighed with each thrust, my breath forced away. Before, he was gentle, sensual, spine-shivering. Now, his delicious silvery sweat stung me, and his hot steel scent dizzied me, and the pleasure of his flesh meeting mine slammed deep inside me like nothing I'd felt before. Sex with Blaze was feversweet and giggly. Kane was just plain weird. This . . . this was something more. Raw. Delicious. Nerve-tingling. Frightening. Not just that our bodies liked each other, fit together like magnets. I felt him. My eyes fluttered closed from the breathless delight of us.

He paused, his breath short and tight. "Don't close your eyes. Look at me. Watch me feel you."

My sex protested with a sharp twitch, longing for more, and I could only obey. I opened my eyes.

His gaze stabbed mine, alight with violet desire for me. My throat dried. His eyes were so sexy, so intense and focused, like I was the only thing in the world that mattered. Desire flashed in my belly. He thrust in me again, slamming my pleasure in hot and hard, and every last sizzle of sensation reflected in his flaming eyes. I'd set this icy iron prince on fire at last, and he burned for me.

Tears pressed hard in my throat as my body responded, flexing against him, drawing him on, showing him what I liked. My heart shuddered with emotion I didn't want as he adjusted his position, found my most sensitive spot and tortured it, the head of his cock rubbing over me again and again until my muscles wept with pleasure. And still he stared at me, hungry, drinking in my excitement, and somehow I couldn't tear my gaze away.

Tension threatened inside me before I was ready. God, this was too much. I felt too much. I couldn't pretend this wasn't happening, that it was just some random orgasm with a guy I'd picked up somewhere and couldn't care less if I saw again. I wanted to come with his taste on my lips. I wanted him to come with my muscles wrapped around his cock, come deep inside me so I felt every spasm.

"Show me." His breath burned my lips, so close, I could taste him, but he didn't break our gaze. He knew what I thought, how I felt, what turned me on. He knew everything. My sex tightened, impossibly tight, so tense that he groaned, fluttering to nudge my hips up to force ever deeper, pushing searing delight into my spine. "Let me have it all. I need you, Ice. Show me."

I bit my lip at unbearable pressure, and with a burning splash the wave broke. Slammed me down. Drowned me in delicious metal flesh. Wash slammed outward from where we met, frothing through my guts, my limbs, dragging hot tingles over my skin. My clit throbbed. My muscles rippled, squeezing him hard. My head swam, my senses inundated. Even better than the last one. Harder, fuller, deeper. And it wasn't finished yet. My pleasure swirled like a whirlpool, sucking back inside me, and now he shuddered and pressed me into the iron roof and gazed deep into my eyes and showed me his own orgasm, his hot flood fresh and stinging inside me, his breath ironsweet and fast and his eyes darkening to the clear blue color of his name.

As he came, he mashed his lips onto mine in a searing, possessive kiss that made me come all over again, and finally I closed my eyes and surrendered to him, our bodies pulsing together, our tongues mingling like the fluids that burned and mixed inside me.

We kissed, and kissed, lips swollen and breath tight and muscles aching but not wanting to let go. I never wanted to let go. This feeling, so safe and warm and protected, so connected, with his flesh deep inside mine and his smell all over me and the rain sticking our skin together. He was everything I dreamed. Everything I ever wanted. A man who knew my soul.

Suddenly, I felt him smile, like he knew what I was thinking. And then he wrapped tender hands in my hair and kissed me more, sighing into me like we'd only just begun.

At last our lips parted, reluctant, and he sighed, flitting up a few inches to ease his weight but not relinquishing his penetration of me yet. The rain eased to a trickle, thunder receding. Sodden strands stuck to his face, and he caressed my cheek with his to scrape them off. "Lady Ice, that was . . ." He shook his head, lost. "I dunno what to say."

"How about . . . kinda nice? Yeah. Totally unexpected? Definitely. A mistake? Absolutely. We don't have to do it again if y—"

"Astounding?" He shushed me with a kiss. "Mmm. No, hang on. Unprecedented? Nope, not quite it. Incredible. Yeah. That's the one." Still out of breath, he dipped more kisses onto my mouth, like he couldn't stop. "You. Are. Incredible. So. Shut. Up. And. Kiss. Me."

I goggled, and obeyed. His lips caressed mine, his tongue now gentle and soulful in my mouth, and my heart teetered one final time and shattered. I was done defending. It was over. He won.

He unsnicked his claws from the iron and gently helped me tug my saturated clothes back into place. A protesting murmur escaped me as he slid out, and I flushed all over again, but I didn't really care. My skin already shone blue from our loving. Let him see how I felt about him. Too late for lies.

He fluttered upward, rearranging his clothes, and lighted beside me on his butt, his silvery wings tucked back. I planted my hands on the roof iron, my fingerpads sticking, and pushed myself up to sitting. I retied my halter and arched my back, stretching my wings behind me to look up at the mist-covered moon. Over muted traffic and the city's nightelectric hum, distant thunder still rumbled, and the sky scudded with fading storm clouds. The smell of rain and wet pavement leached from the ground, misting the air with fresh humidity that tingled my flushed skin.

I wriggled my hips to reseat the popped joints. My aching thighs stuck together with our fluid, but I didn't mind. We hadn't used anything. I could be spawning. I didn't really mind that either.

He didn't say anything, just inhaled deeply and stared at the stars. I inched to the roof's edge and dangled my legs over, peering down at moonlight reflecting on puddles. Normally, I'd be afraid of heights. Tonight, I wasn't afraid of anything. Except . . .

I glanced sidelong at him, and awkwardness crept in like evil green dust under a door. I wanted to touch him, take his hand, lay my head on those wet denim thighs. Was I allowed? Were we . . . something?

Tentatively, I brushed my head on his shoulder. He just kissed the top of my head and shifted with a wince to dig that iron sphere out of his back pocket.

I snuggled closer and grinned, though he couldn't see me. "So. Not a mistake, huh."

"Nope." He pirouetted the mirror from hand to graceful hand, deft like the clever thief he is, titanium glinting green and purple on his wrist.

Could I accept his gift, after this? Take the cure and leave him, when his life was in danger? Take it and stay, even?

I swallowed. "You sure?"

He tugged my knees over his lap, trailing my wings on the steel.

He locked his arm around my waist and rolled the mirror idly over my belly. "Yeah. I know mistakes pretty good. Wanna see one?"

His thighs felt warm and sticky under my butt, his chest sleek against my shoulder. I giggled, warm and content in his arms. "Sure. Just keep it clean, okay?"

He stretched out his hand. The mirror rolled, snickering in his palm. He curled long blue fingers around it, copper claws clicking. And then he tossed the mirror up, and let his hand float away.

The mirror flowered, sharp petals scything, and fell screeching over the edge.

My heart thudded. I jerked forward, breaking his embrace, but too late.

Three floors below, glass crunched.

Splat.

My vertigo abruptly returned, churning my stomach. I scrambled back from the edge on my palms, cold moisture springing on my skin. I opened my mouth, but no sound came out.

He grinned at me, and too late my gaze flashed again to his wrist. His right wrist was now wrapped in rainbow titanium, where moments ago, when we loved, it was bare.

Mirrorswitch. Right before my loveblind eyes.

Indigo—or whoever this was—widened coppery lashes, a wicked golden glint in his eye. "Oops."

23

I scuttered back like a crab, my limbs shaking. "Wh—what did you do?"

Moonlight shone on his face, illuminating a strange silver smile. Back to front. Not quite right. Eerie blue light glimmered in his molten eyes. "It's gone, Ice. Now we can be real."

He reached for me, but I tugged my hand away, sickness thrashing in my belly. "What?"

He lighted up into a sly crouch, his wings flaring behind him, fingers spread on the wet iron for balance. "Now we can be real together. No hiding. No pretense. Isn't that what you wanted?"

My face hurt, like I'd smiled too much. I couldn't pull it straight. My throat ached, and ugly tears skewered my eyes. "But . . . But I needed that. For Kane. You said so. You said I could!" Like a child, I knew. But my mind wouldn't work. My body wouldn't respond. My flesh still ached from our loving, and I'd already lost him.

"*He* said that, not me. Always trying to *cure* you." He spat the word like poison, his eyes flashing scarlet. "I'll never want that for you, Ice. I want you just the way you are."

Disbelief chewed my nerves, and anger spilled like boiling blue ink though my blood. What the hell did he mean? I scrabbled to my feet, dizzy and awkward on the slanting roof, and stabbed a shaky claw down toward my lost mirror. "B—but you just broke my cure! You just killed yourself! Is that meant to be funny? Like, push-me-off-a-skyscraper funny? Your sense of humor really sucks, you know that?"

He unfolded to his full height, rust crackling on his wings like stardust. Puzzlement darkened his eyes. "I thought you wanted it that way. I thought you meant it when you said you loved me."

A horrid laugh clawed at my throat. "Let's not even go there, okay?" Hysteria screeched in my voice, and I clamped my teeth together so I wouldn't sob or scream. But anguish ripped my newly softened heart apart. The worst thing that could have happened. He's dead. I'm mad. What the fuck was he thinking?

He waved static-raveled hands. "Mirror, cure, what the fuck ever. *He* looked into the mirror, Ice, and he got me. Not a disease. Me. You don't need a cure. You need a fix."

My bones frosted to icy shards. It was himself he was talking about. His other self, the right-handed one with the broken heart. My heart hammered in denial. "Christ, Indigo, wh—?"

"Stop calling me that." Fury tightened his mouth, shining scarlet in his eyes, and brown rust flecks cracked from his quivering wet wings. "It's Ebony, okay? Maybe he was doing the talking, but I was there, too. We just made love, and it was pretty fucking mind-blowing if you want my opinion, so the least you can do is get my name right."

Silence, and a dark chill over my heart. I stammered, terrified I understood. "You're not making sense. It's impossible."

"There's no impossible. Don't tell me you haven't figured it out. Ebony, Indigo, one half, other half, skanky mirror whispering glitter in my head." He tugged fiercely at his hair, dragging it into black peaks, and his words spilled faster. "It split us, after she died.

He didn't know. I help him while he's asleep, I itch and I scratch and he feels better. And now he's peeked in the glass again and he sees me, Ice, he wants me dead and he wants you dead and boring and cured and if you're cured you won't love me anymore and I need you, Ice, I can't do this on my own, I hate it but I itch and I burn and I can't stop until they're dead!" He clenched quivering fists in his hair, muscles bunching like he wanted to rip it out, and only with an effort did he relax.

My stomach rippled, sick. Indigo had tried to tell me, but I hadn't listened. I remembered him on the skyscraper rooftop, his claws sharp and eager on my throat. The way he kissed me, his fingers caressing the top of my spine, squeezing, testing the bones, creeping away sheepish. He could've hurt me if he'd wanted to. Could've killed me.

I swallowed. *Courage, Ice. Deal.* "Who's dead, Ebony?"

"Didn't tell you that part, did he? God, it's like a dungeon, living with him. He's so cold and bitter and . . . and closed off that he can't connect with anyone, and all I can ever feel is pain and isolation and death. Until you came along. Ice, please, you have to—"

A scream welled in my larynx, and I bit it back. "Who's dead, Ebony? Tell me!"

He rippled long fingers across his teeth, crafty, and a sweet little smile passed across silvery lips. "Nasty white girl. Bloodsucker boy with blue eyes. Tasty red spriggan."

Horror spiked my throat. I didn't know any white girl, god help her. But Quang? I'd fingered Akash for that. And my dirty vampire admirer, just doing what vampires do. Not his fault. Mine.

I sucked in a breath. *Calm. Placate the psycho you just made love to. He could be making it up. Just stalking you or something.* "Okay. Why, Ebony? How?"

He mimed a quick blow to the chin with the heel of his hand and a slicing motion with his claw, neck height. "Snap, slice, bleed. They hurt you, Ice. I couldn't bear it. And I itch. We itch. I can't help it—"

"Yes, you can!" Rage and sorrow spilled over my skin like hot ashes, burning me. My muscles clenched, my wings twitching to fly away forever. My denial was futile. I didn't doubt him for an instant. I'd felt the strength in those metal fingers. Felt his sweet claw on my vein, his mouth on my pulse. "You killed them for me? That's fucking insane. Okay? You're insane!"

Suddenly he was close to me, his dark scent assaulting my senses with heady memory.

But fear hit me harder. I stumbled back, and my foot slipped down wet iron and crumpled the thin metal gutter. My heart crammed into my throat. My arms waved, grasping for balance. I teetered, and Ebony caught my waist in a warm metal embrace.

I struggled, but he bent to my ear and whispered, and his voice held all the emotion and anguish and awe I'd loved. "Insane? Yeah. But so are you, Lady Ice, and it's wonderful."

His touch sent an unwelcome throb between my legs. Hot water flushed me. I wanted our skin bare again, my breasts warm on his chest, his hot hard flesh moving inside me. I wanted to claw his pretty metal eyes out.

"No!" I pushed him away and stumbled forward to catch myself. My palms slashed on ragged roof iron. My blood spattered blue in dusty raindrops. I scrambled away, stinging. Fear tugged swift needles through the fabric of my soul, and I wasn't just afraid that he'd hurt me or I'd lose my wits again and touch him and tell him everything's okay.

I was afraid he was right. The mirror had changed me into some twisted reflection of myself, and I'd never be the same.

Inside my head, soft glassy chuckles echoed like evil memories. I shook them off, but the whisper wouldn't die. Unease spiked my skin cold. The damn thing was broken. Wasn't it?

I backed off along the roofline, hot tears stinging my eyes. My voice choked. "I'm not like you, hear me? I don't wanna be like you. Keep the hell away from me."

He stared at me, stunned. His bottom lip quivered, and bright silver tears streaked down his cheeks. "You don't mean that. Ice, tell me you don't mean it. Please—"

"I mean it, all right, Ebony or Indigo or whoever you are." Black despair washed my soul. He'd broken my heart. But he'd broken so much more than that. My voice shook to shattered remnants that scraped my throat raw. "You smashed my cure. You lied to me. You murdered! I'll never forgive you. Just stay the fuck away from me."

"But I need you, Ice. You make everything well. Be with me. I love you!"

Hearing those words from his beloved lips made me want to cry. The anguish on his tear-streaked face slashed at my heart, and I wanted to fall to my knees and scream to heaven and hell with all my power that this had never happened.

But it had.

I couldn't soften. I couldn't forgive him. My body trembled, lonely and cold, and my voice cut like glass. "Don't ever say that to me again."

I stumbled down to the roof's edge, my wings straining to support me, and skidded down the drainpipe and away from him.

Ice!" Ebony dives after her, his heart a bubbling mess of terror and guilt. He squeezes the gutter so hard, his claws cut the metal and his fingers sting and bleed. But she's already gone.

Hiding. Out of sight.

Ragged despair claws his lungs, and he shrieks, his throat ripping inside. He tries to focus, and drags in a sick metal-seeking breath, searching for her, the zip on her dress, the jewels at her wrist, the piercing at her pretty belly. Blinding light stabs from all directions. The stink chokes him. He gags, acid burning his tongue. Metal everywhere. He can't find her.

Wild current erupts from his wing tips, arcing blue. The wet iron roof sizzles and blackens. Ozone and burnt metal scrape at his nose like sandpaper, and the quicksilver taste of blood doesn't make him feel better. His eyes sting like poison, and he yowls in agony and dives for the tight comfort of cool titanium on his wrist, crunching his metalsense off. Her honey-sweet fluid still sticks on his fingers, her kiss still fresh and rosy on his lips.

Indigo didn't get her all to himself, oh no. Ebony watched their bittersweet love through smeared black glass, unable to break through, but he was there. He felt her body yearning against his, enjoyed her glorious warmth on his flesh and the incredible heart-wrenching pleasure of making love with her, feeling her sigh and shiver and come on his cock. He felt Indigo's delight like his own, felt every last fiber of his mirrortwinned heart melt into her clear amber eyes.

He slams his body sideways into the roof in rage, just to feel it hurt. The iron crunches, an Ebony-shaped dent. Metallic pain vibrates in his bones, but they don't break. He never breaks. He just hurts, over and over, pain rotting away his sanity like maggots in meat until all that's left is agony.

He can't follow her. She'll only run, and her pale disgust was already too much to bear.

Without her, he's nothing but death.

He jerks aching wings and struggles to the roof's peak, where moonlight shimmers on rain-soaked corrugations, rain clouds at last scudding away. He teeters on the raked edge, and his glamour wobbles drunkenly, sparks showering from shifting images.

His head swirls like black drain water, the cold fingers of *switch* already filtering through his haze, and Indigo's distant sorrowful moan swells closer. Nausea sloshes into his stomach like warm brine. The switch isn't far. His mind sprints in crazy urgent circles, dizzying him. Must get her back. Must. Before Indigo comes.

But icy claws slash into the fragments of his shattered heart, ripping him open like a bloody corpse, and he struggles but his vision shimmers away. With one last defiant thrash, he hurls himself at the stars.

Switch.

Indigo tumbles in dark air, lost. His pulse screams warning. Falling. Instinctively, he flings out aching wings to break his descent, but too late. The ground looms up, alley walls a tight black tunnel he can't avoid. His head smashes through a rusty iron gutter. He screams, twisting. Rough bricks rip at his wings, and his body slams down onto wet concrete, a mess of steel-drenched agony.

His guts wrench tight. He can't breathe. He gasps, cramp punching his diaphragm, and at last blessed air forces in. Bruises swell his body to bursting. Blood spills from his slashed lips in a silvery puddle. He's bleeding all over, his hair dripping with it, his clothes a sticky mercury mess. He grabs something, anything, his claws scraping ruts in rain-streaked ground, and forces his shuddering bones to move. Pain, blood, slashed flesh. It doesn't matter. He only cares about her. Must find her before Joey does, beg her to give him a moment, let him explain that he'd rip Ebony screaming from his heart if he knew how. That he'll find a way, for her, even if it kills him. If she can only forgive him.

Like he could explain. Like it's possible she'll ever forgive him. Ebony did the killing, but it's all Indigo's fault. He shut Eb away so tight that the only way he could feel alive was to kill. And Indigo and Ebony are closer now. He was there, helpless and trapped when Ebony threw the mirror away. His ears still vibrate with the awful smash of precious magic glass. His fingers still scrabble too late for the lost slide of metal. His soul still screams for her.

Fairysharp sorrow slices his heart. She'll never forgive him. Ebony will never give up on her. If Indigo can't get rid of his mirror-twin, he'll damn well never go near her again.

He forces himself to his pain-spiked knees, silver splashing. He can't forget her. He'll never forget her, sugarstrawberry girl who for just a few hours melted away his guilt. He owes her for that. He'll keep her safe as long as he can, until Delilah finally chews the flesh from his bones.

He crackles foil-crumpled wings and staggers to his feet.

A boot slams into his spine, knocking him flat on his face again. Too late the air sparkles with hatred and brass's limy stink.

He gasps again for breath, a stitch crippling his ribs. A rich snaky chuckle slithers in his ears. "Knew you'd come down sometime, fairydirt. Delilah's gonna be pleased to see you."

Fuck. Shoulda listened. Shoulda watched. Shoulda done anything except think about Ice.

Concrete rips stinging skin from his cheek, his palms, his bare chest where Ice dragged his shirt aside. Joey's foot grinds between his shoulder blades, into delicate flight bones that shouldn't be tampered with. Blood rushes like arousal, hardening his flesh there, the pain exquisite. Metalbone vertebrae crunch, slicing his sensitive nerves. He can't help but yowl.

Joey chuckles. "Teach you to break my mirror."

A delighted banshee meow. “Can I hit him, too?”

Joey snickers, black cane thumping the concrete. “Oh, sweet Mina, you most certainly can.”

Indigo’s wings jerk, bloody and useless. He tries to rise, to scrabble to his knees before it’s too late, but the whipcord thrash of leather snaps dangerously in his ears and a swift kick in his temple smashes the lights out.

24

I crouched in the corner of metal walls, shivering in skimpy wet clothes, until he finally climbed out of sight. And then I wrapped my cramping arms tighter around my body and let my tears flow.

God, he wept, like I'd broken his heart instead of the other way round. Ebony really thought I'd understand. That I wouldn't care that he'd murdered for me.

I fisted my eyes, determined. I'm not like him. *I won't be like him, so mirrortwisted and sure that I can't see right from wrong.*

But already the madness festered inside me, the wild urge to destroy. My pulse skewered tight. My skin itched, and I resisted raking my claws over my ribs, my thighs, my hair. My limbs juddered, burning to thrash, dance, sprint away and wreak havoc.

The mirror might be broken, but the spell hadn't dissolved.

I knew I was a danger to myself. Hadn't occurred to me I might endanger others, too.

I clenched my jaw to stop my teeth from chattering. I couldn't just sit here. I had to do something. I'd go to Kane and beg. I'd sleep with him or be his slave or spend a hundred years in hell if I must. I'd get this cure somehow if it killed me.

Aching, I scraped soaked hair from my face and crept out from my metalclad hiding place. Rough concrete cut my feet. I hadn't been sure he wouldn't see me with his metalsight, but it was the best I could do. It savaged my heart to hide from him after we'd been so intimate. But the mirror still ravaged my sense. If he begged me to listen, I'd crumble.

Our pleasure was a lie. Wasn't it? Until I figured out what was real, I had to stay away from him.

I squinted upward, where the moon glowed through thinning pewter storm clouds in the bright, sad smell of rain. The broken gutter silhouetted, still dented where I'd climbed over. Right up there, we'd made love.

I looked away.

A glint of brown glass caught my eye, a beer bottle shattered on the ground.

Shiny. Glass. Mirror.

My heart skipped. I sniffed and wiped my nose, my mind spinning faster. What if the pieces were still here? Big enough to collect? Maybe Kane would accept that. At least Akash or Joey didn't have it.

Hope glowed cautiously in my heart, and I stumbled forward, peering with stinging eyes at rainwashed concrete.

Dirt. Chewing gum, splat. A twist of metal . . . No, that's a rusted tin can. Broken syringe. A bright shard of white-edged glass . . . Could be a piece. I picked it up, and it sliced my fingers bloody. A bit dusty. Probably not. But how could I tell? I cleared my aching throat. "Squidgy? You there?"

No answer.

Despair leaked again into my ragged heart. Just a tiny splinter. Even if it was a part, how could I ever get them all?

Still, I couldn't give up. I eased in a steadying breath, and crept farther into the gloom. Inky shadows grew blacker around me, and the roof blocked my moonlight. Frustration nibbled my toes. I wished I had a torch. A match. Any kind of light.

Flame showered like fireworks against the dark brick wall.

Harsh air scarred my lungs, and my eyes jerked wide.

Huddled in the corner, long pale limbs folded like an insect, dark clothes ripped to show bleeding white skin. Glassy crimson wings. Firebright sparks spitting like hailstones. Splashing red hair, a narrow fae-sharp face.

I crept closer, my heart thudding. "Blaze?"

He stared up at me, black eyes shinybold. Bruises kissed his pointy jaw, and his mouth bled berry dribbles over his chin that he hadn't bothered to clean up. Broken glass shimmered in his hair, and his scent reached my nose, no longer fresh and exciting but somehow smudged, like he'd rolled in something ugly.

I sidled, awkward. I wanted to hug him. I wanted to slap his face and run away. "What you doing here?"

"Following you." Bright, unashamed. Like I wouldn't care. He licked his candy lips, blood spreading.

"Where's Az?"

"No idea."

I swallowed. "You okay?"

He laughed. Not the sweet, cheeky laugh I loved. It scraped my ears, jaded and sarcastic. "Yeah, I'm just great. I love being crazy. At least I haven't killed anyone yet."

The hard glint in his eyes showed he'd heard everything. Nausea roiled faintly. Did he watch us make love, hear me say those foolish things?

Embarrassment crawled my skin. I knitted my fingers together, defensive. "Why you following me?"

He spread his hands in his lap, flicking his gaze downward to make me look, and I leaned over into his hellish circle of light.

A rusty sphere. Empty petals twisted open and dented.

In his other palm lay three bright fragments of glass, a rectangle split neatly in a crooked Y shape. Nothing missing.

I gasped.

He grinned, sharp white teeth shining, and crunched his nose at me like he used to. “This what you’re looking for?”

Hold still, will ya?” Blaze nudged me with a sharp elbow.

“I am holding it still. Get on with it.” I cupped the mirror’s case in my hands, the three glass pieces balanced precariously inside. Moonlight flickered on the raw edges of the cracks, seducing me all over again, and I craned my chin away so I couldn’t look, but my eyeballs kept swiveling back down.

Blaze poked the glass experimentally with one claw. Plink. The edges touched, and a slinky metal whisper hissed in my ears. “See? It ain’t dead.”

He could hear it, too. Maybe we played with things best left alone. But relief shook my limbs that Blaze was in this with me, that I wasn’t all by myself.

I dragged my gaze to the diamond-starred sky. “I don’t care. Just make it look fixed so we can give it to Kane and get our cure.”

“Yeah, well, don’t blame me if he notices.” Blaze dragged sweaty hair from his face and sucked in a deep breath, holding his hand out flat. His fingers trembled, slight but definite.

He was shaking. I could smell it on him, heat and sickness like fever. I swallowed. “Come on, Blaze. You fixed Quang’s counter okay.”

“That’s a chunk of glass. This is a mirror. It’s gotta be all flat and specialshiny and nice. Gimme a sec.” He closed his eyes, chewing his lip until it bled, willing steadiness into his hands. Sweat dripped down his nose and plopped on the ground, and he flicked his eyes open. "Okay. Make a pumpkin. Don't move."

My skin swelled tight in anticipation. *Come on, Blazy. Don't fuck it up.* I held the sphere as steady and level as I could, my palms slick with raindrops and sweat. He extended one delicate finger and dipped his claw lightly to the glass.

Steam hissed, and glass melted in a tiny golden rivulet.

He traced his claw gently along the first crack. Molten glass followed, flowing into the gap. He reached the edge and deftly flicked his claw away. Slowly, the glass cooled, and all that remained of the crack was a thin clear bobbly line.

My chest tightened in disappointment. "It's not shiny."

"Not yet, it ain't." Swiftly he mended the second crack, and the third. Now the glass was whole, marred by a Y-shaped ridge. Blaze bent closer and exhaled. His breath misted the glass, heating the whole thing softly with showering sparks, and when they extinguished, the glass sat sheer and smooth, the sphere's glossy inner surface refracted inside. Mirrorclear. Perfect.

An ethereal giggle swept around me like cold wings and darted away into the dark.

Dread coursed through my blood like cool water. What had we done?

He winked at me, a glint of the old Blaze shining through. "Whaddaya think of that, Spicy?"

I smiled, but tension strained my muscles sore. "You're pretty cool, ya know that?"

"Course. Everyone knows that." He wiped sweat droplets from his face, and his gaze slipped away, uncharacteristically shy. "Look, Ice—"

"Don't wanna talk, okay?" I twisted to push past him, my cheeks burning wet.

But he slipped deft fingers around my wrist, holding me, and urgency cracked his voice with spitting, unignited heat. "I don't like it like this between us."

His touch warmed me, like it used to, sweet and almost forgotten. But too late. I tried to shake him off. "Whaddaya want from me, Blaze? It's over. We ruined it. Just let it go."

He shook his head, just once, fiercely, like he scolded himself. "You're really in love with him, aren't you? You don't love me."

I opened my mouth, and the words stopped awkwardly in my throat. Of course I loved Blaze. Just not like that. We'd hurt each other recklessly, even deliberately. That the mirror set it off didn't change anything.

I swallowed. "Blaze—"

"S'okay. Figures. He's got dignity, I guess. And brains, and a life. But it's okay. It was nice, yeah?" He offered me a crooked Blaze grin, but suspicious moisture jeweled his lashes.

My throat swelled. I squeezed his hand, wishing I knew how to help him. "Yeah, it was."

He hugged me, and planted a steaming kiss on my cheek, his lips lingering shyly. "Once we're done with Kane, we'll go for a drink, just you and me. We'll find you a honeysweet boy who's totally in awe of your awesomeness and mend us that tough little heart of yours. Yeah?"

Tears burned my eyelids, and I hugged him back, clutching the mended mirror on one hand and his hair in the other. My voice choked. "Find you a kick-ass little fairy girl while we're at it. Just try not to fuck her before you say hello, okay?"

He giggled, rubbing his nose on my cheek, and my weary heart warmed. Just for this one fleeting moment, I felt like everything might one day be okay. He nudged my chin up and kissed me, a gentle chaste kiss of loss and apology, and I let it linger.

"I knew it." Cold breeze ruffled my hair, bitter with jealousy, and a chill razor edge bit the side of my neck.

I sprang back, my pulse sliding cold.

Azure twisted her blade, a long wicked curved thing like a pirate's cutlass. The oblique point stung like Joey's poison, and warm blood trickled down my neck. Her pretty oval face distorted, ugly. "Don't run away from me."

I swallowed, bumps erupting on my skin. "Az, for heaven's sake—"

"Shut up." Her static-blue gaze crackled with envy. Her celery hair fluttered in ratty tangles, and she tugged at her dirt-smeared dress with broken claws, fury mangling her voice to an evil croak. "I knew you two were at it. You lied to me all along."

"That ain't true." I tried to back off, but the wall scraped my wings raw. She poked me, and I jerked my chin away, trying to stop her cutting me. Where did she get that thing? It wasn't like her to be so . . . scruffy. Unkempt. Dirty.

That cursed squidgy had poisoned her, just like Blaze and me. And she wasn't fighting it.

Blaze lifted his spark-jeweled arm to push her away. "Jeez, Az, put that fucking thing away—"

"Don't touch me." She swung her blade toward him, threatening, and he halted, his hand raised. She sneered. "You're not my friends. You always hated me. Always laughing at me."

I wanted to rub my bloody throat, but I didn't dare move. "That ain't true, Az. Listen to what you're saying. You know it's n—"

"I said shut up." She swiped her blade at me, metal zinging. Air swirled around her, alive, dragging her dress hem taut. "I've got a new friend now. A better friend than you. And that shiny belongs to her. Hand it over."

My heart blobbed and sank. Delilah had gotten to her. I clutched the mended mirror tight, and the petals we'd coaxed back into shape snapped shut. "But there's a cure. Kane said so. We can all go together."

"Give!" She menaced closer, blade outstretched. Her sour breeze coated my skin with slime. Anger kinked her pretty mouth crooked, showing jagged teeth, but fear glassed her eyes blank. The blade quivered, her hand shaking. "Give it to me! You always get everything. If I get it for her, I'll feel better. She promised."

Blaze edged toward her, flames sputtering from his fingers. His voice tremored, fever sweat igniting like fiery trails over his skin. "You know she's lying, Az. Look at me. Come on. It's me. Blaze. We've hung out for ever and ever—"

"Get away from me!" she screeched, and in a fit of what surely must have been instinct, she flung her weapon away and launched herself at him in a flash of wings.

Wrathful wind howled. Storm breeze dragged my hair sideways, catching the edge of Blaze's burning wake, and with a greedy hiss, his innate flames leapt higher.

Horror clutched my lungs tight, and I lunged between them, foul wind watering my eyes. Blaze's fever sweat was laced with his natural incendiary, and Az's angry wind caught it. He dived onto his back in the air, fluttering madly like a drowning insect to drag himself away, but too late. He'd already caught fire.

His wings exploded in flame, the flammable membranes melting to ragged holes. He splatted to the ground, thrashing and yowling in agony. His hair ignited. Skin bubbled on his chest under the fierce onslaught of heat, his shirt already seared away. The black walls around us glowed with hellish orange fire.

Azure spun up and away in an angry whirlwind. The stink of burned flesh and hair savaged my nose, dragging sour vomit into my mouth. Blaze thrashed on the ground in flames, helpless, and I tried to leap on him, shower him with water and put the fire out.

But Azure landed between us on crouched thighs, a dirty blue angel, wings folded tight like a striking cobra's hood. She grabbed my throat, and her hot breath burned my face, slipping into my mouth. It tasted odd, of pepper and almonds. My tongue swelled swiftly, stopping my breath. Panic rose like floodwater as I struggled for air. What was that? A drug? Where did she get that?

But I couldn't talk. I couldn't breathe. She grinned, her blue eyes cruel, and before I realized she'd poisoned me, I passed out.

25

Blaze doubles up and rolls over and over on the sodden ground, fighting the excruciating compulsion to scream. Bright agony spreads like a cancer though his burning skin, deep into his flesh where the flamefae fluid is, the feverbright liquid that burns.

If he inhales, he'll set his throat on fire and die.

So he rolls, and sinks bright teeth into his cheek until the flesh rips, but he doesn't scream, and when at last he reaches a puddle of rainwater he thrashes like a bathing tomcat until the goddamn flames go out.

He drags in a blessedly cool breath, and at last screeches in desperate agony.

Fuck, it hurts. His skin screams when he tries to move, tight and swollen and sloughed away like wet decay. His ruined wings jerk, melted nerves haywire. He forces his eyes open, and they sting like motherfuckers, but they still work.

He flops panting on his face in the puddle, sizzling the dirty rainwater to steam. His claws scrape the concrete weakly. Fuck her. Setting him on fire like that. Christ, he must look a sight. He hurts all over, and he can't tell where the damage is, can't tell if his face is intact or not.

Dehydration already shrivels his guts, all his moisture rushing to weeping skin that can no longer contain it. He laps weakly at the puddle, scraping his tongue on the concrete, but it's not enough. If he stays like this, he'll die.

He closes his eyes, and his glamour pops weakly like a thinning bubble. Without his looks, life won't be worth living anyway. Sad but true.

He laughs, the pain rampant but somehow sweet. Poor Icy. No cure, if there ever was one anyway. And poor Azure, seduced by a demoness, her fragile confidence shattered.

Anger flares hot inside him, whetting the pain sharper, and he groans. If he were whole, he'd chase after them right now and chew that demon bitch's heart out for them. They're his girls. He'd die for them, even though his life's not worth a damn. Even though Az hates him, and Ice loves someone else. Dying to save them might make his sorry life worthwhile.

If he were whole.

Cuts fade from inked brown skin in his memory, and hope sparks faintly in his heart. He knows a guy who's into making things whole. Akash, his weird new boyfriend. And he's got something Akash wants. He knows where the mirror is, or at least where Az is taking it.

He promised the creepy fucker already, when he thought he'd end up like that poor Indra girl. But he's paid for that favor in full. Surely Akash'll give him one more.

Swap swap. Snap. Gotta be better than a spriggan's toothy blow job. At least Akash didn't bite.

A laugh ravages Blaze's throat, and resolve hardens like cooling steel in his heart. He's not good for much. But he loves his girls, and he's good at pain. Easy peasy. Walk in the park.

He clenches burned muscles, ignoring the panicked chemical rush in his blood, and levers his body up from the ground, inch by agony-rapt inch.

A few suburbs away in another dark alley, an ancient vampire sighs one last sticky breath and stops struggling. The gaping wound in her throat spurts weakening scarlet jets. Her black hair tangles wet on the bricks, blood spreading in a red circle that glints silver in rising moonlight.

"Excellent." Kane stretches his hands, and bloodstains and grime vanish in a puff of hellish steam. He scratches a little stain from his ring, and flicks his fingernail clean. Three DiLucas in one night. Good work.

Angelo slumps against the wall, panting, his white shirt soaked crimson under black leather. He wipes his dripping mouth, sweat gleaming in his dark curls. "Fucking DiLuca bitch. Tastes like shitty Calabrian red." He retches, and dark clots like abortions spew from his lips.

Vampire reflux. Serve him right for gluttony, for doing it all himself when he has minions. Still, every now and then you have to get dirty.

Kane checks his watch. It's late. Akash. Ebony never called back. He should check things out. He tugs his cuffs straight, adjusts his tie, plucks a stray strand of vampire hair from his sleeve. "Leave the body. Let them find it. Tomorrow we'll talk."

LaFaro slips from the shadows, lean and lizardlike in silhouette, and offers a towel. Angelo blots himself clean, still coughing, his voice ragged. "Sure. Nice one. Appreciate the help. Oh, and if you see that succubus of yours? Smack her up for me, will you?"

Sparks flash over Kane's palms, and he digs sharp claws in to keep himself calm. "What?"

"She's a mouthy little whore. You should keep her under better control. You know she's banging her incubus pal every chance she gets?"

"No, she isn't." But he knows it's true. Knows the girl he wants is with her lover now, kissing, sighing, pleasuring. Sour denial crusts Kane's teeth with ash, and green sparks burst from his clenched fist to shower the ground.

Angelo laughs, fangs flashing, and tosses away the sodden towel. His dark eyes glint with gleeful malice. "Whatever you say, man. If it quacks and flaps and shits green on your doorstep, it's probably a fucking duck, okay?"

Rage crackles ice into Kane's hair. "Leave her. She's mine." And he stalks off toward the neon-lit street, his teeth springing sharp. Flame licks his wrists to the elbow. He's not used to being denied. Already the black satisfaction of DiLuca suffering fades. His knuckles itch again to fight, tame, destroy.

And there's a flower-stinking white pest who definitely has it coming.

Growling, he flings his impatient shade into the air on hate-filled black wings.

26

Like my dungeon?"

The demon lady grinned down at me and tossed the mirror from hand to purple-clawed hand. Sleek wine-red hair tumbled down to her freckle-dusted brown shoulders, and her long coppersilk dress glinted with diamonds.

I wriggled on my bottom, my hands cuffed tight behind me, a balcony railing warm and knobbly against my bare back. My wings poked between iron bars, ruffling in warm night breeze, and below, the city glittered wild like a treasure cavern. This wasn't a dungeon. It was a penthouse.

Water trickled on the wall from a river-stone fountain, and soft wind chimes pealed beside an artificial flower bed. The tinted glass door lay open to the summer night, and inside, soft pale carpet graced the floor under golden downlights, window to full-length window. The ceiling gleamed spotless white, the kitchen sparkling steel. No furniture. No stuff. Empty, like she hadn't moved in yet. I rattled my cuffs and kicked my bare feet. "Yeah. It's real nice. Fuck you."

Delilah wrinkled her upturned nose, ice glittering on red lashes. Breeze toyed with her gown. "Defiance. How boring. I hoped you'd cringe at least a bit."

I spat at her. Beside me, Azure struggled and wept in her own shackles, dark blood dripping from her nose onto her grimy white dress. Delilah hadn't kept that promise to her. My head still ached like a fever from Az's poison breath—she'd gotten that foul trick from Delilah, no doubt—and I wanted to strangle her. But I wanted to hug her, too.

A door slammed inside, and uneven footsteps slapped on tiles. Joey DiLuca limped out, leaning on his brass-topped cane, hat tilted rakishly over green eyes. Behind him, Mina dragged a kicking blue-and-silver bundle by the wrist, torn blue hair ragged on her shiny black shoulder.

My blood curdled thick and cold.

Joey tipped his hat at Delilah, stretching bloodless lips in a grin. "Present for you."

Mina hurled her bundle to the floor. Silvery blood splatted on her tight leather pants.

Indigo choked on black tiles, his bruised blue muscles straining against the kind of red neon rubbery restraints they use in cop shows. The kind that get tighter the more you struggle. The kind with no metal in them whatsoever.

She'd tied his wrists. His ankles. His arms, by wrapping it around his wings. He couldn't move.

"Excellent." Delilah laughed, clapping long brown hands, and waved Joey away.

Joey just tapped his cane on the tiles, unblinking. "Your promise."

Delilah's brows lifted ingenuously. "Hmm?"

"The thief for a moment of your time. Don't fuck with my goodwill, demon lady."

She chuckled softly and tweaked his nose with her thumb to a defensive banshee growl. "You've got guts, Joey DiLuca—that's for sure. Well, I suppose one from two isn't bad. We'll talk, eh?" She motioned him away again, and this time he inclined his narrow head and hobbled away, Mina stalking in his wake.

And Delilah turned her lickerish grin back to me.

I wobbled loose-jointed thumbs, but the tight iron stung ruts in my wrists, and I couldn't get free.

On the floor, my beautiful metal fairy writhed and spat blood. "Leave her the fuck alone."

I searched for titanium's telltale rainbow glint and swallowed. Left hand. Indigo. *Christ, don't hurt him. Even if he's Ebony, I don't want him hurt. Do I?*

I yanked my shackles hard against the railing, and frustration and fear cut my voice sharp. "Come on. Punch me, rip my wings off, tear my claws out, whatever. Just get it over with."

"Patience, petal. Oh, do those hurt? Are they too tight?" Delilah pursed bow-shaped lips, clicking her tongue. "Such a silly piece of metal. But so far away. What a pity he can't get up."

She spun away and kicked him in the ribs with a high-heeled foot, eliciting a wet wheeze and a laugh. My stomach squelched to hear him. She kicked him again. I strained against my cuffs, and a defiant yell clambered up my throat. I choked it back, but too late.

Delilah rounded on me, grass-green eyes glinting with laughter. "You two make me spew." Her voice squeaked up in mocking imitation. "'Oh, don't hurt him. Leave her alone. Please.' Who the fuck is that down there anyway? The thief or the murderer? Perhaps I'll just suck you both up like little fairy milk shakes." She brandished the mirror grandly, and petals flashed open with a snap.

My heart quailed. The mirror was dead. Blaze only patched it up. When Delilah found out, she'd kill us all.

But a bright crystal whisper hissed in joyful circles around us, and

Delilah peered into the glass and showed perfect white teeth. "Why, hello, beautiful."

I gaped. No way. Blaze did better than he thought.

"Come now, don't be like that." She clicked her tongue, and the mirror warbled, conciliatory. "That's better. You hungry, pet?"

The mirror giggled.

"Of course you are. What say you to some fairy stew? Hmm, light blue, dark blue, or yellow? Quite a selection."

Indigo spat shining mercury blood. "Don't you fucking dare turn that thing on her."

Delilah laughed, sparks dancing scarlet in her hair to be swept away by the breeze. "Or what, metalshit? You'll curse at me some more? Already too late for you, or I'd shove the fucking thing up your nose and watch you reflect. Perhaps you can choose what's on the menu instead. How'd you like that?"

Indigo struggled, silverfoil wings crackling. "You've got what you wanted. Let them go."

She squatted, her coppery gown pooling, and yanked his black-metal hair back to snap her teeth in his face. "Oh, but I don't have what I want yet. I want your blood, shitworm. But I want your agony first. Teach you to steal from me." She slammed his head down on the tiles and strode back toward me. "On second thoughts, I like him better helpless. You." She pointed a sparking purple claw an inch from my eyeball. "Choose."

I stammered. "What?"

"Choose, you vacant fairy whore. Choose whose soul gets eaten by our little friend." She waved the chuckling mirror in front of my face. "Oh, and you can't choose yourself. That'd be cheating."

Azure sobbed. "You promised me."

I didn't know whether she meant me or Delilah. My heart bled for Az. It wasn't her fault she wasn't the smartest cookie, and the mirror had fooled us all, not just Az. I lifted my chin, defiance blazing in my blood, and stared the demon queen down. "Kill me now, you maniac. I'm not doing it. Fuck you."

Delilah winked at me. "You know what? I've a better idea. How about . . . your cure?"

I gaped, and before I could stop it, the word spilled out, fresh with hope. "What?"

"Ha! Knew that'd get your attention. How about a game before bed? Poor handsome thing's tired, you see." She stroked the humming mirror happily, wrinkling her sharp nose at her reflection. "Only get one cure out of him tonight. Ever, I should think. So who's it gonna be, slut? You can even pick yourself, if you like."

Horror clawed at my bones. I managed a laugh. "Oh, yeah, right. And then you'll kill everyone else. Don't think so."

She made a shocked face. "I'm hurt. Truly. No, I believe I'll set you all free. Should be good for a laugh. Whaddaya say, metalshit?"

Indigo howled like a wounded cat, static crackling in rings on the tiles around him.

I struggled uselessly against the sharp shackles. She did this to torment him. She knew I couldn't waste the cure on myself. Not with my friends counting on me. If I chose poor Az—if I left Indigo as he was—he'd never have peace, either of him. Ebony would keep killing. And if I cured him . . .

Tears spilled onto my face, and my heart tore. If I cured him, poor heartsick Ebony would die. I'd still be crazy. So would Az. So would Blaze, if he was still alive. And Indigo would lose part of himself forever. Who could love a girl who'd killed part of him? Even if that part was a murderer.

I choked back full-on sobs. When did this get so damn hard?

I remembered his eyes as we loved, the warmth, the tenderness of his touch on my face. Cool clarity washed over me, scrubbing my mind clear for the first time in a very long while.

I'd felt so close to him, like we were one. I'd given him my heart, and I couldn't pretend it hadn't happened, even if things ended badly.

So if I really loved him, what did that mean?

It meant I couldn't let him suffer for me. I couldn't let Ebony kill any more innocents for me. I could give Indigo his life back, everything he wanted most desperately, and if that meant Azure would never forgive me and I'd die crazy and unloved, then so be it.

Easy, really.

A shadow shook feathery wings and flapped away, and light shone on my heart.

I sniffled to clear my nose, and stared Delilah directly in those cruel emeraldine eyes. I lifted my elbow as far as the shackles would allow, and pointed. "Him. Cure him."

Sorry, Az.

Indigo cracked his head into the stone, over and over, clenching a scream between stained silver teeth. "Don't, Ice! For god's sake. Please."

But too late.

Delilah smiled, beautiful and triumphant. "How sweet of you. Hear that, rustybrains? She'll drive herself mad for you. She'll die for you, and not a damn thing you can do about it. Sound familiar?"

My throat ached, and my heart hurt like I'd run for miles. His dead girlfriend all over again. And I'd brought it on him with my stupid shiny things.

Indigo growled like a panther and thrashed, still trying to break free. But the red rubber stuff just cut tighter into his flesh.

Delilah laughed. The greedy glass murmured, shining wickedly in her hand, catching the electric light and magnifying it. "Steal this, you fucking maggot." And she stepped over him like a hunter straddling a corpse, and flashed the mirror in his eyes.

Indigo screams, the light searing his eyes like acid on sandpaper. The gnawing beast in the mirror is unshackled now, and it'll never give up. Never let go.

His vision erupts white like burning film. Sour coppery vomit spills into his mouth and chokes him. The horrid plastic rips into his jerking muscles. Bloody talons claw for his consciousness, only it's not Ebony but the mirror, the cursed fucking mirror trying to eat his soul. Cure be damned. The thing will consume him and spit him out twisted, blackened, diseased. Whatever Ice did to the mirror to fix it, the monster inside's gone insane.

Dimly he hears Delilah's hellish cackle, and his heart screams, too. She's getting what she wants, the sly demon trickster. He knows she'll torment Ice to death, torture and scrape and burn until his lovely strawberry girl melts away, and it hurts him deeper than his own agony could ever sink.

Deep under his skin, Ebony spits and claws in screaming rage, fighting the screeching mirror off.

Indigo thrashes helpless wings. Should've kept away from her. Should've gone home and jerked off and never dreamed of loving her. Too late. He's done it again. She's suffering because of him, and he won't have it.

Even if it is her choice.

The thought streaks through him, almost too faint to hear.

No way. It's his fault. And there's only one way to make it right.

Channel the rage. Accept the darkness. Set his monster free. Ebony has no doubts, no cowering conscience. Ebony's fury is unstoppable. If anyone can put an end to Delilah's sadistic plots, it's Eb. Already Indigo's writhing shadow can taste hellblood.

Ice will hate him—worse, despise him—but at least she'll be alive. And at least, for a few precious moments, he had her heart.

With claws of frigid metal will, Indigo grabs his own sanity and rips it open.

The cage inside his head ruptures. Mental bones crack like spread-eagled ribs, and hell bursts out.

Switch.

Ebony yowls in agony, scrabbling in vain to cover his ravaged eyes with rubber-shackled hands too far away. Trapped bloodflow slashes razors in his limbs. The dazzling white thing in the mirror taunts him, screams at him, tempts him to come, come and be slaughtered, but he can't, he won't, not while Ice lives.

She doesn't love him. He knows now she never will. But he can still set her free.

Hatred arcs like lightning in his heart, crackling electric loathing he's bottled up for years, and he releases one last defiant scream and lets the voltage explode.

27

I thrashed and squealed against my shackles, frustration and terror chewing at my nerves. Indigo wriggled and screamed on his back in a cloud of electric-burnt steam. She'd kill him. After all that, he'd die anyway and I'd be left to bear it.

Delilah laughed, malice crackling icicles from her hair, and thrust the mirror closer to his face. "Suck it up, metalshit."

His forearms bunched in agony, claws raking the air, and in a smoky flash his bangle vanished.

Bumps broke out on my skin, and ozone ripped my nose raw. My wings jerked. The bangle snapped into view on his right arm, and in a hail of blue sparks, current erupted.

My hair sprang taut in crackling static. The air sizzled, electrified. My clothes plastered themselves to my skin, and my wrists slammed tight into my back, steel cuffs straining toward him in irresistible magnetic field.

The mirror wailed in iron flux and jerked forward, too, but Delilah held on. She screeched demon laughter, her teeth bristling like needles. "You can do better than that."

Indigo's—no, Ebony's—Ebony's muscles cramped tight with current. His arms convulsed and bulged. His sharp iron-boned wings jerked, sizzling blue current dragging them irresistibly taut, and in a crack of electric thunder the red rubber rope around his chest snapped.

Delilah wailed, and my skin shivered. Ebony's laugh razored. He tore his tied hands and ankles apart with a whip of ultraflex limbs and slashing metal teeth. Mercury blood splatted.

He leapt and hovered, flaring his wings and curling his copper claws like a fierce metal angel. His black hair sprang jagged in sparking green current. Violet neon rage glowed in his eyes, and in a flash of razor-sharp silver, he dived for Delilah.

She stumbled back, brandishing the blinding mirror before her, but her long gown tangled in her heels. They crashed to the ground together in a flail of thrashing limbs, and Ebony sank cruel teeth into her wrist and ripped the shining mirror from her hands.

She howled and struggled, the mirror's beam slashing the night air like a crazy searchlight. Demon blood splashed scarlet, and Delilah kicked and clawed with purple talons, a monster's yellow hellscales breaking out on her skin. Her needle teeth flashed, green ichor spilling onto Ebony's skin in hissing acid burn.

My heart choked, and I thrashed in fury against my chains. Surely she'd kill him. But he just pinned her under his body with a powerful thrust of wings, jammed her throat into the ground with slashing claws, and shone the screaming mirror directly into her eyes.

The howl that erupted from her mouth chilled my blood to ice. The glass door shattered, ripped apart by shuddering frequencies. Shining shards showered, melting on Delilah's smoking scales.

Ebony's claws slashed at her face, demon blood flowing, but as fast as he tore the wounds open, the faster they healed over. Hellflame roiled crimson in her hair, lashing out at his hands with electric fury.

But her eyes burned golden, light streaming in from the mirror like an evil white river, and little by little her struggles weakened.

Her hands fought his, the mirror's light flashing over her face, into her eyes and out. And Ebony fought her down and held her there and laughed as she struggled. Sweat dripped copper on his burnt blue skin, and voltage ripped his silver wings blue. His glinting fangs dripped bloody rage. "Teach you to hurt my girl."

My heart swelled, burning, and tears scorched my eyes and seared down the side of my nose. He'd kill again for me, and it was all my fault. This would never end. I didn't care if the hellbitch deserved it. I hated it.

Fevered fingers snaked around my ankle.

My pulse exploded back into life. Some hellworm come to munch me up. I scrabbled back, blinded by the terrible sight before me, but the grip wouldn't ease.

Something clicked before my eyes like teeth, and terror bit my nerves raw and yanked me lucid.

Blaze snapped his fingers again and hushed me with a match-scented claw on my lips. "Shh. Show me your hands."

Disbelief mushed my brain. "You're . . . You're still alive?" And he bloody was, bless him. Unhurt. The hellish burns were gone, his hair intact, his pretty crimson wings gleaming softly in the night-light. My tears flowed harder. He'd come back for me. Somehow. "How'd ya get in here? What happened? Your burns . . .?"

Secrets flickered his gaze away. "Told ya. I'm cool. Show me your hands."

Behind him, Delilah and Ebony rolled, still fighting, tumbling blue and brown limbs and silvery wings and streaking purple hair. Taking no notice of us. My stomach coiled tight. Eb was strong, even for a fairy. They'd kill each other before this was over.

Urgency rippled my blood, erasing any questions until later. I twisted and shuffled my butt aside so Blaze could reach. "Quick. Get these fucking things off."

Az murmured beside me, her blue eyes pooling wide. "Blaze?"

"Yeah, Az. It's me. Hang on." He jammed one claw into a link of my chain. Heat sizzled, and the metal shone red. I yanked. The cuffs split, and I pulled free in a wash of cool relief. I rubbed my still-cuffed wrists, broken chain dangling.

Blaze winked, devilish, and crawled over to Az. I jabbed him with my foot and hissed a whisper. "Hey! How did you find us here?"

He yanked Az's cuffs apart and jerked his pointy chin toward the screeching demon. "You care? Let's get outta here."

Az tugged her dress straight, sullen. "Why'd you do her first? Huh?"

I ignored her and grabbed Blaze's arm as he started to dart into the shadows toward the glass door. I pointed at Ebony, who still clawed at Delilah's lizard-skinned throat from beneath, her whip-scaly thighs gripping him bare through her ripped dress. "We can't leave him!"

Blaze shook me off, urgent like fever. "Now, Ice!"

A crash cut off my retort. A blur of inked muscle, torn leather, swishing brown hair, a graceful body streaking through the broken window to land on the tiles.

Akash, fresh and unhurt, his curving brown muscles gleaming in a fighting crouch. Dark flame licked over his fingers, fairyfire dancing between his hands like a toy. His sapphire eyes fixed on Delilah, blazing bright, and his voice sang with a banshee's seductive song as he pointed a flame-dripping finger at her. "Demon weakling," he crooned. "Die."

And he launched himself at her, horizontal in a spear of blazing fairyfire.

Flesh and bone slammed together. Skin split. Blood splashed, red and silver. Yowls mingled. Delilah tumbled screeching away from

Ebony, and she and Akash thudded against the balcony. Her skull smacked hard into the iron railing. She spluttered, golden venom splashing from needle teeth, more yellow-green scales sprouting on her neck. Akash sank cruel fingers into her throat and rammed her head into the steel, again and again.

Ebony scrabbled free, the squealing mirror spilling blinding light from his hand. He flexed crumpled foil wings and held the mirror up in two triumphant hands. White-hot light poured out like a beacon, splitting the night air like a scream, and clawed straight into Delilah's eyes.

She roared like a wounded dragon and tried to squeeze her eyes shut, but Akash gripped her scaly cheekbones and forced her scorched lids open. "Die, demon. Go back to hell."

I shook Blaze off and scrambled up to Ebony. I'd forgotten how big he was. My head barely reached his shoulder. I scrabbled for his rust-flecked arm. "Come on. Leave her."

"No." His voice grated, metal on metal. Sweat and blood slicked his dark blue skin. "She dies."

"But we're free! Let's go!" I tugged his arm again, and the mirror's light scorched a smoking path down Delilah's body, away from her eyes.

He shook me off, determined. "It's for you, Ice. She'll never let you be."

"You can't kill her for me!" My voice rose, hysterical. This was all wrong. "I won't let you. Put it down, Eb, or I'll stop you."

He snarled, full of pain and helplessness. "You can't stop me, Ice. No one can."

His rage stabbed my heart, and my courage flowered, not dark and mirrortwisted but true. Death was all Ebony had. All he knew how to give. And he'd never change that without me. Without me, he'd never find anything worth living for, and he'd never stop.

Ebony's dark fingers shook around the rusted iron, but he held the mirror tight and wouldn't look at me. "Leave me. Get out of here."

"No," I said steadily. "I won't let you do it." And I leapt as far as I could into the air and thrust my face into the mirror's burning light.

My lashes singed afire. My eyeballs screamed, the worst pain I'd ever felt, like a great grasping hand ripping through my skull and down my spine and deep into my guts. I couldn't see anything, only blinding white. The force dragged my hair back, stretched my wings taut like drumskins, pulled my skin tight over my bones until it ripped. Air rushed from my lungs, and my throat vibrated. I was screaming, but I couldn't hear anything but my own melting flesh and the mirror, that evil black beast tearing ravenous teeth into my soul.

And then, whiteness tore from my eyes, the mirror tumbling free like a bright arc of flame on my scorched retinas. He'd let the mirror go.

His strong metal hands enfolded my ribs, dragged me down, implored me. Dimly I heard yelling, voices, a scream not mine, and I flexed my aching wings, stretched out my roasted hands, and grabbed.

I didn't need to see to catch it this time. This thing had murmured sweet anarchy in my heart for what seemed like so long, I could feel it. I just knew.

My claws ripped on sharp metal edges, and my wailing heart rejoiced. I clutched the mirror blindly, cruel metal slashing my skin, and rammed my little fist into the glass.

My knuckles ripped and broke with a sick crunch. My fist lacerated on razor petals. The mirrorbeast gasped and roared, thrashing its scaly tail in my heart, and I thudded in a rush to the ground.

Silence.

Slowly, I peeled my raw-scraped eyes. My vision flooded white, then blue, then shimmered slowly into focus. My body ached. Ashes fouled my mouth. The room swam in giddy circles, and I looked down into mirrorswitched colors. Blue blood streamed orange over my slashed hand. My yellow skin glared purple in spiking light. The rusty sphere tumbled away, but I dragged myself after it on my belly, and when I fumbled it up, a mess of shattered glass and dust fell out. Shiny, twinkling, like a pile of pretty diamonds.

A ghostly black bubble twisted up like smoke from the pile of shards. It writhed through the splinters, scattering them, searching for a fragment large enough, any piece it could slither inside and hide. But the glass crumbled like fairy glitter, and with a squeal and a final thrash, the bubble popped, hellblack remnants wisping away.

The squidgy, dead. Good riddance.

The scaly beast inside me whiplashed one final time, and fled.

And then strong rust-brown arms scooped me up in the warm, familiar scent of iron. Fresh breeze ruffled my hair, drying the sweat on my skin. Stars tumbled overhead like jewels, and in the heady sensation of falling, I fainted.

28

Delilah chokes, her own sour blood clogging her throat. She heard the smash of glass. The mirror's gone, and fury chills her heart that she let it go so easily. She struggles to get up, to chase those fairy maggots down, but the stinking angel-thing rams her skull into the floor, sunbright blue eyes glowing with triumph.

Bone splits, and semi-heals with a screech of protest. She's slowing down. He's strong. Too strong. Fear tumbles through her body like a hellstorm. She wasn't ready for this. She didn't know.

Again he slams her to the floor, scales cracking, her needle teeth slashing her tongue to shreds. Pain, real pain, the kind that can't wash away. He's killing her.

She struggles, summoning the last of her compulsion in a shaky black mist that stings her eyes. But he's too strong. It doesn't affect him. He just breathes it in with a pleasured sigh. Wet dark hair plasters in ringlets to his pretty snarling face, and he leaps astride her, holding her down with wrists and thighs. "Give me that mist. I want it." And he jams her wrists into crumbling black tiles and crushes his mouth over hers.

Suction, hot and unbearable, stretching her tongue and tearing her throat raw. Her vision fills with starry clouds. He tastes rotten, of flesh gone sour. His body presses down on hers, impossibly heavy, his arousal threatening, and the black muck of her essence drags agonizingly up her throat like thick acid. She screams into his mouth, eternal terror consuming her. Death. Torment. Hell. Forever. It isn't supposed to end like this.

And then his body rips away, and she's free. Somewhere, glass smashes.

She scrabbles like an upturned bug, instinctively fighting what's no longer there. Agony still cramps her guts. Her heart lurches, and she scrambles blindly to her feet. Her legs won't hold her, and she fumbles at the railing to stand up, her vision slowly clearing.

The second window's a shattered hole, ragged glass dangling. The angel-thing flops wetly on the carpet in a pile of broken glass. A smoking black creature with wiry limbs and streaming blue hair swoops down in crackling blue flame and hurls the angel-thing through the air.

It slams into the wall. Plaster cracks, and the body slumps to the floor, its neck cocked at a crazy angle. Blood slides down the wall from its shattered skull, but still it grins, chokes, tries to laugh. Blood drips from its hair, down its face. It twitches, trying to move, to heal itself, but its neck is broken. It can't raise energy. It can't do anything.

A triumphant cackle freshens in Delilah's torn throat, and she stumbles forward, black hatred festering in her heart.

Kane crouches over the dying angel on bony black legs, smoke hissing from creaking joints. Hellstink curdles the air, and his voice scrapes like metal spikes, black needle teeth spitting obsidian shards. "I warned you, Akash. This is my city."

Akash blinks up at him, sky-blue eyes still shining. Scarlet bubbles inflate and burst on his lips.

Delilah wobbles up, forcing scales back under her brown human-form skin. Her torn dress tangles around her feet, and she rips the skirt away with an angry kick. "Let me kill him. Send the fucker to hell where he belongs."

But Kane thrusts out a lean charcoal-crusted arm and holds her back.

He's strong. Stronger than she thought. She fights, her fingers itching to rip the Akash-thing's skin off, but Kane forces her back. She hisses, sparks showering. "Let me go."

Kane grins, and ash rains from the air. "No, little girl. I've a better idea." He squats like a black hellbird, coarse blue locks tangling around his elbows, and his yellow gaze burns a smoking hole in Akash's bloody cheek. "Go home, Akash from the sky. Tell them what you found here. Tell them that if they come back, I won't be so patient."

Akash's eyes bloom with terror. He chokes and splutters. "Nononot—"

Kane slams his charred palm into Akash's face.

Smoke hisses, the fleshstink delightful. Akash jerks, and his body falls limp, the outline of multijointed black fingers burnt through to his skull.

Kane lights to his feet and changes. Burnt limbs shorten and fill out. Blue hair shrinks to golden blond. Yellow eyes harden to black, and he adjusts his ash-strewn suit and turns his remorseless gaze onto her.

Delilah swallows, cold. She's not ready. Foolish to imagine challenging him yet. She slides damp palms over her hips, nerves tweaking bright. He's better-looking close up. She likes those gentle lips, the soft cheekbones, the guileless look in his eyes. Maybe she can offer herself, placate his temper. Let him think she's apologizing for breaking those stupid court rules.

She licks her lips and edges forward, twirling a curl around one bleeding fingertip. "Thank you. I'm grateful."

"I don't want gratitude from you." He doesn't move away.

Delilah gives a sultry smile, enjoying his dark stormy scent. Her body warms, and she presses close, sliding her fingertips along his suit's rough silk. "Then what do you want?"

She presses her lips to his. He tastes ashen, alkaline, like home. She murmurs and slides closer, and after a moment he responds, a hard, dominant kiss that sucks her breath away and twinges desire deep into her breasts. It's a rare man who outpowers her, and it feels good. Lust and relief fire her blood, and she slides her hand into his lap, ready to do what she must to appease him. Not that it'll be a trial. His body feels taut and lithe, the swelling hardness under her palm delicious. She strokes him, eagerness blotting out her fear.

But Kane steps back a few inches, a polite but definite rejection. "Don't do that."

Unease and confusion blunt her desire. Fuck. Now he'll punish her. It's his right. "I'm sorry, I didn't mean . . ."

But Kane just gives a tiny smile, ash drifting gently from his hair like snowflakes, and flips a glossy card from his pocket. "Next time, call me before you drop by."

Bewildered, she takes it. He walks smoothly away, and the door clicks shut.

Rage crusts her hair with ice. How dare he dismiss her like that? He doesn't care enough about her to punish her, or to accept her peace offering. She's not a threat. She's not even an annoyance to him.

Not fucking yet, she's not. *Just you wait, you arrogant motherfucker.*

The card ignites in her hand, crimson edges on black, and she tosses the burning ash aside and hobbles angrily to the counter for her phone. She claws dirty purple locks from her face and dials, the screen throwing a green glow onto her face. "Joey. Yeah, hi. Look, we need to talk."

29

Salt water burned my throat.

I gulped, and swallowed, searching for more. Warm ocean water streamed over my lips, soothing my face, my skin, my stinging wings. Energy tingled under my skin. Hands caressed my hair. I rolled, and sand plastered my legs. Warm waves lapped over me, the smell of salt and seaweed refreshing in my tired lungs. Distant, weary bliss.

Tender fingers peeled sodden hair from my face. "Ice, wake up."

My heart glowed, and I opened my eyes. Stars jeweled a purple velvet sky, dimming toward the horizon. A seagull wheeled overhead. Salt stung my eyelids. Waves lapped on a midnight stretch of beach, the setting moon painting a bright ribbon across the water.

I blinked, and a dark blue shadow blotted out the sky. His jagged hair dripped, blood and water streaking his chest. He cradled my head on his lap, electric blue waves splashing over his thighs, and he closed glowing red eyes in a sigh of bitter relief. "You're here."

"Yeah. So are you." Salt roughened my voice. I reached up to touch his face, and metal clunked on my wristbones. The broken handcuffs, still tight.

"Let me get that." He traced a sparking claw over the steel, and it hissed and fell apart, ends glowing white. I offered my other hand, and he did the same. His fingers brushed over my wrist, so careful, my tears swelled, and I tried to slide my hand into his, but he pulled away and eased me gently upright, his gaze averted. "Your friends are here. You should go with them."

I sat up. On the sand, Blaze crouched in a dim fiery glow, Azure's sleepy head on his shoulder. Charming little rat. Maybe one day, she'd forgive me, too. I waved, and Blaze waved back in a faint rain of sparks. Beyond the beach above a rock retaining wall, cars slipped by, their headlights scraping faint scrawls in the sea mist. The air swirled in lonely sea breeze, and my heart filled with sorrow. "But what about you?"

Indigo fluttered wearily to his feet on rust-spotted wings. His wet shirt was burned and torn, dark blue skin showing where the cloth plastered to his chest, hinting at curves of muscles, narrow fairy ribs, the dark edge of a nipple. And those tight, dripping jeans . . .

My skin heated. I always made him wet, rain or ocean or the fluid from my body when we loved.

It was a really good look.

But he twisted sparking fingers together, tense, and I knew what he'd say before he opened his mouth.

He sighed, sorrow glowing green in his eyes, and said it: "This can't go anywhere, Ice. You and me."

"But . . . But Ebony's gone. And I'm better. Why can't we—?" My voice strangled, weak. I'd said I loved him. He'd said the same. Would we let that wash away?

"It's just not possible."

I fluttered onto my knees in the warm wet sand, flowing water refreshing my skin, feeding my energy. Even my scorched skin felt healthy and plump with moisture. "There's no impossible. You said that yourself."

But he hadn't. Ebony had. I waited for him to correct me, to deny that anything had changed.

"Yes, I did. I also killed. I also got you hurt. I can't—"

"Oh, you are so damn selfish, you know that?" The words flung out before my brain could reel them in. My pulse thudded, that old exhilaration flowing back. The mirrorbeast might be dead, but my courage hadn't faded.

Unwilling, a smile plastered across my lips. Maybe I'd always been brave, and just hadn't known it.

Indigo stared at me, bewilderment twitching salty drops from his wings. "What do you mean?"

All my frustration and pent-up desire came rushing in like breakers. "Did you see anyone throwing me into the air in front of that mirror? No, I bet you didn't. That was my choice. And how about when we made love, huh? See anyone holding a pistol to my poor helpless little head? Don't think so. That was my choice, too. Fairy wings don't mean I don't have a brain. You don't make me hurt myself, Indigo. I do that on my own. Sure, I understand your girlfriend died and broke your heart. Christ, it makes me want to cry and I wasn't even there. That doesn't make you responsible for her mistakes. And yeah, Ebony killed people. But you weren't there. You didn't do it. Not every fucking thing is your fault, okay?"

I sucked in a breath and held it, waiting for him to scowl scarlet at me and turn away.

But he swallowed, a salty shimmer on his coppery lashes, and shook his dripping head. "You're wrong. It doesn't work that way. Tonight proves that. I'll only ever hurt you."

Waves sloshed around my hips, the tide coming in. I splashed up and down, infuriated. Stubborn, deafhead boy. "Do I look like a child to you? Now isn't the time for your emo think-it-to-death blame-yourself-for-everything bullshit. Snap out of it. I'm here. I'm asking. Do you want me or not?"

My stomach lurched. I felt like stuffing the words back into my mouth. A yes-or-no question had only one easy answer.

But he dropped to his knees in breaking waves and pressed my hand over his heartbeat. My palm tingled, his skin like warm velvet over iron, his pulse light and swift and mingling with mine. "Yes, Ice. I meant it."

I swallowed, my throat suddenly dry. "Then I want in. I've been a shit magnet all my life. If you can make it worse, I'll be surprised."

His pulse quickened under my palm, but his eyes stayed guarded. He slid his hands over my shoulders and shook me gently, like he didn't think I understood. "Ebony, he . . . it's my fault. I shut him away so tight that killing was the only way he . . . the only way I could feel alive. Connected. Just because he's gone doesn't mean I didn't—"

I stopped him with shaking fingers on his lips. "I get it, okay? You have to forgive yourself, Indigo. Everyone's got a dark half. But it's meant to be deep inside, where you can control it. Ebony was never supposed to be out on his own, without the good parts to hold him back. But he's back where he belongs now."

He swallowed. "Can you be sure?"

It sounded weird, talking about him like that. Scary to think that my crazy half was still cackling inside me somewhere, scratching to be free. But it had always been there. The mirror just dragged it screaming into the light. Ebony had always been there, too. That didn't make either of us evil.

Faith warmed my heart, and I stilled his restless hands under mine. His skin sparkled with static at the contact. "I'm sure. And so should you be."

Slowly, he pulled me up onto my knees. The water came up to my hips, playing with my skirt, bathing me in rushing salty warmth. "You know I steal things from bad people. Demons chase me. I get my ass kicked a lot."

"And you damn well better let me come along next time. No way are you keeping all the fun to yourself." Patching him up after an ass-kicking sounded delicious to me. A smile crept over my lips. I wanted to fold him in my arms and kiss him senseless. But I needed him to come to me.

He took my hand, tracing my fingers with a gentle, hesitant claw. "You'd accept all that?"

"Said I would, didn't I?"

"For me?"

Sigh. "See anyone else here?"

He kissed my fingertips, one by one, and then he slid my hand onto his chest and kissed my mouth.

Salt, rust, his delicious iron flavor. His arms enfolded me, so hot and strong, drifting seawater caressing me up to my waist. My mouth sprang alive under his, his tongue on mine, his sharp teeth tingling my skin. I slid my wrists around his neck, buried my fingers in his crisp metal hair, gave myself up to the familiar yet still so unbelievable warmth of his body.

Pebbles splashed around me, and a sharp whistle sang from the beach. "Jeez, please, can we get home sometime this week?"

I giggled. Blaze's idea of a cold shower. "You're just jealous!"

"Get a room," called Azure, giggling, too. "A soundproof one. You guys are a whole box of cream pies. Nausy-ate-*ing*."

Indigo laughed and kissed me again, gentle, possessive. "Wanna go?"

"Yeah." I let him help me up. He shook like a dog, rusty droplets showering.

I squeezed out my hair. Water ran over my body, a sharp and salty glory. I loved it. As we waded toward the beach, I couldn't help but watch him, my delicious dark metal prince. After we'd loved, I'd been afraid to touch him again. Now, I didn't care. I knew I had nothing to fear. I slipped my wet hand in his and held it tight. "So, what now?"

He knotted knobbly blue fingers around mine. "I was thinking, home. Shower. Bed. That kinda thing."

I sighed, content, but my heart sank. I groaned. "I can't. We still owe Sonny five grand."

"Maybe I can help with that."

Excitement sparked my spine. "You got a job on?"

He laughed. "Nope. Got a bank account, though. You should try it."

"God, you're such a human. Next you'll say get a real job."

"Get a real job, Ice."

I swatted him. "No way."

"No hope of a respectable retirement, then."

I skipped, kicking up wet sand, and giggled. "Not a chance."

He stopped me with a searching kiss, his hands fresh and needy on my body, and when he pulled back, I was gasping, my sex aching and my nipples standing out in my wet clothes. Home was sounding better all the time.

He nuzzled his dripping hair on my cheek, and I felt his dark metal laugh. "Good."

Epilogue

"Where is Kane?"

Akash grins and says nothing. Chained in gold to a cold white chair, sunlight burning bright in deathless blue sky. No wind. No scent. Nothing to tell him he's alive.

Shadow leans over him, wings glittering fresh like snow. His frigid blue gaze bores into Akash's soul. "How did he smell? Who are his friends?"

Golden shackles chafe Akash's wrists, tempting. He flexes, digging the sharp edge in harder, relishing the small sting. The sun just stares blankly. Blind. Deaf. Powerless. It was all a lie.

"Where is Indra?" Lightning arcs in Shadow's golden hair. Below, thunder rumbles. He wrenches Akash's head back with a cold white hand, his eyes flashing with fury. "What have you done, minion?"

Inside, Akash drifts away, dreaming of the agonizing shatter of bone, salt's sharp sting on his tongue, the hot wet deliciousness of a kiss. If Shadow speaks, Akash doesn't hear him.

Eventually, Shadow swoops away, and the minions drag Akash to a dazzling white cell. The door slams shut. White walls, a few feet apart. White ceiling. Cold white floor. No windows. No furniture. The sickly sweet stink of honey. Silence.

Akash groans and mutters, and sinks blunt teeth into the webbing of his hand. Flesh crunches. Blood flows, tasteless, staining his pale suit sleeve. It barely hurts.

This nondescript pale body doesn't ache. It doesn't sting. It doesn't feel anything.

Akash rolls onto his back in a crunch of crisp feathers and howls in despair. Hours pass. He howls more.

Intolerable, this emptiness. Eternity is a very long time. One day, Shadow will break him. Unless . . .

A door panel clicks open, and blue eyes pierce a gap in the whiteness like sapphires. The tiny sound springs fresh tears to Akash's eyes. Sensation. He must have it back. He must get away. He can't bear this.

Back to earth. Back to Kane's city. He misses that hellscarlet sun, the smells, the grime. Crafty claws sharpen in his famished mind. Kane bested him once. It'll not happen again. This time, he'll be ready. More drinking, more powers. A proper disguise, something he can wear forever, so Kane will never find him, and he can take all the sensation he wants.

With every ravenous cell of his body, Akash burns to live.

But first, escape this forsaken cell. Shadow has the temerity to call the earth hell.

He crawls toward the door, and the eyes swivel to follow him. Not Shadow. Just another minion. Weak. Corruptible.

Lies tingle on Akash's tongue like a precious, faded memory, and his throat rasps, abused. "A favor. Fresh air. The garden."

The eyes follow him coldly. "It is not permitted."

Akash kneels at the door's foot like a good boy, his wings folded meekly. Tucked beneath him, out of sight under fresh white feathers, his fingers curl with defiant flame. Cruel banshee persuasion prickles in his throat, and he smiles, his voice rich with magical song. "Please?"